BADDA MOON RISING

By

IAN JARVIS

Paperback ISBN 978-1-78705-611-4
ePub ISBN 978-1-78705-612-1
PDF ISBN 978-1-78705-613-8

Published by MX Publishing
335 Princess Park Manor, Royal Drive,
London, N11 3GX
www.mxpublishing.co.uk

Cover design by Brian Belanger

Chapter 1

Goathland nestles in a moorland valley between the market town of Pickering and the ancient fishing port of Whitby. This remote Yorkshire village has been a tourist magnet for two-hundred years, although, in recent times, the popularity stems mostly from its starring role as the fictional Aidensfield in the television drama *Heartbeat*. Daytrippers still descend upon the place to "ooh!" and "aah!" at the filming locations, especially the picture-postcard railway station that hasn't changed in over a century. The platform doubled as *Hogsmeade* in the *Harry Potter* movie franchise and fantasy fans flock to see the steam locomotive that underwent a makeover as the *Hogwarts Express*. If only Hollywood had shot a couple of *Star Wars* scenes nearby, this would truly be Geek Heaven.

Despite the name, there are very few goats in Goathland, but an abundance of sheep roam the lanes and heather-clad hills munching the grass verges to billiard table perfection. This was the reason Tyson Cooper and his small group of travellers had set up camp a mile outside the village. Their caravans stood clustered on the moor, icy March rain beating a frenzied tattoo on the metal roofs. Three men sat in the largest of these – a two-bedroom, aptly-named *Gypsy Wanderer* – nervously listening to Tyson as he paced the carpet. Pausing to glance through the window at the pitch-black terrain, he half-filled a coffee mug with whisky, the bottle rattling against the ceramic as his hand shook.

"It was hideous." The big man guzzled the drink, stammering in his thick Irish accent. "This thing was a feckin' monster from hell."

Tyson was a *big* man in every sense of the term and his trio of cronies had never seen him scared before. An infamous bare-knuckle fighter and winner of over forty unlawful bouts, his questionable party tricks included bench-pressing stolen motorcycles and drunkenly punching horses unconscious. Three years ago, he'd memorably bitten off Billy Walton's ear in a championship boxing match at the Appleby gypsy fair. This framed and somewhat gory trophy was proudly displayed amongst the china plates and other Romany ornaments on his caravan wall. No, his companions knew it would take something pretty special to scare *this* man.

"A monster from Hell," repeated Tyson, gulping more whisky as he paced. "That's the only way to describe it. We'd rounded up the sheep and were getting them in the horse box when it appeared out of the dark. Feckin' huge and black with glowing eyes."

The gypsies glanced warily at one another, unsure of how to reply. Knowing Tyson, any impromptu comment that bordered upon scepticism and disbelief could easily be answered with a broken jaw.

A monster with glowing eyes? Up until now, the local constabulary had been their only concern, and thanks to government cutbacks and policing reductions, especially in rural areas like North Yorkshire, they weren't *much* of a concern. Jim Boscombe of Hatherley Farm hadn't taken kindly to his sheep vanishing. Since the appearance of the travellers twelve days ago, the police had visited their camp four times, but although they knew this shifty bunch were responsible, there was no evidence, the animals having been sold to a crooked Whitby butcher within hours of being stolen. Three lucrative thefts, so far, and no one could prove a thing, but now it seemed they had something else to worry about. *Something a little more frightening than cops.*

"A monster?" One of the gypsies lifted a curtain to squint through the window at the sodden winter moorland. With the darkness and raincloud cover, he may as well have been blindfolded. "Er, well, I don't know what to say. Um, where are the other guys?"

"I haven't a clue." Tyson laughed manically. "They vanished and I drove straight back here. This thing ripped the doors off the horse box and let the sheep out. It tore them off like they were made of *paper*. The lads ran away screaming and I don't blame them." He guzzled down his drink and refilled the mug. "I'm telling you, I don't know what that feckin' monster was, but it's out there somewhere right now and I'm…"

His frightened babbling ended abruptly as the creaking walls lurched and the floor tilted. Crockery smashed and the lighting fused as the caravan was flipped completely over onto its side, the four men falling together in a tangled heap. Animal talons tore through the roof, now effectively the wall.

"What in the name of God…" began Tyson.

The sheet metal was wrenched apart, screeching and groaning as it opened up to reveal an enormous black figure. The wolf stood on two legs like a man, glaring down at them with luminous golden eyes. Seven feet in height and three feet wide between the bulging biceps, its bushy tail snaked, reminiscent of a disgruntled cat. Freezing air wafted over the petrified travellers, an unnatural cold radiating not from the gaping fissure, but the wolf itself. Panting from the exertion of running to the camp and rolling the caravan, the muscular chest rose and fell, clouding breath mixing with the steam that billowed from its rain-soaked pelt.

"Is *that* your feckin' monster?" croaked one of the gypsies.

It was a pretty stupid question; there couldn't be *too* many things like this roaming the moors around Goathland. Tyson didn't answer, but the unsavoury sound of his bowel emptying into his trousers suggested it probably *was*.

The wolf's huge muzzle cracked open to expose sharp white fangs – gigantic razor teeth that, given the choice, none of the travellers would have opted to see.

"Good evening, gentlemen," it said, in a deep rumbling growl. "How are we tonight?"

"Hello," whimpered a terrified Irish voice in the darkness. "Not too bad, thanks."

The cold intensified as the creature moved inside out of the downpour. "Now I realise this may seem like a peculiar demand from a wolf, but I really must insist that you leave the sheep alone. You will remove your caravans tonight and never return. Those sheep are under *my* protection and, if I see any of you people again, I will devour you from the feet up. Do you understand?"

The four men nodded dementedly.

"Mister Cooper," it snarled, the yellow eyes blazing. "You are leaving right now. Do *you* understand me?"

"Yes, yes," whined Tyson. "Absolutely."

"Excellent." Glancing down at its dripping black fur and the rainwater puddle forming around its feet, the werewolf tutted. "Terrible weather, don't you think?"

* * * *

Goathland stands on England's largest expanse of open moorland. A desolate, yet eerily beautiful wilderness of heather and rock, the North York Moors National Park lies within a triangle formed by the Yorkshire Wolds, the Cleveland Hills and the North Sea. Bernard Quist drove across this dark terrain towards the village, his headlights cutting through the sheeting rain and picking out a trio of scampering rabbits on the lane ahead. Slowing down, so as not to harm them, he drew on his cigarette and opened the window slightly to draw out the smoke tendrils.

After leaving the gypsy camp and returning to his car, Quist had *changed* before setting off. In *normal* form, his complexion was conspicuously smoother, his presence didn't lower the temperature and his appearance was far less terrifying. Slim and attractive, with dark wavy hair, he looked to be mid-forties, but he was older – a *good deal* older. The werewolf attack, that changed his life forever, had taken place in 1790 and Quist hadn't aged a day since. On first meeting him, most people noticed his prominent nose, but although it *was* a little on the large side, it was nothing in comparison to the

4

gruesome jutting muzzle of his *other* self.

Hatherley Farm stood on the village outskirts and, parking his Ford saloon on the driveway by the house, he climbed out and took a deep breath of night air, tilting his head and smiling to feel the refreshing rain on his face.

Quist was shorter than his lupine alter ego and an average trim figure replaced the supernatural wolf's muscular bulk. Despite this, he was much stronger than most men and his augmented senses were immeasurably keener. He picked up the sound of cats in a nearby barn, their low mewing to one another easily discernible above the hissing patter of rain on vegetation. The scents of the wet moorland filled his nostrils, along with various farmyard odours, some pleasant, some stimulating, and some emanating from dubious sources he wouldn't wish to step in.

Killing his cigarette underfoot and pulling on a black leather overcoat, Quist paused to peer at the sky as the moon appeared to his right. A distant break in the rainclouds had exposed the bright sphere and it glowed with yellowy light above the sodden heather, almost full and quite hypnotic. He tore his eyes away and shook himself before heading for the farmhouse. Many lycanthropy legends were incorrect, especially those concerning the moon. Bernard Quist and his kind could shapeshift on any night between sunset and sunrise, but the violent bestial urges, that he managed to keep in check, were more powerful during the full phase and he preferred not to transform at this time of the month. Tonight, however, there had been no other way to accomplish his unusual mission.

The farmer's sheepdog came running from its kennel at the rear of the house to greet the approaching man. The collie froze halfway down the drive, took one look at the figure in the long coat, and bolted away yelping into the darkness. This impolite display didn't surprise Quist; animals could always sense the supernatural wolf and tended to instantly vanish. He'd jokingly toyed with the notion of working in pest control – just entering a building and sitting down with a coffee and cigarette would be more than enough to clear out any rats and mice.

Jim Boscombe answered the doorbell. "Ah, you're back?" The farmer waved Quist into the hallway. "I'm guessing it was a waste of time and they told you to piss off, but I can't believe they didn't hurt you. I thought going to speak with those bastards would be a big mistake."

"Yes, you *did* warn me," admitted his visitor. "But as you can doubtless see, I'm fine."

"So what happened?"

"I can't say as they were overly pleased to see me." Quist looked around, breathing in the scents of wood smoke and an unlucky farmyard chicken sizzling in a nearby kitchen range. "But we had a somewhat *frank* discussion and they agreed to never trouble you again. They're vacating the area as we speak."

"What?" Boscombe frowned. "Is that some sort of joke?"

"Of course not. I can assure you, you'll have no further thefts of livestock."

The farmer shook his head, finding it difficult to accept that such a nondescript and well-spoken man could intimidate a group of hardened criminals. His eloquence and vocabulary belonged in a theatre Shakespeare recital. "They're actually leaving?" he said. "I'm sorry, but I can't believe you did it."

"I'm not at liberty to divulge my methods. My approach to this was somewhat unusual, to say the least, but it achieved the desired results." Quist pulled a bulky envelope from his overcoat. "Mister Cooper, their ringleader, apologised profusely and asked me to give you this – the proceeds from the sale of your stolen sheep, minus the fee for my services."

"*Seriously?*" Boscombe gazed open-mouthed at the thick wad of twenty pound notes. "My God! The police couldn't prove anything, but I knew they were the ones responsible and…"

"Your suspicions were well-founded." Quist nodded. "I caught them in the act, rounding up your sheep into their horse box."

"You're telling me you just strolled into their camp and sorted everything out? This is incredible." Laughing, Boscombe slapped the man's shoulder. "As you know, you were recommended by a mate of mine. You did a job for him last year and he said you were a brilliant private investigator, but this is…"

"Consultant detective," corrected Quist, with a quirky, lopsided smile. "Not a private investigator. I'm pleased I was able to assist you with this problem."

Bernard Quist operated as a *consultant detective* from a small agency on Baker Avenue in the nearby city of York. Originally a discreet one-man operation, for several months now he'd been ably assisted by a local youth named Watson, one of the very few people he'd trusted with his dark supernatural secret.

"So my worries are over." Boscombe excitedly counted the money. "I'd say this deserves a drink. I have a decent bottle of malt and we could…"

"That's very kind, but I need to get back to York. Perhaps another time?" Opening the door, Quist peered out at the downpour and tutted. "Terrible weather, don't you think?"

* * * *

Chapter 2

As public car parks go, St George's Field is quite attractive, but this has little to do with the shade of tarmac, the overpriced ticket machines, or modern toilet block. The appeal is purely down to its surroundings and tree-lined location alongside the tranquil River Ouse, with its drifting swans and cruising pleasure boats. One of the central parking areas in the city of York, it lies next to Skeldergate Bridge, a Victorian masterpiece of Gothic towers and ornate ironwork. The iconic fortress of Clifford's Tower rises on a defensive mound to the north of the bridge, and the medieval city walls stand on grassy bankings to the eastern side.

St George's Field hasn't always been used for parking. For centuries, this large patch of land hosted celebrations, circuses and firework displays. Funfairs made regular visits and Royal events were marked with open-air festivals, but after the war, this all stopped when the area was given over to vehicles. Breaking into these soon took over from picking pockets as the principal crime here, but the police tent by the river and the forensic team working around it suggested this *latest* crime was far more serious than a stolen car radio.

An elasticated hood covered Katie Bradstreet's short blonde hair and forensic overalls protected her suit. Hitching up the knees, she crouched on the tarmac. The movement was automatic, trouser creases being the last thing on the Detective Inspector's mind this Monday morning.

"Yes, they're the same," she said, quietly. "A pentacle and a triangle."

The police shelter had been erected in the secluded corner of the car park furthest away from Tower Street. It was March, and although the sun had risen an hour ago at six o'clock, a halogen lamp illuminated the interior, the bright light allowing Katie to examine the symbols close-up. A seven-inch circle enclosed a five-pointed star with a central swirling pattern. Next to it was a small triangle bisected by a line. Ordinarily, geometric designs would attract little police interest, but these grisly motifs had been carved between the breasts of a naked female corpse.

Detective Sergeant Angie Gibson stood behind Katie, watching from the tent entrance. A petite girl of thirty-two, her long ginger hair was gathered back in a bun beneath her forensic hood and her ashen complexion resembled wallpaper paste.

"Just like the others," she said, her voice quavering slightly. "A dead girl, wrapped in carpet, with a star and a triangle cut into her chest. Three sex workers murdered in the same way and then dumped around York over three nights? This is unbelievable, Ma'am."

An elderly bearded man squeezed past Angie to stoop beside the Inspector with a cringe-inducing crackle of joints. Jay Mortimer, the Police Pathologist, was dressed like the detectives in a coverall suit with disposable overshoes. Every officer's prints and DNA were filed for elimination purposes, but if the Scenes of Crime Officer hadn't finished his work, then suiting up was still required. Hairs and skin cells are constantly shed and it was virtually impossible to enter the area without leaving something behind. The brown carpet had been unwrapped by the SOCO and Mortimer gestured to the gruesome symbols on the corpse.

"I finished my preliminary examination before you arrived," he said. "Cause of death is the same as before. A single stab wound here, as you can see. A sharp stiletto blade pierced the heart."

"You believe the girls were alive when these designs were cut?" said Katie. "And then they were stabbed through the centre of the star?"

"That's correct," said Mortimer.

"Why would the killer do that?" asked Angie, shaking her head. "What are these symbols supposed to be?"

"That's for you to find out," said the Pathologist. "There are no other marks apart from here…" He gently rolled the dead girl onto her side. "Lividity markings on the shoulder blades and buttocks, suggesting she died on a flat, hard surface, most probably the floor. She lay there for a short period post mortem allowing these to form."

Katie leant over the body to see the purple discolouration. Circulation ceases with death, but gravity still does its work and blood sinks to the lowest level. "Yes," she said. "Again, this is exactly like the first two victims."

"We have no ligature bruising," continued Mortimer. "No signs of a struggle and her fingernails are clean."

"So she wasn't tied up." The Inspector nodded. "But she didn't put up a fight when this madman cut his weird designs. That means she was out cold and, if there are no bruises where he knocked her unconscious, it means she was drugged."

"Highly likely," agreed Mortimer. "The toxicology tests found chloroform traces in the first two victims, both in the blood and around their mouths. Is this her? Your missing girl?"

"Yes, that's Shannon Lunn." Sighing, Katie rose from her crouch. "She's been missing since lunchtime yesterday."

"We'd better call on her sister, Ma'am," said Angie, checking her notebook for the address. "She can make an official identification before the autopsy."

"It's now almost seven." The Inspector glanced at her watch. "You estimated that Heather Campbell was killed around nine o'clock on Friday evening and Tania Ford died around the same time on Saturday. Shannon here was found by an early dog walker two hours ago, so I'm assuming she died last night?"

"Yes, before midnight." Doctor Mortimer wiped clean his thermometer spike. The device always reminded Katie of the kitchen instruments that were stabbed into meat during cooking. "Her liver temperature and the rigor mortis would suggest over six hours ago. Yes, it was probably around midnight and the lividity points to her being dumped here shortly afterwards."

"It's insane." Angie grimaced. "Every evening this lunatic is killing a young sex worker. *Jesus*! This is a really nasty one, Ma'am."

Her superior slowly nodded. *All* murders were nasty, but the deaths she normally dealt with tended to involve robbery, or a volatile combination of enraged partners and alcohol or drugs. Two decades in the North Yorkshire Police had taught the forty-two-year-old Katie Bradstreet that the majority of victims were butchered without any thought whatsoever, let alone the intellectual planning found in the pages of Agatha Christie. Occasionally it was different. Occasionally, as Angie said, it was *really nasty*.

Heather Campbell's body had been found on Saturday, dumped on a quiet section of Knavesmire Road by the racecourse. Tania Ford turned up in an alley behind the National Railway Museum yesterday morning. Both murders had taken place the night before, and now there was Shannon Lunn here in the corner of this large car park. Each naked corpse had been marked with the triangle and the pentagram with its central stab wound, and each was wrapped for convenient disposal in a roll of cheap brown carpet.

The Sergeant cleared her dry throat. "I have to say, Ma'am, this is incredible. We never got anything like it in Northallerton."

"We don't get *too* many like it here in York." Katie smiled grimly. "Regretting your move to the big bad city?"

"Not at all." Angie shrugged. "But you know what I mean."

Inspector Bradstreet's usual Sergeant, Tariq Aslam, was currently on sick leave with a broken arm and ribs following a car accident three weeks ago. Angie Gibson had temporarily taken his place, transferred onto Katie's team from the North Yorkshire Police Headquarters in Northallerton. This young woman was highly intelligent and extremely capable and the Inspector would be sorry to see her go when Aslam returned in April.

Angie gazed at the dead girl's waxy features and gestured to the design between the breasts. "Who the hell would want to do this to a young kid? What kind of maniac are we looking for here?"

"I don't know," said Katie. "But we have three signatures of sorts. They're all sex workers, he always uses the same carpet to wrap them, and he marks them all with these weird symbols."

She hated signatures. They pointed to sociopaths, and meant you could forget about easy solutions with violent partners and muggings that had gone wrong. The three victims had minor records for soliciting and drugs, but they didn't appear to know one another and, so far, there was nothing definite to link them.

The Inspector pushed back the tent flap and left the shelter with Angie. She took a breath of the crisp morning air and looked around at the police vehicles and activity. The two officers turned to Skeldergate Bridge as a bright flash drew their attention to the onlookers on the parapet.

"Oh, hello," said Angie.

Several more bursts of light followed, high-quality flashes as opposed to those found on phones. It was impossible to photograph the body, but the detectives outside the police tent and the forensic team working around it would make for juicy tabloid pictures.

"Ah, the gentlemen of the press," drawled Katie, sarcastically. "Well they certainly have their headline."

"Yes." Her Sergeant nodded. "Unless someone shags a celebrity and steals the front page."

Police were blasé with death and the gallows humour was used to combat the horrors they witnessed. Despite the jokes, no officer actually enjoyed being around corpses. At least Katie *hoped* none of them enjoyed it.

"*Soap star love-rat is a flop in bed, claims blonde nobody?*" She let out a dry laugh. "No, not even *that* will prevent tomorrow's front page from reading: *Cleopatra Killer Slays Number Three.*"

According to popular legend, Cleopatra was brought to Julius

Caesar rolled in a carpet. Katie didn't know which paper had christened Heather Campbell's murderer the *Cleopatra Killer*, but the rest had followed suit. Classical knowledge wasn't a strong point with their readers, so the tactful tabloids carried pictures of Elizabeth Taylor as the Egyptian Queen next to their shots of the deceased girls.

Angie shrugged. "I suppose their name is a little more imaginative than the *York Slasher* or whatever."

Two of Katie's Detective Constables walked across the car park, Zoe Planer and Gary Mitchell, both of whom had been liaising with the forensic personnel by the van. The pair were in their late twenties and had been on the Inspector's CID team for the last few years.

"What does the SOCO have for me?" asked Katie. "I don't suppose the killer accidentally dropped his wallet and I.D?"

"We're not that lucky." Mitchell smiled bitterly and pointed at the tarmac. "But we have decent tyre tracks. Our suspect reversed through this patch of oil just outside the shelter. They look like the same van tracks that we found in the grass next to Heather's body, but CSI won't know until they get the photographs to the lab."

"CSI?" Katie peered curiously at Matthew Carson, the man Mitchell had just been speaking with. "How long has our Scenes Of Crime Officer been CSI?"

"Didn't you know?" Zoe Planer smiled. "Since Matthew realised it sounds sexier than SOCO when people ask him what he does. SOCO sounds like a clown you'd hire for a kid's party."

"The lab just phoned him," said Mitchell. "We have the results on the touch DNA he found on the first two victims. Our killer left plenty of skin cells on the bodies. The bad news is he isn't in our database."

"*Marvellous*," snarled Katie. "So whoever our friend is, he has no previous criminal form." She grimaced as a black saloon rushed into the car park, pulled up by the forensic van, and a thin middle-aged woman climbed out. "Oh, *great*. Here we go."

Angela Morton was the new Superintendent at the York Police Headquarters and Katie hadn't exactly warmed to her. Morton reminded the Inspector of a long-haired rat in a designer suit, and not a particularly *pleasant* rat. Lacking empathy, Morton was aloof and manipulative, but Katie's aversion stemmed from her unfeeling practise of placing career advancement before everything. The Superintendent had been expecting to use her time in York to coldly work on her next promotion, yet her first week had been inconveniently filled with three unsolved murders. This wouldn't endear her to the Chief Constable.

"So we have another one?" snapped Morton, walking over. "Unbelievable. I see the press are here too, up on the bridge watching us. I want this madman caught and the investigation wrapped up as soon as possible. Do I make myself clear?"

"Oh, absolutely, Ma'am," said Katie. *And to think, she'd been planning to piss around and pointlessly draw this out for months.*

"Why is the killer marking his victims with those symbols?" demanded the Superintendent. "That's the most obvious question, but you have no idea what they mean."

"Not so far, Ma'am." Katie nodded. "The larger design has a squiggle added, but basically that five-pointed star is a witchcraft pentagram. I presume I'm not the only one who's thinking of Hammer horror films and the occult?"

* * * *

Chapter 3

York was crowded this damp Monday afternoon, but then again, York is *always* crowded. International tourists flock here throughout the year to admire its historic sights and the wealth of Tudor, Elizabethan, Georgian, Edwardian, and Victorian buildings. Over two miles of medieval defensive walls surround the city and, within these fortifications, narrow cobbled streets and passages known as "snickleways" lead sightseers from one architectural marvel to the next. The jewel in York's crown is the 13th century Minster, the largest Gothic cathedral in Europe and an absolute must for every tourist's snapshot collection.

College Street, a quiet backwater of cobblestones and mature ash trees, lies beneath the Minster's eastern transept. Gargoyles glared down from the ornate parapets above as a small crowd walked along the pavement led by a solemn tour guide in a black cloak. Most of the group gazed at the exquisite half-timbered frontage of Saint William's College on their right. Built in 1461 for the Chantry Priests, the place hasn't changed since that time, but *these* people hadn't come to learn about old buildings. The guide stopped outside a diminutive house just past the college. Around twenty-five strong, the warmly-wrapped crowd fell silent as he ran a hand over the wall.

"A sensation of foreboding," he said. "I always channel the emotions of fear and melancholy when I approach this building." The guide pointed up. "And whenever I gaze upon *that* tiny window."

Amongst its many claims to fame, York has more ghost tours than any other British city, with a dozen different walks like this one exploring the streets, a Ghost Bus Tour, and even a Supernatural Cruise sailing along the River Ouse. This particular tour had a slight edge on the rest, in that it was run by a psychic medium named Kyle Tarot.

The afternoon light was dismal, but it sparkled on Kyle's

pentagram ring as he massaged his brow in concentration. The silver ring was part of his professional image, complimenting a trim beard and his working outfit of black cloak over an indigo velvet jacket. An attractive thirty-seven-year-old, the devilish facial hair enhanced his lean features, the enigmatic look having been developed six years ago when he changed his name from Kyle Lewis.

"The vibrations are strong today." Kyle closed his eyes and stroked the stone. "The more sensitive of you may feel them. Can you sense the sadness in the air?"

Some members of the group nodded – the more suggestible ones who had always suspected they were "a bit psychic" themselves. They peered apprehensively at the little window he'd pointed out.

"The fourteenth century was a ghastly time," said Kyle. "The Black Death ravaged Yorkshire. In just *one* year, 1349, this plague claimed over four-thousand souls here in York. When anyone showed signs of infection, their house was boarded up with the family locked inside in a futile effort to prevent the spread." He touched the building again, slowly running his fingers down the masonry. "Unfortunately that's what happened here. They sealed the family inside with their little daughter and left them to die."

John Watson stood listening on the edge of the crowd with his employer Bernard Quist. "Hey good, uplifting entertainment, Guv," murmured the young man, raising his eyebrows. "Nothing like a story about dead kids to brighten a wet Monday afternoon in March."

Quist gave his assistant a lopsided smile.

Watson was a good-looking black youth of nineteen. He'd worked at Quist's detective agency on Baker Avenue for the best part of a year and, although he enjoyed the varied assignments, he'd already decided that today's squalid job wouldn't be featuring in his *top-ten list of thrilling cases.* Lean and wiry, with short curly hair, Watson wore a bright yellow sweater beneath a green canvas blouson, with blue jeans and fluorescent trainers – a vibrant contrast to Quist's calf-length leather overcoat and drab grey jacket.

"The plague eventually left York," continued Kyle Tarot. "When this house was opened up again, something unimaginable was discovered. The daughter was found dead in that room, but this girl hadn't died of the infection like her family. She'd starved to death."

The crowd gasped in unison.

Kyle nodded. "Some were lucky, in that they were immune to the pestilence, but with this poor child, her immunity was her curse. Because the boarded-up plague houses were avoided, no one heard her pitiful screams. No one came to her aid as she slowly starved to death surrounded by the rotting corpses of her family."

"How *lovely*," whispered Watson, dryly. He blew warmth into his hands before nudging his boss. "Hey, Guv. Here we go again…"

"Yes." Quist raised his phone. "I've already spotted them."

Two of the tourists on the opposite side of the crowd were locked in a tight embrace, the man running his fingers through the woman's blonde hair as he kissed her. Pretending to photograph the tour guide, Quist turned his phone slightly and fired off three snaps.

"Wow!" Watson cringed. "It looks like she's choking on a sweet and he's trying to clear out the blockage with his tongue."

"An intriguing observation," muttered Quist, changing his camera setting and filming a short video. "Human nature never fails to fascinate me. I wonder which part of the horror story prompted this bout of unrestrained passion?"

Kyle gestured to the bedroom window. "Many have seen the child's spirit since that time," he said. "She gazes out from there looking for the rescue that will never come. Passers-by see her waving to attract attention. The current occupants of this house are accustomed to folk knocking on their door to tell them that someone upstairs seems distressed and appears to need assistance."

"Have *you* ever seen her?" asked a woman, dabbing her eyes.

"I have indeed," admitted Kyle. "Yes, on many occasions,

and I've heard her pitiful sobbing too. Some people envy my gift, but being attuned to the spirit world isn't always pleasant." Nodding sadly, he swirled his cloak and left the house. "Okay, everyone, if you'd like to follow me this way, please?"

The guide led his group into Minster Yard, the vast cobbled area that encircles the cathedral. They passed the twin western towers and the huge doorway in the south transept to make their way along High Petergate, a narrow, medieval thoroughfare of Tudor buildings and timber-fronted shops that leads to Bootham Bar.

Quist checked his video footage of the kissing couple as he walked, allowing his assistant to move away and stroll beside a young girl who was equally busy with her phone.

Watson smiled to himself. *It was rare to find any girl under thirty who wasn't busy looking at a phone.*

The young woman was striking, with lengthy jet black hair, black lipstick and too much eye-shadow, suggesting a definite affinity with the Goth culture.

"Good tour," said Watson, grinning. "Are you enjoying it?"

"I've heard it all before." She looked up from her mobile to return his smile. "It isn't the first time I've taken this ghost walk."

"So you must *really* like it. Hey, here's a thought – how do you *like* the idea of a drink afterwards? I'm into the paranormal too and we should have a chat about these scary stories we're hearing."

"Do I look like the sort of girl who goes drinking with strange men?"

"Well, I'm not *that* strange." Watson shrugged. "Okay, I have a ginger cat named Mick Hucknall, and I've been known to dunk my chips in lager, but apart from that…"

"Sorry," she laughed. "But I kind of have a date."

"Ah, pity." He clutched at his heart and adopted a sham wounded expression. "Whoever it is, he's a lucky man."

"Let's hope he doesn't get *too* lucky." She pointed to the guide in the cloak. "It's a date with my Dad."

"Your Dad's the psychic? Wow, that's pretty cool. Funnily enough, my *own* psychic senses are telling me you might like to go out somewhere another time." He reached into his jacket for a business card. "Give me a ring if you fancy it."

"John Watson?" She read the information and gave a low whistle. "So you're a private investigator at the Bernard Quist Detective Agency? Now that really *is* cool."

"Yeah." He gave a modest shrug. "I suppose it is."

This was the reason he'd had the cards printed. So far, the teenager had handed out none to potential clients, but several dozen to attractive girls.

"I'm Charlotte," she said. "Yeah, I might be in touch."

Kyle Tarot paused at the fortified gateway of Bootham Bar, the miniature stone castle that separates High Petergate from the bustle of traffic beyond.

"The Screaming Skull is our final story," he said, gesturing to the building. "We're now standing at the end of the street named Bootham, an area of York steeped in paranormal phenomena. Along this road you'll find the Grey Lady of Moatside Court, the spirit of Guy Fawkes haunting his old school and, of course, the establishment's infamous ghostly werewolf."

"A school with a ghost werewolf?" echoed an American in the crowd. "Seriously?"

"Whooo!" Watson nudged Quist and lowered his voice. "Anything to do with you, Guv?"

His boss gave him a deadpan look.

"Witnesses have been seeing the spectral creature for centuries," said Kyle, nodding. "Always at the full of the moon. Sometimes the wolf is seen lurking in the moonlit halls of the school itself, and sometimes running across the cricket pitch behind."

"Cricket pitch? Howzat?" called out Watson, unable to help

19

himself.

"That sounds so scary," said one of the women tourists. "But why on earth would a school be haunted by a ghost werewolf?"

"We may never know." Kyle smiled enigmatically and used the line he always employed at such times. "Where the supernatural is concerned, sometimes it's best not to question too much. Sometimes it's best just to accept."

* * * *

Many towns have an *Eagle and Child* public house, named after the legends of vicious eagles snatching babies from cradles. Widely perpetuated by gamekeepers, the ridiculous myth provided an excuse to kill them, not that shooting enthusiasts need justification to massacre birds of prey, or any *other* wildlife. Oxford has the most famous *Eagle and Child*, where regulars Tolkien and Lewis would boozily chat about Hobbits, elves, witches and wardrobes. For over two-hundred years, York had a pub with this name on the Shambles, but the more recent *Eagle and Child* stands halfway along High Petergate, tastefully converted from the restaurant that stood there for several decades. The Rolling Stones were customers – the rock band leaving their (now framed) wall graffiti upstairs – but as this Tudor building was constructed in 1640, it has doubtless boasted many more celebrated visitors over the centuries.

With beamed ceilings and exposed floorboards, the inn's olde worlde rooms are spread over three levels. Quist and his young assistant sat by one of the front windows in the busy downstairs bar. The detective's overcoat was folded on the chair beside him and Watson smirked at his grey jacket, black trousers and beige shirt. Compared to his boss's dreary wardrobe, the clothes worn by middle-aged geography teachers would appear flamboyantly camp and daring.

"I'm wondering, Guv…" The youth took a gulp of lager and began chomping his way through a bag of bacon crisps. "Have you ever thought about making a porn film?"

Sipping his beer, Quist regarded him curiously. "That's an unexpected and somewhat peculiar question. I hardly think anyone would want to watch me *in action*, so to speak."

"Ooh, I don't know." Watson laughed. "You're a good-looking guy, even with that, er, bigger than average nose. No, don't be daft; I mean *filming* a porno. We're halfway there already, taking sleazy videos of people kissing and groping."

"Oh, I see." The detective glanced past the entrance to the corner by the opposite window where the couple from the ghost tour were seated. "I have to concede, our footage of Alan Turnpenny is somewhat sordid, but ideal divorce evidence for his wife's solicitor."

"Adulterous Al," Watson watched the pair cuddling and shook his head. "Wow, what a catch."

Yes, this was definitely NOT the most thrilling assignment he'd been involved with. Alan Turnpenny lived with his family in Leeds, but managed a York sales company and this was a typical working day for him. Client appointments had been rearranged, enabling him to take his current girlfriend Bethany for a drink before heading to her apartment for thirty minutes of rolling around on the bed. *What girl could ask for more from a relationship?* thought Watson, smirking. *True romance was far from dead.*

Bethany had been spoiled this afternoon. Aware of her obsession with astrology and the paranormal, her lover had squeezed in a ghost walk before the lager and sex.

"Bloody hell," gasped Watson, crunching crisps, He watched as Turnpenny's hand slid beneath the table and Bethany began to giggle. "Well, I've got to say, Adulteress Al really knows how to show a girl a good time. He's a real old-fashioned smoothie, isn't he?"

"Good Heavens," murmured Quist. "Whatever is he doing?"

The youth raised his eyebrows. "Well, I don't think he's winding his watch down there."

The incredulous detective lifted his phone, zoomed in with the camera and clicked off a swift photograph.

Bernard Quist hadn't always been a detective, nor, for that matter, had he always been Bernard Quist. Born into the wealthy Quist family of Northumberland, he was christened Richard and his signet ring still bore the RQ initials. Since the supernatural attack in 1790, along with the resultant life change and furry makeover, he'd never aged and to avoid suspicion (and poor jokes about paintings in attics), he changed identities and moved around every few decades. A similar name was always used – Richard Quayle, Bernard Quinn, Robert Quist – and over the years, he'd excelled in many professions. Quist ran a small London law firm in the 1850s and practised as a medical doctor in Victorian Edinburgh, but this modern age of digital records and computerised background searches meant that such occupations were no longer possible.

"Boring adultery," sighed Watson, swigging lager. "So, you take me along on the crappy cases like this, but when it comes to the exciting stuff, you piss off on your own."

"I *had* to go alone last night," said Quist. "I'm sure you'll appreciate that?"

The teenager winked. "I just wish I could have seen the faces on those gypsies when you threatened them as the big bad wolf."

"You'd need to travel to Ireland to see them. I took the precaution of fitting an inexpensive tracker beneath one of their vehicles to ensure they left the Goathland area. They drove through the night to Liverpool and caught a ferry to Dublin."

"Brilliant. You must have really scared them. Hey, Guv, how do you get gypsies to take a bath?"

The detective shrugged.

"You leave it unattended on your front lawn."

"Droll." Quist nodded. "And a little racist."

"Racist?" The grinning youth finished his crisps without

offering any, tilting back his head and emptying the bag down his throat. "A sexy black guy like me?"

Watson knew bacon-flavoured snacks were off limits to the detective. To control his dark supernatural side, Quist was unable to consume meat, or *anything* containing animal products. A strict regime of veganism, yoga and meditation allowed him to manage the ferocious urges, along with his adherence to an ancient rule – to remain in control of the wolf, he could never take a human life.

The teenager was decidedly grateful for the latter whenever Quist shapeshifted in his presence. The majority of werewolves were a little less approachable and not quite so friendly as his boss. In lupine form, Quist's glowing eyes were amber, whereas most had red eyes after surrendering to the savage impulses and embracing the beast within. The detective had grown tired of his assistant jokingly comparing this to the colours of the lightsabers wielded by goodies and baddies in *Star Wars*.

"Yeah, frightening off criminals." Watson nodded. "That certainly beats this divorce stuff and serving papers. The usual cases we get are so boring compared to the paranormal shit."

Quist glanced around the busy room to ensure no one was listening and lowered his voice. "Let's be honest, the first time you encountered *paranormal shit*, as you so eloquently phrase it, you almost died of fright. Besides, we can't be involved with such challenges all the time. I can't just magic up a case involving the supernatural."

"Good pun. Speaking of supernatural, it's the full moon tomorrow. Aren't you worried about Rex?"

Rex Grant was a friend in London. This young man had been close to death when Quist saved his life with a werewolf bite, but the good deed had an obvious downside. Being responsible for Rex's secret furry condition, the detective had been monitoring this fellow lycanthrope and teaching him how to cope, especially at this time of the month when the lupine impulses were at their strongest. Both men followed the strict vegan diet and yoga regime and the even *stricter* rule of never killing a human with tooth and claw.

"I'm confident he'll be fine," said Quist. "Rex is accustomed to handling the lunar phases now. Besides, he's currently holidaying in Jamaica with some lingerie model he's dating."

"Ah, that's good." Watson nodded. "If he's in a different country, the moon won't be full."

Quist raised his eyebrows. "You're inferring that, when the moon is full in Britain, it will be a crescent in, say, Australia?"

"Exactly," snorted Watson. "It isn't rocket science. I thought you were supposed to be clever?"

The detective regarded him with a peculiar expression, wondering if this was an attempt at humour. He saw that it wasn't and returned to sipping his beer.

"You'll just have to keep an eye on the news." Watson laughed. "Watch out for any reports of people being ripped to shreds in the Caribbean. Hey, speaking of murders, what do you reckon to this Cleopatra Killer?"

"I *reckon* the gutter press have truly excelled themselves with that ludicrous name." Quist shook his head. "But three young women killed over three nights here in York is beyond belief, isn't it? I heard about the third murder on the radio earlier. The police discovered the poor girl on St George's Field this morning."

"Horrible." Watson shuddered. "It makes you think."

"Absolutely," said Quist. "I'm thinking why would the murderer dump his victim in the corner of the car park right *next* to the river instead of *in* the river?"

"That's some pretty morbid shit."

"Just an observation. This individual clearly has a vehicle to transport the bodies. I can understand him wrapping them in carpet to assist in moving them, but why leave them in locations where they'll be discovered? Why not drop his victims in the river which would carry them away?"

"I don't know," admitted Watson. "But here's an idea, Guv. Maybe lunatic psychopaths think differently to us."

"Perhaps, but the water would also destroy any traces of his DNA. Thanks to the winter rain, the Ouse is currently high and fast. His victims would be carried out past Goole and into the Humber before dawn. The chances are they'd never be seen again."

"Yeah, what a *lovely* thought." Watson gestured to the door as a black-haired girl with Goth make-up walked in. "Well, on a lighter, more upbeat note, look who's here."

The detective watched as Kyle Tarot followed his daughter into the pub and headed for the rear room beyond the bar. The girl spotted Watson and gave a mischievous wink as she passed.

"Oh, yes," said Quist. "The guide from the ghost walk, and the attractive young lady that I noticed you were so interested in."

"She's called Charlotte," said the teenager.

Quist nodded slowly. "She looks slightly familiar."

"She *looks* slightly tasty," corrected Watson, smirking. "She seems to like me and, let's face it, who can blame her? The guy who runs the walk is her Dad."

"Really?" Quist gave a lopsided smile. "He should have brought his clientele in here. They'd see far more spirits in a pub than on that lamentable *psychic* tour of his."

* * * *

Chapter 4

Charlotte found a vacant table in the Eagle and Child as her father ordered at the counter. Kyle Tarot had removed his cloak after the ghost walk and bundled it into a carrier which the girl hung on the rear of her chair. The pub was busy and Kyle noticed that some of the male customers were staring at his daughter. Paying for the drinks and turning to look at her, he realised why and shook his head resignedly. She'd slipped off her Goth coat and wore a tight black T-shirt with no bra. Charlotte was sixteen, but could easily pass for someone in their early twenties.

Kyle grimaced as he carried the beer and orange juice to the table. *Very soon now this girl was going to start breaking hearts and his would probably top the casualty list.*

"Are you going to be okay getting home after we've eaten?" he asked, handing her a bar food menu. "You can take my cloak. I have a session of private readings, so I have to go to..."

"Dad, please," laughed Charlotte. "I'm not a kid."

"Those murdered girls weren't kids either, so be careful out there. I *mean* it. I'll give you the taxi fare to make sure you're safe."

"Well, unless the Cleopatra Killer is a taxi driver."

"Don't joke about it." Kyle grinned. "Hey, I wasn't sure that afternoon ghost walks would work. There isn't much atmosphere in daylight, but we had twenty-seven customers so maybe I was wrong."

Charlotte nodded. "One of them was nice. I chatted with him and he gave me his business card."

"What? Did you tell him your age?"

"Are you serious? That might have put him off."

"Exactly," snapped Kyle. "You're sixteen, for God's sake."

"Er, *yeah*, which was legal the last time I checked."

"*Legal*?" Kyle shook his head, astounded. "Charlie, you're still a schoolgirl. You only turned sixteen last month and already you

26

have smarmy businessmen chatting you up..."

"He gave me a business card, but he was a private detective, not a businessman. Actually, he's in the next room."

"Is he indeed?" Her father glanced around suspiciously.

"Hey, I thought you were cool." She smiled mischievously. "Anyway, despite the outraged parent crap, you *are* cool. How many girls can say their Dad is psychic?"

Kyle chuckled and drank his beer. "Get it right, Charlie. I'm psychic *and* clairvoyant. It means the same to most people, but psychics feel atmospheres and emotions. Clairvoyants actually speak with the deceased."

"Whatever. You *look* cool too."

"It's all for the punters, as you know." Kyle stroked his beard and wiggled his pentagram ring. "That's why I changed my name and wear the cloak when I'm working. There are thousands of psychics and a memorable persona is the best way to get repeat business. People prefer readings from a black-garbed clairvoyant called Tarot than some plain old psychic called Kyle Lewis."

"If you're psychic, you'll know I'm having a sandwich." Charlotte handed back the menu. "The grilled chicken wrap."

"I can't have anything spicy." Kyle read through the food. "I'd better get the same. I need fresh breath for the readings."

"You're out every night doing your readings and ghost walks and now you have these extra afternoon tours. I hardly see you."

"It can't be helped." Shrugging, he headed to the bar to order the food. "We need the money."

Charlotte waited until he returned. "As we're talking about your work, I've been meaning to ask for a while – does it ever bother you? Lying to people is your profession and we both know that basically you're a con-man. Do you ever feel bad about it?"

"No, I provide a service," said Kyle. "People come to me for comfort and they leave feeling safe in the knowledge that their dead relatives are happy. If they have *real* problems, I refer them to appropriate agencies." He tapped the pocket of his velvet jacket containing his notebook. "I have a list – cancer support, counsellors and suchlike. The church lies to bereaved people every day. Vicars charge a fortune at funerals to tell you your loved one is in a better place, far more than I charge for the same message."

"Yeah, the psychic business is an easy way to make cash," conceded Charlotte. "I might take it up as a side-line when I go to college."

Kyle grimaced, but covered this by scratching his nose. The plan had always been for his daughter to enrol in a good art college after finishing school, but higher education plans cost money and the Tarot bank account wasn't exactly overflowing. Charlotte remained blissfully unaware of just *how* bad their financial situation actually was.

"You're a bit young," he said. "Image plays a big part and clients expect psychics to be older than you. I visited plenty of mediums for research when I began and they're usually a particular type too. Bank managers never discover they can talk to the dead and resign to help people with their power. If psychics aren't unemployed when they start out, they're mostly shop assistants or hairdressers, the kind of job where they mix with women. Once they discover how much cash women waste to hear simplistic claptrap from clairvoyants, it doesn't take them long to realise they could do the job themselves."

"You got into this because of your aunt, didn't you?" asked Charlotte.

"Well, I thought if *she* could do it, so could I." Kyle laughed. "Your Mum was an accountant and I was the househusband looking after you. She was the breadwinner and, after we lost her, I needed money. I'd been stupid enough to let the life insurance lapse and that's why I felt guilty and drank so much back then. The house was paid off on her death, but I made the mistake of taking out a remortgage to see us through until I found a job. Watching how my aunt operated, it soon dawned on me that this was something I could easily do. Something lucrative requiring no qualifications or training."

"And then you fell out with her." Charlotte shrugged. "To be honest, I always liked her."

"Let's not talk about that." He smiled tightly. "I went to a spiritualist church to research the job. I don't know what I expected, but certainly not the charade I saw. I couldn't understand why no one else could see it was an act, with every medium performing the same routine and using identical catchphrases. I saw through it in *one* night, so why didn't the people who went there every week?"

"Amazing."

"I haven't a clue what happens when we die, Charlie, but I know we don't talk drivel through someone who charges money to hear it. The clients don't seem to notice, but if the spirit world is real, then the IQ must take a nosedive after death, because the departed aren't renowned for intelligent conversation. Spirits will vaguely mention holidays, uniforms and pet cats, but you can forget about *real* dialogue or insightful glimpses into the next life."

Kyle paused as the two sandwiches arrived, glaring as his daughter's nubile figure was given a lingering look by the waiter.

"Thanks, pal," he snapped irately, turning back to her. "I knew it'd be easy enough to put on a better show than the spiritualist mediums and I booked private readings to learn how psychics operated one-on-one. Incredibly, they all had the same act, using cold reading with the same psychological tricks and key phrases."

"And you became a clairvoyant – just like that?"

"Like I said, Charlie, I'd remortgaged the house. I owed a fortune and our home would have been repossessed."

Debt has a malicious tendency to escalate, especially when mixed with alcohol, and Kyle had consolidated his various loans into one "simple" monthly repayment which wasn't as simple as the finance company had made out and extended into the distant future. He had the sickening feeling that his debts would be paid off when people were commuting to work in flying cars.

"Yeah, six years ago, I became Kyle Tarot." He chewed on his chicken wrap. "After your Mum's death, changing my persona was probably an unconscious attempt to leave behind the emotionally-shattered Kyle Lewis. On the plus side, I'm a good psychic and I've helped lots of people. You have to understand that the clients *want* to believe in my powers and they attach significance to whatever I say. If I mention a man with a limp or something in the pocket of an old coat, you'll see them racking their brains to make these things fit into their life. That's why there are so many psychics and why so many are rubbish. If their customers are so eager to believe in life after death, the clairvoyants don't have to try too hard."

Charlotte nodded. "Do the television psychics work differently to you?"

"The programmes use editing and cut out the waffle. You've watched their awful shows. If those clairvoyants could genuinely glean *real* information from empty rooms, don't you think the police would use them? Imagine taking them into a building recently used by terrorists. Within minutes, they'd tell you their whereabouts and names, but instead, these people are strolling around *haunted* houses making blonde presenters scream."

"Yeah, we know psychics are con-men..." His daughter frowned. "But spirits *must* exist..."

"Only in the same world as Santa Claus and the Tooth Fairy."

"But so many people have seen them."

"Well, some people *want* to see certain spirits and most see them next to the bed as they're dropping off to sleep. Their recently departed grandfather appears and, when they sit up, he vanishes. How stupid would you need to be to not realise you've fallen asleep, dreamt it and jolted yourself awake to an empty room?"

"Would you call *me* stupid?" asked Charlotte, quietly. "Because it was next to the bed where I saw Mum."

"Really?" Putting down his sandwich, Kyle reached across and took her hand. "You've never mentioned this before."

"It was a few weeks after we lost her. Mum told me I wasn't to worry and said she'd always love us both. I didn't say anything because I knew you'd be upset, but I told your aunt and she said that my Mum was…"

"My aunt was a con artist just like me," snapped Kyle, irately. "If she was spouting rubbish about your Mum, I'm not really interested in what *she* said."

"That's why I never told you. So you think it was a dream?"

"I think you were a little girl, you missed her very much and you were thinking about her as you were drifting off to sleep." He squeezed her hand. "Whatever it was, it's really lovely, Charlie."

His daughter smiled. "It's hard to believe that all those famous people are fakes. Those celebrity psychics like Doris Stokes…"

Kyle laughed. "Doris wasn't even good at faking it. She used audience plants and a host of other well-known tricks. The top psychics hardly ever bother with private readings because so many idiots are prepared to pay for their shows. To get the big money, you need to be a showman up at that level, filling venues three nights a week and boasting a list of famous clients on the side."

Charlotte nodded. "I've noticed how celebrities always visit clairvoyants. The showbiz world seems to be obsessed with it."

"That's true," agreed Kyle. "Just a few days before her death, Princess Diana visited a Sheffield medium who could see the future, but guess what? She never spotted the Paris car smash. She saw nothing of that funeral where Britain came to a silent standstill and the world watched Elton John singing in the cathedral."

"Wow. So that ruined her?"

"Absolutely not." He shook his head. "They flocked to her

after that, because once you're famous, it doesn't matter how rubbish you are. People are drawn to fame and, if you're a celebrity psychic, you can charge serious money. All you need is that break, that scrap of fame to set you apart from the rest, and this woman achieved it simply by being Diana's clairvoyant."

Charlotte winked. "Well, obviously that's what *you* need to do and I can have a Porsche for my seventeenth birthday."

"Obviously," laughed Kyle. "Yeah, I'll just become a top celebrity psychic. I mean to say, how hard can it be?"

* * * *

Chapter 5

Liam Piper believed that dressing sensibly in winter was for wimps, homosexuals and people with larger IQs. Combatting the icy March weather with a Leeds United T shirt, the burly youth stood outside the Alpha Inn in Acomb, leaning drunkenly against the front wall with a cigarette trembling in his fist. Although Piper would never admit to the girly weakness of feeling cold, he was absolutely freezing this Monday afternoon. He shivered uncontrollably, but *this* shivering was mostly due to the inexplicable unease he felt as he watched a shaven-headed man in a crumpled blue suit.

Piper had never seen him before; he certainly didn't frequent the Alpha Inn. Around thirty and cadaverously thin, the man had parked a red Transit van on the pub forecourt and now appeared to be waiting for someone by the rear doors of the vehicle. Piper often popped outside for a smoke and normally spent the time staring slack-jawed at his phone. Today the mobile remained forgotten in his pocket as he gazed instead at the stranger, almost mesmerised by this bizarre character.

The drooling weirdo reminded him of a reptile. His bright green eyes didn't seem to blink, and every few seconds his tongue extended, as if tasting the air, before running over his lips to collect the copious tendrils of dribble. He'd clearly missed quite a bit, as his jacket lapels and shirt front glistened with matted saliva.

"Mmmh, it's a lovely afternoon," said Rakkat, his voice a rumbling growl. He turned to fix his inebriated observer with a frigid green glare. "It'd be a real shame to ruin it, so I hope we don't have a problem, big boy?"

"Er, no, not at all." The brawny drunk shuffled nervously, slurring as he held up his shaking cigarette. "There's no problem, mate. I just came out for a smoke."

"No problem? Oh, I'm so glad to hear it."

Rakkat stood ten feet away, but even at that distance the stench of his breath was repulsive. The Alpha wasn't the friendliest of taverns and most of the regulars could handle themselves, but something – some sixth sense – told Piper that aggression would be very foolish here.

"Well, Liam, I guess this is a bit of a clichéd line…" Rakkat's skeletal features cracked into a ghastly, drooling smile. "But just who the fuck are you looking at?"

"No one." Piper turned away quickly and the trembling increased. It was colder than usual this afternoon and he folded his arms tightly over his protruding beer belly. "No, I'm not looking. Like I said, I came out for a smoke."

He couldn't understand it. *Why the hell was he feeling scared when this ashen-faced bastard looked so emaciated in his loose-fitting suit? He should be able to wipe the floor with him. One good punch would probably put him in intensive care. And how on earth did the man know his name was Liam? He wisely decided not to ask.*

"Ah, sweet child." Rakkat's smile widened as a fair-haired young woman left the pub, a mobile phone grasped in her hand. "I do believe it's Sara, isn't it?"

"Er, yeah, I'm Sara." Catching her breath as the icy air hit her, the scantily-clad girl eyed the man warily, seeing the grubby suit and the drool stains on his chest. "How did you know?"

"Oh, I know a great many things."

"Is that so?" Sara shuddered. *This cold felt wrong and somehow… unnatural.* "Who are you?"

"Merely a lonely stranger hoping for a little romantic company." Rakkat gave a chivalrous bow and gestured to the van. "Look, my dear child, your chariot awaits."

Sara Ritter operated as a discreet prostitute. Supplementing her job in the Solaris Massage Parlour two streets away, she picked up clients in the Alpha Inn most weekend evenings. Occasionally, when she needed more coke, she'd work during the day like this. She had certain standards, however, and this salivating creature didn't come anywhere close to meeting them. Something about his green eyes and his voice – the low growling – caused the hair to rise on her neck. Her profession had its fair share of risks, which had furnished her with an inbuilt alarm system, and every warning bell was loudly ringing.

"Er, no," she said, peering apprehensively at the van and gripping her phone tighter. "I don't think so. No, I'm busy."

This skinny creep probably might not be too bad if he didn't look so grey and so... dead. Sara recoiled slightly. *And then there was his unbelievable breath. It smelled like a blocked toilet – a toilet blocked by a decomposing cat. No, she definitely wasn't entertaining this hideous guy. Besides, clients never took kindly to being vomited on.*

"Don't be foolish, sweet child." Chuckling and throwing open the rear doors of the Transit, Rakkat began to sing. *"Sara, you're the poet in my heart. Never change and don't you ever stop..."*

Still leaning against the pub wall, Liam Piper's eyes widened. There were poor vocalists and really lousy ones, but this horrific noise was something else entirely. He'd heard the Fleetwood Mac song before and although it wasn't his kind of music, he remembered it being pleasant and melodic. If anyone were deranged enough to release this guttural snarling as a cover version, they wouldn't be selling too many copies.

Rakkat stopped his singing and turned again to Piper. "Hey, big boy, didn't Mummy teach you that it's rude to stare?" He wiped a spill of drool from his chin. "Believe me, Liam, staring at me can be suicidal."

Gulping, Piper tossed down his half-smoked cigarette and hurried back into the warmth of the pub.

Sara suddenly spotted the van wing mirror and the face reflected in the glass. With its rear end facing her, she hadn't realised before, but this stinking nutter wasn't alone. There was someone else sitting in the driving seat. *Was he wanting a threesome?*

"No, like I said, I'm busy." Shivering in the cold, she shook her head and began walking past the vehicle. "I have somewhere I need to be and…"

Rakkat's arm shot out to grasp her wrist, his other hand sliding into his jacket pocket. The open van doors shielded the pair from passing traffic and he glanced around to ensure they were unobserved. Jerking her arm angrily, Sara noticed the bloody cuts on his wrist; a crude symbol about four inches in diameter had been carved into the grey flesh.

"What the hell do you think you're doing?" she snapped, the icy chill prickling her skin with goosebumps. "You have two choices, darling. You can either let go of me right *now*, or you can explain to everyone who comes running out of this pub why I was screaming so loudly."

"Ooh, no, I believe there's a *third* choice." Whipping out a moist cloth from the plastic bag in his pocket, Rakkat clamped it tightly over her face, looking around again as she struggled.

Sara stared into his green eyes as the overpowering chloroform fumes filled her throat and lungs. Her mobile clattered on the forecourt tarmac as Rakkat caught her slumping body, effortlessly scooping her up and laying the unconscious girl inside the rear of the Transit. Slamming the doors, he glanced around a final time before kicking Sara's phone away, strolling to the front and climbing into the passenger seat.

"*Sara,*" he sang, stroking the gashes on his wrist as the driver pulled out onto the road, "*you're the poet in my heart…*"

* * * *

Chapter 6

Kyle Tarot sat in a house on Wormstall Street, one of the less salubrious areas in the York neighbourhood of Clifton. A dog barked by the broken fridge in the garden and a wailing baby competed for attention with a loud reality show in the next room. Dressed in tight jeans and a low-cut top, Chelzee Grimes sat opposite him at the kitchen table, the third of his seven psychic readings. Her friends waited their turn in the lounge, drinking fizzy wine and staring at phones. On meeting clients, Kyle profiled them, checking their clothing brands, tattoos and a host of other things. Some were harder to read than others, but this group would be straightforward and, as always, they *wanted* to believe in his gift, which made it easy. *The fact that they were actually paying someone money to hear about their futures already told him quite a bit about them.*

Cold reading enables psychics to appear far more informed than they actually are. Most psychologists would outshine Kyle at this technique, but naturally, would never claim their talent was supernatural. Salesmen, con-men, mentalists and advertising people all use cold reading to some extent, but clairvoyants have constructed their entire profession around it.

In order to give an accurate *reading*, psychics need general insights into human nature, along with a basic knowledge of current trends. People see themselves as individuals, but many think alike in a multitude of ways. Kyle asked questions and dropped hints whilst watching for involuntary "tells" – changes in expression and posture. If what he'd hinted at was correct, he'd pursue that avenue, but if he was wrong, the client showed that too and he changed direction. He'd go *fishing*, mentioning lots of things and observing these signs – a child with a violin, a vet's bill, marital troubles, a celebration, a red car, someone moving home. They never remembered what he got wrong. Only what he got right.

If the client was the age for teenage children, he'd tell her she was having problems with them, uncannily knowing they were surly and quarrelsome. Pets and babies were mentioned; everyone knows a pregnant girl or someone who recently gave birth. Kyle memorised the year's "must have" baby names – Andromeda, Alopecia, Galadriel, Chlamydia – because the girls who paid for his services invariably chose one of these. Younger clients were sometimes pregnant when they came to him. Often they hadn't told anyone, so his psychic knowledge of their condition was amazing.

Basically Kyle told them things they already knew, but they needed to trust his gift before he could speak to the departed. Only when he'd proven his powers – by telling a suntanned girl that she'd recently been abroad and that her ex-boyfriend was a bastard – did he contact the spirit world, in this case Chelzee's grandfather.

"Yes, Chelzee," he said. "The uniform belongs to a nurse. It was the nice nurse who looked after your granddad."

Like every psychic, he always mentioned uniforms. Everyone is familiar with someone who wears one; even supermarket workers have a uniform. The technique was to say that he could see it and they'd tell him who wore it. They may know someone in the forces, they could have been arrested, or like Chelzee, a relative may have been hospitalised. They found the association and told him, but went away thinking *he'd* told *them*.

"Was your granddad in pain for a while, Chelzee, or did he pass over quickly?"

"Oh, quickly. He was only in five days before he died."

"That's right," nodded Kyle, "because he's telling me he was fortunate. He was there less than a week and he was spared the pain. He wants you to know that he didn't suffer."

If the spirit was providing this information, anyone with sense might wonder why Chelzee needed to be asked. Luckily, sense was something she seemed to lack. He found himself questioning the sense of her parents too, for spelling Chelsea's name *Chelzee*.

Kyle paused for a moment. Using pauses was good; silence feels awkward in conversations and people get an urge to fill it. If he didn't speak, they spoke instead, volunteering information and often telling him what he needed to hear.

"What was it you always called him?" he murmured. "Not granddad. He says you called him…"

"Gramps."

"That's right. Gramps is saying you're thinking about a change in your life." He always kept it vague. Everyone contemplates change and she'd soon tell him what it was. "He says the change you're considering is a good one." Kyle smiled to himself. *Like anyone would decide they needed a bad change.*

"Yeah, you're spot on." Chelzee paused in her gum-chewing to inflate a pink bubble which burst with a loud *plap*! "I'm thinking about changing jobs. It's shit where I work."

"Gramps says you should." Kyle followed the golden rule of telling them what they wanted to hear. "He says you'll be rid of that nasty little cow who works there, and the other one with the loud mouth. He's giving me the letter D."

Clients found nothing unusual in this, but why anyone, who had no interest in word puzzles during life, should suddenly acquire a taste for them after death was bewildering.

"He means Donna." The girl gave a brusque laugh. "And big fat Chantelle."

Whenever he performed group readings, Kyle liked to chat with the party over a coffee beforehand. A wealth of information could be gleaned from mundane banter, but tonight's conversation had centred around the York murders and he'd had to rely on cold reading. Normally this was fine, but Charlotte's college fees dominated his thoughts which could easily lead to mistakes.

"Gramps says a change of job will be good for you, and

what's this about Magaluf? A holiday?"

Every year there was *the* place to holiday, but Kyle never told the client she'd been there. That was too specific and he could be wrong. He'd simply say he was sensing *Tenerife* and, if she'd visited, she'd be amazed he knew. If she hadn't, she was probably planning to go, or would know someone who had.

"Yeah, Magaluf," said Chelzee. "It was a weekend away with the girls."

"Gramps is glad you enjoyed it, but he thinks you overdid it a bit with the merrymaking. He's also warning me about a young man. He's saying he has lots of tattoos and he likes a drink. In fact he drinks a bit too much and he drives too fast. Does that make sense?"

"Hah!" She rolled her eyes. "He means Tezza."

"Gramps says Tezza's no good for you." Stroking his brow, Kyle glanced under his hand at Chelzee's legs. The jeans were so tight, he was able to count the change in her pocket. "He's saying you deserve better."

"Well he's history now. He shagged Abbie behind my back."

After taking her details when she made the appointment, Kyle could have discovered most of this from Chelzee's social media; it was simple to get accepted as a false friend and read up on the recent past. Had she been influential – a professional with wealthy associates – he'd have used Facebook, but cold reading was less time-consuming. The internet had been a godsend for psychics. Once he had a name, it was incredible what he could Google, and all television mediums accessed websites on their mobiles to glean on-the-spot facts.

He closed his eyes in concentration. "I'm seeing the number four; look out for that and smoke, perhaps coming from a window. Yes, you should be careful of fire. I'm also seeing two presents, one large and one small. I'm not sure if they're for you..."

Kyle shook himself, realising he'd lazily lapsed into fishing in an attempt to speed things up, mentioning unrelated nonsense and leaving it to the client to sift out relevant items. This was the rubbish spouted by mediocre psychics who topped up their benefits by operating from council houses. He grimaced and lowered his voice.

"Now, Chelzee, we need to talk about this abortion…"

The gum-chewing abruptly stopped.

Something so private was never mentioned, except to close confidants, and for a psychic to hit upon such a colossal secret was absolute proof of their gift. Clients were oblivious to the number of terminations that took place and the trick was never to be specific. He always said *this abortion* and paused to let them fill in the rest. It could be the client herself, her sister, daughter, or friend. If they were unaware of a termination, then it was obviously someone close that they didn't yet know about. From her shocked reaction, Chelzee certainly knew about *this* one.

"It was the correct thing to do," he continued. If Chelzee was the one, she'd assume he was speaking directly to her. If it was a friend, his ambiguity still worked. Keep it vague and never say *you* or *they*. "Guilt isn't necessary, because it was morally right. Gramps has a young spirit with him who's saying it would have been wrong to be born into the world at that time."

"What's he talking about?" Chelzee shook her head. "I'm booked in for the operation this Friday. I don't understand."

Kyle had been preoccupied with college fees and he cringed at his clumsiness. "Understanding isn't always important," he said, smiling supportively. "Where the supernatural is concerned, sometimes it's best not to question too much. Sometimes it's best just to accept."

* * * *

Kyle walked along Terry Avenue, leaving the city centre behind and heading towards his home in the suburb of Nunthorpe. Huge confectionery firms once operated in York and many streets bear their names. This narrow thoroughfare alongside the Ouse was named after the inventor of the Chocolate Orange, Joseph Terry, the evil nemesis of countless dieting women. After crossing Skeldergate Bridge, Kyle could have continued on Bishopthorpe Road, but he preferred strolling by the water. More a footpath than a street, Terry Avenue passes a low-rise apartment block just after the bridge, then quickly takes on a rural feel as it reaches the sprawl of Rowntree Park. This quiet route helped Kyle to think, and his current financial situation gave him *plenty* to think about.

He'd made a decent amount tonight, but a third had already been spent on a taxi ride into town and a few drinks in one of the pubs. *Well, more than a few.* Sighing, he knew it didn't really matter. The money he'd blown wouldn't have made a dint in his crippling debt and it would take a lot more than seven psychic readings to send Charlie to college.

Trees and bushes lined the narrow street and an owl called from the overhead branches. Slightly inebriated, Kyle smiled to hear the hooting and tried shrugging off his monetary worries. *Yes, not only was this way home quieter and slightly shorter, but it was more pleasant. Well, it was usually more pleasant.*

Tonight, with the lack of vehicles and pedestrians, it felt a little creepy. The moon was almost full, and glancing across the river to his left, he realised why. The police had discovered a girl's body over there on St George's Field this morning and he could make out the cordon tape that still surrounded the car park corner. Shuddering, Kyle walked faster, before deciding he'd better make a quick stop.

"When you have to go..." he muttered, stepping into an opening on his right.

He stood behind a bush to urinate, gazing into the darkness of Rowntree Park. Joseph Rowntree owned the largest of the York chocolate companies and created this twenty-acre recreational area in memory of his employees who died in the Great War. Kyle was grateful that he'd also created this handy gateway. A fox yelped somewhere in the trees, then hearing a vehicle approaching, he glanced over his shoulder to see a Transit van drive past without lights. The moon reflected silver on the dark roof and he watched curiously as it executed a U-turn to stop on the riverside grass some twenty feet away. Kyle could make out the shapes of two people inside, one of whom had long hair, and the lack of headlights suggested a courting couple.

"Well, who's a lucky girl?" he mumbled to himself, grinning drunkenly. "You've found someone romantic enough to shag you in the back of his works van, have you?"

A slender man in a suit climbed from the passenger seat and stood for several moments, his bald head slowly turning as he checked the park and lane for movement. Shivering as an icy breeze wafted over him, Kyle zipped up his trousers and realised he was invisible here in the shadows concealed by shrubbery. Seemingly satisfied, the man opened the back of the van to rummage inside. Kyle wondered if he was about to bring out the girlfriend for an alfresco romp, then froze as a roll of carpet was dragged onto the grass.

"*Jesus!*" he mouthed. "You have to be kidding." He watched the man dump the bundle beside a clump of bushes and close the rear doors. "Oh, no, you really *have* to be kidding."

Could this be... No, of course not. No, this was just someone fly-tipping. Kyle gulped, his heart thudding as the man climbed back into the vehicle. *Yes, it was just an old carpet.*

"KE55 WCK." Reciting the moonlit registration as the van accelerated away past him, he fumbled for his notebook. "What's the point?" He laughed uneasily and scribbled it down with a shaky hand. "You know it's only rubbish, you idiot. It's just an old carpet." He stepped out of the gateway, heart pounding faster as he crossed the narrow lane. "Come on, you've got to do it, but please let this be nothing."

Six feet in length, the carpet roll lay partly under the bushes by the water. Gritting his teeth, Kyle pulled back the uppermost fold.

"Oh *Christ!*" He clapped a hand to his mouth and jumped back as if someone had punched him.

No, of course it wasn't rubbish. From the moment he saw it, he'd known exactly what this was going to be.

Glazed eyes stared from a white face. Kyle had only seen three bodies before – his parents and his late wife – and although he'd never profess medical knowledge, he knew beyond any doubt that this girl was dead. He also knew now that death looks far more terrifying by silver moonlight. His heart felt like it was about to burst and he realised that, for several seconds, he'd forgotten to breathe.

Jesus, it was a naked corpse wrapped in carpet. A woman who'd been murdered.

Shaking uncontrollably and unclamping the fingers from his mouth, his eyes moved down from her blonde hair and waxy features to the disfigured chest. A triangle and a five-pointed design had been carved into the pallid flesh between her breasts, a criss-cross of cuts that appeared gloss-black in the cold lunar rays.

What the hell had those maniacs in the van done to her? Full sobriety had now returned and, shaking worse than ever, he wished she'd stop staring at him. *Oh, God, it was a murdered woman.*

Taking large gasps and staggering backwards, Kyle scrabbled for his phone and thumbed in 999. "What?" He tried again, but the mobile bleeped, its battery dead. "Of all the times to…" He gave a manic laugh and peered along Terry Avenue. "I don't believe this. I really do *not* believe this."

He had to find a pub with a phone or maybe a passing police car. If he ran back along the lane, he could call in the pub at…

"Wait a minute…" Kyle stopped breathing again as the tiny seed of an insane idea began to germinate.

He shook himself. *What was he thinking? No, it was so*

ludicrous, only an imbecile would consider it. He really had to find a phone and report this as soon as possible.

Kyle raced up the lane and stopped abruptly, his hammering heart almost audible. "Wait a minute though. But what if..."

Yes, it might be immoral and crazy, but this was exactly what he'd talked about with Charlie in the pub earlier. *All you need is that break – that scrap of fame to set you apart from the rest.* The seed of the idea grew and began to flower. *If he took care and everything was done right, then here was the fame he'd spoken of. His debts would be history, the house would be safe for his daughter and her college fees would no longer be a problem.*

Trembling and panting slightly, Kyle gazed at the dark shape by the bushes, wrestling with the chaos of emotions before reaching a decision. *Whoever she was, this poor girl was dead and there was nothing he could do about that.*

"I'm sorry," he whispered, setting off for home. "I really am so sorry, but you need to lie there just a little longer."

There was nothing he could do to help her, but if this insane idea worked, he could certainly help Charlie.

* * * *

Chapter 7

The York police headquarters stands south of the city centre in a quiet area of landscaped grounds off the main Fulford Road. The four-storey building was busier than usual this Tuesday morning, but Katie Bradstreet knew that three murders over three consecutive nights will tend to do that. It was seven-thirty and the Detective Inspector sat with her Sergeant in one of the interview rooms, both women wearing smart grey suits.

"Kyle Tarot?" Katie read from a black business card. She glanced at Angie Gibson and turned back to the man on the opposite side of the table, running a cynical eye over the goatee beard and pentagram ring. "So what's your real name?"

He licked at his parched lips. "That *is* my real name."

"And you're psychic? A psychic called Kyle Tarot?" She tossed down the card. "Well I'm DI Bradstreet. That's *my* real name. I was called in early because they told me you have information about my investigation?"

"That's right," confirmed Kyle, his heart thumping. "I believe what I have to tell you concerns the murders. I'm certain I can…"

"Would this information be supernatural?" asked Angie. The ginger-haired Sergeant rolled her eyes. "Obtained from the shadowy land of the dead?"

"Did I come by it through my gift?" Kyle made another attempt to dampen his bone-dry lips. "Er, yes."

His mouth felt like hot sand and a vein pulsed visibly in his neck. He hadn't slept since finding the girl's body, but adrenaline erased all traces of fatigue. The most difficult part had been screwing up the courage to walk in here, and now. no matter how obscenely unethical this was, he had to make it work. Kyle hated himself, but knew he had to stick to the planned story.

"You need to understand my gift," he said. "Details don't

46

come to me in a clear manner. I don't see things how others see them and the spirit information I channel is sometimes vague, like clouds passing over the…"

"Yes, thank you." The Inspector climbed to her feet and briskly buttoned her suit jacket. "But I'm a busy officer working a murder investigation and I don't have time for this crap."

"What?" Kyle frowned. "I came here to help you with…"

Katie laughed. "Do you know how many psychics crawl out of their holes and come to *help* with every murder and missing child? Instead of getting on with *real* work, we're obliged to listen to them. It's a misconception that the police call on psychics for assistance. No, the parasites simply turn up, like you, to offer their fake services. Once they've spouted their garbage, they can go to the papers and tell them how they've helped." She picked up Kyle's business card. "They can advertise on these as a *psychic who aids the police.*"

Kyle cleared his throat. All of this was true, of course, and common practice in the clairvoyant profession.

"We *have* to listen," added Angie. "Because, who knows? You may be the killer and this could be your eccentric way of confessing."

Katie tossed down the card. "There's only one thing I'd like to use *that* for and it isn't large enough or absorbent enough. My Sergeant here will deal with this."

"Er, right." Kyle turned to Angie as the older detective marched out. "Well your friend isn't very open-minded…"

"Let's not worry about that." Angie smiled tautly. "Why don't we get this over with?"

"*Get this over?*"

Kyle shot her an incredulous look and felt worse than ever, the guilt physically hurting, like a machete buried in his guts, or a particularly bad prawn curry. He lied about the supernatural every day, but that was during readings with clients. He'd never blatantly lied to the police before.

"Look, I'm here to assist you," he said. "I know how this must seem to people who don't understand such things, but I really *have* channelled something which might…"

"Okay," sighed Angie. "So tell me about it."

"I couldn't sleep last night. Shortly after midnight I made a connection with a young girl, a girl with golden hair surrounded by fear and death." His insides twisted themselves into tight knots. *The girl in question was still lying in the bushes on Terry Avenue.* "That's why I called here so early; I needed to tell you about this as soon as possible."

Not reporting what he'd seen was appalling, but using this situation to his advantage was worse and, no doubt, illegal. He stamped down the guilt. *He had to keep a clear head.*

"A blonde girl?" Angie feigned interest. "Is she dead?"

"Yes, she passed into spirit very recently." Kyle narrowed his eyes. "I can still feel her distress. I often channel fear and confusion with the recently departed, but this was more like panic. This poor girl suffered a violent death before her time. She told me she was like the others and I believe she means the murders you're investigating."

"I see." The Sergeant nodded curtly. "Have any of the other victims spoken to you?"

"No, this golden-haired girl is the only one."

"Did she give you the name of her killer, by any chance?"

"I'm afraid not."

"That's a shame," drawled Angie. "I was hoping to close this case before lunch."

"I made notes so I didn't forget." Kyle took out his pocketbook. "Like I said, the information doesn't come in a logical fashion, but in a mystifying jumble. There's water – a river, I think. She isn't *in* the water, but beside it." He closed his eyes. "Yes, it's the River Ouse, and I sensed this golden hair. *You have beautiful hair,*

Little Angel, her mother used to say to her. *It's like spun gold.* Her Mum always called her Little Angel."

"Right," said Angie, deadpan. "That's nice."

"I channelled a sweet fragrance too. Not flowers, but *actual* sweets: chocolate and caramel. I believe the smell was sent spiritually to guide me to her location. It was the scent of Rowntree chocolate."

"Mister Tarot..." sighed Angie. "This is all very interesting, but why don't we leave it there? I'll get back to work and you can go and see if you can channel something more useful."

"I also channelled a van," said Kyle. "A dark van that doesn't belong to the golden-haired girl. She's scared of the van. Why does she fear the dark Transit van so much?"

"I can't imagine," said Angie. "Maybe it belongs to the killer. Then again, over ninety percent of the psychics who call in police stations like this mention the good old van. That and a river or a lake."

"I connected with a man too, a young, thin man with a shaven head. I don't know who he is, but I sensed darkness and I didn't like him. I also channelled the word *Keswick*." He held out his notebook showing combinations of letters. "It isn't the man's name or his location, but I think it's to do with the van; possibly the registration. Look – KES WICK."

"Ah, yes," said Angie. "Yeah, that's helpful."

"Wait, I think it *is* the vehicle registration." Kyle closed his eyes again. "I'm seeing it right now – the number of the Transit van. No, not Keswick, but KE55 WCK."

"Right." The Sergeant smiled tartly. "So instead of telling you who murdered her, this dead girl decided to give you an anagram?"

Kyle shrugged. "Where the supernatural is concerned, sometimes it's best not to question too much. Sometimes it's best just to accept. You can't apply your police logic to this. Maybe she didn't know the killer's name."

"Oh, of course. I didn't think of that."

49

Kyle gulped. *It was time to go for it. Once he crossed this line, there was no going back.*

"I think the sweet scent was a clue, guiding me to Rowntree Park. Yes, she's lying beside Rowntree Park, next to the river, and there's a symbol on the van. No, wait. No, it isn't on the van, but on the girl herself – a red star."

"A star?" Angie stiffened.

"A five-pointed star in a circle with a swirling pattern. I can see it clearly – a pentagram in blood, and a triangle too." Kyle clutched at his chest as if it pained him. "I don't understand. Does any of this make sense to you?"

* * * *

"This *psychic* is the killer," said Angie. The Sergeant stood with Katie Bradstreet and Superintendent Angela Morton outside the interview room. "It *has* to be him."

"I agree," said Morton. "I think you should…"

"You could be right," broke in the Inspector, glancing at her superior and gritting her teeth. "But we can't arrest him yet."

"But he described the symbols on the body," snapped Morton. "The only people who know about them are the murderer and a few police who…"

"Oh, come on, Ma'am." Katie leant against the water cooler, her fingers drumming angrily on the plastic. "Quite a *lot* of police, plus forensics and medical staff. Those officers tell their partners and God knows who else. The partners tell their friends in secrecy…" She jerked an angry thumb towards the interview room door. "Or maybe even their psychics."

"I suppose so," conceded Angie. "He could have overheard two of our people talking carelessly in a pub."

Morton ran a hand through her long hair and seethed. She'd been hoping to ring the Chief Constable and let him know she'd apprehended the Cleopatra Killer.

"No," said Katie. "Much as I'd love to cage this charlatan for wasting our time, we've nothing to actually hold him on. Yes, he knows about the pentagram design, but that's all."

Zoe Planer hurried from the incident room to join them in the corridor. "Kyle Tarot," said the young Detective Constable, reading from a printout. "Believe it or not, that's his legal name. He changed it officially from Kyle Lewis six years ago and he's been operating as a clairvoyant since that time. He also runs one of those ghost tours in the town. A widower with one daughter, Charlotte Lewis, he's lived on Terry Street in Nunthorpe for the past twelve years. He has a driving ban for drinking, but no criminal form."

"Vehicles?" asked Katie. "Anything that might match our tyre tracks at the crime scenes?"

Zoe shook her head. "He sold his car after the ban."

"His knowing about the killer's symbols makes him the closest thing we have to a suspect," said Angie.

The Inspector nodded slowly. "The first thing we need to do is take a voluntary DNA swab for elimination."

Gary Mitchell threw open the incident room door, his face grey. "Ma'am," he said. "We've found another girl,"

"Dead?" asked Morton. She saw the Constable's expression and felt stupid for asking.

"The body has just been discovered," he said. "A blonde-haired girl, just like your psychic told you, wrapped in carpet, and with the pentagram and triangle markings."

"Good God!" Katie closed his eyes.

"The body was left next to Rowntree Park." Mitchell motioned to the interview room. "Again, just like he said."

"Unbelievable!" said Angie. "This has to be his lunatic way of confessing."

"Right," said Morton, excitedly. "We have our killer."

"But we still need evidence." Katie turned to Planer and

Mitchell. "Zoe, get a warrant and search this place of his in Nunthorpe. Gary, I want a swab from Tarot right now to match against the DNA we found on the victims. Angie and I need to see this latest crime scene... wait." She paused. "That vehicle registration he mentioned – he was as specific about that van as he was about the pentagram and blonde hair."

"You're right, Ma'am," said Angie. "The van has to be relevant."

Katie nodded to Zoe. "Before you get the warrant, run a check on KE55 WCK." She glared at the interview room door. "If he decides he wants to leave, arrest him on suspicion, otherwise no one speaks to this guy until Angie and I get back from Rowntree Park."

* * * *

Chapter 8

Murders are often solved on minuscule details reported by members of the public. The killers and their victims are remembered, the detectives in charge of high-profile cases are occasionally remembered, but no one even hears about the witnesses. So many people provide crucial details and not one of them has a name. Kyle sat in the interview room and took a deep breath to steady himself.

Well today this so-called Cleopatra Killer would be caught and everyone, especially the tabloids, would know Kyle Tarot's name.

To openly disclose what he'd seen would have made him another anonymous eyewitness, but this made him something very different. Several hours had passed since he walked into the station and he still couldn't believe he'd had the audacity to go through with it. The fame he'd spoken about with his daughter was so close and his one-sided romance with the loan company would soon be over. He shrugged off the swell of guilt.

Lying like this was criminal, but those poor girls were dead. There was nothing he could do to change that fact and, despite how he'd gone about it, he'd soon be responsible for catching their killer. If there was a way to ensure that he and Charlie kept their house – a way to ensure her security and to fund her through art college – then surely it would be wrong not to go for it?

It wasn't as if this was harming anyone.

As soon as he got out of here he could move on to the next step and contact the media, but first he had to actually *get out*. Police scepticism had been anticipated, along with the obvious suspicion that he was the murderer, but he hadn't envisaged how truly nerve-wracking this subterfuge would be.

Two female detectives sat across the interview table and, from their dark expressions, Kyle Tarot didn't appear to be their favourite person. It was also quite clear that both gave more credence to the earth being flat than to his amazing clairvoyant abilities.

"So once again for the recording, please…" Angie Gibson folded her arms. "You're assisting us of your own free will. You've provided a sample of DNA and you don't require a solicitor to be present for this interview."

Katie Bradstreet sat beside her Sergeant, frostily eyeing their suspect.

"That's right," said Kyle, glancing at her. "But I'm sensing anger here. Anger and confusion about the…"

"*No*," snapped Katie, her hand shooting up. "Don't even *think* about trying your cold reading with me."

The Inspector masked her rage by pausing to rub her brow, running her fingers through her short fair hair. *This man had probably murdered that girl in the park and now he was sitting here "sensing" her fucking anger. The psychic medium act was really annoying her and she needed to calm down.*

The British judicial system was peculiar, to say the least, in that it bent over backwards to assist and protect the criminal in every possible way. The police, on fairly unremarkable wages, would spend huge amounts of time catching wrongdoers at the taxpayer's expense, only to have someone (on ten times their salary) arrive in a Porsche and get the villains released back onto the streets. Police officers had no great affection for solicitors spouting "no comment", but just for once, Katie wished this character had demanded his right to representation. *It would have been fascinating to see how their smug advice worked with a man who talked to the dead.*

"Why on earth would I want a solicitor?" Kyle gave a puzzled shrug. "I'm here to assist you."

"Of course, Mister Tarot." Katie paused after speaking the stupid name and made a mental note to rinse with disinfectant. "And you've given us permission to search your house without a warrant."

"I *have*, but I don't understand. Surely that isn't normal

practise with a witness?"

"You're right, it isn't," agreed Angie. "But you're hardly a *normal* witness, are you, Kyle?"

"Well I've nothing to hide, so it isn't a problem. I gave you all the information I channelled. Wouldn't your time be better spent checking the van I sensed, or searching for the girl I connected with? The frightened girl with the golden hair?"

Katie pictured the crime scene they'd inspected earlier and held back the swell of anger. "Believe me," she hissed, "I'll decide on how best to spend our time."

The Inspector turned as Gary Mitchell opened the door and silently gestured. She followed him out into the corridor.

"Your psychic didn't invent the registration KE55 WCK," said the Constable, handing over a sheet of paper. "It's the license plate of a red Transit van owned by Tennant's Rentals on Denham street."

"Is it currently hired out to Tarot, by any chance?"

"We don't know yet, Ma'am. Tennant's is a small family firm and they close on Tuesdays. We've tried the owner's home address, but there's no one there right now and the only telephone number we have rings the business."

"Damn! Keep trying them."

"The SOCO has just been in touch too," said Mitchell. "The tyre tracks beside Rowntree Park are a definite match with the tracks we found at the other crime scenes. He believes they *are* van tracks."

"Okay, thanks, Gary." Katie returned to the interview room and her seat beside Angie. "Well, we've found the mysterious vehicle from your spooky dream," she said, holding up Mitchell's paper. "KE55 WCK. Yes, apparently the number you channelled is real and registered to a Transit van owned by Tennant's Rentals."

"You've traced the license plate?" Kyle smiled, excitement building inside. "Hey, that's good, isn't it?"

He was no expert on police procedure, but knew that if he didn't stay here willingly and co-operate like this, they'd arrest him. His plans didn't involve sitting in a cell for the next twenty-four hours and, once they checked the rental records, everything would be fine.

The Inspector shrugged. "The problem is, the company is closed today and we've yet to locate the owner."

"Ah." Kyle gulped as the elation quickly subsided. "I see."

"Are you familiar with Tennant's?" asked Angie. "Have you ever hired a van from there?"

"What?" He shook his head. "No, I haven't."

The Sergeant sat forward, staring at him. "You need to try looking at this from our side. You come in here with knowledge of the latest murder. You know things that only the killer would know, but you claim it's all thanks to your supernatural powers which…"

"Latest murder?" echoed Kyle.

Katie nodded. "We've just been to see her and it wasn't pleasant. Sara Ritter is her name. A golden-haired girl, just like you said. Her body was dumped next to Rowntree Park, again just like you told us."

"That's right," said Kyle, kneading his brow. "Yes, I can see her clearly now, and yes, Sara *is* her name. Her mother used to call her *Little Angel Sara*."

"How sweet," muttered Katie, gritting her teeth. "Sara's body was found by the ubiquitous early-morning jogger on Terry Avenue. I often think that if the public didn't walk dogs and go out running, our parks and woodlands would stink of rotting flesh. So you knew about a dead blonde beside the park before she was found and you knew about the symbols carved into her body."

"Sara wasn't the only victim marked in that way," said Angie, quietly. "We made the decision to withhold the killer's pentagram signature from the media."

Kyle had guessed right. He had a feeling that, like the carpet, the symbols would be common to all the victims and it was just the kind of information the police would suppress.

"The preliminary examination puts her death at around eight, or perhaps nine o'clock last night," said Katie. "Where were you during that time period?"

"*What?*" stammered Kyle. "You think *I* did this?"

The Inspector smiled tightly. "Oh, I know the chances are remote, but we're thinking that might just be possible. So where were you?"

"I was working, performing psychic readings in Clifton, and then I took a taxi to a pub, the Postern Gate."

"Can anyone corroborate that?" asked Angie.

"My clients, of course, the driver, I suppose, and plenty of people in the pub. They probably have cameras in there. Look, I gave you that van registration. As soon as you find out who hired it, you'll know..."

"Or perhaps you saw the van parked in the rental yard," said Angie. "Perhaps you simply used the license plate to embellish your story of visions and..."

"Hang on a moment," snapped Kyle. "If I'd killed this poor girl, why on earth would I walk into the station and tell you about it?"

"That's an interesting piece of jewellery." Katie gestured to his silver ring. "You have a liking for pentagrams, don't you, Mister Tarot? You have one on your business card and another on your ring there. Coincidentally, the killer uses a very similar design. Do you suppose we could take a closer look?"

Kyle shakily slipped it from his finger.

"Thanks." Angie held open an evidence bag and he dropped it in. "I wouldn't be surprised if we found DNA traces in the engraving."

"Please believe me..." began Kyle.

"Isn't it time you stopped playing the confused innocent?" sighed the Sergeant. "You killed those women, didn't you? Why did you mark them with those weird symbols?"

"Where's the stiletto dagger?" added Katie. "And where's the van?"

"No, no, no." Kyle laughed nervously. "This is crazy. I honestly have no idea what you…"

"Crazy?" barked the Inspector. "I'll tell you what's crazy. You walk in here and tell us you've had a psychic dream about a dead woman with a star cut into her chest…" She took a deep breath. "No, this has gone on long enough. Mister Kyle Tarot, you are under arrest on suspicion of the murder of Sara Ritter. You do not have to say anything, but it may harm your defence if…"

Kyle's stomach turned over. Things weren't exactly going to plan and it didn't look like he'd be a wealthy tabloid celebrity any time soon.

* * * *

Chapter 9

Bernard Quist's York detective agency stood on the corner of Fishergate and Baker Avenue, close to the ancient fortifications of Fishergate Bar and the Postern Tower. Occupying the first floor of a Victorian building above a kitchen showroom, the office was frugally furnished with just a leather-topped desk, three swivel chairs and a filing cabinet. Quist claimed, he'd filled his mind with so many interesting facts, that meditating upon these didn't allow him the time to fill his office. Watson wasn't sure whether or not this was a joke.

The detective stood at one of the two windows, contemplatively smoking a cigarette and staring out at the Tuesday evening twilight. The five o'clock rush hour traffic moved slowly along the street, and beyond the opposite row of shops, the medieval circuit of city walls basked in the amber glow of floodlights. Quist gazed up at the darkening sky.

"The first night of the full moon," he purred. "The lupine urges are strong, but as you know, I've trained myself to resist the power of this enigmatic celestial body."

Watson didn't answer and, turning, Quist rolled his eyes to see him engrossed in his mobile phone. Holding a Pepsi tin in his free hand, his assistant slouched in one of the leather office chairs with his trainers propped up on the desk.

The distinct contrast in personalities often puzzled people on meeting the two men, but the detective had deliberately chosen his young employee *because* of their differences. As a result of changing identities and moving around to protect his supernatural secret, Quist had lived alone for many years, lasting friendships being awkward for someone who never aged. Constantly striving to remain *under the radar* had left him feeling isolated and he'd needed someone to help reconnect him to humanity and the modern world. Someone with a lively, jovial outlook, and this streetwise and astute nineteen-year old was perfect.

"Amazing." The detective tutted. "Why on earth do you stare at your phone so much?"

"Huh?" Watson glanced up. "I'm checking my social media and shit. Why? What *should* I be doing?"

"Oh, I don't know." Quist blew a cloud of smoke. "Maybe something useful?"

Watson no longer complained about his boss smoking in the workplace. There was little point mentioning health risks when Quist could only be harmed by silver, fire and decapitation. Slicing off the head tended to kill most things, supernatural or not.

"Here's a thought," said Quist. "Perhaps you could try mastering the skills of detection. You could learn how to utilise elementary deduction in solving problems and answering questions." He turned back to the window. "Questions such as who could *that* be calling upon us?"

Frowning, Watson glanced towards the silent reception room, waited three seconds, then sighed resignedly as a rapping sounded. As usual, his boss's lupine senses had picked up footsteps approaching along the upstairs passage, a noise inaudible to the teenager's human ears. Slipping the phone into his canvas jacket, he headed through the small reception area and opened the door.

"Hey, hello there." The youth grinned to see a familiar female face with black lipstick and too much eyeliner. "Nice to see you again."

"Hi." Dressed in a black raincoat and jeans, Charlotte Lewis appeared tense. "Can I come in?"

"Absolutely." He threw the door wide. "I'm guessing you decided to take me up on that offer of a drink?"

"Actually, I'm here because I need your help."

"Really?" Watson looked puzzled. "Er, what kind of help?"

"*Detective* help, of course." She held up his business card.

"This *is* a detective agency, isn't it?"

"Oh, right." The youth laughed. "Yeah, come on through."

"Greetings, young lady." Quist smiled warmly as she walked into the main office. "I saw you on your father's ghost walk yesterday. You're Miss Tarot, aren't you?"

"Hi." Running a nervous hand through her long black hair, she looked around the magnolia-painted room. "No, my Dad's called Tarot. He changed his name a few years back, but I'm still Charlotte Lewis."

Watson opened his mouth, tempted to ask why he chose such a ridiculous name, but decided against it. Suggesting her father was stupid probably wouldn't strengthen his chances of a date.

"Please take a seat, Miss Lewis." Quist gestured to one of the swivel chairs by the desk. "I overheard you speaking with Watson out there in the reception. Difficult as it is to believe, you *aren't* here because you've fallen for his romantic charms, but because you require our services. How can we assist you?"

"I have a problem." Charlotte sat, but her posture was stiff and she looked apprehensive. "It's a *big* problem with my Dad. He's been arrested."

"Is that so?" Hoping to impress, Watson perched himself on the edge of the desk and attempted Quist's deductive technique. "Mmh, let's see now, your Dad runs those ghost tours for cash in hand. He claims to be a psychic medium and tells the tourists that phantom werewolves haunt schools. I'm guessing he's been arrested for fraudulent clairvoyant practises? Maybe performing without a street license, or possibly income tax evasion?"

"You're way off." Charlotte hit him with a derisive glance. "No, he's been arrested for murder."

"Good heavens!" Quist sat behind the desk. "Murder? Who do the police suspect he's killed?"

The girl took a deep breath. "You know those dead women

they've been finding around York…"

"*Fuck me*," gasped Watson, wide-eyed. "You mean your Dad's the Cleopatra Killer?"

Sighing, Quist wearily massaged his brow. "I'm sorry, Miss Lewis," he said. "Believe it or not, my assistant is quite an asset to this firm, but on occasions he appears about as professional and tactful as a drunken rugby player on a stag night. Please tell us what happened."

"The police are holding him in their cells." Charlotte glowered at Watson, her expression suggesting his proposition of *going out for a drink* was unlikely to materialise anytime soon. "I honestly can't believe this. He rang to tell me he'd been arrested and said that I shouldn't worry. He says that, by tomorrow, everything will be okay, but he didn't have time to explain why on the phone. "

"I see." The detective nodded slowly. "Er, so why exactly are you here?"

"Because I *am* worried – I'm worried out of my frigging mind. Let's say he's been wrong plenty of times before."

"Your sentiments are understandable." Quist nodded. "But what is it that you'd like Watson and I to do about this?"

"Well, prove to them that he's innocent, of course. They have the wrong man and this whole thing is absolutely crazy. If you knew my Dad, you'd know he'd never hurt a fly."

"Charlotte…" Watson grinned uneasily. "The cops don't just pluck guys off the street and charge them with multiple murders for no reason. What do you suppose made them grab your Dad?"

"True," agreed Quist. "Mistaken or not, they must have some justification for this extraordinary course of action."

"The thing is…" Charlotte cringed. "He, er, he saw a dead girl in a dream vision and told the police about her – about where her body was and some other stuff. They interviewed him about it and then arrested him."

"Ah," said Quist. "And with him knowing the location of this crime scene, the police naturally suspect he may be responsible."

Watson raised his eyebrows. "Does he have many spooky dreams like this?"

"Visions?" She shook her head. "No, this is the first time anything like this has happened."

Quist chose his words carefully. "So how do *you* feel about this… this unexpected paranormal occurrence?"

"I'm not sure…" Charlotte looked evasive. "Dad always says where the supernatural is concerned, sometimes it's best not to question too much. Sometimes it's best just to accept."

"Very profound, Miss Lewis." The detective nodded. "But how do you *really* feel about this?"

"Oh, I don't know," stammered Charlotte, slumping miserably in the chair. "Of course Dad doesn't have psychic visions because he *isn't* psychic, is he? None of them are. The thing is, he says he had this supernatural experience, he tried to help the cops and now they think he's a killer. Look, to be honest, I've no idea what the hell is going on here, but I just want him home."

"I'm so sorry." Quist smiled sympathetically. "Your anxiety and confusion are to be expected, but I genuinely fail to see how we can be of assistance."

"No." The girl's mouth fell open. "There must be *something* you can do for him?"

"Well, not *really*." The detective gave a sad shrug. "The police will hold your father for twenty-four hours, and he asked you to wait until tomorrow, by which time he claimed everything would be fine. Now that strongly suggests to me that he knows a little more than he's telling. More than he could explain to you in his obligatory telephone call."

"Yeah, he must have a reason for saying that," agreed Watson. "Sounds like he has some trick up his sleeve, so why not do as he says and…"

"Well, thanks a lot, guys." Charlotte shook her head angrily. "You're a *real* help."

"The police are only allowed to…" Quist paused, his eyes suddenly narrowing. "Wait a moment. Charlotte *Lewis*, and your father works as a psychic? I don't suppose, by any chance, you're related to a certain *other* psychic named Vera Lewis who operated on the Scarborough seafront?"

"Vera was Dad's aunt," said Charlotte. "Yeah, she called herself Madame Selene."

"Oh, of course." Quist nodded slowly. "As you were sitting here, I *knew* I recognised you from somewhere other than yesterday's ghost walk. Yes, Vera passed away recently and you were at the funeral, were you not?"

"Was she?" Watson frowned. "I don't remember."

"You were possibly staring at your phone?" suggested Quist.

"*You* were there too?" asked Charlotte. "You were friends with Vera?"

"She assisted us with a case." The detective smiled. "I only knew the lady briefly, but yes, I considered her a friend. Come to think of it, I don't recall seeing your father at the crematorium."

"No, he wasn't there. Dad had a big fall out with his aunt and he didn't get on with her." The girl shook her head. "Sorry, but I don't remember you being there either."

"Watson and I were sitting at the rear," explained Quist. "Noticing strangers will have been the last thing on your mind."

"Dad still doesn't know I went," said Charlotte. "I bunked off school that day and never told him."

"I'm sorry to hear there was a need for such subterfuge," said Quist. "This hostility between them? Is it something you're able to speak about?"

"It was nonsense really." She sighed. "Dad never believed in

Vera's psychic powers and, after we lost Mum, she tried to give him a spirit message from her. Things were still raw and Dad went ballistic at the idea of her lying in that way. He never spoke to her again. It's probably because I was a kid, but I was never sure whether Vera was a genuine clairvoyant or not. Dad says *none* of them are."

"I can assure you..." said Quist. "In her last days, Vera was most *definitely* genuine."

"They fell out six years ago," said Charlotte. "He never made up with her before she died and I really wish he had."

"That's family feuds for you," snorted Watson. "No one spoke to my Uncle Dave after he got drunk at Marianne's birthday party, pulled down his trousers and did his impression of..."

"Perhaps another time?" broke in Quist. "Please continue, Miss Lewis."

"I once saw Mum by my bed." Charlotte smiled slightly, trying her best to recall the night. "It wasn't long after she passed away. I'm sure Dad believes I was dreaming, but at the time, Vera said it was real. She told me not to mention our conversation to Dad, because it would upset him again, but it really *was* Mum's spirit visiting me. I suppose you think that's silly?"

"Hey, believe me," said Watson. "I've seen plenty of weird shit. To me, ghosts hanging around bedrooms are nothing."

"Yes, who can say for certain?" Quist lit a cigarette, drawing thoughtfully on the tobacco. "As I mentioned, Vera once assisted us with a case, so I suppose we owe her this."

Watson grinned. "So you've changed your mind, Guv? We're going to help her Dad?"

"Ah." Quist raised an eyebrow. "You must be psychic."

* * * *

Chapter 10

Walking with Watson across King's Square, Quist paused on the cobblestones to gaze wistfully at the three limestone towers rising above the rooftops ahead.

York Minster is gigantic. Construction began in the thirteenth century utilising the ruins of an earlier cathedral, which itself was built upon the basilica of the vast Roman fortress that stood here two-thousand years ago. 525 feet in length, the nave lies east to west and its transept north to south, the two forming an enormous crucifix. The twin western towers stand 185 feet tall, with the central Lantern Tower soaring a breath-taking 233 feet above the city. As with all architectural treasures of such size, a continuous preservation programme is necessary and visitors are lucky not to find maintenance being carried out. Scaffolding was currently erected around the main tower, allowing stonemasons to work and, as a bonus, providing every visitor with comedic aspirations to laughingly say: "*Begun in the thirteenth century? I thought it'd be finished by now.*"

Quist stared at the Minster, his hands in the pockets of his leather overcoat. The limestone gleams white by day, but takes on a golden radiance after dark, courtesy of several dozen spotlights. Tonight he was more concerned with the full moon above the building, its beams highlighting the winter clouds with a ghostly sheen.

"Guv?" Watson realised his boss had stopped and turned to see him staring heavenwards. "Are you okay? You're not going to start howling, or any shit like that?"

Shaking himself and smiling, the detective turned off the square and onto St Andrewgate. The pair headed along the narrow thoroughfare to the converted Victorian granary where Watson's friend Gareth Lestrade lived in a top floor apartment.

"So, basically we're doing this because of Vera?" said

Watson, climbing the stairs. "The psychic we met in Scarborough?"

"Correct," said Quist. "With her father in custody, Charlotte Lewis will be worried out of her mind, but knowing that someone else believes he's innocent and is working to help him will provide her with comfort. Vera helped us and I feel we owe her a favour. Wouldn't you agree?"

"Yeah, but I can't see how this is *much* of a favour. I mean, we can't *really* help Charlotte, can we? The cops have arrested her Dad for murder, and we're talking about a high-profile investigation. It isn't often they get four killings over four nights. You say we believe he's innocent, but we have no idea."

"I agree." Quist rang Lestrade's doorbell. "But we can take a look at their reports and discover *why* they suspect him."

"We can make a good guess." Watson laughed. "Er, possibly because he saw the last victim in a *psychic* vision and told them where the body was?"

"Yes." Quist gave a lopsided smile. "If Tarot *isn't* psychic, as his daughter claims, then how did he come by the information? If nothing else, this should prove interesting and you know how much I relish such puzzles."

Gareth Lestrade answered the door and ushered them in. Pale-skinned, with blonde hair, the bespectacled young man was clearly an aficionado of science fiction and comic books. Signed cinema posters and framed issues of Spider-man decorated his walls, and starship models rubbed shoulders with movie memorabilia in glass cases. Lestrade worked freelance, troubleshooting computer problems for companies, and his profession clearly paid well. His income was occasionally boosted, however, by payments from Watson's boss – no-questions-asked payments for illegally hacking encrypted sites and supplying information.

"Welcome back to the cyber-cave." Lestrade gestured to the computer equipment by the window. "Every time you ask to visit, it's for my internet skills." His smile widened. "Before Watty started working for you, he used to call for a beer and a chat about shit like UFOs, or the best time travel films."

"We really must rectify that one evening," said the detective. "I enjoyed the *Time Machine*, both the 1960 film *and* the H.G. Wells novel, but yes, as you say, this visit *is* internet related as usual."

Quist had once dined with Wells in 1907 and had found him both charming and interesting, something he couldn't speak about to too many people without the risk of being sectioned.

"Okay." Lestrade sat at his monitor surrounded by networked computer banks. "So what can I do for you?"

"You're pretty clever, Guv." Watson perched himself on a stool beside the large screen. "If you learned about computers and how to hack them, like Gazza here, you'd save a fortune."

"Ooh, I'd rather you didn't." Lestrade laughed. "I've grown used to your *fees for services rendered*."

"Invaluable services." Quist smiled thinly and sat next to him. "I need you to access the police records again, Gareth."

"No problem." The young man began tapping at his keyboard. "It won't take long, as you know."

"I've often wondered about this." Shrugging off his overcoat, the detective nodded to the computer. "I know you have an illicit way into their website – a secret *back door*, as you refer to it – but what about when they update their system?"

"That won't happen anytime soon." Lestrade advanced through pages of script. "The government won't give the cops the cash they need, so they have to make cutbacks. One of the drawbacks is we have less officers on our streets, but an advantage, for *me* at least, is the North Yorkshire Police can't afford to modernise their computers."

"Hey." Watson gestured to the constabulary crest on the screen. "Looks like we're in."

"That's right." Lestrade glanced at his friend's boss. "So what exactly do you want to see here?"

"The investigation reports on the recent York murders," said Quist. "The so-called Cleopatra Killer."

Lestrade raised a curious eyebrow, but he no longer questioned this private detective's bizarre requests. "Er, *right*." He worked through various menus and gestured to the keyboard. "Okay, there you go. As always, be *very* careful. Feel free to scroll the page using *that* key, but for God's sake don't touch anything else and don't click on anything. We don't want them to know we were ever in here. I'll navigate the pages for you when you're ready."

"Don't worry," murmured Quist, reading.

"I guess it's similar to social media?" said Watson. "When you're checking out some ex-girlfriend's page and you crap yourself for accidentally clicking *like*, or whatever?"

"Something along those lines." Lestrade laughed. "But accidentally clicking *like* here would be a touch more serious."

"Inspector Bradstreet is heading the investigation; we've met her before," said Quist, scrolling through the report. "Mmh, we know most of this from the media. The locations of the bodies, the way they were wrapped in carpet and the fact that all four were sex workers. Fortunately, the police don't appear to have found anything linking them to Charlotte's father..." He paused. "This is interesting. Their dates of birth are here and each was born between late August and September. That means they all had the astrological sign of Virgo."

"You spotted *that*?" said Watson. "Is it a coincidence?"

"Four victims with the same star sign?" The detective glanced at him. "What do *you* think?"

"Honestly? *I* think it sounds like weird serial killer stuff."

"The police aren't attaching importance to it," said Quist. "They possibly haven't noticed, but it appears as if the murderer purposely chose girls born under Virgo. He either knew them, or had some means of discovering their dates of birth."

"Well…" Watson shrugged. "People need to give those details in lots of different situations."

"Yes, but the most pertinent question is why Virgo?" Quist stiffened as he scrolled the text. "Ah, now this is *far* more intriguing than star signs – the manner in which they died. Each victim was drugged and symbols were cut into their chests. Good Lord, they were then stabbed in the centre of the design with a stiletto blade."

"Shit!" whispered Lestrade. "*That* wasn't in the news."

"Ugh, they have pictures." Watson winced at the SOCO photographs. "Oh, hell, Guv. It's horrible."

"Indeed." Quist nodded sadly. "This is clearly ritualistic, isn't it? Each girl was killed in the same way and these triangles are classic representations of the elements – air, earth, fire and water…" He leant forward. "But I don't recognise the main design."

"It's a pentagram," said his assistant, smugly. "Watching late-night horror films hasn't been a complete waste of my time."

"He's right," said Lestrade, slapping his friend's back.

The detective sighed. "I'm fully aware that the star within the circle is a pentagram, but I'm referring to the overall design; the pentagram is merely part of it. You'll notice that the lower two points of the star are extended. It's the same in each photograph, so it isn't accidental, and this central swirling pattern is unfamiliar. It's almost like a Caduceus, but without the wings."

"Er, if you say so, Guv." Watson frowned. "Maybe a witchcraft symbol?"

"Possibly." Quist stroked his nose thoughtfully. "Looking at these triangles depicting the elements, I'd say *probably*. Now, Gareth, could you find me the information on a suspect named Kyle Tarot?"

"Seriously?" Lestrade laughed. "These murders could be to do with witchcraft and they have a suspect called *Tarot*?"

"They *do*. I'd like to know *why* he's a suspect."

Lestrade worked his way through the menu. "Ah, here you go. There's a witness statement by him."

The detective read it. "Yes," he said. "As his daughter informed us, he claimed to have psychic visions of the last victim. He gave them her exact location by Rowntree Park and..." Quist smiled grimly. "Oh, apparently, he saw the symbols on her body too, symbols which the police withheld from the public."

"*Ah.*" Watson winced. "So *that's* why they arrested him."

"But that appears to be the *only* reason," said Quist. "According to this, they have no evidence, so they can only detain him for twenty-four hours."

"Good news for his daughter," said Watson.

"Yes." Quist stroked again at his large nose. "Those carved designs on the victims – could I see them once more?"

"Here you go." Shaking his head, Lestrade returned to the investigation report. "Like I always say, you can't beat looking at dead women with no clothes on."

"Thank you." Smiling tartly at the sarcasm and taking out his phone, Quist photographed the onscreen pictures for reference. "I presume there must be a database for this kind of thing?"

Lestrade nodded. "There's an international database of tattoos and symbols shared by cops, Interpol and the FBI." He clicked on a report. "But it looks like they've already conducted a search for these designs. Yeah, look, it's all here. They know the triangular ones are the elements, like you said, and they believe this other star thing is North African and linked to ritual magic."

"Ritual magic," echoed Quist, quietly. "Intriguing."

* * * *

Askham Richard lies in the open countryside five miles west of York, an attractive village with an inn, limestone cottages, and a large quacky duck pond on the green. Over the years, Quist had moved around Britain, quietly residing in many areas, before choosing this rustic spot two summers ago. Briar Cottage, his ivy-clad home stood on the outskirts, isolated and set back from the rural lane. Rambling roses obligingly rambled over the porch, wisteria smothered the east gable, and a walled garden bordered the rear meadow. Quist would have loved house martins beneath the eaves, hedgehogs snuffling on his path and singing robins, but knew this wasn't possible. The local wildlife sensed his dark supernatural aura and stayed well away. He'd once sadly mentioned this to his assistant, who laughingly compared him to *a known nonce sitting in a deserted kid's playground.*

Watson sprawled on the detective's Chesterfield couch in the lounge, warming himself by the black-leaded open range where a pile of freshly-ignited logs crackled and spat in the grate. His boss's home was very different to the Spartan office. Antiques, curios and bric-a-brac filled the beamed room and paintings of the Yorkshire Dales decorated the stone walls.

Quist returned from the kitchen and passed the teenager a can of lager. "Here you go," he said. "I always keep a stock for whenever you're here. I know you don't appreciate the single malts I drink." Setting down a crystal glass and pouring a whisky, he took a sip and sighed. "Ah, this is Askaig from Islay. Ten years old."

"No, I'm fine with this, Guv." Watson ripped open the tin and gulped the beer. "Yeah, that's the right vintage and temperature for me. Are you going to be okay for driving me home later?"

"No, I'll call you a taxi." Folding up his shirt sleeves, Quist headed to one of his large bookcases. "I'll be too busy here attempting to find that mysterious symbol."

"A mysterious symbol which, I should point out, has bugger all to do with us. We've done our bit for Charlotte. We now know the cops have nothing on her Dad, so why are you bothering with this?"

"Because it's highly intriguing."

The detective switched on the hi-fi and the youth winced as

Borodin began to quietly play. Quist claimed classical music helped him think, and although Watson's musical tastes were vastly different, he had to concede that it made *him* think too. He invariably thought: *I wish he'd switch off this crap.* He watched as his boss searched through hundreds of old volumes, most of which were devoted to the occult, anthropology and mythology.

"Weird, isn't it?" said the teenager. "So how did her Dad know about the markings on those dead girls?"

"Four answers spring immediately to mind," said Quist, thumbing through a book. "Kyle Tarot could actually *be* psychic and he's telling the truth about seeing them in a vision…"

"Yeah, right."

The detective smiled. "He could have been told about them, of course, or overheard someone discussing them…" He turned to Watson. "Or he could have *found* that last victim and seen the symbols in the flesh, if you'll pardon the awful pun. The fact that he knew her location would strongly suggest the latter."

"And then he lied to the cops about the psychic stuff?" Watson laughed dryly. "Wow, that would take some balls."

"Indeed, but what *is* that star symbol?" Quist took a drink of malt and returned to his bookcases. "More to the point, why did the killer mark his victims with it? I have countless books on the occult and magic and, with any luck, I'll find it here. The police database claimed it could be North African."

Watson took out his phone as his boss searched. "Are you thinking the killer could be a witch or something?"

"I'm familiar with witchcraft symbolism. No, this design suggests ritual magic – an adept of the occult, not a witch. Or more probable, someone who believes he is."

"Ah, right." Nodding, Watson sipped his lager. "A loony."

"As you know from past investigations, ritual magic *does* work if performed by a genuine practitioner with the correct knowledge and training, but we don't know if that is the case here. Four women, all with the Virgo star sign, have been murdered and their bodies marked with these designs. We *could* be looking at an occultist, but this killer is more likely to be some deranged individual with an unhealthy obsession with the dark arts and horror films."

"Like I said, a loony." Watson shuddered. "Either way, those poor girls are dead. After all the shit I've seen with you, it's still hard to believe there are *real* occultists out there who perform rituals. It's still bloody scary too."

"Genuine occult circles are rare, but yes, they *are* most certainly out there." Quist strolled to the fire and stabbed at the logs with a poker until flames erupted. "Many of these serious groups are harmless, performing, for the lack of a better phrase, *white magic*, but some are more dangerous."

"Black magic?" The teenager grinned uneasily. "You mean they've gone over to the *dark side*?"

"You might say that." Quist smiled grimly. "They perform rituals to gain wealth and improve their position in life, but mostly to acquire power. Such people have a thirst for power. Only last year, the body of a man named Bradley Curtis was discovered on the moors above Pickering. Esoteric markings had been carved into his flesh and a circle was found nearby, large enough to perform a ritual within. It was quite obvious that some dark rite had taken place, but no one was ever arrested and the police investigation is still open."

"I don't remember a witchcraft murder being in the news."

"The death was reported, but not the occult angle. I was hired by a landowner over there to assist with his daughter's divorce. He knew one of the police officers on the case and told me about it."

"Bloody hell, Pickering is a bit close to home," muttered Watson. "To think there could be a coven of Satanic nutters operating less than thirty miles away. I know there are supernatural things out there..." He gestured to his boss. "Well, in *here* too, but I think I preferred the time before I met you, when I thought magic was all about rabbits in hats and women being sawn in half."

"Magic." Quist lit a cigarette, warming himself by the fire grate. "The infamous occultist Aleister Crowley spelled the word *magick* differently. He added a letter K to differentiate serious ritualistic workings from the performances of conjurers. You need to understand that magic is actually a science, an ancient and well-guarded science that harnesses ethereal energy and causes change to occur in conformity with the will."

"That sounds as clear as mud." Watson peered at his mobile. "But from what I've seen with you, I'll go along with it."

"Imagine time travelling three-hundred years into the past and taking out that phone." Quist returned to searching through his books as he spoke. "Imagine showing videos on it to people back then, those ridiculous cat videos you love so much. Without a doubt, you'd have been burnt as a witch."

The youth glanced up from the mobile. "Your point being?"

"When you witness ritualistic magic, you feel amazed and frightened, but you're simply seeing a science you don't comprehend, much like Tudor people seeing cats water skiing on your phone." He pulled out a book and flicked through the illustrations. "Yes, somewhere in one of these I'll find that symbol and…"

"The Sussamma Star," said Watson. "Used in a fabled occult rite that enabled the initiate to locate hidden treasure."

"*What?*" The detective turned slowly and saw that his assistant was reading aloud. "You're telling me you actually found it on the internet as I was speaking?"

"Yeah." He held up his phone and grinned. "I did a search for *four dead women, Virgo* and *pentagram symbol on chest…*"

"Let me see that." Quist snatched the mobile and scrolled down the screen. "Oh, it's Roundhay. Yes, this is the mythology section of a history website run by the Reverend Miles Roundhay."

"Do you know him?"

"I know *of* him. Roundhay is something of an expert on the Roman occupation of Yorkshire, their history and also the folklore. I have his books over here." Quist walked back to the shelves, pulled out a thick volume and turned to the index. "If this ritual is mentioned on his website, Roundhay may go into more detail in his written works. Mmh, Sussamma, you say? Yes, here it is. The Sussamma Ritual, used by..." He paused. "Ah, used by the Badda cult."

"Guv?" Watson noticed his expression. "Are you okay?"

"Er, yes." The detective shook himself and began to read. "Yes, the symbol is shown here, taken from illustrations etched onto slate in Morocco; it's exactly the same. Roman historians document historical fact, but Roundhay is a passionate student of mythology. He's collected all the legends surrounding the Roman Badda sect and what we know of their rites. He explains here how the Sussamma Ritual was supposedly a divination rite involving the sacrifice of four virgins for each of the four elements, air, earth, fire and water..."

Watson frowned. "Hey, like the triangles on the bodies."

"That's right, and apparently these sacrifices had to be carried out over four consecutive nights leading up to the full moon." Quist nodded slowly. "Exactly like the four murders here in York."

"Shit," whispered the teenager. "Are you thinking..."

"I don't know." Quist drew on his cigarette. "Four virgins were required for the Sussamma Ritual and the York victims were all born under the Virgo star sign." He gazed at his assistant. "No, surely not? Incredible as it may seem, could the York killer have been performing this ancient Badda ritual?"

"It certainly sounds like it, Guv." Watson shook his head. "But a divination rite to locate stuff with human sacrifices? It all seems a bit over the top just to try and find your lost car keys."

"If it actually worked, theoretically this rite could be used to locate *anything*."

76

"It'd need to be something frigging huge to go to these criminal lengths. There's one good thing – if some nutter *was* doing this crackpot ritual and only *four* girls are needed, it means there won't be any more murders."

"Hardly a *good* thing, Watson, but yes, I take your meaning."

"If this isn't some crazy coincidence, what do you reckon this killer's looking for?"

"We don't know if we're right about this," pointed out Quist. "If we *are* right, we don't know if this is a genuine occultist, or just some psychopath with an interest in the dark arts and a book of folklore such as this one by Roundhay." He sipped his whisky. "One thing I *do* know, the Yorkshire Museum in the city centre is currently hosting an exhibition on the Badda cult."

"What?" The teenager's eyes widened. "Now that *is* a coincidence, isn't it?"

"No, Watson, that's a *huge* coincidence."

Falling silent, the detective tapped his ring finger against his drink, tinkling the metal on the glass, something his assistant had seen him do many times when he was thinking. Watson knew about the signet ring with the RQ initials and wondered how many times he'd absent-mindedly done this over the centuries. As it wore thin, goldsmiths had thickened the band, but it had certainly aged well.

"We were looking into this as a favour to Charlotte," said Quist. "The intention was to see what the police had on her father and hopefully reassure her. But if the occult is involved in these murders, it changes things. It all becomes rather intriguing, doesn't it?"

"I might have known," grinned Watson. "You're always the same once you get a sniff of anything like this. I take it you've no intention of passing this information about magical rituals to the cops and leaving them to deal with it?"

"You know the police don't take such things seriously." Quist shrugged. "No, I believe we should investigate ourselves and see where it leads. It's only yesterday that you were lamenting our lack of supernatural cases."

"True, but what is there to *actually* investigate? Where on earth would we start?"

"We'll begin by visiting the museum tomorrow to take a look at their new exhibition. I happen to know a little about this particular cult."

"Hardly surprising." The youth laughed. "You know a little about *most* things."

"My *condition* has provided me with the time to learn, but the Badda cult is somewhat pertinent to me. Some folklore authorities believe that werewolf mythology began with this ancient sect."

"Wow. Really?"

Quist nodded slowly. "They were a secretive group based in the Atlas Mountains of North Africa. These people worshipped a hunter God, a dark deity that took the form of a huge wolf."

"North Africa?" Watson looked puzzled. "But the book with the symbol is all about the Romans in Yorkshire."

"That's right. Like many other mystical sects, such as the Minerva cult, it was brought to Britain by the Romans. I've researched the history of our city, as you know, and the Badda cult once worshipped at a temple in York."

"So, if these murders *are* sacrifices in a Badda ritual, you think the cult might still be operating?"

"I wouldn't have said so." Finishing his whisky, Quist narrowed his eyes thoughtfully. "This particular sect was wiped out over two-thousand years ago."

* * * *

Chapter 11

Originally the riverside estate surrounding St Mary's Abbey and then a Victorian botanical park, the Museum Gardens lie in the centre of York. Ten acres in size, the landscaped grounds slope down to the Ouse and still boast a wide variety of exotic trees and shrubs. The parkland reeks of history, with the Yorkshire Museum standing central, the ruins of the 11th century abbey forming a picturesque backdrop, and an old astronomical observatory on one of the pathways. Down by the water, the beautiful half-timbered Hospitium – although built in 1300 – is so perfectly preserved, it looks to have been recently constructed for a film set.

Watson strolled along a winding path with Quist, his hands deep in the pockets of his green canvas blouson. It was crisp this Wednesday morning and the youth watched squirrels racing after each other in the frosty vegetation beneath the trees.

"Come this way," said Quist, leading him across the lawns to the eastern side of the park. His black leather coat flapped around him like a vampire's cloak. "Although you reside in York, you're probably unaware of this. I know history isn't your greatest passion, but after last night's conversation about Romans, you may find it to be of interest."

"Yeah?" Watson followed him and peered at the remains of a wide limestone tower, some twenty feet in height. "You can't mean these old walls?"

"*Old walls?*"

"I've passed here hundreds of times, but your shocked face tells me it's something important." The teenager laughed. "Either that, or you've just had an accident in your trousers. So what exactly am I looking at?"

"You're looking at Rome." Quist's eloquent voice was tinged with reverence. "SPQR. The mighty Rome herself, still here after two millennia and thrusting up indefatigably from the earth. This, my young friend, is York's famous Multangular Tower."

"Not *that* famous, Guv. I've never heard of it."

"Why am I not surprised?" sighed the detective. "You were fortunate enough to be born in this wonderful city, yet you remain ignorant of its treasures. This tower is two-thousand years old and formed the western corner of the battlements that surrounded the Roman fort of Eboracum. Note the ten sides, hence its name. York is filled with Roman remains, but this is one of the examples you can see above ground."

"I suppose that's pretty cool," conceded Watson, shuffling his cold feet. "If you're into really old crap." Five stone coffins were arranged on the grass in front of the wall, so weatherworn, he'd assumed they were horse troughs. "Hey, I've just realised what these things are." He pointed. "Were there once people in them? You know, *dead* people?"

"Well, I doubt the Romans chiselled them out for fun." Quist checked his watch. "I rang Charlotte Lewis last night and told her not to worry. I explained how the police had no evidence on her father, but I also asked her to meet us here for a chat."

"Great." Watson smiled. "It'll be nice to see her."

"Yes, but please try not to drool too much. Come along. We need to take a look at the new exhibition before she arrives."

The pair headed back through the gardens to the museum. Resembling a stately home with a Greek temple attached to the frontage, the huge building had been designed in a Grecian classical style with giant fluted columns supporting the portico roof projecting over the front steps. The teenager licked his lips. Constructed of honey-coloured sandstone, this place subliminally reminded him of cinder toffee and left him peckish.

"Just look at this." Quist gestured upwards. "A superb construction, isn't it?"

"Well…" Watson shrugged. "It's definitely a construction."

"It was founded in 1830 by the Yorkshire Philosophical Society." Quist climbed the steps. "The museum houses several permanent biology and archaeology collections, but they also host temporary exhibitions such as the one we're here to see."

"Museums?" Watson shook his head. "Now why do I prefer football and science fiction to museums?"

The double doors opened into a bright, modern reception, with a gift shop and a desk staffed by two middle-age women.

"Good day to you," said Quist, purchasing the tickets. "How are we this fine morning?"

Watson tutted as the blushing women fussed unconsciously with their hair. His boss often affected females in this way, his lupine pheromones stimulating them on a supernatural level. It was unintentional, but also unavoidable.

"Shouldn't you get a concession for being over sixty?" whispered the youth. "Quite a *bit* over sixty."

Quist ignored the joke. "This Badda exhibition of yours opened two days ago, didn't it?"

"That's right," said the older woman. "Monday. It's only on display for the next fortnight. You'll find it at the far side of our Roman galleries."

"I'm quite interested in the Badda cult," said Quist. "I wonder which of your curators would be the most knowledgeable on the subject? Who is in charge of the exhibit?"

"Oh, none of *our* people," she said, glancing at the trim body beneath his open overcoat and giving a flirty smile. "You'd be best speaking to Doctor Sawtelle. He brought the exhibit here from London last week. He liaises with the Chairman and various members of the York Museums Trust, but he's the one in control. I believe the doctor is in there right now."

"I see." Quist headed through the reception with Watson

following. "Thank you."

His assistant laughed quietly. "Yeah, the girls certainly swoon over the scent of the big bad wolf, don't they?" he murmured, amazed. "If you could bottle that shit, I reckon you could sell it like Rohypnol."

The first gallery was dedicated to Roman York and a banner hung above the door with the words: MEET THE PEOPLE OF THE EMPIRE. A series of large rooms with lofty ceilings were filled with glass cabinets and statues of Gods and Emperors, but Quist paid them no attention and headed for a separate room at the far side of the building. Watson ignored the displays too. Museums had never really been the teenager's *thing* and, on his list of favourite pastimes, looking around museums was somewhere between basket weaving and having his teeth drilled.

"Ah, this is it," said Quist, entering the side chamber and pausing to take in the scene.

The lighting was subdued, to create an enigmatic air, and the Badda exhibition had been tastefully laid out like a temple, with illuminated cabinets on the periphery and carefully-positioned spotlights trained on the collection of artefacts. The centrepiece was quite spectacular – an immense granite altar with upright iron incense burners on either side and a gigantic stone head positioned on a raised column to its rear. The latter had clearly once topped a tall statue and Watson gazed up at it with wide eyes. It was the head of an evil-looking wolf, but an exaggerated creature with a wide projecting muzzle reminiscent of an alligator.

"Bloody hell," mumbled the youth. "Look at that gruesome twat. He reminds me of you, Guv. Er, no offence like. You know what I mean? You when you're er, not yourself, as it were."

"That will be Badda Oushane," said Quist. "The wolf God they worshipped." He peered at a white marble bust beside the door and read the information card. "The Roman Prefect Aquila. My word, the features are remarkably lifelike and positively radiate cruelty."

"Yeah, I don't know who he is, but he looks hard-faced," quipped Watson. "He has a bit of a stony expression there. He, he, I should be doing stand-up."

Several people studied the cases of pottery and paraphernalia, but Quist spotted a black girl with a clipboard of papers peering into a cabinet at the far side of the altar. Attractive and in her late twenties, with coffee-coloured skin and short black wavy hair, she wore a smart blue suit and scribbled notes on a pad.

"Good morning," said Quist, strolling over to her. "I have to say, it's an excellent display, isn't it?"

"Hey, thank you." The young woman smiled warmly. "Yes, we've attempted to capture the dark mystery of the Badda sect and I think we've done a pretty good job."

"Hello there," said Watson, treating her to his best sexy grin. "I guess you work here?"

"Not at the Yorkshire Museum, but the British Museum in London. I'm up here with this exhibition for the next couple of weeks." She shook hands with them both. "I'm Doctor Blake. Well, it's Melissa. Mel, if you like."

"Yes, I *like*," said the teenager. "You're far better looking than *my* doctor. Hello there, Mel."

"You have amazing artefacts," said Quist.

"You can say that again," agreed Watson.

The detective gestured to the huge altar. "I'm assuming they weren't found in York?"

"No, all of these are North African." Melissa looked around the room. "The Atlas Mountains were the stronghold of the Badda sect. Unlike other cults, they were highly secretive and had no interest in expanding. Their temple was discovered buried in a valley there in the nineteen-twenties and you're looking at pretty much the entire contents, give or take a few wooden and leather items which had perished over time. Everything you see here was shipped to the British Museum where it's been on display ever since."

"The good old British." Quist laughed quietly. "We certainly didn't mind appropriating the treasures and history of other nations, did we? Nations perceived as being inferior to us. I've always been surprised that Tutankhamun didn't end up in the British Museum."

Watson sighed as the girl smiled sexily at his boss and involuntarily moistened her lips with a flick of tongue. *As usual, it seemed the wolf pheromones were doing their thing.*

"It's rightly viewed as stealing in these more enlightened times," agreed Melissa. "But, to be honest, many priceless artefacts would probably have been lost if we hadn't *stolen* them back in our Empire days."

"I suppose that's true," admitted Quist.

He walked to the altar and ran a hand over the polished stone surface. Some eight feet wide and four feet in height, it was fashioned from a single block of black granite and carved symbols decorated the sides. His eyes narrowed suspiciously and he leant forward, then swiftly reconsidering what he was about to do, he straightened up.

"Incredible," he murmured. "I understand they worshipped a deity named Badda Oushane, a hunter god?"

"There he is." Melissa gestured to the stone head glowering down above them. "Or rather what's left of his temple statue; earthquakes had crumbled the body to rubble before it was unearthed. We're in his month right now. March was the time when the Badda sect would honour their God with sacrifice and celebrations, thanking him for their fruitful hunts over the winter period."

"Sacrifices," repeated the detective, stroking the gleaming black surface of the altar. "Yes, one can only imagine the rites that took place over two-thousand years ago upon this."

Nodding excitedly, Melissa placed her hand beside his and gasped slightly as their fingers came into contact. "Absolutely," she said, her pupils instantly dilating. "This is one of the best parts of my job. Every day I get to actually *touch* ancient history."

"One of the *best* parts?" mumbled Watson, rolling his eyes. "Hey, I wonder if they have any vacancies here."

"I'm quite interested in the Badda rituals," said Quist. "I imagine you know all about their mystical rites?"

"*She* doesn't, but I do," announced a voice behind them. "I'm the expert on this cult."

Quist and Watson turned to see an overweight man in a grey suit. Somewhere around fifty, he was balding and sported a short beard, the sort of thing men with double chins often cultivate in the belief that it gives them a jawline. He gazed at the two men with a frosty expression.

"Ah, hello," said the detective. "I presume you're Doctor Sawtelle?"

"That's right." Sawtelle returned Quist's polite smile, but his grey eyes remained cold. "I wasn't sure whether to interrupt. I noticed you holding hands on the altar and thought I might be intruding upon the moment?"

Quist answered the preposterous implication with a brisk laugh. "Very nice to meet you," he said. "Yes, I was just commending Doctor Blake on this splendid display. I appreciate how you've depicted the layout of a Badda temple here, illustrating how Badda Oushane's statue would have been positioned behind the altar with the incense burners flanking it. This deity always appeared in the form of a wolf, didn't he?"

"He did." Sawtelle glanced at the lupine face above them, a hint of sarcasm in his voice. "I'd say the stone head there is something of a giveaway."

Quist nodded. "I assume you're familiar with the legends surrounding that? The werewolf mythology?"

Sawtelle studied the detective for a moment. "Yes, I'm aware of the various stories." He laughed dryly. "But I'm a Doctor of History and Archaeology, not bullshit."

Quist shrugged. "Some believe the two go hand-in-hand. Folk tales have often pointed the way to historic truths and finds."

"Is that so?" drawled Sawtelle. "Well, not in my experience. I believe in science, not fairy stories." Rudely dismissing him, he turned to Melissa. "Where's Rogers? I can't find her."

"I'm not sure," said the girl. "She could be in the basement with the…"

"Oh, never mind." He strode away. "I'll find her myself."

"Nice guy," said Watson, smirking as he watched the doctor leave. "Yeah, good people skills."

"Tell me about it." Melissa pulled a sour face. "You should try being under him."

The youth's eyes widened. "He's your boyfriend?"

She laughed dryly. "No, under him in the hierarchical sense. Edwin is my boss."

Another girl entered the exhibition and joined them by the altar. Watson ran a swift eye over the slinky figure beneath her chic white office blouse and black trousers. She was a few years younger than Melissa, perhaps early twenties, with expensive designer spectacles and her long blonde hair tied up in a bun.

"Hi, Tamzin," said Melissa. "Edwin is searching for you. Have you had any luck finding it?"

"The tiara?" She glanced at the two men. "I'm afraid not."

"Rogers," growled Sawtelle, reappearing at the exhibition entrance. "I spotted you walking in here as soon as I left. If I didn't know better, I'd say you're avoiding me. Has it turned up?"

"Not so far," said Tamzin, uneasily. "I've rechecked the packing crates, but they're all empty as we expected."

"Unbelievable." Sawtelle shook his head. "You two are supposed to be in charge of these artefacts, so how come *I* spotted it wasn't here and *you* didn't?"

"Am I to take it you've lost something?" enquired Quist.

"Oh, well done," snorted the doctor. "Ten out of ten for that analysis."

"We've just discovered one of our smaller relics is missing," explained Melissa. "The Moon Tiara."

"Is it valuable?" asked Watson.

"Two-thousand years old?" said Sawtelle. "What do *you* think?"

"Moon Tiara?" repeated Quist, thoughtfully. "Would this also be known as the Moon Crown?"

"That's right," said Tamzin. "It's a small iron band etched with African runes. Are you familiar with the ritualistic paraphernalia used by this cult?"

"Not really," admitted the detective. "Just this particular item. Funnily enough, I was reading about it last night."

Melissa turned to her portly superior. "I know it's listed on the itinerary, Edwin, but I can't see how it can have been misplaced. The chances are it's still in London and I've rung Mike to have him check down there."

"Let me know when he calls back." Sawtelle sighed angrily. "This is what happens when you pack an exhibit and drive it across the country for no reason." The doctor glared at Quist and Watson as if it was somehow *their* fault. "Instead of leaving it in the British Museum where it belongs, the curators decided to send it *here*."

"I'm sure the people of Yorkshire are grateful for the chance to view this excellent collection," said Quist. "*I* certainly am."

Melissa smiled at him. "We came here because of the York connection," she said. "The idea was to celebrate the centenary of the temple's discovery, but we missed the date."

"We're a fortnight late," said Sawtelle. "But the whole idea of temporarily moving the exhibit is ludicrous, as is the cost." He let out a short laugh. "All this upheaval for two short weeks. Plus, these relics are African and have no *real* relevance to Aquila and his time in York."

"I disagree," retorted Melissa. "This is the actual temple used by Hanka and Aquila in Morocco. The York temples are long gone, so this is the only surviving example."

"Aquila?" asked Quist. "Hanka?"

"The Prefect Aquila," explained Tamzin. "He was the Roman soldier who brought the Badda cult to the city."

"Ah." The detective glanced at the marble bust by the door. "I noticed the gentleman over there as we entered."

"I like to think he greets our visitors," said Melissa. "York was the only place in Britain where this minor religion was ever practised – the only place, in fact, outside of what's now Morocco. Hanka was the Badda Priestess who accompanied Aquila from North Africa, hence our display to inform the public about this unique period in York's history."

"Listen," broke in Sawtelle, brusquely. "I'm giving a talk on this tonight in the Tempest Anderson Hall. If you'd like to learn about Aquila and his time here, I suggest you buy a ticket and come along." He marched away. "You can book at the front desk."

"Yeah, good people skills," repeated Watson, nodding. "With that kind of friendly warmth, he should be a children's entertainer."

"As usual, Edwin isn't in the best of moods." Melissa cringed, before turning to the young woman beside her. She clasped a friendly hand around her shoulder and squeezed. "Anyway, this is Tamzin. The three of us are in charge of the exhibition. I'm Edwin's assistant and Tamz is *my* assistant."

"You opened on Monday, didn't you?" asked Quist.

"Yes," said Tamzin, "but we arrived last week to supervise the unpacking and setting up."

"Edwin may claim he didn't want to spend three weeks in

York," said Melissa, smiling thinly, "but he's certainly milking the budget. Tamz and I have rented an apartment above an old chocolate shop on Stonegate. Edwin has booked himself into a suite in the York Grand."

"Very nice," grinned Watson.

"This missing Moon Crown," murmured Quist. "You don't know where it could be?"

"If they did, it wouldn't be missing," pointed out Watson.

"A fairly stupid question," confessed Quist, smiling. "I wonder, out of the visitors you've had here so far, has anyone expressed an interest in the crown?"

"No." Melissa shook her head. "Why do you ask?"

"How about anyone showing a deeper interest than usual in the Badda cult?" continued the detective. "Perhaps someone requesting a private viewing before you officially opened, or enquiring about the rituals as I did?"

"Er, I don't know." Melissa gave him a quizzical look. "To be fair, those are pretty odd questions."

"Well, to be fair, he's a pretty odd bloke," laughed Watson.

"This sect..." Quist gestured to the altar. "As I mentioned earlier, I'm quite interested in the legends surrounding their wolf deity and the occult rituals they performed to him. Do you know anything about their sacrifice rites?"

"Not a great deal." Tamzin shrugged. "We're more versed in the history and archaeology than the esoteric side."

"Edwin's the authority on that," said Melissa. "He doesn't talk about it much and, if I'm honest, I find it all a bit creepy, but he has something of a fascination with the occult and the dark arts."

"Really?" said Quist, innocently. "Well, how interesting."

* * * *

Chapter 12

Quist strolled slowly through the Roman Gallery exhibits, stooping to read the information cards with hands clasped behind his back. His assistant followed, looking around the museum with indifference. The bored teenager peered into a stone coffin, intricately carved and far more pristine than the weathered examples lying outside.

"Correct me if I'm wrong, Guv," said Watson, frowning. "But I thought we came here to see the Badda cult stuff?"

"We did," confirmed Quist.

"So what are you doing looking at all *this* shit?"

"I'm waiting." Quist watched through a glass display case as Melissa Blake and Tamzin Rogers walked out of the Badda exhibition chatting to each other. "Waiting for those two to leave."

"Oh, right." Watson nodded. "Well, if you want my opinion, that room was much more interesting with the gorgeous black girl and the blonde *inside* it."

"Yes, your attraction to their good looks didn't escape my attention, but I don't want any staff becoming curious and questioning what I'm about to do." Returning to the dimly-lit chamber, Quist headed for the central altar display and lowered his voice. "I noticed something earlier, but I couldn't check anything with Doctor Sawtelle and his assistants present."

"Noticed what?" quizzed Watson.

Ignoring the question, Quist walked to one of the upright incense burners that stood six feet tall on either side of the altar. Glancing around to ensure none of the other museum visitors were watching, he raised himself on tiptoes to sniff the wide metal dish on top, then turned to the altar itself. He studied the huge stone block, before taking out a pen, accidentally dropping it on the floor beside the black granite and stooping to retrieve it.

"Intriguing," he murmured, shrugging his overcoat straight and smiling grimly.

"*What's* intriguing?" whispered Watson.

"The scent of this thing close up."

"So what does it smell of?" The youth regarded him curiously. "A stone altar, by any chance? Care to share whatever you're thinking, Guv?"

"All in good time." Quist looked around the busy room. "I intend to confirm my suspicions before misleading and unnerving you with speculation. We really need to inspect this place properly when it's empty. By the way, it's somewhat significant that the Moon Tiara is missing."

"That crown thing Mel talked about? Why's that?"

"After you left last night, I did quite a bit of reading on the Badda sect. Various books and internet sites mention the Sussamma Ritual and explain how the Priestess would need to wear a headdress known as a Moon Crown during this divination rite. It's shown in carved illustrations on tablets. The ritual infuses the iron crown with energy and guides the wearer to their lost objective."

"And the exhibition crown has vanished," gasped Watson. "So you're thinking someone took it to use? Whoever it was, he murdered those girls?"

"Everything seems to fit, doesn't it?" Quist nodded slowly. "I believe we were right. The victims were killed during the correct lunar phase, they were all Virgo, their bodies were marked with the Sussamma symbols, and now we learn that the Moon Tiara has disappeared. Yes, I believe some occultist performed this dark rite and those unfortunate women were the requisite sacrifices."

"Whoever this nutter is, it's lucky the exhibition arrived here with the crown at exactly the right time of the month."

"I don't think *luck* enters into this."

"The ritual is used to find lost things. What do you reckon

they're searching for?"

"I have no idea, but I'm certain I'm right about this and I intend to find out." Quist glanced at his watch. "I believe we're done here for the time being and our young friend Miss Lewis should have arrived by now."

The pair headed back to the museum reception where Charlotte stood waiting by the main entrance. As usual, the girl wore a Goth outfit – a black denim jacket over a lacy Victorian-style dress and stiletto ankle boots. Watson noticed she'd neglected to apply her black lipstick and eye-liner.

When your father's in a police cell, he mused, *make-up is probably the last thing on your mind.*

"Hi there," said the youth, walking over. "Are you okay? I know last night can't have been much fun with your Dad locked up."

"It wasn't too bad." Charlotte sighed. "I slept at a friend's house rather than staying at home by myself. By the way, thanks again for ringing me, Mister Quist. It made me feel a lot better."

"Good, I was hoping it would reassure you," said Quist. "Come along, Miss Lewis. We should talk."

Slipping a paternal arm around the girl's shoulders, he led her out through the main doors and between the stone columns. The temperature was still chilly, but the sun had broken through the clouds and the bright parkland was filled with tourists.

"Would you mind calling me Charlotte?" she said, walking down the steps. "The *Miss Lewis* stuff sounds like a job interview or something."

"They all spoke like that in *his* day," laughed Watson.

"What? In the 1980s?" The girl smiled timidly. "I say I *slept* at a friend's, but to be honest, I didn't sleep *much*. I just don't know what to think. I know you told me they don't have any evidence, but…"

"No, they don't." The detective gave her a heartening grin.

"This police arrest was a huge mistake. Trust me, Charlotte, your father is going to be fine and I can assure you he'll be released today."

A large antiquated tricycle stood by the building, fitted with a wide awning, a counter and a gleaming chrome percolator. Quist often called at this mobile coffee stall when visiting the Museum Gardens and he was acquainted with the friendly couple who ran it. He paid for three steaming cups – a black coffee for himself and lattes for Watson and Charlotte.

"I'm guessing they do snacks here?" said Watson, hopefully.

"How remiss of me." Quist shook his head resignedly. "I'm forgetting how it must be over sixty minutes since your last meal." He bought three slices of caramel shortbread, one for the girl and two for his assistant. "I should have known you'd be ravenous."

The trio carried their drinks to one of the benches set out around the museum frontage. They sat facing the parkland and, crossing his legs, the detective turned to Charlotte.

"Just as a matter on interest..." he said, "Does your father have any interest in the occult? Witchcraft and magic?"

"No," she said. "Despite working as a psychic, he thinks all that kind of supernatural stuff is rubbish. Why?"

"I had to enquire, but I'd already guessed the answer." Quist sipped his coffee. "Anyway, the good news is you'll be reunited with him today after the official twenty-four hour holding period has ended. As I explained, the police have nothing to implicate your father in these crimes."

"That's brilliant if it's true" said Charlotte. "But how can you be sure? Why did they arrest him?"

"We've been doing a little research. I'm afraid your father gave the police information which they believe only the killer could have known, privileged information which was never made public. The victim he told them about had occult symbols on her body and he claimed he saw these in his psychic vision. He described the markings perfectly."

"*Shit*," whispered Charlotte. "So it's no wonder they suspected him."

"This isn't as serious as it may sound," pointed out the detective. "This *privileged* information could have been obtained from numerous sources and the authorities will know that. So would any half-decent solicitor. The law allows the police to detain suspects for twenty-four hours and that time will have been used gathering evidence to support their suspicions. Be assured, there *isn't* any."

"Like the Guv says..." Gobbling his shortbread snack, Watson took her hand and nodded reassuringly. "He'll be out and back home today."

"This makes me feel a lot better." Charlotte squeezed his fingers before turning again to Quist. "I've been thinking about when we were talking in your office. You said you believed my Dad's aunt was a genuine psychic medium."

"She *was*," he confirmed. "Towards the end of her life, Vera Lewis acquired a supernatural gift. The phenomena is uncommon, but sometimes it occurs when certain people are approaching death. She used her new talents to help us, assisting Watson and myself with an investigation."

"I see." The girl frowned. "So if she only became a *real* psychic just before she passed away, then Dad was right. She must have been a fake when she told me about getting a message from my Mum's spirit."

"Who can say for certain?" said Quist, quietly. Curling an arm around her shoulders, he gave her a hug. "The supernatural is something of a grey area, Charlotte. Yes, Vera's gift manifested itself in her final days, but perhaps it was there beneath the surface throughout her life. Perhaps she occasionally had genuine insights into the spirit world and *that* was one of them. Whatever it was, I'm sure Vera meant well and she was attempting to comfort you."

94

Charlotte nodded. "Like I told you, Dad went crazy. He knew she was a charlatan and it was too soon after Mum's death for him to hear that kind of nonsense. Hey, wait a minute..." She sat up straight. "Maybe the psychic gift runs in the family and that's what happened here. Maybe Dad had some sort of genuine psychic insight when he saw the symbols on that dead girl and went to the police."

Watson and Quist glanced dubiously at one another.

Drinking her coffee, Charlotte studied the detective. "Do *you* believe in all that sort of thing?"

"I definitely believed in Vera in her last few weeks," he said. "Er, listen, about your father's psychic abilities..."

"Well, look who's here," drawled a woman's voice. "It's Mister Quist, York's very own consultant detective."

Quist twisted around on the bench to see Detective Inspector Bradstreet and another female officer walking to the museum, both wearing beige raincoats over grey suits. He smiled to himself, knowing that the police would have identified the Badda symbols on the murder victims, just as he'd done. Like him, they would *also* be suspicious of a Badda cult exhibition arriving in York at the same time as the killings.

"Ah, Inspector, it's good to see you again," said Quist, rising to his feet. He turned to the red-haired girl beside her. "I notice you have a fresh face with you, and quite a pretty one too. Where's D.S. Aslam?"

"My Sergeant is on sick leave following an accident." Katie nodded to Angie. "This *pretty face* is Detective Sergeant Gibson."

"Very pleased to meet you, Sergeant," said Quist. "But how unfortunate about Aslam. Nothing too serious, I hope?"

"A car accident," said Katie. "Certainly nothing to concern *you*."

"Consultant detective?" echoed Angie, looking Quist over with interest and guarded amusement. "Er, I'm guessing that's like a private eye or something?"

"He prefers consultant detective to private investigator," said Katie, with more than a hint of sarcasm. "Mister Bernard Quist here runs a small agency in York and you'll soon discover he has the curious knack of somehow becoming involved in our *stranger* investigations. Take *this* as a perfect example. Would you believe he's drinking coffee outside the Badda exhibit with the daughter of our suspect?"

"And Watson," pointed out Quist's assistant, munching shortbread and cheerfully raising his cup.

"We're here because I'm fascinated by the wonderful history of this city." Quist gestured to the museum. "Especially the Roman era. We came to view the new exhibition."

"With your friend here?" Katie gestured to the young Goth, eyeing her guardedly. "Tell me, how long have you known Charlotte Lewis?"

"Oh, not very long," admitted Quist. "She's a client."

Charlotte glared at Katie. "So how's my Dad?" she asked, sarcastically. "Has he broken under questioning yet and confessed to mass murder?"

"Your feelings are understandable," said Angie. "But I'm afraid we can't discuss anything. I'm sure you know that?"

"Right." Charlotte laughed dryly. "Just so long as he isn't bruised too much from accidentally falling down your stairs."

"They stopped all that a while back," said Watson, grinning. "The moment the cops got CCTV cameras in their stations, the suspects stopped walking into doors and tripping."

"Now, now," chided Quist, turning back to the Inspector. "Am I to take it you share our interest in ancient Rome, or are you visiting the museum in a professional capacity?"

"The latter," said Katie.

Feeling her face flush hotly as he smiled, she unconsciously brushed back her short blonde hair. *For God's sake, why did she always become sexually aroused near this man?*

"Would this be in relation to the recent killings?" asked Quist. "The murders for which this young woman's father has been wrongly implicated?"

"He implicated himself," said Angie, curtly. "And like I just said, you know we can't discuss this."

Katie glanced at her vibrating phone and saw it was Constable Mitchell calling. "Hello, there, Gary. What do you have for me?" She listened at length, raising her eyebrows and glancing at Charlotte. "I see. That's incredible. Okay, we'll be right there."

"Developments?" asked Quist, sipping his coffee.

"Yes." The Inspector nodded for Angie to follow her and hurried towards the main gate. "You *could* say that."

* * * *

Chapter 13

The shaven-headed man sat quietly on the interview room chair. His wrists were handcuffed to the table in front of him and blue police-issue overalls covered his skeletal frame, the breast of which was soaked with saliva. Smirking, his green eyes remained fixed on the wall mirror, almost as if he could see the invisible group standing behind the glass. Katie and Angie stared back from the observation booth with Superintendent Morton and Zoe Planer.

"His name is Aaron King," said the young Constable. "I checked with Tennant's Rentals the moment they opened this morning and this is who hired the Transit van KE55 WCK last Thursday. They gave me his address in Brompton Court and Constable Mitchell and I called there with uniform. The van is parked behind the house and there's quite a bit of blood in the rear."

"I see," murmured Katie.

"It was weird, Ma'am," continued Zoe. "He didn't answer the door, but it was ajar so we announced who we were and entered. He was sitting on a chair in the kitchen. Just sitting there, grinning and drooling, as he's doing now."

"But you say he confessed?" asked Morton. The sharp-faced woman smiled excitedly. "He's definitely our killer?"

"We're waiting for his DNA results," said Zoe. "But yes, Ma'am, he confessed immediately. He claims he killed all four girls."

"Do we have the murder weapon?" asked Katie.

The Constable shook his head. "We're still searching the area. He rented the Brompton Court property last Thursday, the same day as the van. He has a roll of carpet in the kitchen, which looks identical to the one used to wrap the victims, along with two plastic bags of clothing and personal items belonging to the four girls." She gestured to the grisly symbol beneath King's right cuff. "Have you seen what he's done to his wrist?"

"Yes," said Katie. "It's similar to the main design cut into the victims, with a few more squiggles."

"He was wearing this around his neck too." Zoe handed her an evidence bag containing an old medallion on a chain. "The only time he showed any resistance to his arrest was when Constable Mitchell and uniform wrestled this off him."

"Some sort of occult amulet by the look of it," said Katie, examining the cryptic symbols on the iron disc. "Well, it all sounds fairly conclusive. So what do we know about him?"

King's grin was beginning to unnerve the Inspector. The thin man wasn't just staring at the mirrored glass, nor impossibly at the concealed group of police, but straight at *her*. She shook herself and glanced at the uniformed officer who stood guarding the interview room door. His pale expression suggested he'd rather be elsewhere – probably in a lavatory.

"We don't know much," admitted Zoe. "He's a heroin user. You can probably tell that from his malnourished appearance, but he also has a huge amount of needle scarring on his arms and legs."

"So he's been using for some time?" Katie turned to her with a puzzled look. "We know the killer isn't in our DNA database. Are you telling me King is the only heroin addict in York who *hasn't* been arrested for something or other?"

"He *is* in the main database," explained the Constable. "He has arrest records for shoplifting, disorderly behaviour and other minor stuff. We have his photo and prints on file, but not his DNA."

"Surely samples were taken when he was fingerprinted?" asked Superintendent Morton.

"You'd assume so, Ma'am," agreed Zoe. "But, for some reason, they're missing from the database."

"Brilliant," muttered Katie. "See if you can find out why."

"King has no personal effects at Brompton Court," continued Zoe. "The only documents there are the rental agreements for the property and vehicle." She handed the Inspector an evidence-bagged driving license. "We found that in the van and, according to the date, he's twenty-nine years old. I checked with DVLA and the only address they have for him is a flat in Acomb that was demolished a year ago. I also checked with Social Services and they have records of an addict named Aaron King living rough on the streets of York. He picks up methadone on a regular basis from one of the clinics."

"Living rough until Thursday?" Katie watched the motionless man. "So how did a homeless addict pay for a van and a house? More to the point, *why*?"

"Well, to abduct those women, of course." Morton snorted derisively. "He needed somewhere to kill them and a vehicle to transport them."

"According to the rental firm, he paid cash," said Zoe. "That makes sense, as he has no bank or credit card records."

"Exactly," said the Superintendent. "He probably robbed his drug dealer. I honestly couldn't care less where the money came from. We have our killer, this is over, and that's all that matters."

Katie shuddered. "Why is he drooling like that all the time?"

"The drool is nothing," said Zoe. "It's the stink. Before we got him into those police overalls, we noticed his suit trousers were crusted with dried urine..."

"*Suit?*" Angie turned to her. "Is that the latest trend with the York drug addicts?"

The Constable shrugged. "I wondered about that too. It was a bit of a mess, what with the drool and urine, but it appeared to be fairly new."

"No need to bother about such things," said Morton. "He probably found it in a skip."

"His breath is horrendous too," said Zoe. "It's been getting a lot worse since we brought him in."

The wiry man continued to stare at the Inspector like a

hideous, grinning cadaver, his green eyes gleaming. Katie gulped. *Yes, he WAS staring at her, but how the hell could he be? The glass on his side was a mirror.*

"I've experienced bad breath before," she said. "And he's been sitting there smirking long enough, We need to interview him."

Zoe shuffled uncomfortably. "He has a funny way of talking that creeps you out, Ma'am. A bit like those weird green eyes."

"Thanks, Zoe." The Inspector left the booth. "I must remember not to soil myself with fright."

Morton followed them into the corridor. "I've asked Doctor Lennon to join you and take a look at this character," she said. "He doesn't exactly appear *normal* and the criminal psychologist may be able to help."

"Good idea, Ma'am," said Katie. "Zoe, I understand Mitchell is still at King's house? I need you to get back there to help him and work with the SOCO. See what else you can find out about this man."

"I checked Tarot's alibi." Zoe opened her notebook. "It's sound enough. He was in the Eagle and Child with his daughter and then at a house on Wormstall Street. At the time of Sara Ritter's death, he was performing palm readings, or whatever it is he does. He then took a taxi to the Postern Gate on Piccadilly where he spent the next couple of hours; he's on their CCTV. He has solid alibis for the other three deaths too."

"The lab rang me on the way here," said Katie, nodding. "It isn't Tarot's DNA on the victims. I was sure he had something to do with this, but he's been here twenty-four hours."

"Release him," said Morton, grinning. "We have the killer, plus a confession and evidence to back it up. Like I said, this is over."

Angie turned to Katie. "But you're right," she said. "Tarot *must* be involved. How else could he know those details?"

"Maybe he really *is* psychic?" suggested Zoe.

"Well, thousands of them practise in Britain." Angie

shrugged. "Surely *some* of them must be genuine. He knew where the body was and he knew about the symbols. He knew her name was Sara, and the van registration…"

Katie shook her head. "Actually I told him her name and he turned it with the *little angel* nonsense, making it seem like he knew."

The Sergeant frowned. "I don't remember…"

"If he's any good at his job, you shouldn't. That's how they work."

"It doesn't matter," said the Superintendent. "Release Tarot."

* * * *

Katie had to agree with Zoe about Aaron King's creepiness. Once you got close, the skeletal man was far more than unnerving – he was downright terrifying. She'd felt edginess with prisoners many times – gangland sociopaths who enjoyed violence the way other men enjoyed football – but this was different. The handcuffed creature sitting at the table filled her with actual ice-cold dread.

King never seemed to blink, unless it was some trick and he closed his eyes quickly when no one was watching. She really wished he *would* close them – anything to conceal that green stare. Most of the time it remained fixed on her face, the unhinged smirk never leaving his lips. Zoe had been right about the stench too. Every outward breath made her feel physically sick. Katie glanced at the heating vents at the base of the wall and wondered why they weren't switched on; it was freezing in the interview room.

"Mister King," said the Inspector. "Do you understand that you've been arrested for the murders of four women?"

"King?" The laugh was deeper than expected for such a thin man and his stinking breath wafted across the table. "Mmh, that's nice; it makes me sound regal, doesn't it? And Stephen King wrote horror stories, didn't he? I hope you guys like horror. Yeah, you can call me King if that's what turns you on."

"Well, that *is* the name on your driving license."

"Some of us have more than one name, Blondie."

Katie's stomach lurched and she gagged slightly. The stench around the man reminded her of the early stages of decomposition. "I see," she said. "So which name do you go by?"

"Rakkat." The eyes seemed to glow green and he ran a tongue over his lips. Drool oozed through his stubble to dangle in tendrils from his chin. "I've had lots of names, Blondie, but you can call me Rakkat."

"Is that East European?" asked Katie, shivering slightly. *Someone should definitely turn on the heating; the room felt like a mortuary, but mortuaries had a nicer smell.* "Your surname or Christian name?"

His laugh was close to an animal growl and the sound covered her in gooseflesh. The uniformed officer by the door shuddered.

"*Christian*? Ooh, absolutely not, sweet child. No, it's just Rakkat."

"Well, if it's all the same," said Katie, "I'm going to call you by the name on your license."

"Your people removed my amulet," he snarled. "They really shouldn't have done that. Why don't you let me have it back?"

"That isn't going to happen," said Angie.

"Well, it's going to smell a lot worse in here if I don't wear it." He stared at the Sergeant. "Hey, Ginger, you feel different to your sexy friend Blondie here. I just love your red hair and I sense an affinity with you. Have we met before?"

"Trust me…" Angie shook her head. "I'd definitely remember *you*."

Leaning towards Katie, Rakkat licked the drool from his lips. "You're a yummy little thing, aren't you, Blondie? How would you like to be in a horror story? *My* horror story?"

"Thanks." The Inspector fought the urge to recoil from his breath. It really *did* smell like rotting flesh. "But no thanks."

"*Angie, Angie…*" Rakkat turned to her Sergeant and began to sing, the guttural sound raising the hair on Katie's neck. "*When will the clouds all disappear? Angie, Angie, where will it lead us from here?*"

"That's enough," said the Inspector.

"Oh dear!" Salivating again, he sat back. "You don't like songs by the Rolling Stones?"

"I'd *like* to know how you knew my Sergeant's name was Angie."

"I heard you talking out there in the corridor."

"I see. You mean through our soundproofed door?"

"Oh, I have good hearing, Blondie." The green eyes ran over Katie's breasts. "*Very* good hearing. I can hear your heart beating right now, sweet child, and it's beating so deliciously fast. Mmmh, is that because of me?"

"Speaking of names," said Angie, "do you know Kyle Tarot?"

"No, but I like that name. It's not as cool as Rakkat, of course, but I *do* like it."

"Try as I might," said Katie, "I can't seem to place your accent. Where are you from originally? Certainly not Yorkshire."

Rakkat grinned. "I really don't think you want to know where *I'm* from, little girl."

"Actually I *do*. You rented a van and a house in Brompton Court six days ago, but you don't appear to have any finances. How did you pay the hire charge, the deposit and advance rent?"

"Ah." He laughed again, a bubbling, maniac sound. "Yes, I had to be on my best behaviour that day. I had to be shaved and dressed up nice and smart to pay for them."

"Really? So where did you live prior to that?"

"Before Thursday? Apparently I was living on the streets. A gentleman of the road I believe such people were once called."

"*Apparently?*" Angie frowned. "Don't you remember?"

Rakkat chuckled and declined to answer.

"Why did you carve that symbol into your wrist?" asked Katie.

"My seal?" Rakkat lifted his arm as high as the tethered handcuffs would allow and leered. "Mmmh, do you like it, Blondie?"

"Not particularly. I've seen too many designs like that recently. Did you carve the symbols into those young women too?"

"The pretty virgins? Yeah, before I killed them. I already told your sexy friend Zoe when the police called at the house."

"And you'll sign a statement to that effect?" asked Angie.

"Bring it on, Ginger." His tongue curled over his lips and licked in a wide circle, the eyes narrowing into horrific green slits. "Yes, let's get this confession signed. You took my amulet and it's starting to feel tight in here."

"Tight?" repeated Katie. "In the interview room? What do you mean..."

"Not the room, you silly little girl..."

The door opened and Angie turned to the recorder. "Doctor Malcolm Lennon has just entered the interview."

Katie watched as the psychologist settled himself in the spare chair beside her Sergeant. He'd been observing with Morton in the booth next door and had obviously decided this was the moment to join in. She wasn't sure if Lennon's usual tactics of surprise entrance followed by friendliness and compassion would work here.

"Hi, Doc." Rakkat gave him a frightening grin, drool pouring from his teeth. "How are we?"

"I'm fine, Aaron. Thank you for asking." Lennon rubbed his hands briskly. "I say, it's a little chilly in here, isn't it?"

"We're discussing the murders," said Katie. "The four girls killed by Mister King."

"I'd prefer to discuss Aaron here." The psychologist motioned to the prisoner's wrist. "Your design is interesting."

"Blondie and Ginger don't like my seal." Rakkat eased back his sleeve against the edge of the table and held up his handcuffed forearm to show the star. "I wouldn't be around if it wasn't for the amulet and this, but it's a real bind too. *Bind.* Hey, that's funny. How about *that* for a pun?"

The doctor peered at the gruesome symbol. It hadn't scabbed over yet, suggesting the cuts were very recent, but although they were deep and required stitches, there was no flow of blood.

"Does it hurt?" asked Lennon. "It looks rather painful."

"Oh yes." Rakkat dipped his head to lick the pentagram, saliva running down his arm. "Of course it hurts, but the pain is good. The pain is so sweet."

"Yes, sometimes it *can* be good, can't it?" Lennon nodded. "Sometimes when we hurt ourselves, the pain can enable us to forget a greater pain. Something can weigh us down, and cutting into our arms, hurting ourselves in that way, can make us forget the…"

"Ooh, Doc, you should be showing me your ink blots." Rakkat laughed, the hideous sound turning the psychologist's stomach. "Sometimes I don't feel pain or anything at all for such a long time." He inhaled deeply, his eyes flickering ecstatically. "And then I get the chance to feel again; to feel flesh and skin." He turned to Katie. "I haven't been allowed to kill this time, sweet child, and killing you would be so exquisite."

The Inspector folded her arms. "You haven't killed, apart from the four women you claim to have murdered? I just love consistency." *One thing was for certain, they wouldn't be needing Lennon, or any other shrink, to diagnose King as a fucking lunatic.*

Rakkat ignored her. "So luscious to watch your expression as I tear out your lungs and feast upon them. Who knows, sweet child? This isn't over yet and I may get the chance. I really hope we can have our own little horror story."

"I shouldn't hold onto that hope," said Katie. "This is most definitely over."

He winked. "Don't bet your life on it, Blondie."

"I agree with what you say, Aaron," broke in Lennon. "I believe that pain can be good, but what makes *you* believe that?" He gestured to the carved symbol. "Why is *that* pain good?"

"This pain is of the flesh," muttered Rakkat, his voice low and throaty. The saliva began to pour again. "The warm human flesh. The flesh that feels…"

Lennon leant forward to catch the mumblings.

"Doctor…" Katie shook her head. "Be careful."

It happened with unbelievable speed. The handcuffed Rakkat kicked back his chair and lunged over the table, sinking his teeth into the psychologist's face and twisting his jaws, wrenching like a crazed pitbull. The uniformed officer leapt from his posting at the door as the flesh tore gruesomely. Dropping to the floor screeching, Lennon cradled his cheek, blood pulsing between his fingers. Katie grabbed the sniggering Rakkat in a headlock, pinning him to the table.

"Do you still agree, Doc?" Rakkat swallowed the meat and licked gore from his mouth. "Do you still think that pain is good?"

* * * *

Chapter 14

Brompton Court led off the southern end of Galton Road in Acomb, a small cul-de-sac of ten semi-detached dwellings. Quist and Watson stood behind a bush, watching a shabby house some forty feet away and the police forensic team working in its overgrown garden. The afternoon sunshine was bright, but the evergreen shrubbery concealed the two men.

"So why are we here?" asked the teenager.

"Tarot has been released," said Quist.

"Hey, good news for Charlotte. Did Gazza tell you this when he rang you in the car just now?"

The detective nodded. "As you know, Lestrade has been checking the police website and ringing me with every development. They have a new suspect in custody named Aaron King and this is his address." He gestured to the house. "This man admitted to the murders and they have solid evidence to back up his confession."

Watson glanced up, noting the broken streetlamp, the bushy conifer hedge that shielded the property and, apart from the forensic vehicles surrounding King's van, the air of deserted seclusion.

"Well..." he murmured. "If any psycho nutter needed a sheltered base with no one watching him coming and going, this is ideal. So, again, why are we here? You listened to Gazza for ages and then raced over here like a loony."

"Yes, it was because of the name."

"Aaron King?"

"No, he's calling himself Rakkat." Quist smiled tightly. "I wanted to see the house and get a general feel of the place. Ever since we became aware of the possible occult angle, these murders have been intriguing me more and more. I researched the Badda cult last night and came across several references to Rakkat. It was a demon in ancient African mythology, a creature that was supposedly used by the sect. It would enter a host body to carry out their tasks and..."

"*What*?" Watson hit him with an incredulous look. "I know it shouldn't surprise me, Guv, what with you being a frigging werewolf and everything, but are you saying you actually believe in demons? Demons that possess people like that?"

"Demon is the wrong term," said Quist. "They're actually dark elemental entities. Transdimensional beings from another mystical plane of existence."

"Ah, right." The youth let out a caustic laugh. "So why didn't you just say that?"

"The Christian church were responsible for naming the more sinister elementals *demons*. They mixed them into their own folklore about fallen angels to use in their anti-pagan propaganda."

"Okay..." said Watson slowly.

"The Badda cult were supposedly capable of reanimating fresh corpses to use as physical hosts for this creature." The detective took a deep breath. "Now this suspect Aaron King may be a mentally unwell murderer who has read the right occult books and picked up the name Rakkat, or..."

"Or?" echoed Watson.

"Or his dead body may be actually hosting this elemental."

"You can't be serious, Guv?"

"I truly hope I'm wrong and he's just some lunatic," sighed Quist. "But after our visit to the museum, I'm certain that at least *one* genuine occultist is behind this and they've performed that horrific Sussamma Ritual. Whether King is hosting Rakkat or just insane, I'm *also* certain that he's working for them."

"Yeah, you got a bit weird near that altar," said Watson. "What did you see?"

"Like I told you earlier, I need to confirm my suspicions later tonight." He shook his head. "Something is very wrong here."

"Four girls are dead." Watson laughed nervously. "Yeah,

something is *definitely* wrong."

"According to the short police report Lestrade read out to me, Aaron King is a heroin user in his late twenties. He was living rough on the streets until last week when he somehow managed to rent this house and hire a Transit van."

"So you're wondering how he afforded this place and got the cash to rent a van? Maybe he stole it? Homeless addicts *have* been known to steal."

"Watson, you know that when addicts steal, they use the money to buy drugs. King was also wearing a new suit. The charities who hand out clothing to the homeless provide practical warm garments, not suits."

"Okay." The youth nodded. "Using deduction, maybe he needed a suit to appear respectable when he rented the house and hired the..."

"But *why* did he hire the van and rent this property?"

"To pick up the girls and..."

"So one morning this homeless heroin addict decided to become a serial killer?" Quist shook his head. "I don't accept that. As I say, something isn't right and King can't possibly have made those payments. Someone else is clearly behind all this; probably more than one person, and they're controlling King."

"A black magician or an occult group with plenty of cash?" Watson scratched his head. "But if you're right about the demon thing, why would they need it?"

"Dark elementals are far more powerful than humans. That would prove useful when abducting victims and carrying corpses, but I believe Rakkat is now serving another planned purpose. The divination ritual is complete, the occultist will have located his prize, but rather than have the elemental vanish, Rakkat, or rather his host Aaron King, is the ideal scapegoat for the murders. The police have their killer in custody and, with their investigation neatly concluded, they won't search any further for the *real* murderer, the adept who stabbed those girls with a sacrificial dagger."

"We still don't know what they were looking for with that divination rite."

"No we don't," murmured Quist. "The thing is, if Rakkat is real and he *is* using King's body as a host, then the adept who conjured up this entity is genuine too. If they're proficient enough to place elementals in human hosts, it's safe to say their Sussamma Ritual will have been successful and they'll have found whatever they were searching for."

Hearing an approaching vehicle, the detective yanked Watson further back behind the shrubbery as a car drove past them down the cul-de-sac to pull up by the house

"Come," he murmured, watching Katie Bradstreet and Angie Gibson climb out. "Let's see what Mister Tarot knows and if he'd care to share it with us."

* * * *

Gary Mitchell and Zoe Planer met the Inspector and her Sergeant in the hallway, both wearing forensic coverall suits.

"How's the psychologist?" asked Mitchell. "I heard what happened from Zoe. It must have been horrific."

"He's at the hospital," said Angie. "It was like an animal attack. That lunatic ripped off part of Lennon's cheek and actually ate it."

"*Fuck!*" mouthed Mitchell.

"Yes, I couldn't have put it better myself," admitted Katie, looking around. The grubby carpet and cheap décor were past their best and typical of these low-priced furnished rentals. "So how are things going here?"

Mitchell led the detectives towards the kitchen. "The SOCO is finishing with the scene. So far there's nothing here to tell us who Aaron King is and the neighbours are no help. They never set eyes on him. Matthew has a few things for you, but they're pretty strange."

Overhearing the voices, Matthew Carson, the Scenes of Crime Officer, appeared from the kitchen and slipped off his forensic mask. "Gary is right," he said. "There isn't anything in this house belonging to your suspect, and that includes food and waste in the bins. He hasn't been eating here."

"It seems he hasn't been eating at *all*," said Katie. "Well, apart from Doctor Lennon's cheek. The Police Doctor claims he has malnutrition."

"Well, he *is* a heroin addict," pointed out Angie. "They're not known for their healthy appetites."

"Addict or not, there are no traces of heroin here." Carson shook his head. "No drugs or drug paraphernalia. Now you might think that's unusual, but let me show you *unusual*."

The SOCO led them into a dining kitchen and gestured to a solitary brown armchair.

"How *lovely*," drawled Katie, seeing the discoloured fabric and wrinkling her nose at the stench of ammonia. "I take it I'm looking at urine stains?"

Carson nodded. "Yes, the material and padding are both soaked, just like King's trousers when you arrested him. The weird thing *is*, the only DNA belonging to your suspect is in this one room and most of it is in that chair."

"He hasn't used the bed or the bathroom?" asked Katie, puzzled.

"I'm saying he hasn't been *anywhere* in the house except for here. He's been sleeping and urinating right there in that chair. I know it's difficult to accept, but between going out in the van to abduct those girls, it appears he just sat here."

"*What?*" Katie laughed dryly. "You're telling me he's been sitting here since last Thursday when he rented the place? No, Matthew, that's too bizarre."

"This is crazy," whispered Angie. "So King was obviously drinking water, but not eating or bothering to visit the toilet?"

"And it gets stranger," said Carson. "I don't believe his victims were ever inside this house."

Angie frowned. "But we were told you found blood…"

"I found four obvious patches in the lounge when I arrived, one from each victim, but I strongly suspect the blood was brought here, like the clothing and other evidence belonging to the girls. From the spill pattern, it appears to have been poured from a container."

"Planted evidence?" said Katie.

"I'd say so." The SOCO nodded. "Planted in a hurry too by amateurs. I can tell you with certainty that King's four victims weren't killed in this property. I should have found hairs, skin cells and DNA, but apart from those four blood pools, there's nothing. The van parked outside is a definite match for our tyre tracks and the interior is covered in DNA from the victims. He definitely used that vehicle to transport them, but not to *this* house. He didn't kill them in the van either."

"Could he have cleaned up?" asked Angie.

"No, the sort of deep cleaning required to destroy evidence is really obvious."

"Oh, Morton is going to fucking *love* this," mumbled Katie. "So, from the planted blood and bags of clothing, someone clearly wants us to believe this is our murder scene. Perhaps the same someone who paid for this house. There's no way a homeless addict could get the deposit and rent together."

"And the cash for the van," added Angie.

"Exactly. I don't buy the idea that King stole the money. I believe someone else paid for all this, but why?"

"Well, Tarot's house isn't the crime scene either," said Angie. "It's been searched and the place is completely clean."

"So where *were* these four girls killed?" Katie turned to the

Sergeant. "And speaking of DNA, why wasn't King's in our database? I looked at his file and he's been arrested nine times. Check with the officers involved and see whether or not they took samples."

"Will do, Ma'am," said Angie, puzzled. "One or two might have decided not to bother swabbing for his DNA, but surely not *all* nine of them."

"This is getting weirder and weirder." The Inspector looked around the room. "Why would someone want us to believe those girls died here?"

* * * *

Chapter 15

The suburb of Nunthorpe lies to the south of the city, sandwiched between the riverside Rowntree Park and the flat meadows surrounding York's racecourse. This peaceful little area is mostly comprised of neat terraced streets, the rows of redbrick houses built in the latter part of the 1800s for workers in the confectionery factories. Kyle Tarot's semi-detached house on Terry Street stood on the eastern edge of this neighbourhood, with a front garden of flower tubs and a small expanse of parkland stretching from the rear of his property to the banks of the Ouse.

Answering his doorbell and grinning widely, Kyle ushered Quist and Watson into the front hall and shook their hands enthusiastically.

"It's good to meet you both," he said, showing them through into the lounge and picking up a mug of coffee. "Charlotte told me about how you agreed to help her, but there was really no need for her to worry. The police have completed their checks. My DNA and prints don't match anything from their crime scenes, obviously, and I have solid alibis for all of those murders."

A glass-topped table, a large television, and a dark green suite filled the room. Charlotte sprawled with a magazine in one of the armchairs, and, smiling at her, Quist ran his eyes over several framed photographs on the wall. The similarity between the young Goth and the dark-haired woman in these pictures was remarkable and he could see it was her late mother.

"Hello again," said Charlotte, sipping tea. "Yeah, you were right about everything. They released Dad earlier today."

"I'm pleased to hear it," said the detective, sitting on the couch with Watson. "I told you they couldn't hold him longer than twenty-four hours."

"Would you like a drink?" Kyle held up his mug. "Tea,

115

coffee, or maybe something stronger? I want to say thank you for taking the trouble to look into this for Charlie and for putting her mind at rest." He glanced pointedly at Watson. "She's only just turned sixteen, you see, and she was quite frightened when I was arrested."

"Honestly, Dad." The girl laughed and shook her head. "Sometimes you can be so embarrassing."

"Sixteen?" Watson winked at her. "I've got to say, you look and act older."

"Yes, well she *isn't*." Kyle's frigid smile suggested he wouldn't be welcoming Watson into the fold as a beloved son-in-law anytime soon. He turned to Quist. "By the way, do I owe you anything for this? Is that why you're here?"

"You don't owe money," said the detective, crossing his legs, "Just an explanation."

"Er, right…" Kyle sat in a chair beside his daughter. "What do you mean?"

"The suspect in police custody is a young man named Aaron King," said Quist. "He's confessed to the murders and they discovered evidence of the crimes in his property."

"That's why the cops let you go," said Watson, nodding.

"But this man King is a penniless drug addict," continued Quist. "He was living rough on the streets, then suddenly he acquired a new suit and was able to rent a house and hire a van for several days. It's quite obvious he had an accomplice who funded this. I'm certain that accomplice isn't you, Mister Tarot, but I'd very much like to know who *is* behind this."

"Why?" asked Charlotte, puzzled. "My Dad's in the clear now and this addict doesn't concern you. Surely what you're talking about is a police matter?"

"I *do* have my reasons." Quist studied her father. "I'd be very interested to know what you saw that night."

"Yes, whatever." Kyle sipped coffee and closed his eyes.

"The vision was clear, but as always, it was complex…"

"Very good." The detective smiled wryly. "but I mean what did you *really* see on Tuesday evening by Rowntree Park?"

He shook his head. "I'm not sure I understand what you…"

"Mister Tarot…" sighed Quist. "We both know you're about as clairvoyant as Watson's cat. The police checked your alibi and confirmed you were in the Postern Gate public house on Piccadilly. Before that, you were performing psychic readings in Clifton…"

"How do you know about my alibi?" asked Kyle.

The detective ignored his question. "The shortest route to your home from the Postern Gate would take you along Terry Avenue and right by the location where Sara Ritter was found. I know you witnessed something there that evening. Something which provided you with a van registration and the killer's signature symbol."

Charlotte frowned and turned to her father. Squirming in his chair, Kyle could actually feel his colour draining.

"From her perplexed expression," said Quist, "you clearly haven't told your daughter the truth."

"Dad?" said the girl.

"You saw Aaron King disposing of the girl's body," said the detective. "You saw this at night, because you never mentioned that the dark van was red; you couldn't distinguish the colour when you read the registration in the moonlight. You described King as bald and slender, but you never mentioned his eyes. The police reports refer to how remarkably green his eyes are and, had it been light, you would have noticed and told them. Such a feature would have added *colour* to your *psychic* vision, if you'll pardon the pun."

Focussing on keeping his hand steady, Kyle sipped his coffee, praying that his fear wasn't showing. The moment he came clean and admitted to this, it was all over. This lucrative new life he was planning would be finished before it had begun and his career as a celebrity clairvoyant would be ruined.

"Is this true, Dad?" asked Charlotte.

"He's wrong," muttered Kyle, the familiar guilt tearing at his stomach. "Er, it's like I said – I channelled those visions with…"

"Visions," repeated Quist. "Yes, you obviously decided to impart this information to the authorities as supernatural visions. I imagine the objective was to cash in on these murders by going to the media with your sensational story. When you were arrested you told your daughter not to worry; you said to wait until Wednesday and everything would be okay. The firm where King hired the van is closed on Tuesday, so you knew you'd be in the clear once Tennant's opened the following morning and the police checked their records."

Kyle sat in silence for several seconds until Watson spoke.

"Or maybe he really *is* psychic," said the teenager, grinning.

Charlotte's shocked face suggested Quist's explanation was slightly more credible than her father's paranormal story. "Oh, Dad, I don't believe this," she gasped. "You actually found a dead body and didn't ring the cops? You just left it there? What were you *thinking*?"

Kyle slumped in the chair, rubbing his eyes. "I was thinking about the financial mess we're in," he muttered. "We're really in the shit, Charlie, and I've always shielded you from the truth. I was thinking about the money for your college fees and…"

"That doesn't matter," said Charlotte.

"Yes it *does*," said Kyle. "And yes, you're right, Mister Quist, but how on earth do you know about the Tennant's rental company?"

"I've been keeping up to date with the police investigation," said the detective. *Keeping up to date* was mostly down to Lestrade's illegal skills, but he neglected to mention this. "So returning to my original question, what did you *really* see that night?"

"Just what I told the police," mumbled Kyle, ruefully. "But yes, I saw it for real, as you guessed. It didn't last long, but it was horrible. I was standing in one of the Rowntree Park gateways when they arrived and left that poor girl's body. They just dumped it like it was *nothing* and then drove off."

"*They*?" echoed Watson.

"Er, yeah." Kyle stared at the carpet. "The bald guy wasn't alone in the van. There was someone else driving."

"As I said, there *had* to be an accomplice." Quist nodded. "Can you describe them?"

"Not really. To be honest, I'd had a few drinks and it was too dark. The courtesy light didn't come on when the door opened."

"Doubtless it was switched off," said Quist. "Anyone with sense would do that during the disposal of a corpse."

"Yeah, Guv." Watson glanced at him. "Let's face it, we *all* do that when we're dumping bodies."

"I think it was a woman, but I'm not sure," said Kyle. "At first I thought it was a courting couple, so I might have assumed it was a woman. I just don't know."

"I presume you neglected to inform the police about this?" said Quist.

Kyle nodded, squirming in the chair. "Like I'm telling you, I couldn't really see the driver. I got the impression she had long hair, but when I told the cops about my vision, I didn't mention this other person because, er…"

"Because?" prompted Watson.

"Well, it sounds stupid and they'd have thought I was mad, but her eyes seemed to be, er… *glowing*."

"I see," murmured Quist, thinking for a moment. "Listen to me, Mister Tarot, I would strongly suggest you discard any ideas you may still harbour about profiting from this. Inspector Bradstreet is far from stupid and she will have made the same deductions I did."

"Yeah, the Inspector was pretty clear." Kyle sighed. "She knows I was lying about the psychic visions, but she can't prove it. I felt bad about this to begin with, but now…"

"Now you should leave things well alone," broke in Quist.

"Do you know who John Humble was?"

Kyle shook his head.

"Humble made the infamous hoax tapes during the Yorkshire Ripper police investigation. He became known as Wearside Jack and received eight years in prison for perverting the cause of justice. Bradstreet could charge you with something similar or, at the very least obstruction. A judge wouldn't take kindly to someone attempting to profit from these murders."

"He's right," agreed Watson.

"Fortunately for you," said Quist, "the police found Aaron King because of your information, despite the mercenary way in which you provided it. You saw another person in that van, but with King being a destitute drug addict, I'm sure they'll have already realised he didn't work alone. Besides, you don't have a description of this driver or any further information that would prove useful. If you have any sense, you'll now keep a low profile and hope Bradstreet forgets about your *psychic* lies."

Watson nodded. "I reckon if you appear on the front page of a tabloid as a celebrity clairvoyant, it'll jog her memory."

"I agree." Charlotte glared at her father. "I can't believe you didn't tell me the truth. Not just about this, but about how we have no money. I'm not a kid and you don't need to *shield* me, as you put it."

"Yes, I'm sure you have plenty to discuss." Quist stood up and headed for the door. "If there's nothing further you can tell us about that evening, we'll leave you both in peace. You'd better give me your number in case we need to get in touch again."

Kyle handed him a psychic business card and, smiling tightly at the embossed pentagram, Quist shook his head and pocketed it.

"At least he *did* help the cops," said Charlotte, following them into the hall with her father. "They have their murderer."

"Yes, that's what we're all supposed to think," said Quist.

"Huh?" Kyle looked bewildered. "I know you don't believe

this Aaron King guy paid for the van, but you're saying you don't believe he's the killer?"

"I'm fairly certain he isn't." The detective turned to him. "You claim the van driver was possibly a long-haired girl? That's interesting."

"Long hair?" Watson frowned. "Call me weird, Guv, but I'd say the glowing eyes are *more* interesting."

* * * *

The long-haired girl walked along Norwood Avenue in Clifton, a cul-de-sac of tall terraced houses. Smartly dressed, she carried a bulky shoulder bag and, looking up at the large yellow moon over York, she smiled to herself. This was the second evening of the full phase and, so far, everything had gone to plan.

The terraced street terminated in a small builder's yard behind a wrought iron gate. The sign on the wall read *Jon Oldacre* and the girl knocked on the door of the adjacent dwelling, the last house on the terrace. A chubby middle-aged man answered with a pint mug of tea in his burly fist.

"Hello, love." He smiled warmly. "Can I help you?"

"I'm sure you can," she said. "You're a builder, Mister Oldacre, but I understand your firm isn't exactly large and you take on smaller projects for cash-in-hand?"

"Yes, it's a family business." Jon nodded. "Just me and my two lads. Er, when you say I work for *cash*, I still put the money through the books and pay tax, of course. If that's why you're here, I can show you my accounts with…"

"No need to worry about all that. I'm led to believe you own a small mechanical digger, the sort of thing used for excavating graves and ditches?"

"That's right." He gestured to the metal gate. "It's in the yard there."

"Good." She smiled. "I'm here to offer you a job and, just like you, I don't care about income tax. I need you to do a little excavation work. It's a simple one-man job that shouldn't take long, but I ought to mention this will be at night because, to be honest, it isn't strictly legal."

"I see." Jon looked evasive. "Well, I don't know…"

"Mister Oldacre, I know you've been warned several times by the council and successfully prosecuted twice. You were fined for tearing down mature trees with preservation orders, and fined again for demolishing a Grade Two listed building. People hire you because larger, more reputable building firms would turn down such work."

"Hey, they were mistakes." Jon let out a nervous laugh. "You know how it goes. Rich folk want things removing from their properties and they don't always tell you about preservation orders and suchlike…"

The woman shook her head. "That doesn't interest me, but I think this will interest *you*." Opening her shoulder bag, she took out a plastic carrier. "Five-thousand pounds in tax-free banknotes and another five when the job is completed. No questions asked."

"Er, right…" Jon gazed into the carrier of money and grinned. "But there *are* three questions, darling. *What* is it, *where* is it, and *when* do you want me to start digging?"

"Tonight." The girl laughed and checked her wristwatch. "An acquaintance of mine will accompany you and explain everything. I need this work completing before dawn."

* * * *

Chapter 16

The Tempest Anderson Hall is situated beside the Roman galleries on the ground floor of the Yorkshire Museum. The Victorian plasterwork on the ceiling and walls provides a stark contrast to the sloping bank of modern seating that faces the stage. This lecture theatre can accommodate almost three-hundred people, but the Badda cult talk this Wednesday night had attracted less than a third of that number and the small crowd filled the front of the auditorium.

Quist and his assistant sat at the end of the second row, the teenager stifling yawns and trying his best to stay awake in the comfy seat. Doctor Sawtelle spoke on the small podium, punctuating his talk with a series of photographs on the large video screen to his rear. Historical lectures had never been Watson's favourite way to spend an evening and, so far, this chubby academic had done little to change his mind. The youth curbed another yawn. *The past hour had been filled with slides of temples, pottery, and stone tablets covered in crap pictures and gibberish writing.*

Watson had learnt that the Badda cult had originally been a Berber tribe in a remote village hidden in the Atlas Mountains of North Africa. They worshipped some mystical wolf God named Badda Oushane, they practised mysterious rites, and they were highly secretive. *He'd also learnt that, the next time his boss suggested something like this, he'd pretend to have a bad stomach upset.*

Sawtelle clicked his remote control to change the slide. A picture of a marble bust appeared behind him.

"So that's as much as we know about this sect," he said. "Admittedly, our knowledge doesn't amount to much due to their clandestine nature. They appear to have been fiercely protective of their mysterious rites and their..." He chuckled. "Their black magic."

Watson glanced at Quist, who nodded slightly.

"Now we'll take a look at how the sect came to be here in

York." Sawtelle gestured to the photograph, the silvery light of the screen glinting on his balding head. "This is the only known depiction of the Prefect Aquila – we have it on show in the exhibition here. As you can see, his features are noticeably malicious and ruthless and, by all accounts, he wasn't a particularly *good* man."

"It isn't a particularly *good* lecture," mumbled Watson, wincing as he received a sharp jab in the ribs from Quist's elbow.

"An imposing man of formidable strength, Aquila commanded a cohort of 480 infantry." Sawtelle changed the slide to one showing Roman reenactors in uniform. "Prefects were a social class down from the senators, and heading an auxiliary unit didn't have the same status as commanding a unit in the legions. These soldiers weren't equipped to the same standards and were seen as lower quality troops, but being a Prefect created opportunities for these officers to advance their careers. Because they were often garrisoned in regions with no other Roman forces for hundreds of miles, they acted independently and had the freedom to show their initiative. This is exactly what Aquila did."

Quist leant forward to study the screen as the doctor brought up a map.

"Aquila was stationed in what is now Morocco," said Sawtelle, gesturing to the illustration. "He was based in the Roman city of Volubilis, an isolated outpost on the south-western edge of their empire. This was originally a Berber city and the capital of ancient Mauretania. A visit to the present-day ruins of Volubilis is quite stimulating."

I'll bet, thought Watson. *Yeah, I'll book a ticket tomorrow.*

"As they expanded into these exotic lands, the Romans came across countless religions and seemed to have a weakness for them. Many cults, such as Minerva, Orpheus and Isis, were taken on board and the Roman fortresses had shrines to these new deities alongside the shrines to Jupiter and their own Gods. They certainly took to

Christianity. Yes, in the early days they fed a few to lions, but look how Rome promoted that particular sect later."

Watson smirked as the doctor laughed at his own wit and paused for the audience to join in. The silence was broken by someone coughing and he tetchily continued.

"Volubilis was close to the village of the Badda sect. According to the Roman records, which we possess in the British Museum, Aquila heard fearful whisperings of this cult in the nearby mountains and decided to investigate." Sawtelle brought up an old monochrome slide of a half-buried temple. "The Badda village is long gone, but this was their place of worship, the only example ever found, and everything from this 1920s excavation is on show next door in our exhibition. The Prefect was soon seduced by this sect and, not only was he initiated into the religion, but he became the lover of Hanka, one of the five Badda Priestesses."

Quist looked up as a figure quietly appeared to his left. "Ah, Inspector," he whispered, moving his overcoat from the empty seat beside him and smiling at Katie Bradstreet. "Good evening. I'm afraid you've missed most of the talk."

"Yeah, you must be gutted," mumbled Watson.

"Mister Quist." The Inspector sat and lowered her voice. "And Watson too. Keeping up with your Roman history, I see?"

"Just like you, apparently." Quist's smile widened. "I've also been keeping up with your current investigation. So it would appear Kyle Tarot is innocent?"

"Innocent of murder," said Katie. "But Mister Tarot is still implicated in this. He knew things that only the killer could know."

"Well, he *does* work as a psychic," said Watson.

Katie hit him with a sarcastic smile, then turned as Sawtelle coughed loudly on the stage. The doctor glared, unaccustomed to people talking during his lectures.

"At this point," continued Sawtelle, "legend mixes with the

factual records. The Priestess Hanka was said to have been remarkably beautiful, but also very jealous of the main Badda Priestess. She had her lover Aquila murder this woman and Hanka and the Prefect ran the sect themselves. Aquila initiated his own soldiers into the cult and, once he'd learned enough about the mystical rites, he had his men wipe out the Badda village, massacring the entire sect and taking their treasures."

A man on the front row raised his hand. From the pad and pen in his hand, Quist deduced he was a local journalist. "What treasures?" he asked.

"Yes, don't bother waiting until the end for questions," said Sawtelle, finding it difficult to conceal his contempt. "If anyone has anything to ask, feel free to interrupt. These weren't conventional treasures, but mystical artefacts supposedly infused with magical power, the main item being a knife known as the Oushane Blade." The doctor switched slides again to show a Roman standard bearing a golden eagle. "Now at some point around 115 AD, the Ninth Legion who were stationed here in York, were sent north to deal with the tribes of the Brigantes. Aquila and his cohort were called away from Morocco to guard York until they returned."

"What happened to the Ninth?" asked a woman, who had clearly taken the sarcastic invitation for questions literally. "Didn't they mysteriously vanish?"

"We don't know what became of them," admitted Sawtelle, stroking his trim beard. "There's no documented trace of the Ninth Legion after 117 AD, and various theories have been proposed as to their fate. The point is, by this time, Aquila's entire cohort were initiates in the Badda cult and the Priestess Hanka accompanied them to York. He introduced the religion here gradually, first constructing a small temple in the grounds of the York fortress, but the skeleton staff left behind by the Ninth became unnerved by this. They didn't much care for the dark practices of the sect, so he built a larger temple south of the river in the Colonia, the fortified settlement inhabited by the Roman civilians. Once again, it's said they became more and more frightened by the cult, so Aquila went outside the fortress and constructed a full-size Badda temple – just like the one in the Atlas Mountains – where he and his people could worship and carry out their rites in secret."

Quist lifted his hand. "Do we know where?" he asked.

"No." Sawtelle peered at the detective, recognising him from their chat in the exhibition. "All we know is that it was somewhere in the forests to the west of the fortress. Aquila and his men worshipped and performed magical rituals there for over a year, but there was much bad feeling amongst the other Romans and local tribes which quickly turned to fear. People often vanished and the locals believed the sect were sacrificing them, which was almost certainly true. It's claimed that human remains were found in the woodland half-eaten."

"So the Badda cult were involved in cannibalism?" asked the journalist on the front row, an excited look on his face.

Sawtelle laughed, partly at the way people were more interested in unseemly aspects like treasure and cannibalism, and also at the way this had begun to descend into a free-for-all of questions.

"These are only legends," he said. "There are always plenty of fantastical myths. Take the Oushane Blade I mentioned, which Aquila brought here from Morocco. It supposedly bestowed immortality upon the owner, provided they knew how to use it. It's only folklore, you understand, but this knife was a jewelled dagger in a golden scabbard with a blade fashioned from wolf bone."

Quist cleared his throat and raised his hand again. "Wolf bone?"

"That's right," said Sawtelle. "As we all know, their deity Badda Oushane was a Hunter God taking the form of a huge wolf. Cult members would sacrifice someone and then draw their own blood with this dagger." He mimicked the action of cutting his palm.

"It would happen during a full moon ritual in the correct month and they were then transformed into a Hunter God themselves. "

"I see," said Quist, swallowing dryly. "Which month would that be?"

"Coincidentally, it was *this* one, March. The month dedicated to Badda Oushane, when the deity was thanked by the sect for their fruitful winter hunts. Aquila himself is said to have performed this rite, cutting himself with the blade like Hanka before him. The ritual was known as the Oushane Sacrament."

"That's rather intriguing," murmured Quist.

"Old legends usually are." Sawtelle smiled tartly. "Intriguing if you enjoy rubbish as opposed to history. I spoke with you earlier today and, as I mentioned then, I believe in science, not nonsense."

"So what became of the Prefect Aquila?" asked another person.

"It didn't end well for our friend." Sawtelle smiled grimly. "This was a turbulent time for the empire, which protected Aquila's new cult and their dark practises from the eyes and ears of Rome. In 119 AD, however, it became evident that the Ninth Legion had been wiped out and the Emperor Hadrian brought the Sixth Legion to York from Germany to replace Aquila's cohort. He didn't like what he found and he *certainly* didn't like the horrors and obscenities of the Badda cult."

Quist sat forward, listening intently.

"Viewing this religion as a crime against Rome and the God Jupiter, Hadrian stamped out the sect in a matter of days. Aquila's men were rounded up, beheaded and burnt on pyres, but a different fate lay in wait for the Prefect and his Priestess Hanka. Hadrian decided their crimes deserved a far worse punishment and he had the pair buried alive. The legends claim they were entombed inside the Badda temple itself, along with their occult artefacts, and the entire construction was secreted for eternity beneath a mound of earth."

Quist looked puzzled. "If this Oushane Blade was mostly made of gold and jewels, why didn't Hadrian keep it and melt it down?"

"Superstition, apparently." Sawtelle shrugged. "He believed it to be cursed."

"And you say this temple cum tomb is lost?" asked a woman. "Hasn't anyone ever looked for it?"

Sawtelle sighed testily. "As I've already stated, no one knows where it is, just that it was somewhere outside the walls of the Roman fortress and concealed for posterity by Hadrian. We assume it was built over long ago and the remains are long gone."

Quist turned to Watson. "This is why they performed the Sussamma Ritual," he whispered. "This *has* to be what they were searching for."

The teenager nodded. "The tomb?"

"Exactly, or rather what's inside – this Oushane Blade. An occult adept with the right knowledge of the Badda rites could ritually cut themselves with it and gain immortality by becoming a *Hunter God*."

"Yeah." Watson gulped. "I'm guessing you mean a werewolf."

* * * *

The main entrance into the Tempest Anderson Hall isn't via the Yorkshire Museum front doors, but through a separate door in a large sandstone porch on the northern face of the building. The crowd began to leave the lecture theatre and Watson noticed Melissa and Tamzin smoking and chatting by the wall outside. The night air was chilly and both girls wore warm coats.

"Hey, hello again, you two." Melissa drew on her cigarette and smiled. "So how did you find the talk?"

"Fascinating," said Quist, taking out his own cigarettes.

"It was okay," agreed Watson, deciding against mentioning

how bored he'd been. With this sexy black girl and her blonde friend choosing careers in history, his true feelings probably wouldn't enamour them. "A good lecture, if you're into Romans and shit. Your boss seems to know his stuff."

"He does." Tamzin laughed dryly. "And he certainly loves the stage."

"We were at the back," said Melissa, lowering her voice in case Sawtelle should appear amongst the stream of exiting people. "We've heard it before, of course, so we left early. Thankfully Edwin didn't notice. He sees it as an insult if anyone walks out of his talks."

"He enjoys power," said Tamzin. "Public speaking gives him a feeling of being in control, but he doesn't like talking to the public on a personal one-to-one level."

Quist lit a cigarette and nodded. "Mmh, I couldn't help but notice how he spoke to us this morning."

"More to the point, how he spoke to you girls," said Watson. "Is he usually like that?"

Melissa grimaced. "Pretty much."

"Why is he always so rude?" asked the youth.

"Basically he's a creep," muttered Tamzin, adjusting her large designer spectacles. "He's sexist and…"

"He's also our boss," pointed out Melissa, with a rueful look. "So we tactfully grin and bear it. Edwin and I are both doctors, but he's our department head and outranks me at the British Museum." She puffed on her cigarette and smiled. "Anyway, what's the story with you two? Are you history students or something, or is this just an interest of yours?"

"Student?" Watson laughed, whipped out a business card and presented it. "Private investigator, actually. Anything you want investigating privately and I'm your guy. Well, me and the boss here."

"Wow." Tamzin gasped. "A real private eye."

"Consultant detective," corrected Quist.

"Speaking of work," said Watson, "what do you do *afterwards*? You're only up here for two weeks and a *real* private eye is the ideal person to show you girls the sights of York."

"Yeah." Melissa laughed. "Probably far better than one of the countless tour guides I've seen."

"Absolutely." Watson took out a pen and drew a smiley face on the reverse of the card. "There you go, Mel. That's how you girls will be grinning when you've had one of *my* tours of the pubs and clubs."

"We might just take you up on that," said Melissa.

"Ah, Inspector." Quist nodded courteously as Katie Bradstreet left the lecture theatre. "I wonder, are you on duty at the moment, or do you have a little time to spare?"

"Over the past week it's felt as if I'm *never* off." Katie buttoned up her raincoat. "Why do you ask?"

"Watson and I are popping for a swift drink and I'd very much appreciate your company." Quist lowered his voice. "I have something to tell you that I feel will be advantageous."

Sawtelle appeared through the exit and turned off the lights on the large panel beside the door.

"Are you the last to leave?" asked Tamzin.

The doctor shook his head. "No, there are still people in there," he said, sarcastically. "But I thought I might leave them inside for the night." Locking the door with a bunch of keys, he took out his mobile and stabbed in a code.

"Interesting," said Quist. "I take it you're able to control the museum alarm system with your phone?"

"As I told you earlier, I believe in science, not legends and fairy stories." Sawtelle looked pointedly at the detective and held up the mobile. "Behold, the wonders of science."

* * * *

131

Chapter 17

Katie Bradstreet had visited the Last Drop on Colliergate many times. Named, *not* after the last drop of ale in a glass, but the last drop through the nearby gallows trapdoor, this atmospheric tavern has wooden floors, high-backed pews and brick walls covered in old paintings. The Inspector and Watson sat at a table beneath a poster of the famed highwayman Dick Turpin, someone who had taken a *last drop* in York himself. The place was bustling with evening clientele and Katie unbuttoned her suit jacket, watching as Quist ordered drinks at the busy counter. He'd slipped off his leather overcoat and she ran her eyes over his grey jacket and black trousers.

This was crazy. Why did she always find him so attractive?

"So what's it like working for a private eye?" she asked, turning back to Watson.

"Consultant detective," said the youth. "Yeah, I have to say it's pretty good. We get some… *interesting* cases."

"You seemed to find Doctor Blake *interesting*. I saw you giving her your number."

"Can you blame me?"

"We were called away from the museum this morning, but I returned later to ask her a few questions about the Badda cult. She's quite an intelligent woman. Isn't she a little out of your league?"

"Oh, you girls." The youth laughed. "I know what this is; you see Mel as competition. Sorry, luv, but you're not my type."

The Inspector stared blankly.

"No, he isn't joking," said Quist, joining them with a tray. "Try not to be too devastated, but you really *aren't* his type." He handed out the drinks. "Here we go. A lager for Watson, a slimline tonic for the CID detective who is always on duty, and a beer for the *consultant detective* who isn't. I overheard you talking."

"You have exceptional hearing." Katie gauged the distance to the bar and the volume of surrounding chatter. "Why do you refer to yourself as that?"

Watson grinned. "He says clients prefer to have their personal shit handled by a discreet consultant detective than a private eye."

"Ah." Katie nodded. "I say they should have their shit handled by a *real* detective."

"Come, come," said Quist. "The police are vastly overworked and understaffed. Besides, you have no interest in the messy divorces and similar cases we handle." He sipped his drink. "Centurion's Ghost. Mmmh, excellent."

"*Centurion's Ghost*, eh?" She held up a beermat showing a spooky picture. "So what's the story there?"

"*What*?" Watson looked shocked. "You're telling me you've never heard about the Treasurer's House? It's York's most famous ghost story, and for a city with around twenty ghost walks and an endless supply of paranormal crap, that's really saying something."

"It may be famous, but as a busy police officer, I have better things to do with my time than listen to nonsense."

The teenager leant forward. "The Treasurer's House is behind the Minster. It's medieval, but this happened in the nineteen-fifties. A plumber was working in the cellar when he heard a trumpet and almost shat himself when a bunch of Roman guys came marching through the wall."

"Well fancy that," said the Inspector.

"They looked knackered from fighting and marched across the cellar straight through the opposite wall, but the weird thing is…"

"Oh?" She laughed. "You're saying there was something weird about this incident?"

"He could only see them from the knees up, as if they were walking on a deeper surface below. Years later, when they dug up the cellar, they realised the house had been built on a Roman road and the cobbles ran eighteen inches below the floor level."

Katie gasped theatrically. "That's why their lower legs weren't visible?"

"It's so obvious when you think about it," said Quist, smiling to himself. His assistant had picked up most of this on Kyle Tarot's tour. "You can laugh, but this plumber, Harry Martindale, always maintained his story was true, even when he joined the police and spent thirty years on your force."

She nodded. "Yes, I'm aware Martindale was one of our officers and, yes, I *do* recall his story, but I don't have time for the supernatural."

"You should never dismiss it," said Quist, "because one day it may have time for *you*."

"Wow, that's so profound." Smirking, Katie sipped her tonic. "You said you had something to tell me and I'm guessing it concerns this kind of thing? There are aspects of this case that I can't discuss, but I'm not blind to the fact that the occult plays some sort of warped part. That's why I went to the lecture – to brush up on this Badda sect and see if there could be a link."

"Oh, there's definitely a link," confirmed Quist. "What do you make of those occult symbols on your murder victims?"

"I assume Tarot told you about those? I know you're friendly with his daughter."

"We hear you've let him go," said Watson. "You don't seriously believe he's involved with the murders, do you?"

"Not directly," admitted Katie, "but he knew things about the last victim which..."

"I think we can both guess at how he came by that *psychic* information," said Quist. "On his way home from town he saw the van and whoever dumped the body. He saw those symbols for real."

"That's my theory," said Katie. "Although he's sticking to his story of psychic visions."

"I presume he's too scared to back down." Quist shrugged.

"He probably feels that an admission would lead to prosecution for deception. I'm certain he can't help you any further, even if he admitted he'd seen the van for real. He doesn't know anything more than the information he gave you."

"Has he told you that?" she quizzed.

"Inspector, I can assure you it isn't worth your time pursuing Kyle Tarot when the real murderer or murders are out there."

"Hey, thanks for the advice," said Katie, "but I think it might be better if I decide for myself how to run my investigation."

"Well, as you suspected, the occult *does* play a part in it – a huge part. I'm sure you're aware that the symbols cut into the victims are Badda designs, but did you know they're required for a specific magical ritual, and are you aware that each girl was born under the Virgo star sign? That isn't a coincidence; the killer had some way of discovering their dates of birth."

The Inspector frowned, recalling how King had referred to his victims as virgins. *Could that have anything to do with their Virgo star signs?*

Wondering how to broach his next question, Quist decided to just ask it. "I understand your new suspect claims his name is Rakkat?"

"Tarot didn't tell you *that*," snapped Katie. "How the hell do you know?"

"Your officers chat in public. Sometimes they chat loudly enough to be overheard with my *exceptional hearing*. The point is, this is an ancient demonic name. Rakkat was an elemental entity, well known to the Badda cult in North Africa."

The Inspector laughed harshly. "So you think Aaron King might be possessed?"

Quist lowered his voice. "According to the reference works, the Badda sect were able to reanimate freshly deceased bodies by performing a mystical rite, carving a symbol known as the *Oushane*

Seal onto the right wrist and placing a magical possession amulet around their neck. This bound the Rakkat entity to them and forced it to do their bidding."

"Is that so?" Katie stiffened slightly, remembering King's amulet and the way he'd described the grisly wrist carving as his *seal*. "By reference works, you mean books of fairy stories? Don't tell me you actually believe this?"

Quist smiled. "I have the luxury of being able to research things which the police would naturally view as a waste of time. It doesn't matter whether or not *you* believe in the Rakkat entity. *Someone* does, and someone is performing the Badda rites. The four murders were sacrifices, one for each element, in a rite known as the Sussamma Ritual. You can find it in several books and read for yourself how those symbols had to be cut into the chest."

"He's right," said Watson. "It's a divination rite, used to locate stuff."

"Yeah?" Katie rolled her eyes. "*Stuff* such as…"

"The Badda temple," said Quist. "After listening to the story of Aquila tonight, I now deduce they're searching for the lost temple where this Roman lies buried. According to Doctor Sawtelle, the Oushane Blade is buried with him, a mystical dagger which grants immortality to whoever uses it during…"

"Oh, come on," scoffed Katie. "*Please.*"

"You don't believe such things." Quist nodded. "But if someone *did* believe it, you can imagine how the concept of immortality might drive them to such terrible lengths. The occultists behind this certainly believe it and, if their four-night sacrifice ritual worked, they will have already located Aquila's tomb. Now I realise this may sound far-fetched…"

"Far-fetched?" The Inspector shook her head. "The phrase I'd use is *utter bollocks.*"

He continued undeterred. "As Doctor Sawtelle explained, no

one has ever found this temple, so it obviously lies below ground. These people will need to dig, so it would be prudent to check for new excavation activity in the area west of where York's Roman fortress was situated."

"This is ridiculous." Katie grimaced. "I can't believe I actually came here to listen to this."

"I understand your feelings," said Quist. "But you must be aware that occult groups exist? There are circles right here in Yorkshire who practise the dark arts for whatever reason. Last year a man was discovered dead on the moors near Pickering. I understand the police suspected an occult connection?"

"I'm aware of the incident you're referring to," said Katie, warily. "But how did *you* know about the connection?"

"Oh, I heard something. I don't recall where."

"Really?" she drawled. "Your exceptional hearing again? Yes, the victim was a heroin dealer named Bradley Curtis. We initially believed the murder was drugs-related, but he had occult markings on his body, a circle was found cut into the turf, and there were traces of candle wax and other things. We suspect whichever lunatics killed him were some sort of witchcraft group, but that doesn't make the occult real. It just makes lunatics real."

Quist smiled grimly. "Don't make the mistake of confusing real occultists with those idiots who sometimes kill cats in graveyards for kicks/." He moved closer. "Tell me, does Aaron King have noticeably green eyes, by any chance?"

Katie froze as she lifted her glass. "Why do you ask?"

"I take it the answer is *yes*." Quist stroked his large nose. "Intriguing. The ancient texts speak of Rakkat having bright green eyes. It was how you could always recognise this particular elemental when it controlled a deceased host. I mentioned how the host would have a symbol cut into the right wrist and an amulet around the neck. I noticed, from your earlier reaction, that this definitely relates to your suspect?"

Katie didn't confirm this. "Look," she sighed. "I can accept that some people perform witchcraft rites in their suburban houses or out on the moors. Their kinky ceremonies probably involve sex and I assume they spice up their lives. I know there are many respected magical reference books and I can also accept that some people perform the complex occult rituals contained in them. What I *can't* accept is that those magical rituals actually *work*."

"Genuine adepts are invariably intelligent," said Quist. "They study the esoteric arts the way physicians study chemistry and they view magic as a science. Those girls were killed just after this Badda exhibition appeared in York. Don't you find that strange?"

Katie's eyes narrowed. "What's your point?"

He touched the Inspector's hand on the table and her stomach fluttered. Her face flushed and she ran her tongue over her lips.

"Inspector," he said. "I'm convinced an occult group are searching for Aquila's tomb. That exhibition contains all the ritualistic artefacts they need to perform…"

Katie's phone suddenly vibrated and she snatched her hand away. "Hello, Bradstreet." She cleared her throat and stroked back her fair hair, realising his proximity had caused her to become stimulated as usual. "Hi, Angie. Yes, what do you have for me?"

Quist watched her eyes widen.

"You're joking?" she hissed.

"Are you alright?" he asked, as she jumped to her feet. "Bad news?"

"I have to go," snapped Katie. "We'll continue this in the near future."

"Bradders is in a hurry" muttered Watson, watching the flustered woman leave. "Looks like some shit is going down,"

"*Bradders?*" Quist peered at him. "Well, this isn't good. From her reactions, it would seem this suspect Aaron King has all the

138

classic characteristics associated with Rakkat. Bright green eyes, a carved design on his wrist and an occult possession amulet."

"Yeah, so I definitely don't want to meet him." Watson gulped his lager. "You know something, what you said to her just now made me think."

"Oh, yes?"

"You said these adepts view the occult as a science." The youth frowned. "It's probably a coincidence, but I couldn't help thinking of how Sawtelle is always going on about believing in science."

"Yes, at the museum just now he mentioned *the wonders of science*." Quist nodded slowly, tapping his signet ring against his glass. "Mmh, as you say, it's probably a coincidence."

* * * *

Chapter 18

Speeding into the grounds of the police headquarters and braking hard outside the glass doors, Katie leapt from her car and raced inside. Angie Gibson met the Inspector in the main reception area. The Sergeant looked pale-faced and anxious.

"Less than ten minutes to get here," said Katie, glancing at her watch. "How is he now?"

"It isn't good, Ma'am." Angie gestured to the lobby stairwell. "He's still unconscious. He's grown worse since I rang you."

"You say King collapsed and didn't appear to be breathing?" Katie keyed in the combination for the door and hurried down the steps to the basement level. "I assume the doctor is with him?"

Angie nodded. "He's giving CPR, but King isn't responding."

The pair ran along the detention corridor to an open cell door where the station custody Sergeant stood outside. Katie looked in to see Aaron King flat on his back with Doctor Steve Wallace kneeling beside him. King's complexion had never resembled a Miami Beach lifeguard, but now it was the ghastly colour of congealed semolina pudding. The police doctor pumped at the prisoner's chest, each downward thrust forcing stench from the open mouth.

"*Jesus!*" hissed Katie. "So how is he?"

"Worse than he looks." Pausing his chest compressions, the doctor blew into King's mouth, gagged at the stink, and then checked his carotid artery. "He's fading fast and this CPR isn't working."

"Worse than he looks?" Katie squat beside the spread-eagled man. "Well let's be honest, Steve. He looks like shit."

Cringing at the horrendous smell, she mentally crossed her fingers, hoping to God that Wallace didn't ask for assistance with the first aid. *The very last thing she wanted to do was clamp her lips over King's vile drooling mouth and breathe for him. Keeping down her stomach contents would be impossible, and cleaning a public toilet with her tongue would be far preferable.*

Katie turned to the custody Sergeant. "Angie phoned to say he'd collapsed. What exactly happened?"

"*Nothing* happened, Ma'am." The uniformed man shrugged uneasily. "I checked on the prisoner fifteen minutes ago and he was singing some old song like he always does. A couple of minutes later it went quiet and I checked again to find him like this."

"His pulse and breathing are virtually non-existent," snapped Wallace, irately. "Where's the ambulance I asked for?"

"The paramedics are on their way." Angie checked the corridor wall clock. "They should be here anytime now."

"He's far too cold." The doctor pumped again at King's chest, his breath clouding as he spoke. "It's like the Arctic in here. Don't you people have any heating in these cells?"

The custody Sergeant almost burnt his hand as he felt the radiator, but had to agree. The air was freezing.

"We don't think he's eaten anything for a week," said Katie. "There was talk of force-feeding him as soon as he was transferred to… She shivered and glanced at the custody Sergeant as an icy wind whipped down the passage. "Yes, get someone to sort out the heating, They can start by closing whichever window is open."

"Damn, wait a moment…" Wallace checked the prisoner's pulse again, pressing against the artery for several seconds, before sighing and climbing to his feet. "Ring the ambulance and tell them not to race through any red lights on the way here. I'm afraid he's gone."

"*Shit!*" The custody Sergeant shook his head. "I can't believe this, Ma'am. Like I told you, he seemed absolutely fine fifteen minutes ago, singing and laughing to himself…"

"I'm not laughing," growled Katie, grimacing. "King was the prime suspect in a high-profile murder investigation. We've had him less than a day and he's just died in *our* care. It's bad enough when drunks choke on their vomit in the cells, but the media will absolutely love this, not to mention our new Superintendent. I can't imagine *she'll* be throwing a fucking party when she hears about this."

"Did he mention feeling unwell?" asked Angie. "Did he say anything at all?"

The custody Sergeant wiped his brow with a trembling hand. Cell deaths were traumatic, but he was already shaken from just being around this stinking prisoner; the man had genuinely terrified him.

"Nothing that made any sense," he stammered. "No, he was perfectly okay and he said something about how I should tell the little sweetie that it isn't over. He was looking forward to seeing Blondie in a horror story and killing her slowly."

Katie shuddered. The heating must have kicked back in, because the detention corridor was beginning to warm up, but it felt as if ice-water had just been tipped over her spine. She was in no doubt that this insane message was meant for her, but all things considered, there was very little chance of Aaron King *killing her slowly* now.

Squatting on the cell floor again, the doctor began to check the body.

"Hey, wait a minute…" Katie moved closer as he lifted an eyelid. "His eyes are brown."

"Oh, well-spotted, Detective," said Wallace.

The Inspector shook her head. "No, I mean Aaron King has green eyes."

"She's correct," said Angie. "They were green. The prisoner had very conspicuous green eyes."

The puzzled doctor looked up and saw the custody Sergeant nodding his agreement.

"Well I don't intend to argue about such trivia," said Wallace. "But, as you can clearly see, *these* eyes are brown and you'll find my medical degree will back me up when I tell you that eyes do *not* change colour."

Katie recalled her conversation with Bernard Quist about the demon Rakkat having green eyes. She shook herself and felt stupid for even thinking about such utter nonsense. *But why had King's eyes turned brown?*

A gurgling, bubbling noise came from the lower half of the corpse and an unbelievable, almost tangible stench filled the cell. Katie reeled, coughing and choking. She'd experienced something similar once before, when a bloated suicide pulled from the river had inconveniently burst open.

"What on earth…" Retching, the doctor rolled the body and unzipped the prisoner's overalls. He recoiled and swiftly covered his mouth. "Good God! I don't understand. I don't believe this…"

"Ugh!' The custody Sergeant stepped back, gagging. "He's shat himself."

"It isn't excrement," stammered Wallace. "No, this can't be right. His organs appear to be decomposed and liquefied. A build-up of intestinal gas is forcing them out through his relaxed anus."

"*What?*" hissed Katie. "*What the hell are you talking about?*"

"This is impossible." The doctor retched again and let out an uncomfortable laugh. "I mean, I just felt his pulse. He had a *pulse*, for God's sake, but if I didn't know better, I'd say this man has been dead for several days."

* * * *

Chapter 19

Floodlights illuminated the Yorkshire Museum, the abbey ruins and historic buildings in the surrounding parkland. People strolled the moonlit pathways, but luckily for Quist and his assistant, none appeared to be interested in the sandstone porch where they lurked in the shadows. Watson kept watch, his nervous eyes darting about the lawns and trees, as the detective squat by this side entrance into the Tempest Anderson Hall.

"Are you sure about this," whispered the youth, zipping up his canvas jacket. The boredom he'd felt on their earlier visit had been replaced with apprehension and fear. "I don't mind telling you, Guv, this isn't doing my bowels any favours."

"I have to check something," said Quist. "Something which would be difficult to examine properly when the place is open."

"You can pick locks?" Watson squinted in the darkness to make out two slender metal probes. "Cool, but for God's sake hurry up, will you?"

He watched as the curved tools were carefully twisted in the keyhole and shook his head resignedly. Because of his furry secret, Quist was forever drawn to supernatural puzzles and threats, perceiving it as his moral duty to help wherever he could. Watson had grown accustomed to his boss's bizarre investigative methods, whether he was paying Gareth Lestrade to hack computer systems, or unashamedly breaking into a museum like this. He turned back to the gardens, cringing. *It no longer surprised him, but it still bloody well scared him.*

"Breaking and entry," he whispered. "This is so wrong."

"But necessary, and no *breaking* is involved. No one will ever know we were here." Quist turned the twin picks. "Some locks are easier than others. This is archaic, but instead of updating it, they obviously rely on their modern alarm system."

"Oh, right." The teenager grinned uneasily to hear the tumblers finally click. "Which kind of leads to my next question."

"The alarm won't pose a problem." Quist rose to his feet, took out his phone and rang Lestrade. "Hello there, Gareth, did you manage it? Ah, thank you, young man."

Watson winced, waiting for the clamour of klaxons as the door was eased open.

"The wonders of science," whispered Quist, derisively quoting Sawtelle and stepping inside. "When I discovered the alarm could be operated remotely by phone, I knew it must be computer-controlled. I spoke with your friend Gareth and had him hack into the museum database. I've just confirmed that he's disarmed the system. I'll have him switch it back on after we've left and locked up."

"You're sure?" Watson checked the park again for witnesses, before following and quietly closing the door behind them. "The alarm could be silent and linked straight to the cops."

"True." The detective gave a lopsided smile. "I suppose we'll soon find out."

The porch door opened into an antechamber which in turn connected with the theatre where Sawtelle had given his lecture. Leaving the lights off and relying upon enhanced night vision, Quist led the way through the darkness and into the Roman galleries. He headed straight for the room housing the Badda exhibition with his assistant remaining close behind, glancing about anxiously and trembling.

These chambers were far spookier by night, decided Watson.

Most places would be spooky when empty, dark and totally silent like this, but the museum was very different. The full moon shone through the high windows, coldly highlighting the multitude of marble statues, granite sarcophagi, and Roman busts that seemed to glare angrily at the intruders.

"Bloody hell," murmured the youth, his voice sounding

louder than normal in the deathly quiet. "I really don't like this, Guv. It might sound stupid, but it feels like these statues are watching us. At any moment, something might climb out of these stone coffins."

"You're right – it *does* sound stupid." Quist led him into the Badda temple exhibit. "Ah, here we are."

Watson swallowed dryly, the action hurting his throat. "So what exactly are you looking for here?"

"Confirmation," whispered Quist.

"Oh, of course." The teenager peered fearfully at the stone wolf's head, his eyes now accustomed to the dim light. "Er, confirmation of what?"

"Something I came across this morning." Nearing the altar, he slipped off his overcoat. "Would you be good enough to hold onto this?"

Watson watched in the gloom as the detective swiftly stripped off his clothes and passed them to him. He grimaced to see the pale skin of the naked man gleaming in the moonlight and knew what was about to happen – he'd witnessed this many times, but it never got any easier.

"So you obviously don't think I'm scared enough?" he muttered. "Is there really any need for this, Guv?"

"I'm afraid so," said Quist, dropping into a crouch.

The exhibition room was already cold, but Watson felt the temperature plummet. *According to his boss, shapeshifting leached supernatural energy from the surrounding atmosphere, or some such weird shit.*

The detective grunted in pain as crunching bones visibly altered, his crackling features sprouting into a lengthy animal muzzle and his entire body growing in bulk. Thick fur covered his rapidly changing form, and falling human teeth clattered on the tiled floor and turned to dust as fangs instantly replaced them. An enormous black wolf finally rose on two legs and turned to the shivering teenager, its amber eyes smouldering eerily in the dark.

"Yeah, that's more like it." Watson wrapped his canvas jacket tightly around himself to combat the icy air. "The stone werewolf head there isn't terrifying enough. Let's have the real thing, eh?"

"I don't usually shapeshift during the full moon, as you know," growled the monster, stretching its powerful frame. "But like this, my senses are greatly heightened, including my sense of smell." He strode to one of the upright incense burners beside the altar and sniffed at it. "I'm also taller, which allows me to smell the bowl on the top of this."

"Very nice, Guv," muttered Watson, peering at Quist's glimmering yellow eyes and gulping. "Yeah, that's handy."

"Indeed." The wolf moved to the altar and dropped onto all fours, padding around the base of the stone block and snuffling at the sides. "I picked up a scent from this earlier today when I *accidentally* dropped my pen. It was the scent of bleach."

"Amazing." Watson watched with wide eyes. "You look as if you're searching for somewhere to cock your leg up and take a piss."

"Bleach," repeated the wolf. "Those incense burners and this entire altar have been thoroughly scrubbed with it. The floor too. Intriguing, don't you think?"

The teenager shrugged. "Really enthusiastic cleaners?" he suggested.

"Yes, enthusiastic in their efforts to destroy evidence. This whole area has been bleached and…" Creeping about and sniffing at the floor tiles, the creature suddenly stiffened, the black fur rising on its back. "Oh, hello, they missed something." Narrowing his eyes at a familiar scent, he padded to a display cabinet that stood against the wall. "They missed *this*."

"What are we looking at?" quizzed Watson, joining him and squatting.

"Blood," growled the wolf, baring its huge razor fangs.

"Human blood has splashed the wall and the base of this cupboard. They've sponged it off with bleach, but tiny amounts remain in the cracks behind the skirting here."

Quist felt a rush of excitement at the delicious smell and tried hard not to lick his lips. Closing his eyes, he concentrated to stem the lupine urges. They were always intense at this time in the lunar cycle.

"Guv?" Watson shook his shoulder and prayed he didn't twist and snap at his hand. "Er, are you okay?"

Taking a deep breath, the wolf stood upright on its hind legs and peered through the glass doors; the cabinet was filled with ancient daggers and knives. "Don't worry, I'm fine," he said. "Just a minor struggle with my... er, *other* self over the blood. This is why I never like to change at the full moon."

Quist held out his front paws, bizarrely transforming them into hairy fingers, before reaching into the coat that Watson held. He took out the two lock picks and slipped them into the keyhole. His assistant grinned with amazement as the door swung open and his boss's tail began to involuntarily wag.

"Compared to the lock on the external door, this is rudimentary." Moving its elongated muzzle closer, the wolf sniffed the air in the cabinet and raised a lupine eyebrow. "Yes, as I thought." It lifted out the daggers and quickly smelled each in turn, almost as if they were fine Cuban cigars. "Ah, it's *this* one."

"What about it?"

"I'm sure the police will be interested in this particular knife." He held up a thin-bladed dagger, turning it in the moonlight. "It's their murder weapon – the one used in the four killings."

"You can smell more blood?" gasped Watson.

"No, I can smell more bleach. I detected the scent the moment the display case opened and this is the only item inside to have been cleaned with it."

"Maybe it's normal hygiene. Maybe the cleaners are just

being…"

"Watson, this is a priceless historic artefact over two-thousand years old." Quist read the label aloud. "*The Hanka Dagger.* Mmh, Hanka was the Badda Priestess brought to York by the Roman Prefect. Museum cleaners do *not* touch this; they don't touch any of the artefacts. When you handle this, you wear gloves and clean it with the utmost care, using cotton buds and specialised fluids. You do *not* scrub it with bleach."

"Point taken," said Watson. "So what's going on here?

"Isn't it obvious?" The wolf looked around the exhibition room visualising the scene. "My suspicions were correct, as I feared they would be. The Sussamma Ritual *did* take place and those girls were killed right here with this sacrificial dagger."

"Human sacrifices?" Warily eyeing the knife, the youth glanced around the dark chamber too, certain he could feel it growing colder. "All four of them? Right here on this altar? Shit."

"As I deduced, the people responsible for this are clearly well versed in the Badda cult magic." Spotting a storeroom door, Quist strode over and tried the handle. Using his picks, he quickly unlocked it. "Pass me my torch, would you? It's in the left pocket of my coat."

"Mops and cleaning stuff," said Watson, eyeing the contents as the wolf shone the beam inside. "What are you looking for?"

"Those." Quist gestured to a pile of folded black curtains on a shelf. "The ideal thing for hanging over the windows at night and preventing outsiders seeing lights in here. Ah, and look there."

"What?" Watson saw the half-empty box of aerosols. "You mean the air freshener?"

"Correct. Deodoriser for spraying the room to remove the aroma of the incense they burnt in those thuribles over there. Thuribles which have been scrubbed out with bleach."

"I don't get it, Guv." The teenager shook his head. "They killed those girls *here* in the museum? Four of them over four nights?

Whoever did this would need to be crazy to take such a huge risk."

"Unless they had no option," murmured the wolf, looking around again. "This place must have been significant to their magic and whoever is responsible for this clearly has access. They were able to come and go here at any time."

Watson nodded. "Like Sawtelle, you mean?"

"Yes, like Sawtelle," said Quist. "This exhibition arriving in York at just the right time isn't a coincidence, that much is certain, but as you've just pointed out, why perform the ritual *here*?"

"Yeah, why not some private building where it's safe?"

"Indeed. This place was obviously used at night, with candles and the windows blacked out, but even so, such an undertaking was ludicrously dangerous." The wolf nodded grimly. "As I said, perhaps they had no option."

Watson gazed at the bust of Aquila by the entrance. "That Roman nutter supposedly sacrificed someone then sliced himself with that magic knife. Do you reckon it worked? Did it turn him into a werewolf?"

"Whoever is searching for the dagger is certain of it." The wolf smiled, moonlight glinting on its teeth. "The Oushane Blade would be quite a prize if you believed in such things as werewolves."

* * * *

Chapter 20

The Thursday morning traffic crawled past the Fishergate junction with Baker Avenue where Watson stood at the first floor window of the detective agency. Wearing a bright orange sweater, the teenager prepared two coffees, peering at the busy thoroughfare as he stirred the mugs. He noticed how the windowsills across the street sported rows of wire spikes to deter roosting birds, and smiled at the pristine ledge outside *this* window. Pigeons and starlings wouldn't come anywhere near the boss and his supernatural aura.

Quist sat at the office desk behind him, its leather surface strewn with several open books on Badda legends and Roman mythology. Leafing through one and scribbling notes, he paused to answer his phone.

"Good morning, young man," he said. "What can I do for you?"

Watson brought over the coffees as Quist listened at length.

"I see. Well, thank you for that." The detective thumbed off the phone and massaged his brow. "Incredible."

"Well?" said Watson, blowing steam from his drink.

"Unfortunately I was right."

"Naturally." The teenager grinned. "About what?"

"That was your friend Gareth. He's still monitoring the police website for me and that was an update on developments. It seems their suspect Aaron King died in custody last night."

"*Shit*! I wonder if that's why Bradders rushed out of the pub?"

"The time of death would support that assumption. Due to certain irregularities, they decided to carry out the post mortem as soon as possible and the report has just been filed on their system. It's somewhat bizarre, to say the least. King's internal organs appear to have been rotting, as if he'd been dead for days."

Watson's mouth fell open. "So someone actually used this

guy as a dead host, like you said? This Rakkat, the elemental thing inside him, was real?"

Quist sipped his coffee and nodded slowly. "I was hoping their suspect had read occult books and fancied himself as the Rakkat demon. Highly unlikely for a homeless addict, admittedly, but far preferable to the horrific alternative. Yes, it was real, Watson. This man King obviously died last week. More likely he was murdered by the occultists, who then used his fresh corpse for the entity they had conjured up."

"Wow!" The teenager ran a nervous hand through his short curly hair. "After all the crazy shit I've seen with you, it's still hard to believe there are people in York capable of putting demons inside dead bodies and having them walk around."

"Indeed." Quist nodded bitterly. "I deduced King would have a symbol cut into his right wrist and, from the Inspector's reaction last night when I mentioned it, I knew I was right. Lestrade just read me the autopsy report which confirms it." He gestured to the books on the desk. "According to these reference works, it's known as the *Oushane Seal*. The people responsible are clearly proficient in the ancient Badda rituals."

"This Rakkat thing…" His assistant shuddered. "The church called them demons, but you say they're elemental entities? Where will it go now that this guy King is dead?"

"It's difficult to explain, but such creatures exist in energy form and don't adhere to our physical laws. This elemental will have returned to the timeless dimension it was summoned from."

"Good." Watson let out a short laugh. "From what you've told me, this definitely wasn't something I fancied meeting."

"I seem to recall you moaning the other day about how you prefer our supernatural cases to mundane divorces and…"

"But there's *spooky, cool supernatural* and there's *being ripped apart by a super-strong demon supernatural*. Now this Rakkat thing has gone, this mystery just got a lot more exciting." Sitting back in one of the office chairs, the youth lifted both legs and rested his trainers on the desk. "So you still think these occultists are searching for the magic knife in the lost temple?"

"Yes, but I doubt it's still lost," said Quist. "If the Sussamma Ritual worked, they'll have the location and they're probably excavating for it as we speak."

"But we've no idea where."

"Unfortunately, no." The detective stroked thoughtfully at his large nose. "Once they unearth that dagger, they can perform the sacrifice rite that Doctor Sawtelle spoke of – the Oushane Sacrament. If it works, they would become like me."

"Murdering someone and cutting themselves to hopefully become werewolves?" Watson shook his head. "Well, each to their own."

"Speaking of temples…" Quist picked up one of the volumes he'd been reading. "This book by Miles Roundhay goes into great detail on the Badda rites. Many of their secrets were translated from stone tablets and potted scrolls discovered in the Moroccan excavation. For the Sussamma Ritual to work correctly, he claims it needed to be performed in a consecrated Badda temple in order to evoke the necessary ethereal energy. That explains why they used the museum."

"Ah, right." Watson nodded. "The only Badda temple in existence is set out in there."

"Exactly. They could easily have constructed a makeshift temple somewhere private, but the real thing would be much more powerful and worth the risks they took." Quist hurried to his filing cabinet and brought out a map of York. Brusquely swiping the youth's feet from the leather surface, he unfolded it on the desk. "I wonder…"

Watson peered at the streets. "What are you thinking?"

Quist studied the topography, then took a highlighter pen from the desk drawer. "In his lecture, Sawtelle explained how Aquila constructed three temples here in York. The first two were small and *inside* the Roman stronghold."

"Okay."

"Their fortress covered over fifty acres, with the central basilica positioned where the Minster now stands. The outer walls would have enclosed the area that now contains the Yorkshire Museum, like this..." With bright yellow pen strokes, Quist carefully drew the outline of the fortress over the modern thoroughfares. He marked a cross on the museum and gazed at it. "The exhibition arriving here at the right time isn't a coincidence. They needed a Badda temple for their ritual, so they brought one here, and the altar will have been reconsecrated to their wolf deity." He tapped the map. "But just look at the museum's location. Could this exact spot have increased the volume of energy?"

"Er, *right*..." Watson frowned. "But speak English, Guv."

"You're aware of electricity, but there are many other forms of energy and occultists tap into them when they perform their rites." Quist gyrated his hand in the air. "Ethereal energy is all around us and often utilised in magic, the same energy harnessed by my supernatural side when I shapeshift."

"Right." Watson nodded. "I'm kind of with you so far."

"Looking at this outline, it's very possible that the museum now stands above Aquila's first temple. Shrines to the lesser deities were constructed on the edge of the Roman fortress and the outer perimeter ran right by the museum building. The Badda temple in the exhibition could actually be positioned above the buried ruins and, if so, that would definitely boost the power and their chances of success."

"Great theory." The teenager shrugged. "But the temples you're talking about vanished nearly two-thousand years ago. How could these occultists know where they were?"

"Good point," admitted Quist. "I don't even know if I'm correct about this, but although he claims otherwise, Sawtelle could be aware of their precise locations. We know he has a deep interest in the dark arts and he brought the exhibition here at the perfect time for this ritual – in March, during the correct phase of the moon."

"So you're thinking he's involved?"

The detective gave a lopsided smile. "I believe there's a good chance."

"Well, he's a bit of a twat, that's for sure," said Watson. "But I've watched plenty of horror films and he doesn't seem like an evil magician."

"It's just my opinion, of course, but Hollywood possibly isn't the best authority on such matters. Plus, you should always keep an open mind and never allow appearances to fool you." Quist drank his coffee and studied the fortress outline. "Be a good chap and get that, would you?"

The teenager looked baffled, then sighed as a knock sounded on the outer office door. He headed through the reception room and Quist glanced up from the map as he returned with Katie Bradstreet.

"Inspector," he smiled. "Good morning. I see you're alone?"

"Apparently so," said Katie. She wore her beige raincoat and, Quist saw, a slightly pensive frown. "It might have escaped your notice, but I'm a grown-up girl, Sometimes I *am* allowed out by myself."

"True, but you coming here without another colleague suggests you wish to converse about something off the record. Something... shall we say *odd*?"

"Yes, let's say that." Laughing dryly and walking to the office window, Katie stared out and took a deep breath. "Our prime suspect Aaron King died in custody last night and there were..." She hesitated. "There were certain *peculiarities* surrounding the death."

"Oh, I don't doubt it," said Quist. "The *most* peculiar thing being that King was already dead. His body expired sometime last Thursday and something evil was animating it."

She turned slowly to him. "You know I can't possibly accept that crap."

"Yet you came here." Quist sat in his swivel chair and crossed his legs. "And something is compelling you to continue listening."

"His insides seemed to be actually rotting," said Katie, quietly. "The police doctor is talking about obscure tropical diseases, but yes, it was almost as if our suspect was dead, as you say. His eyes changed colour too. King had bright green eyes, but after he died in the cell they changed to brown. Now I know that's impossible..."

"A bit like his rotting guts?" suggested Watson.

"Look, I feel stupid coming here." The Inspector laughed ruefully and scratched at her short blonde hair. "But I'm aware you know about this kind of weird stuff and I guess it can't do any harm to listen to your opinion. *Listening* is all I intend to do. Don't expect me to take you seriously."

"I fully understand your reservations," said Quist. "I've spent the past couple of nights studying the rites of the Badda cult. I've been through all the textbooks and, as I told you yesterday, there are many references to a creature named Rakkat that was often used by this sect. I think you'll find that Aaron King *did* have brown eyes, but Rakkat, the elemental that inhabited his corpse, has green eyes. Whenever he made an appearance, Rakkat's eyes were always described as bright green."

"Yes, his eyes changed and his insides were..." Katie paused and turned back to the window, the passing traffic in the street below providing her with a welcome sense of reality. "But I'm a police officer and I can't accept demonic possession."

"Not demonic possession," corrected Quist. "A fresh corpse is reanimated through magical rites by placing an elemental entity inside it."

"Right." She let out a harsh laugh. "Well, when you put it like that, it's much easier to cope with."

Quist nodded. "Would I be correct in thinking it was always icy cold around your suspect?"

"*What?*" Katie twisted to face him, her mouth falling open. "How could you know about..."

"It's the energy transference," said Quist. "I was speaking to Watson about this just before you called. There are many forms of energy – some which we've discovered and harnessed and other more esoteric forms, such as ethereal energy, that have yet to be properly identified by science. This elemental creature would need to drain ethereal energy from the surrounding atmosphere to maintain the host body and keep it functioning. This invariably causes a temperature drop which...."

"No, this is all too much." Closing her eyes, Katie shook her head. "But there *were* other weird things. He seemed to know stuff like the names of my officers..."

"A simple form of telepathy," said Quist, nodding. "Yes, an elemental would have that."

"Oh, telepathy, of course." The Inspector laughed quietly. "So, just for one minute, assuming this utter lunacy is right, why would *anyone* want to reanimate a fucking corpse?"

"Someone has been performing a magical ritual involving four sacrifices," explained Quist. "The Rakkat creature was used as a servant, abducting the victims and disposing of their bodies afterwards, but it was also needed it as a scapegoat."

"Scapegoat?"

"None of the victims were dumped in the river or buried, because whoever did this wanted them found. They rented a house and a van in Aaron King's name, planted evidence in his property and then had him, or rather Rakkat, admit to the crimes. The police were presented with a nasty little murder spree, the killer was swiftly caught, he confessed to everything, and then conveniently died."

"You're saying they wanted it all neatly tied up?"

"Exactly, but they never expected Kyle Tarot to appear and give you the registration of the van they were using. That unexpected event will have caused them to rush in setting up the rented house as a crime scene for when you called there. Their haste may well have resulted in mistakes."

"It did." Katie nodded slowly. "Our forensic people soon realised that the blood we found at King's place was planted. But who are *they*?"

"Adepts of the occult," said Quist. "Most probably a small magical circle rather than a lone individual, and these people are the real thing, Inspector. I don't know who they are yet, but it wouldn't harm if you were to discreetly look into the background of Doctor Edwin Sawtelle."

"You suspect *him*?" Katie frowned. "Why?"

"The Badda exhibition arriving in York at the perfect time for these sacrifices isn't a coincidence and the doctor brought it here. The murder weapon is in the museum too. It's in a glass case labelled the *Hanka Dagger*, one of Sawtelle's artefacts."

"What?" gasped Katie. "But how could you know that?"

"Please trust me and examine it," said Quist. "You were supposed to think those women were murdered in King's house, but that was to divert suspicion from the real crime scene. They actually died in the museum."

"I know it's hard to take in," said Watson. "But those poor girls were sacrifices in an occult ritual."

Quist nodded. "The rite was performed over four nights in the exhibition room upon the Badda altar. The altar, its surroundings and floor have been scrubbed with bleach, but you should check the skirting board on the right side of the knife cabinet. Specks of blood have been missed, in the crack where it joins the wall, and I'm certain it will match at least one of your victims."

"I'll ask again, how do you know all this?" Katie shook her head. "I can't just go in there and search the…"

"Inspector, believe me," said Quist. "I know how difficult this is to comprehend, but I'm afraid it's all real."

"You need to trust him on this," said Watson. "I used to think the supernatural was a load of crap, but I've seen shit you can't imagine. He's not kidding about this occult stuff."

"It's real," repeated Quist. "Occultists have been sacrificing women right here in York and the suspect you had in custody wasn't *really* Aaron King. Incredible as it seems, there was something inside his corpse – an elemental controlled by these dark adepts."

Katie stared at him. "I remember last night when you said they were probably searching for that Roman tomb? They want the magic dagger that's buried in there?"

"I'm now certain of it" said Quist. "You should look into excavations in the area that were carried out over the last two days."

"I answer to superiors," sighed Katie. "I have a new Superintendent breathing down my neck and I can't channel police resources into such a search without hard evidence." Checking her watch, the Inspector grimaced and headed for the door. "Listen, you've certainly given me plenty to think about, but you know we have procedures. You must know I can't investigate the supernatural."

"I suppose not," sighed Quist. "But it won't do any harm if Watson and I look into this and keep you updated, will it?"

* * * *

159

Chapter 21

Wearing a smart grey suit, Melissa Blake walked through the Roman galleries and found the Yorkshire Museum far busier than usual this Thursday lunchtime. The doctor smiled knowingly. It would have been nice to believe these visitors had developed a healthy interest in history and culture, but no, the March weather was responsible for this. The afternoon was freezing, a stagnant mist was spreading across the Plain of York, and the city tourists had wisely decided to do their sightseeing indoors.

She paused at the entrance to the Badda exhibition, noticing Doctor Sawtelle unlocking one of the display cabinets. He took out a dagger and Melissa frowned curiously to see him examine it, slowly and reverently turning the knife in his hands.

"Good afternoon, Doctor Blake."

"What the fu…" The girl jumped at the sound of Bernard Quist's voice behind her, then laughed timidly. "Hey, you scared the hell out of me. I didn't hear you walking up."

"Sorry, Mel." Watson grinned. "Yeah, we're part Apache."

"I'm aware that you're working," said Quist. "But I wonder if you could possibly spare us a few minutes? We'd like a brief chat and it shouldn't take long."

"Sure. About what?"

He glanced around. "Perhaps somewhere more private?"

"Ooh, sounds interesting," said Melissa. "Okay, this way." She led them through the gallery. "Thursday is our free afternoon. I'll be leaving soon with Edwin and Tamzin, so you aren't interrupting anything."

The two men were ushered into an empty side room bearing a *Staff Only* sign. Plastic chairs surrounded a canteen-style table, and an upright water dispenser stood in the corner beside a push-button coffee machine.

"Is this about the Badda exhibition?" asked the doctor. "Or something to do with your job as…" She smiled awkwardly. *"Private investigators.* To be honest, I feel a bit weird saying that."

"He prefers *consultant detective,*" corrected Watson, following her inside and closing the door. "Don't ask."

"Actually, it concerns both." Quist watched as she placed a cup in the vending machine and pressed for a latte. "I know you said you were unfamiliar with the mystical Badda rites, but have you ever heard of something named the Sussamma Ritual?"

"I don't think so." She held up two more cups. "Would you like a drink?"

"Yeah, coffee with milk and two sugars," said Watson, sitting at the table. "Any biscuits? Preferably chocolate?"

"Black for me, please," said the detective. "So you've never heard Doctor Sawtelle mention this rite?"

"As I said, no." Melissa placed another beaker in the machine. "What *is* it exactly?"

"A form of magical divination," said Quist. "The Badda cult used it to locate things. But their temples are the reason for our visit. Would you happen to know their exact locations here in the city?"

"Well, as you're aware, no one knows where the main temple was." Melissa brought the drinks to the table and sat beside the two men. "The two smaller ones were built very near here. The first was somewhere within the Roman fortress, most probably against the perimeter boundary wall. That was the way with all minor *imported* deities like Isis and Minerva. The second temple was just across the river in what was then the Colonia for the Roman civilians. As to their *exact* locations, I haven't a clue. Edwin is the one to ask."

"Thank you." Quist took the offered coffee and smiled thinly. "But something tells me he'll be reluctant to divulge the information and I need to know as soon as possible."

"Whatever for?" Melissa looked puzzled. "And why are you

asking about that Sussamma thing?"

The detective hesitated. "Because, difficult as it is to accept, someone has just performed that dark ritual right here in York."

"You're joking? How on earth do you know that? Are you talking about a witchcraft coven or something?"

"A group with far more power," said Quist. "Those recent killings in York weren't murders. I'm afraid they were sacrifices."

"No." The doctor laughed uneasily. "No, that isn't *difficult* to accept, it's *impossible*. Human sacrifices in modern-day York? What the hell would make you think such a thing?"

"Did you find that Moon Tiara you were searching for?" asked Watson.

Melissa frowned. "I'm surprised you remember that. No, we think it's still in London."

The detective shook his head. "It's missing because it was needed for this particular rite. The Sussamma Ritual requires four sacrifices over four nights leading up to the full moon. The release of life energy infuses the Moon Crown with power and guides the wearer to their objective."

"This is crazy," snorted Melissa, disbelievingly. "*What* objective?"

"The main temple." Quist paused to sip his coffee. "I believe they're searching for Aquila's burial place and the mystical artefacts there, specifically the Oushane Blade."

"You think someone would steal museum relics and actually murder people to find a Roman grave?" The girl laughed again. "That's insane."

"By now, I'd say they've already located the temple and there's a good chance they possess the dagger. As you know, from Doctor Sawtelle's lecture, if used correctly in the Oushane Sacrament rite, the blade would supposedly bestow eternal life."

Watson nodded. "Definitely something that would tempt

certain nutters to murder."

"Those are just legends," snapped Melissa. "I honestly can't believe I'm listening to this." She drank her coffee and eyed the detective warily. "So what's *your* interest in this black magic conspiracy theory? It can't be one of your private investigations?"

"No." Quist gave one of his quirky, lopsided smiles. "It's rather difficult to explain, but I see it as my duty to look into this."

"Whatever." She took a deep breath. "Look, I know the occult may have been involved in those recent killings. The police were here yesterday asking questions about the sect. They mentioned how a psychic had seen Badda symbols on one of their murder victims in some sort of clairvoyant vision. That was weird enough, but now... I'm sorry, but this is utter garbage."

Melissa ran a hand through her hair in a subconscious grooming gesture. Her pupils had dilated and her lips were fuller.

Watson noticed and rolled his eyes. *Here they were talking about human sacrifice and she was still getting turned on by Quist's presence. They could keep the changing to a wolf shit, but he'd pay good money for this particular lycanthropy side effect.*

"I appreciate your scepticism, and I'll spare you the details of possession rites and elemental entities." The detective sipped his drink. "The thing is, whether you believe this or not, I need to find those temples to stop these murderers before…"

"Oh, come on." Melissa smiled derisively. "You mean these *occultists* who may not exist."

"They exist," said Quist. "If they haven't yet excavated the tomb, we may actually catch them in the act. Another sacrifice is needed when the Oushane Sacrament is performed and that means there will be *another* murder which we can hopefully prevent."

"So why not go to the police?" quizzed the doctor. "Surely *they're* the ones who should be preventing such things?"

"They tend to think the occult is bollocks," said Watson.

"Really?" gasped Melissa. "How surprising."

"You told us how Doctor Sawtelle has an interest in the dark arts," said Quist. "But he seems reticent to speak of it. He always claims to prefer science to fairy stories."

The girl nodded. "He downplays it with strangers, but he has a huge fascination with the occult." She pulled a sour face. "Speaking of fairy stories, surely you don't suspect he's part of this? He isn't my favourite person, but I can't see him sacrificing women surrounded by black candles. To be honest, I can't see *anyone* doing that."

"Believe me," said Quist, "*someone* is most definitely doing it. Does Doctor Sawtelle have any friends here in York?"

"I don't know." Melissa thought for a moment. "There *are* a couple of men he speaks to. I've seen him with them here and at his hotel, but I've no idea who they are."

"Can you describe them?" asked Watson. "Black cloaks? Goat masks?"

"Yeah, right." She grinned. "I haven't taken much notice, but they're white and... well, *normal* looking with London accents. Oh, come on, you can't be serious about this?"

Quist didn't answer. "I know the doctor has the museum keys and he's able to control the alarm system on his phone. Clearly he can come and go here at any time of the day or night."

"Well, he *has* been visiting the museum after dark over the past few nights, but I imagine that was to prepare his lectures and..." She narrowed her eyes. "I wonder why he..."

"Yes?" prompted Quist.

"Er, I saw him doing something with the Hanka Priestess Dagger just now."

"Stabbing a girl with it?" suggested Watson, smiling.

She laughed nervously at the joke. "I'm sure it was nothing, but it just seemed suspicious. It was probably my imagination."

"Probably," said Quist. "I recall you saying that the arrival of the exhibition here in York was delayed by a fortnight. That would have ensured the temple was here for the full moon and, more pertinent, the four-day lead up to it. The Badda cult rituals always centre around the full moon."

"Edwin was the one who changed the date." Melissa nodded slowly. "What are you suggesting?"

"The exhibition arrived at the perfect time for this divination ritual and provided whoever performed it with a fully equipped Badda temple. The sacrifices were carried out here, using the altar, that Hanka Dagger, the Moon Tiara and other ritualistic paraphernalia."

"In the museum?" Melissa shook her head. "Just assuming you're right with these crazy ideas, why? Surely it's too risky to do anything like that here?"

"It *is* risky, but unavoidable," said Quist. "I believe this place was necessary. The rite had to take place in a Badda temple and I also suspect this museum could be directly above the first of the original temples constructed by Aquila."

"Seriously?" She glanced at the floor. "Below here?"

"The ritual took place at night using candle light," said Quist. "The adepts will have been quiet and there are black sheets in the storeroom that will have been used to cover the windows."

Her eyes widened. "You've been in the store?"

Watson winked. "He's rather good at guesswork."

"Well, it sounds like *most* of this is guesswork." Sighing, Melissa took out a card and passed it to Quist. "Here, you may as well take my mobile number. I still can't accept any of this, but I don't suppose it will hurt to keep my eyes and ears open for anything *unusual*."

"Thank you." The detective nodded. "I fully understand your reservations, but any help is appreciated."

Finishing her coffee, Melissa stood up and led them out of the staff room, straight into the path of an irate-looking man.

"There you are." Sawtelle strode through the Roman gallery, his harsh tone was as sarcastic as ever. "Entertaining gentlemen on the firm's time?"

"Come on, Edwin." She laughed at the chubby doctor's derisive joke, assuming it *was* a joke. "We're virtually finished here for the day."

"Doctor Sawtelle." Quist smiled warmly. "I was just speaking to Doctor Blake here about Aquila and those first temples he built. I'm attempting to find the exact locations."

"Really?" The man eyed him suspiciously. "Why would you want to know *that*?"

"Historical interest. I'm also curious about the occult rites of the Badda cult, especially the Sussamma…"

"The original temple was constructed inside the fortress," broke in Sawtelle, tersely. "The second in the Colonia. I mentioned this in my lecture, but perhaps you weren't listening?"

"Yes, and what an excellent lecture it was," said Quist. "But I was hoping for the precise sites. If *you* don't know, then I suppose I'd better speak to an expert."

"I *am* the expert," said the doctor, icily.

"This is merely a personal theory…" Quist watched for changes in his expression. "But I suspect this museum is built right above that first temple."

Sawtelle stared silently.

"I need someone who could hopefully substantiate this and provide me with the exact site of the other Colonia temple. I'm thinking I should perhaps approach the Reverend Miles Roundhay."

"*Reverend*?" scoffed Sawtelle. "You mean the dog crackpot?"

"Dog crackpot?" echoed Melissa.

The doctor ignored her. "Yes, Roundhay has had things published, but he's hardly an authority. The way he makes his money should tell you all you need to know about him. He's just some amateur historian and I wouldn't waste your time."

"Yes, I'm aware of the Reverend's er, line of work," said Quist. "But where history and archaeology are concerned, amateurs are sometimes the most passionate people in the field. If you can't help, then he's the obvious person to speak to. He's written several books on the Romans in York and one on the Badda cult."

"Good luck with him," snapped Sawtelle. "Watch out he doesn't accidentally marry the pair of you."

* * * *

"You're shitting me?" Watson sat in Quist's parked car peering incredulously at his boss. "What, seriously?"

"Seriously." The detective searched the internet on his phone. "Roundhay became ordained as a Reverend through a website, simply to enable him to legally officiate at canine weddings. He charges a large fee for his unique services and has a pet psychic present to communicate with the dogs and translate their vows."

"And people actually pay him for this?"

"It's a funny old world, Watson. You'd be surprised at the number of owners who want their cherished pets legally married in white dresses and tuxedos. The church doesn't allow dog marriages in their consecrated buildings, but that will change when they realise how much people are willing to spend. The ceremonies are usually held in hotel function rooms, and some gay couples have been known to pay tens of thousands for lavish events."

The youth laughed. "Hang, on. How can pet psychics communicate with dogs that aren't dead?"

"Well, they *can't*, of course. Just like they can't communicate with dogs that *are* dead. Fortunately, the clients of pet clairvoyants are gullible beyond words." Quist found the Roman history website that Watson had come across on Tuesday evening. "Ah, here we go."

"He marries dogs." The teenager shook his head. "But you still trust this guy to help us?"

167

"You mustn't allow his lucrative profession to fool you. Miles Roundhay is one of the leading experts on the Roman occupation of York. As you know, I have his three books on Eboracum and the one on the Badda cult and they're truly excellent. He regularly lectures at historical societies, but an extensive knowledge of Rome doesn't pay the bills. Ah, look at this…" Quist held up the phone and pressed the dial button. "His history website has a telephone number."

"His history website?" Watson grinned. "Yeah, I guess he has a separate site for the loonies who want dogfood wedding cakes with a bone on the top."

"Reverend Roundhay?" said Quist, speaking into the mobile. "You don't know me, sir, but I found your contact number on your website and I believe you can help me. I'd like to meet for a chat."

"Ask if he does discounts for cats," whispered Watson, smirking.

"No, this isn't about weddings." The detective lit a cigarette and dropped the car window. "I'm Bernard Quist, a consultant detective in York, and you may be… yes, *consultant detective*. You may be able to assist with something I'm currently working on. I've read all four of your books and found them highly informative. This concerns the Badda cult in York, particularly the locations of the first two Badda temples that were constructed in the city and the legends concerning the site of the larger one."

Watson waited as his boss listened.

"That's correct," said Quist. "I'm also interested in the rites performed by this sect, specifically the Sussamma Ritual and the Oushane Sacrament. I wonder if my assistant and I could call on you as soon as possible for a brief discussion? Why, thank you so much."

"Does he live in York?" asked Watson, as the detective slipped the phone into his pocket and started the car.

"Wetherby." Quist turned out of the misty museum grounds. "It's thirty minutes away, so we'll head there now. Hopefully, he'll have the information we need, especially the main temple site where Aquila was buried alive."

"But the experts say it's completely lost."

"True, but experts stick to established fact and hard evidence, when it's often possible to glean clues from folklore, mythology and place names. For many years now, Roundhay has been collecting the Yorkshire legends and deciphering them. No one bothers to question why their street is named *Temple Lane*, or *Altar Rise*, but when searching for an ancient place of worship, such things could prove to be extremely significant."

"Yeah, I suppose I can see that."

"Even old songs and local nursery rhymes can contain hidden information and point the way. As we all know, Ring-a-Ring o' Roses was about the plague."

"Really?" Watson sat quietly for a moment, then turned to Quist with a mischievous smirk. "Okay, here you go. There was a Roman Prefect named Aquila. He was a big bloke, just like a gorilla. His bird was called Hanka, and although he was a wanker, when he turned into a wolf, he was a killer."

"Exquisite poetry," drawled the detective, nodding. "Yes, it seems you *were* listening during Sawtelle's lecture."

* * * *

Chapter 22

Wetherby lies midway between York and Harrogate on the Great North Road – ironically, once a Roman road connecting London to Edinburgh. The ancient route ran through the centre of this pleasant market town and, because of this, several old coaching inns still line the main street. The icy mist had yet to reach here and Quist drove across the river bridge where afternoon tourists stood looking down at the weir. Formed by streams high in Langstrothdale, the River Wharfe weaves through glacial valleys and tumbles through dozens of villages before it reaches Wetherby. It was usually shallow beneath the bridge, but melted snow had engorged the waters and Quist knew the surging weir would look spectacular against its backdrop of mature woodland.

"Wetherby," said Watson, peering out from the passenger seat of the detective's metallic blue Ford. "Whether the weather be cold, or whether the weather be hot, we'll weather the weather, whatever the weather, whether we like it or not."

Driving into the Market Place, Quist drew on his cigarette and turned to peer curiously.

"Good, eh? His assistant grinned. "It's an old poem they taught us at school."

"Apparently your schooldays weren't a complete waste then? You know next to nothing about algebra, logarithms, history and geography, but you remember obscure nonsense poems?"

Watson laughed. "It was junior school. I also learnt some shit about the Duke of York having ten-thousand men, the wheels on the bus going round and round, and London Bridge falling down..." He waved through the window at a good-looking girl jogging along the pavement. "Ooh, falling down, *my fair lady*."

Shaking his head, Quist left the town centre on Linton Road, the main western route out of the town, that curled away towards Harrogate. Miles Roundhay lived off this road in a quiet cul-de-sac of detached houses named Sterndale Close.

Save for a resident polishing his car to the subdued sound of Radio 2, the street was empty and Quist pulled into the Reverend's gravel driveway behind his white Range Rover. The large house was Victorian Gothic, constructed around the end of the last century in red brick. The detective climbed from the car and killed his cigarette underfoot, peering up at the bay windows and the high gables covered in dark ivy.

"Nice place," said Watson, closing the passenger door. "Dog marriages obviously pay well, just like you said. Hey, what if a rich Labrador is marrying some skanky gold-digging poodle? I wonder if the Rev can arrange pre-nuptial agreements through that pet psychic of his?"

"It may be wise to tone down the sarcasm," advised Quist, heading for the porch to ring the bell. "Bearing in mind we're hoping for this gentleman's help."

"Good afternoon," said the Reverend, smiling jovially at the pair as he opened the front door. "You must be Mister Quist." He ushered them into a large hallway. "Come on in out of the cold."

Miles Roundhay was a short, steely-haired man with a grey moustache and spectacles. He wore casual trousers and a V-necked sweater which showed off his Minister's collar.

It was amazing what you could buy on the internet these days, thought Watson. *This clever guy had actually bought himself an official and very profitable career as an ordained man of the church.*

"Hey, that's appropriate." The teenager pointed to the white dog collar as he entered, then winced as Quist jabbed his ribs with an elbow.

"Very pleased to meet you," said the detective. "This is my assistant Watson. I must say, it's good of you to spare the time."

"Not at all." Roundhay closed the door and shook his hand. "Every historian loves to chat about their passion with fellow enthusiasts. You asked about the Badda sect and their mysterious story has always been a huge interest of mine."

He turned to shake with Watson, but the youth was gazing open-mouthed at the gilt-framed photographs that covered the walls. Each featured a different pair of dogs, all smartly attired in tuxedos and wedding dresses. Some, especially the owners of West Highland terriers, had opted for traditional Scottish outfits with tartan kilts.

"Wow, look at the happy couples." Watson trembled, trying his best not to explode with laughter. Many of the bitches gripped flower bouquets in their teeth. "Yeah, you can see that most of these are deeply in woof. Sorry, deeply in *love*."

"My wedding gallery." Roundhay smiled proudly. "I officiated at all of them. Pet owners call here to arrange and tailor ceremonies and it's good for them to see these other successful unions. As I understand it, however, you're here to talk about Roman history, not canine marriages?" He waved a hand. "Please, if you'd care to follow me?"

The Reverend led the way along a passage and Watson tore himself from the hall photographs. *He'd never realised how ludicrous a Rottweiler could be made to look in a dress and white veil.*

Roundhay's study lay at the end of the corridor, the room filled with bookcases and filing cabinets. A walk-in bay window provided a good view of the side garden, and his desk was positioned in the recess to benefit from the daylight.

"So you're private investigators?" said Roundhay. "On the phone you mentioned two of the Badda rituals. I'm rather curious to know how such things figure in your work?"

"I'll explain in a moment," said Quist, spotting the desk. "That looks intriguing."

A street map of York lay open on the surface, large-scale and highly detailed, with the individual houses and even their gardens depicted. Roundhay had superimposed the outlines of the Roman fortress and civilian Colonia over the modern topography, just as Quist had done on his own map earlier, only this careful illustration was far more accurate.

"I got this out ready after you called." Roundhay smoothed the paper. "You wanted the sites of the York temples and here they are. The one inside the fortress walls, and the temple in the Colonia."

"Excellent," enthused Quist. "Are these the *exact* locations?"

"Well, of course. You don't think I randomly threw darts at the map?" The Reverend laughed. "No, this has all been thoroughly researched. Aquila's tomb, however, is another matter. No one knows for sure where this notorious Prefect built his full-size Badda temple, the replica of the Moroccan one, but we *do* know it was in the forest to the west of the fortress."

The detective nodded. "Any theories would be welcome."

"Oh, I certainly have theories." Adjusting his spectacles, Roundhay stooped over the map. "I've made some guesses in pencil, working from the little we know and all the various legends. You might say these are *educated* guesses and I'm certain that one of them is the correct location, or as near as damn it."

"Wonderful." Quist studied his markings.

"You were right, as usual, Guv." Watson grinned. "You said he was *the* guy to ask about this."

"Guesses aren't good enough for the authorities, of course." The Reverend sighed. "These potential sites are all in residential and listed areas and they won't allow excavations based on *amateur* theories." Opening a drawer, he brought out a folder of papers. "By the way, you asked about the Badda rituals and these are my notes."

"I've read your exceptional books," said Quist. "Including the one on the sect. Is this new material?"

Roundhay nodded. "Historical research is never complete. We make discoveries every day and constantly expand our knowledge. Yes, this is more recent work that doesn't yet feature in my published works." He patted the folder. "But I'll ask again, why would private eyes be interested in lost temples and ancient rituals?"

"Consultant detectives," corrected Quist. "There's a very good reason, but it's somewhat difficult to believe."

"Try me," shrugged Roundhay. "Funnily enough, you aren't the only ones with an interest in this. A woman has been calling here over the last year and we've had several lengthy chats about the cult and the locations of their temples. She took several photographs of this very map."

"Is that so?" Quist's eyes narrowed. "Would you happen to know her name?"

"Yes, she was a history student named Jane Smith."

"Right." Watson glanced at the detective. "Well, that doesn't sound invented, does it?"

"Do you happen to recall what she looked like?" asked Quist.

"I do indeed," said Roundhay. "A very attractive lady and she..." Turning at the sound of his doorbell, he smiled apologetically and headed for the hall. "I'm sorry. If you'll excuse me?"

"Someone just found out their dog's pregnant," whispered Watson, as he left. "They'll be wanting a fast wedding before the embarrassing bump starts to show."

Ignoring the joke, Quist inspected the map. "Ah, the original temple lies right beneath the Yorkshire Museum. So I was correct."

"As usual," said the teenager, pointing. "Look, the second one is here."

Quist nodded. "Yes, the fortified Roman Colonia would have covered that area south of the river. It's on Rougier Street with buildings above it. Mmh, why does Rougier Street ring a bell?" He waved a finger over the six pencil markings to the west of the fortress outline. "But never mind that. These are more interesting. These crosses are the Reverend's *educated guesses* and one of them is probably the temple where Aquila lies buried..."

Squealing car tyres drew their attention to the window. Watson stepped into the deep bay which allowed him to see the street where a black car accelerated away from the house.

"Hey, look at this dickhead," he said, grinning at the dust cloud. "He's in a hurry, isn't he?"

"He certainly is," agreed Quist, joining him to peer out. He frowned slightly. "Wait a moment. No, surely not…"

Leaving the study, the detective ran along the passage to the hall and found Roundhay sprawled on his back by the open front door. "*Damn*," he hissed, rushing to his side and seeing the hole in his forehead. "No, no, no."

Watson followed him and froze. "He's *dead*?" he stammered. "You have to be fucking joking? No, he *can't* be dead."

"I'm afraid he *can*." Quist stooped to swiftly examine the body. "Good Lord, the poor man must have been killed the moment he opened the door to his caller. A small calibre entrance wound and larger exit wound on the rear of his skull. He was shot in the head at close range and the gun was obviously fitted with a silencer. I heard the dull pop, but I was engrossed in that map and didn't realise what it was."

"*Really*?" Watson leant unsteadily against the wall and let out a tense laugh. "You thought it might have been someone opening a bottle of champagne?"

"I certainly didn't think it was *this*."

Clamping a hand over his mouth, the shaking teenager stared at the red hole above Roundhay's eyes. *Before working with Quist he'd never seen a dead body, but since then… well, he didn't like to keep count, and none of the corpses he'd come across had slipped away peacefully in their sleep.* He shook his head. *It never got any easier.*

"I honestly don't believe it." Watson tore his gaze from the body to peer at the empty street. "That BMW just now…"

"You noticed the make of vehicle?" Quist glanced about for witnesses before closing the door. "Well done. Yes. I think it's safe to say the driver of that speeding car was responsible. I don't suppose you saw the registration?"

"No, I didn't." The youth ran a nervous hand through his hair. "Maybe a dog owner who was pissed off with a crap wedding, or are you thinking this was something to do with our visit?"

"The latter," said Quist, grimly. "That's enough canine wedding jokes, Watson. I feel responsible for this and I'm in no mood for humour."

"Hey, this isn't *your* fault, Guv?"

"Isn't it?" The detective rubbed his eyes. "I beg to differ. Someone knew we were coming here to speak to Roundhay and they obviously wanted to silence him before we could learn anything."

"The only ones who knew were Mel and Sawtelle." Watson's frightened eyes were drawn to the gallery of wall photographs. "Bloody hell, will you look at that?"

A dark splatter of brain matter ran slowly down one of the pictures, surreally concealing the blushing bride – a dachshund in a Vivian Westwood dress.

"Never mind *that*." Quist took out his phone and the card with Melissa's number. "I'm fully aware of who knew about our visit and I need to check on them. How do I speak face-to-face with video on this?" He handed it to his assistant and pulled him to a blank wall. "I've never used it and I need you to connect me. Quickly."

"Hi there," said Melissa, her face appearing on the small screen with the museum's Roman gallery behind her. "Why are you on camera?"

"Oh, is the camera on?" Quist ensured there was nothing to his rear that might indicate the location. "This is what occurs when you mix middle-aged fuddy-duddies like me with modern technology. Sorry, but the phone is new and I'm still working out how to use it. Is

Doctor Sawtelle there?"

Melissa shook her head. "Edwin left shortly after you. I told you this was our afternoon off. You only just caught me before Tamz and I head home too. Would you like his number?"

"Hi," said Tamzin, appearing over her shoulder to wave.

"Hello, Tamzin." Quist smiled. "No, that's alright. It isn't important and I'll catch him later."

"Hey, did you speak to Miles Roundhay?" asked Melissa. "Could he help you with the temples?"

"No," lied Quist. "I'm afraid something else came up. I'll try contacting him tonight."

The detective thumbed off the mobile. "Both girls are at the museum," he said, gazing at the corpse. "We can safely rule them out, but as you heard, Sawtelle left there shortly after us. Speaking of which, we need to get away from here right now."

"Are you serious?" gasped Watson. "You mean you're going to leave a dead body here without ringing…"

"I feel wretched enough about this," snapped Quist. "This man would probably be alive if we hadn't called on him today, but yes, I'm afraid we're going to leave him." Hurrying back to the study, he grabbed the map and folder of notes, quickly wiping the desk surface he'd touched earlier. "Calling the authorities would be unwise. We'd be suspects and we have more important things to do than spend the remainder of the day in a police interview room. Come on, we need to leave quickly."

"Okay, Guv." The youth glanced again at the body and gulped. "Er, yeah, whatever you say."

Rubbing down the handle as he closed the door and jumping in the car with Watson, the detective pulled out of the driveway and headed steadily up the cul-de-sac. The neighbour two doors away was still polishing his vehicle to the sound of Abba, blissfully ignorant of the Reverend's murder and his departing visitors.

"Ah, look at this." Quist watched a police car turn into the street and pass them. "Where are they heading?"

Watson glanced anxiously over his shoulder as his boss reached the junction. "Hey, they've gone straight to Roundhay's house. Wow, we only just left there in time. Somebody must have heard the gunshot and called them."

"No, a silencer was used and the neighbours were oblivious to everything." Pulling out onto the main road, Quist nodded knowingly. "That's interesting. Whoever murdered Roundhay must have notified them."

"*What?*"

"They probably claimed to be a concerned resident and said they heard a violent disturbance."

"Why would they do that?" demanded the teenager.

"The only explanation is that the murderer saw my car outside and wanted the police to find us there."

"Again, why?"

"If we were in custody on suspicion of murder, we'd be safely out of the way. We've been asking a lot of questions about Badda rituals and the locations of temples. I can only assume our occultist friends have something important planned for this evening and don't wish to be disturbed."

"Apart from our cop pal Bradders, the only people who know we've been digging into this supernatural shit are Sawtelle, Mel and Tamzin."

"Unless Roundhay rang someone and told them we were visiting him, which I somehow doubt. I'm sure we can rule out Inspector Bradstreet, and we know the two girls were at the museum when he died..."

"But not Sawtelle." Watson frowned. "If you're right, what could these occultists be doing tonight?"

"I don't know." The detective thought for a moment. "I'm

sure the Sussamma Ritual will have been successful, so they could be unearthing the main temple under the cover of darkness. If they've already raided Aquila's tomb and possess the blade, they could be attempting the Oushane Sacrament. Sawtelle said it had to be performed in March."

"Slicing yourself with a knife to hopefully become immortal? Not something I'd fancy myself." Watson laughed uneasily. "You think Sawtelle would be crazy enough to try it?"

"I think it's a definite possibility." Quist took out his phone. "Why don't we learn a little more about him?"

* * * *

Chapter 23

"I still can't believe we left a dead body back there in Wetherby," muttered Watson. "That poor guy."

"I feel sickened by it," admitted Quist. He drove by the York War Memorial and turned into Station Rise. "But it couldn't be helped."

This straight thoroughfare wasn't always a *street*. Before the city railway station was built outside the medieval walls in 1877, train tracks ran along here, terminating in the original station just beyond. Quist pulled into a parking space outside the Grand Hotel and gazed at the Edwardian façade of red brick and decorative sandstone. Opened at the turn of the last century as the palatial headquarters of the North Eastern Railway Company, the building underwent a restoration in 2010, converting it into this five-star hotel and spa.

"I can't help worrying about the cops showing up," said Watson. "You can imagine how it would look if anyone spotted us at Roundhay's place and told them about…"

"No one saw us." The detective gave his shoulder a reassuring squeeze. "Believe me, we left no physical evidence and I checked for witnesses and traffic cameras as we drove away. That's why I took the side streets across Wetherby rather than the main route through the Market Place. Sawtelle and Melissa knew we intended to contact Roundhay, but apart from the gunman, who doubtless saw my car in the drive, no one is aware that we were at his house."

"The gunman who was possibly Sawtelle." Watson frowned. "What about phone records? You phoned the Rev thirty minutes before he died and…"

"Yes, the police will naturally check his calls as part of their investigation." Quist nodded. "And yes, I will almost certainly be the last person to contact Roundhay, but I can explain that away as a simple enquiry into the Badda cult. Don't worry."

"Okay, Guv, if you say so." Watson grinned uneasily and peered up at the hotel. "Sawtelle obviously doesn't care about spending the British Museum's cash, does he? For some reason he must prefer *this* to a bed and breakfast."

Smiling and taking out his phone, Quist rang Gareth Lestrade. "We've arrived," he said. "I realise it's only been fifteen minutes since I contacted you, but did you have any luck finding the room?"

"Luck?" scoffed Lestrade. "Believe it or not, the encryption on a hotel computer is a little easier to hack than the police system. By the way, you always expect to find me at home when you call. Don't you think I have a social life?"

"Gareth," sighed Quist, "you have over two-thousand pristine comic books in your cabinets and an extensive collection of *Star Wars* figurines. Whenever I ring, I assume you'll be either watching a science fiction movie or glued to one of your computers."

"Yeah, yeah," drawled Lestrade. "Well anyway, your guy Sawtelle is in one of the suites. I've just texted you the details."

"Thank you." The detective checked his messages. "Ah, yes, here it is. And you're certain you can override his door lock?"

"No worries. The rooms there are all connected to the housekeeping database. Just let me know when you reach it."

"Very good. Now this may seem an odd request..."

"Odd?" The young man laughed. "Hey, you *do* surprise me."

"I wonder if it's possible for you to delve into his background? Watson just performed a rudimentary search for Edwin Sawtelle on his phone, but the information he found mostly concerns his history lectures and work at the British Museum."

"I'll see what I can do," said Lestrade. "But no, that doesn't sound *odd*, not compared to some of the weird shit you've been involved with. What exactly are you hoping to find on this guy?"

"We're aware that Sawtelle has a keen interest in the occult, so hopefully links to anything connected with that, witchcraft and

181

ritual magic."

Lestrade laughed again. "Ah, now that's more like it – weird shit."

The detective hesitated. "I understand there's something known as the *Dark Web*, a secretive and unsavoury area of the internet used by terrorists, paedophiles and other undesirables?"

Listening beside him, Watson turned. "That's right," he said. "I guess if Satanists use websites and forums, that's where Gazza will find them. Humansacrices.com, or something."

Quist smiled. "Yes, Gareth, if it's possible for you to access this *Dark Web*, you may discover clandestine occult groups. It would be interesting to know if a respected academic like Doctor Sawtelle has ever frequented such a distasteful area of the internet and left any traces of his visits."

"Okay, leave it with me," said Lestrade. "With the advanced equipment I use, the *Dark Web* isn't quite so dark."

Pocketing his phone, Quist climbed out of the car with Watson and pulled on his lengthy overcoat. Two smartly dressed hotel concierges in bowler hats held open the glass doors as they reached the Grand Hotel main entrance.

"Thank you," said the detective, walking into the opulent reception area. "Most kind of you."

The pair crossed a chequered marble floor resembling a giant chess board and, ignoring the staircase behind the front desk, Quist turned right, leading his assistant along a thickly-carpeted corridor to another flight of steps at the far end.

"Always display assured confidence, as if you're a resident," murmured the detective. "No matter how you're dressed, the staff will only approach to question you if you seem hesitant or lost."

"Or if you look like you're here to break into a room," added Watson, unhelpfully.

They headed up the steps and traversed various landings to

reach the top floor. Quist checked the room number on his phone and rapped on Sawtelle's door.

"Er, Guv…" Watson glanced around nervously. "What are you going to say if he answers?"

"Your friend Gareth checked the room log," said Quist. "The electronic lock registers when the guest exits and enters, and this particular guest left ten minutes ago." Several seconds passed and he knocked again to make certain. "No, it would appear we're fine." Glancing up and down the passage, he rang Lestrade. "Hello, Gareth. Yes, we're outside the room now, so whenever you're ready."

The lock buzzed as the young man unlocked it remotely from his computer terminal.

"Amazing," muttered the detective, entering. He pulled on latex gloves and passed a pair to Watson. "Come on, we need to search this place fast. Sawtelle may return at any moment."

The three-room suite was huge and lavish, with large windows looking onto a spectacular view of the Minster. Quist closed the door and headed for the bedroom off the lounge.

"Always check the bedroom first," he whispered. "We have a natural instinct that compels us to keep important items near to us when we sleep."

"Wow, how big is that frigging bed?" gasped the youth, following him in. "You could play tennis on that thing."

"Take a look under it and check beneath the mattress too. Needless to say, be very careful to leave everything exactly as you found it."

"You think that dagger could be here somewhere?"

"It's possible and if so…" Quist opened one of the wardrobes and grimaced to see a safe bolted to the wall. "Ah. If he *has* found the Oushane Blade, I've no doubt it will be in there."

"Yeah, and that's something Gazza *can't* unlock." Watson looked in the bedside cabinets. "So what else are we hoping to find?"

"Anything unusual." Quist swiftly searched through the desk drawers, taking care not to disturb the layout of contents. "Basically anything connected with the occult. Hopefully there will be an address book somewhere. Doctor Blake mentioned he has two London friends and they may be listed in his contacts."

"*Address book?*" His assistant laughed quietly. "Hey, you're not living in 1790 anymore, Guv. I think you'll find most folk have all that stuff in their phone."

"True." The detective gave a lopsided smile. "Try to forget I said that."

The hurried search took less than five minutes and, checking his watch, Quist opened the door. "That's enough," he whispered. "We'd better not push our luck. Let's go."

Watson followed him out and the door locked automatically as they closed it behind them.

"Well, everything in there seemed kind of normal," pointed out the teenager. "So what do you think, Guv?"

"I *think* it's all rather peculiar," murmured Quist, heading back along the corridor. "Peculiar and a little suspicious. If Sawtelle was an occultist, I'd have expected to find something indicative of that – ritualistic paraphernalia, notes on the Badda rites and magical grimoires. He'd keep such items close to hand and certainly not at the museum."

"Well, we saw he has a room safe."

"Yes, but it isn't a particularly *large* safe, is it?"

"Okay." Watson shrugged. "Maybe his hooded cloak, goat's head mask and other shit are with the friends that Mel told us about?"

"Maybe." Quist nodded. "And maybe you watch too many late-night horror films."

* * * *

Chapter 24

People have walked along Stonegate since the time of Christ, but no one knows how this atmospheric York street came by its name. Two-thousand years ago, this was the Roman Via Praetoria, the main route through their fortress, connecting the military basilica to the civilian Colonia across the river. Some historians believe it acquired the name simply because the Romans paved the way with stone. Others point to the thirteenth and fourteenth centuries when, for many years, the street was used to transport masses of limestone from the Ouse to build the Minster. Whichever story is correct, this cobbled thoroughfare is now one of York's most distinctive medieval streets, with beautiful old shops sporting antiquated signs, wooden corniced windows and bullseye glass.

The icy fog was thickening, but it didn't matter to Edwin Sawtelle as he was in no mood for gazing at the surrounding architecture. A doorway stood between an ancient apothecary and a half-timbered chocolate shop and he marched up to buzz the intercom. The chubby doctor wore an expensive black coat with a red scarf. The time was a little after four, and many of the daytime shoppers were making their way home, the weather hastening their pace.

"It's Edwin," he grunted, as the intercom unit crackled into life. "Open up."

The electronic lock clicked and, brusquely shoving the door wide, he climbed the steps to Melissa and Tamzin's apartment above the confectionery shop.

Tamzin let him in. "Hi there." She gave a puzzled smile. "We weren't expecting you."

Ignoring her, Sawtelle looked around the lounge. The place had a Victorian feel, with polished floorboards, plaster coving and diminutive chandeliers. A kitchen diner stood at one end where Melissa was making coffee at a breakfast bar. Two doors led into the bedrooms and Sawtelle smirked, knowing that only *one* of these would be in use.

"So can you guess why I'm here," he snapped, unbuttoning his coat.

Melissa shook her head. "We've finished work for the day," she said, tinkling a spoon in the coffee mugs. "We didn't think we'd see you until…"

"The Hanka Dagger," said Sawtelle.

"I beg your pardon?"

"You know what I'm talking about; you saw me checking it." Loosening his scarf, he sat on the couch and crossed his legs. "I knew it looked wrong, with a strange sheen to it, so I went back later to examine it properly. That knife has been bleached, for God's sake."

Melissa frowned. "And you think *I* did that?"

"Well, one of you silly bitches did. Who else could it be?"

"It's time we discussed your attitude, Edwin." The girl bristled with anger. "I know why you speak to us like this. I never responded to your crude seduction attempts when I began working for you. It's because I won't sleep with you and…"

"Well, let's face it, you sleep with *anyone*." Sawtelle nodded to Tamzin and leered. "You *even* sleep with Rogers here."

"Yes, my sexuality turns you on. I've always known that."

"A bisexual black girl?" He laughed. "What can I say? I'm a red-blooded male. But you're clearly trying to change the subject, so I'll ask again. What did you do to the Hanka Dagger and, more to the point, where are the missing relics?"

"What?" Tamzin glanced at Melissa. "Missing…"

"The Moon Tiara." Sawtelle folded his arms. "The pair of you lied to my face. You told me you'd spoken to Chapman in London. You said he'd misplaced it at his end and he was looking for it. I've just been in touch with him and he's never heard from either of you. The crown was definitely sent to York; he wrapped it and put it in the

186

crate himself."

"I see," murmured Melissa.

"Three amulets have disappeared from the same ritualistic display. The description cards have gone too, presumably so I wouldn't notice the empty spaces in the cabinet. You're in charge of these artefacts and you unpacked the smaller items yourselves. They didn't just vanish, so what have you done with them?"

Melissa nodded slowly. "Actually, you're wrong."

"No, those relics are…"

"You said I sleep with *anyone*, but you're wrong. Apart from the ones I'm attracted to, like my Barbie Doll…" Melissa walked by Tamzin and paused to kiss her. "I only sleep with people who can assist me."

"What's *that* supposed to mean?" demanded Sawtelle.

"Well, for example…" She walked behind him and leant on the couch, speaking close to his ear. "I was screwing Professor Harwood. I wanted him to transfer Tamz and I to your department and to appoint me as your personal assistant. We soon developed a mutual understanding and he did as I asked. I was also sleeping with Doctor Lambeth for two months."

"*Lambeth?*" he gasped. "He's over seventy."

"Yes, and very grateful. So grateful, he agreed to send the Badda exhibition to York."

Sawtelle shook his head. "I honestly can't believe this."

"I'm afraid I had to have sex with that awful director Jessops too. The exhibition date was wrong for me, so I persuaded him to delay it being moved up here." Leaning closer from behind, she stroked the doctor's neck, her breathing shallow and fast. "We had to be in York right *now*, you see, when the phase of the moon is correct."

"What on earth are you talking about…"

Melissa's hand flew over the couch to plunge a knife deep into the man's chest. A gush of crimson gore spurted onto his shirt.

"Yes, Edwin," she said. "You *are* a red-blooded male."

Sawtelle grasped at the knife hilt, spluttering and coughing, and Melissa moved around the couch to face him. Panting and shaking with the adrenaline, she watched as he lurched forward and slumped to the floor dead.

"What the fuck, Mel?" Tamzin gaped at the body. "I didn't see you take the knife from the kitchen. I had no idea you were going to…"

"Kill him?" laughed Melissa. "Yes, it's amazing how easier it gets. The idea of murder terrified me before the first Sussamma sacrifice. I threw up and I didn't sleep a wink afterwards, but by the fourth, I was fine. Now look at me."

"Surely there was some other way?"

"Tamz, he knew we'd bleached the knife and that we took the crown and possession amulets. How were we supposed to explain that?" She stifled another frantic laugh. "Killing those four girls was necessary, but this felt different. I actually enjoyed this."

"But what will the Priestess say? If this should jeopardise her plans…"

"Her plans?" snarled Melissa, trembling. "None of this would have been possible if we hadn't brought the temple here and supplied the crown and amulets. She might have planned this, but we took all the risks and I had to screw those horrible men. Plus, you know how she has an obsession with loose ends. Realising that those relics are missing made Edwin a definite loose end."

"I suppose you're right." Unable to tear her eyes from the corpse, Tamzin shook her head. "She wants rid of the private detectives too. We won't be returning to our normal lives after the Oushane Sacrament, so why go to such trouble?"

"It's in case the ritual should fail. For obvious reasons, she doesn't want anything pointing to us and yes, Quist and his friend know far too much." Still shivering, the doctor debated for a few moments. "But the ritual *won't* fail and, you're right, we *aren't* going back to our mundane lives. I was just thinking..." She turned to Tamzin with a manic smile. "Three adepts were needed for the Sussamma Ritual, but not anymore."

"What are you saying?"

"We only need each other. Like I said, we've done most of the work and taken most of the risks. I'm saying *we* could perform the Oushane Sacrament, just you and I."

"But the Priestess is in charge," gasped Tamzin. "This whole thing is *her* operation. She researched and conceived the entire..."

"Barbie Doll." Melissa kissed her deeply, ending the babble of words. "I've never liked that woman. Listen to me, we can do this ourselves and she won't know. The builder uncovered the temple with you last night and you say the sacrifice is ready?"

"Leanne?" Tamzin nodded nervously. "Yes, she's a junkie and very pliable. She thinks I'm taking her to a party."

"Good." The doctor checked her watch. "It gets dark at six-thirty. We're supposed to be opening Aquila's tomb after midnight, but we'll go to the temple earlier and take the blade for ourselves."

Tamzin ran both hands through her blonde mane, closing her eyes as she considered the insane plan. *This was so wrong, but then again, murder and pretty much everything else she'd taken part in over the past week had been wrong.*

Tamzin's mother had been a witch and her attraction to the supernatural had been nurtured from childhood, fate lending a hand when she began work at the British Museum and met Mel. This beautiful black woman had discovered her interests and taken her under her wing, both as a lover and an occult student. She introduced her little "Barbie Doll" to her magical circle and they performed rudimentary rites together. Then, three months ago, the Priestess contacted them with an incredible proposition and everything changed. This powerful occultist had researched the Badda cult and knew all about the Oushane Blade. She knew what it could do and persuaded Mel to bring the temple to York at the correct time. Their assistance in this venture would be rewarded with the opportunity to use the blade themselves and join the Priestess in immortality.

Tamzin shuddered. *Now Mel was acting crazy and fully intended to defy this woman. Hopefully she knew what she was doing, but Tamzin had never seen her like this.*

"This is too risky." She gulped. "We haven't known the Priestess long and we don't know what she's capable of. You seem different and a little… Well, this isn't you…"

"Maybe this *is* me," laughed Melissa. "The *real* me. Do you realise how powerful we'll be after the Oushane Sacrament? No one, including the Priestess, will be able to harm us. Trust me, Tamz, we can do this and we'll never be found afterwards."

"We just disappear?"

"Yes, the fresh start in North Africa that we spoke of. We're both tired of the British Museum and, with our lupine power, we'll be able to do anything. Go anywhere." She gestured to Sawtelle. "We don't even need to dispose of his body. It can walk out of here as a host for Rakkat."

"We already *have* a reserve host to get rid of the builder and the detectives," said Tamzin. "Our drug addict Ryan Farmer. The Priestess has me supplying him with heroin for when we need him."

"Fortunately for Mister Farmer, it's looking like he won't be required." Reaching into the lounge bureau, the doctor brought out one of the stolen Badda amulets and draped the chain around Sawtelle's neck. "No, Edwin will do instead. Give me a hand."

Tamzin stooped to take one of the arms and Melissa grabbed the other, the girls dragging him across the varnished floorboards into the centre of the room. Tamzin brought a wet towel to wipe the blood as Melissa chalked a circle around the body and scribbled cryptic symbols. Pulling the knife from Sawtelle's ribs with a sickly slurp, she wiped it on his shirt and passed it to Tamzin.

"Here, carve the seal and I'll get the ritual." Hurrying to the bedroom, the doctor returned with a file of papers and a black candle, lighting the latter and placing it by the corpse. "It's lucky the Priestess printed copies of the Badda rites for us to learn word-perfect. Not only do we have the possession rite here, but also the Oushane Sacrament for later."

Tamzin completed the grisly wrist symbol and stepped out of the circle, watching as Melissa opened the file of occult incantations to read aloud over Sawtelle's body. The possession spell was short and sounded like gibberish, but both girls knew its power and had seen it work before, shortly after the Priestess injected Aaron King with a lethal heroin overdose.

"There." Melissa stepped back, grinning excitedly. "He's nice and fresh, just like King, so it shouldn't take long. The Priestess wants rid of the workman who excavated the temple and now those private detectives too. I agree with her. I can't imagine why they've involved themselves in this, but Quist is too clever. I can't believe how much he knows."

"They went to Wetherby," said Tamzin, timidly. "Do you suppose they know about the Priestess? How she visited Miles Roundhay and interviewed him about the temple locations?"

"I doubt it." Melissa shrugged. "I rang her the moment they set off to see him and she got there before he could say anything. Quist thinks I'm helping him, but he obviously isn't certain about us. After Roundhay died, he rang on his camera phone; that was to make sure we were in the museum and nowhere near Wetherby."

Tamzin nodded. "The Priestess saw Quist's car in the drive, but he lied to you saying he wasn't there."

"That's why I rang the police anonymously and said I'd heard a gunshot. If Quist and Watson were found with Roundhay's body, it would get rid of them for a while until Rakkat got rid of them permanently." Melissa took out her mobile. "Speaking of which, I think I should arrange a meeting."

Tamzin held her free hand as she spoke.

"Mister Quist. Hello there, it's Mel – Doctor Blake. Yes, I'm worried." She smiled at Tamzin. "Edwin has been acting suspiciously and you were right about him being an occultist. I have some information for you and we really need to talk. It's best if you don't come to our apartment; he could easily turn up here. Lendal Bridge is close by. I'll meet you there at six-thirty."

Tamzin felt the temperature fall rapidly and, glancing at the corpse, she saw it had begun to twitch. The electric lights dimmed slightly as Rakkat's bright green eyes flickered open.

"Loose ends." Melissa switched off the phone and gave another manic grin. "Yes, I can see why the Priestess hates them so much."

* * * *

Chapter 25

With ornate metal parapets and painted lampposts, Lendal Bridge is arguably the most attractive of York's three road bridges. The Victorian span crosses the Ouse between a pair of medieval stone towers and, standing in the middle on the upstream side, Watson leant on the handrail and waited with Quist. Thanks to the dismal weather, darkness had fallen earlier than usual this Thursday evening and the detective used the glow of a lamp to look through Roundhay's notes. Rubbing his hands to warm them, his assistant gazed at the museum on the northern riverbank, not that he could see much. The freezing mist had thickened, hazing the gardens and covering the river below him with eerie drifting tendrils. He peered over the nearby buildings at the Minster, where the central floodlit tower, currently encircled with scaffolding, loomed high above the fog.

"Crap place to meet." Watson turned up the collar of his green canvas jacket. "So what do you reckon Mel wants to tell us?"

"We'll soon find out," murmured Quist, reading. "Roundhay was constantly researching the Badda cult and this new material is rather interesting. He talks about the Oushane Sacrament, the sacrifice ritual to attain immortality. The Moon Crown has to be worn and it must take place on the last night of the full moon in the deity's month of March." He nodded grimly. "That's tonight."

"So you could be right? That could be why the Rev's killer wanted us arrested. We were doing too much snooping and it would get us out of the picture while they piss about with their magic knife."

"Probably, but here's something else – a more detailed description of the Sussamma Ritual with a detail we *weren't* aware of. Apparently the rite requires three adepts working together, no more and no less, if it's to succeed."

"Really?" Watson frowned. "Well, we can forget about the three running the exhibition. They're the least likely occultists ever.

The two girls are *normal*, Mel's helping us, and they can't stand Sawtelle. From the way he speaks to them, the feeling's mutual."

"Remember what I said about allowing appearances to deceive you. *Three* adepts are needed and…"

"And according to Mel, Sawtelle has two friends up from London."

"Exactly," said Quist. "*According to Melissa*. She was the one who told us about his deep interest in the occult, but after seeing his room…" Spotting Inspector Bradstreet approaching with DC Gary Mitchell, he slid the notes into his coat pocket. "Ah, Inspector, there you are."

"Here I am," said Katie. Like Mitchell, she wore a raincoat over her suit. "So what is this? Why did you ask to meet here?"

"I don't know yet," he admitted, checking his watch. "Melissa Blake from the Badda exhibition will be arriving at any moment. She has information for me and I wanted you to hear it too."

The usual attraction tingled inside Katie, the sexual sensation she always experienced around Quist, but tonight the full moon had accentuated the supernatural allure. Staring at his mouth, she wanted to kiss him as he spoke, but gritted her teeth and averted her eyes.

"Have you checked the museum yet?" asked Watson.

The Inspector shook her head. "I told you earlier, I can't just go barging in there because of bizarre suspicions."

"The new exhibition is your crime scene," said Quist. "Those four murders were committed in there and…"

"How could you possibly know that?" quizzed Mitchell.

"It doesn't matter *how* I know. Just find a reason to get your forensic people inside. Someone performed an occult ritual there and you *will* find the evidence."

"Occult?" scoffed the Constable, grinning. "Why should we listen to some private eye?"

"Consultant detective," corrected Quist. "I suspected Edwin

194

Sawtelle was involved in the killings and I believe Doctor Blake may back me up. She claims he's obsessed with the occult. He certainly knows the Badda rituals, he has full access to the exhibition after hours and Blake claims he's acting suspiciously. That's why I asked you here. If you won't believe *me*, then maybe you'll listen to *her* – a Doctor of Archaeology at the British Museum."

"Acting suspiciously?" echoed Katie. "What does she mean?"

"Er, just off the top of my head…" Watson pointed past her to a dishevelled figure approaching along the bridge pavement. "Maybe she meant *that*."

The Inspector turned. "Doctor Sawtelle?"

Quist saw the grinning doctor, the hair instantly rising on his neck. An open overcoat flapped about his portly frame and dry blood covered his shirt. The evening temperature wasn't exactly tropical on the bridge, but a noticeable pocket of coldness surrounded him, a cold that wasn't natural.

"Hey, look at this." Sawtelle winked at Katie, drool running over his short beard. "I was sent for this big-nosed guy and the black kid, but look what I get as a bonus – Blondie, my favourite cop. Hello, sweet child."

"*What?*" mouthed Katie. *The deep voice sounded like Aaron King and he'd used that same stupid nickname.* "Is that blood?"

"My friends are tying up loose ends," he growled, openly salivating. "These guys know far more than they should."

"It's Rakkat." Gripping the Inspector's arm, Quist backed away. "I wasn't expecting this. Don't let it near you."

"Trust me," croaked Watson. "If *I'd* been expecting it, I wouldn't be here."

"Don't be ridiculous." Katie gave a tense laugh, unable to tear her gaze from Sawtelle's eyes. *Why were they green and why did they appear to glow so eerily?* She noticed the drool-covered amulet around his neck, like the one King had worn. "Doctor, what are you doing here? Why do you have blood on your…"

"Your *friends* sent you?" snapped Quist. "Who are they?"

"Ooh, that would be telling." Leering at the Inspector, Rakkat began to sing the old Johnny Cash song. "*Well there ain't no need to doubt, there ain't no two ways about it. As sure as your name's Katie, you put me here.*"

"What's going on?" demanded Mitchell, bemused.

"Who *did* put you there?" Quist glanced at the blood on Rakkat's hand as the creature began to slowly circle them. "I see you have the Oushane Seal cut into your wrist. Who performed the possession ritual?"

"Mmmh, I sense something from you." Ignoring the question, Rakkat gazed at him and let out a bubbling chuckle, his foul breath wafting over the group. "You're different to these others. You're my kind of guy, aren't you?"

"Hardly." Quist looked around anxiously, knowing he couldn't use his lupine strength without exposing himself.

"Guv?" Watson moved back to the bridge parapet. "What do we do?"

"What's going on?" repeated Mitchell. He'd never met Sawtelle and this man reminded him of someone on day-release from a psychiatric care home. "Is he usually like this?"

"No." Watson shivered. "He's usually a twat, but this is different."

Katie unconsciously backed away too, her heart racing. *Had Sawtelle suffered a breakdown? Why was it so cold and why did she feel so scared? This escalating fear was absurd, but she couldn't shrug it off. Why were his eyes bright green? His voice was different too and deeper. This was crazy, but it WAS Aaron King's voice.*

The Inspector fumbled for her mobile with shaking fingers. Her mouth had turned to chalk and icy sweat moistened her body. She gestured to Mitchell. "Gary, I want you to detain this man. I need to ring the station and let them know about..."

"I was ordered to kill the private eyes," growled Rakkat. "But like I said, I've got you as a bonus." His gruesome smile widened as Mitchell grabbed his arm. "Mmh, and *this* one too."

"It isn't Sawtelle," said Quist. "Mitchell, let go of it. If this creature says it's going to kill us, it will. It's powerful enough to tear us to pieces."

"For God's sake," sighed the Constable. "I don't know what you're talking about, but..." He grunted as Rakkat head-butted him, flattening his nose with a nauseating crack.

"Move!" Quist yanked the Inspector's arm. "Move fast."

Katie's irrational fear turned to sheer terror, some primal sense shrieking *RUN*. Sprinting along the bridge with Quist and Watson, she glanced back to see Sawtelle holding her unconscious Constable upright and lapping the blood from his face. *No, this wasn't Sawtelle. Reason and logic argued otherwise, but this revolting creature was NOT Doctor Sawtelle.*

"Ah, Katie baby." Rakkat dropped Mitchell in a heap. "No one can accuse me of being unsporting. I'm counting to ten and then I'm coming for you, Blondie."

Stone steps led to the riverside at the end of Lendal Bridge and the trio virtually tumbled down the dark flight. All thoughts of police procedures had taken a back seat and Katie ran behind the two private detectives, her open raincoat flapping like a cape.

"That's their pet demon?" gasped Watson, petrified. "You're saying that's the same thing that was inside Aaron King? I thought you said it had gone?"

"Evidently it's back in a new host," snapped Quist. "I wasn't prepared for this."

Reaching the bottom, they raced along Wellington Row, the tarmacked pathway beside the riverbank. It was deserted and dark here, the Victorian lamps on the water's edge supplying poor illumination in the fog. Rakkat landed cat-like on all fours behind them and, realising he'd leapt from the bridge above, Katie turned and winced to see his left foot sticking out at a sickening sideways angle.

"I told you this wasn't over, Blondie." The creature giggled, spraying saliva. "Do you remember how I wanted to tear out your lungs? Well this time they've allowed me to kill and I intend to take my time and enjoy this." He noticed the broken shin. "Mmh, this body is too heavy, but, hey, when it isn't *your* body, you don't need to worry about damage." Laughing louder, he rotated the ankle in a crackle of bone.

"Keep moving fast," yelled Quist, running past the building that housed the York City Rowing Club. Roosting geese on the banking exploded onto the river in a squabbling panic. "It's playing, but it'll soon get bored and carry out its orders."

"It's pointless running, Blondie." Singing loudly, Rakkat twisted the splintered limb into a more practical shape. "*Katie baby, you're my special lady…*"

"This way." Quist turned left after the club and headed for the Memorial Gardens. He didn't want to use his strength with the Inspector as a witness, but knew he might *have* to and the foggy darkness in the parkland could provide cover.

Watson and Katie glanced back, both whimpering to see Rakkat bounding after them along the riverside. Reminiscent of some grotesque ape, the bulky body was hunched over and its knuckles padded the ground, but the moans of fright had been triggered by its eyes. Here in the misty gloom, they could see now that those terrifying eyes were actually lit with a cold green glow.

Circular and surrounded by trees, the Memorial Gardens were two-hundred feet wide and a pair of surly teenagers loitered in the gateway smoking marijuana. Barging between them, the trio rushed inside and across the open lawn.

"Hey…" The largest youth was more used to shoving people

around and taking their handbags than being shoved himself. He pulled a knife from his jacket. "What do you think you're…"

"Hello boys." Rakkat appeared behind him and rose from the running crouch. "It might be a sensible idea to get out of my way."

"What?" The thug gaped at the pouring saliva. "Just who the fuck are you talking to…"

Pushing him aside, Rakkat felt the knife slam into his ribs and glanced down at the protruding hilt. "Ooh, that went into a lung." He laughed and oxygenated blood frothed up to mix with the drool. "It's lucky I'm carrying a spare."

In one swift movement he pulled out the weapon and slashed the teenager's throat. His friend rushed forward, then crumpled to the ground choking as a punch burst his windpipe. Rakkat pounced on him, clawed open his abdomen and wrenched out a mouthful of entrails. Energised and aroused by the steaming gore, he threw back his head and let out a hideous howl.

"Shit," croaked Watson. He sprinted past the cenotaph towards the gateway on the opposite side of the park. "I think it's stopped pissing around and things just got serious."

A furious snarling sounded behind them, the guttural noise growing louder. The elemental had speeded up its pursuit and Quist knew they couldn't possibly escape it. *He'd need to use supernatural strength to protect Watson and Bradstreet and then deal with the consequences later.* The growling grew closer as they burst from the gardens into Leeman Road, the panic and momentum carrying all three out onto the roadway and into the path of a speeding car.

"Damn!" Quist grabbed his companions and twisted his body to protect them from the impact, the screech of car tyres drowning his voice. "No!"

Watson experienced an eerie sensation, not unlike swimming underwater, as time decelerated. He'd heard of this *slow-motion effect*, the phenomenon described by accident victims, and he looked into the driver's face, a wide-eyed mask of shock and clenched teeth. The drunken man managed to swerve as he braked, somehow missing them by inches, but his relief turned to horror as a crouching shape flew out of the park gateway, smashed into his bonnet and vanished beneath the wheels.

Still clinging tightly onto Quist, Katie was unable to help herself and kissed him hard on the lips. She instantly regretted the unconscious action and broke away.

"I thought we were dead," she gasped. Shaking and fighting for breath, she watched the car accelerate along the empty street and screech out onto the main road. "Why didn't he stop?"

"Who can say?" panted Quist. His lupine senses had detected the smell of alcohol from the open window; the driver had almost certainly been over the legal limit.

"This isn't over," growled Rakkat. The broken body lying in the gutter pushed itself up onto one arm. "But it soon will be."

"*Jesus*," groaned Katie. The horror joined forces with the exertion, causing her to retch before she turned to run. "It's still alive."

"Don't worry." Quist caught her hand. "The danger is over."

Watson gaped at the creature and saw this was true. In his current condition, Rakkat didn't pose much of a threat. *He couldn't have looked worse if he'd argued with a grizzly bear.*

"I need to speak to you." Rakkat grinned at them, crimson foam bubbling over his lips. Pulling himself into a twisted sitting position, he felt around his shattered torso to find smashed vertebrae and a broken pelvis. "Come closer so you can hear."

"Don't go near it," warned Quist.

"*Really?*" Watson let out a hysterical laugh. "Hey, thanks for the advice, Guv."

Snarling and wrenching at its back, Rakkat rolled across the tarmac, lashing out with a makeshift bone dagger and narrowly missing Katie's leg. She clasped a hand to her mouth, gagging as she realised the bleeding shard had been torn from its own pelvis. Throwing itself sideways, it lunged at Quist, attempting to bite his leg and snapping several teeth in a ghastly chomp of jaws.

"That's enough!" he said, jumping back. "Your host body is destroyed and this is finished." He turned to Katie. "Can you feel the temperature? The cold you experienced around it before is worse as far more energy is now required to maintain this damaged body."

The Inspector jerked her head in a terrified nod.

"I shouldn't have wasted time having fun." Rakkat's laughter turned to coughing and he vomited dark blood. "Still, you can't blame me for having one last try, can you?"

"You've failed," said Quist. He looked around for witnesses and saw that Leeman Road was still empty. "Isn't it time you were leaving?"

"Ah, I suppose so." Coughing again, it began to sing. "*I'm leavin' on a jet plane, I don't know when I'll be back again...*"

"Hey, dickhead..." Watson spoke loudly over the gargled song. "Be a good elemental and just fuck off, okay?"

"Yeah, yeah." Rakkat grinned at Quist as a blast of freezing air began to flurry around his host body and whip up gravel. "I imagine we'll see each other again. Like I said earlier, I can sense you're my kind of guy."

The trio watched as the miniature tornado increased and a violet glow enveloped Rakkat. Spluttering a last mouthful of bloody drool, he collapsed onto his side, the bright green eyes fading to grey.

* * * *

Chapter 26

Katie stood on Leeman Road staring at Sawtelle's corpse as the localised squall of wind vanished as swiftly as it had arrived.

"Oh, my God!" Her mouth fell slackly open. "Did you see that? Did you see the weird purple light? The wind?"

"I saw them," whispered Watson. "Shit, I saw them."

"I felt it too," said Katie, weakly. "I sensed something the moment he arrived on the bridge, but I hoped it was imagination. I felt that same unnatural cold and the intense fear with Aaron King. Oh my God, I saw its eyes shining in the dark back there. This is *real*, isn't it? This is fucking real."

"I'm afraid so." Quist lifted his overcoat to squat by the body and tug up the doctor's sleeve. "Look, the Oushane Seal has been cut into the wrist. King and Sawtelle were both dead when the occultists carved this and recited the possession ritual. The seal opens the host body for the elemental, but controls it too, ensuring it follows orders."

"Yes, King had that," confirmed the Inspector. "I remember there was a sort of cold breeze when he died in the cells, but he definitely didn't *light up*."

"Really?" Raising a curious eyebrow, Quist removed the thin chain from around Sawtelle's neck and scrutinised the symbols on the ancient metal disc. "From my research, this is obviously a Badda possession amulet."

"It's the same medallion Aaron King wore." Katie nodded, shakily taking a plastic bag from her raincoat. "It's also evidence."

"I'm no expert on elemental possession," admitted Quist, dropping it in. "But as King was being held in police custody, his amulet will obviously have been taken from him for safety reasons. Perhaps that factor dictated Rakkat's different exits in the two hosts, or perhaps it was just that he'd spent much longer inside King's putrefying body."

"Yeah," drawled Watson. "Just what I was thinking."

"Rakkat," repeated Katie, quietly. "A supernatural entity. I didn't believe you before and now I honestly don't know what to say." She cleared her throat. "Er, listen, when I kissed you, it was a release of tension. I wasn't in my right mind and…"

"Yes, I understand," broke in Quist, smiling. "Please forget about it."

Still trembling, the Inspector heard the wail of nearby police sirens and realised they were sounding from the direction of Lendal Bridge. "It looks as if they've found Mitchell," she stammered, taking out her phone. "I really hope he's alright. I have to call this in, but I don't know what to tell them"

"It's just a thought," said Watson, "But I shouldn't mention singing demons."

They waited as she spoke on the mobile, Quist glancing up and down the foggy street. There were no pedestrians and, although the occasional car passed by with headlights dipped, no one stopped to check on why someone was lying in the gutter. Watson guessed these drivers would assume that the woman on the phone was already ringing for assistance. Or maybe, like many people in this modern age, they simply couldn't care less.

"This is absolutely insane," said Katie, finishing her call. "But now that I've seen it, I know you were right."

"There's something I ought to mention," said Quist. "We travelled to Wetherby earlier to speak with Miles Roundhay, an expert on the Badda cult. He was shot dead by someone. We didn't see the gunman, but you might want to check the area traffic cameras for a black saloon, probably speeding, at around two o'clock. We don't have a registration, but Watson believes it was a BMW."

"Watson *knows* it was a BMW," corrected the teenager, still shivering uncontrollably. "Watson knows his cars."

"*What?*" hissed Katie. "I'm aware of a fatal shooting in

Wetherby this afternoon, but you're telling me you were *there*? You left the scene of a murder?"

"We *had* to, but apart from the killer, no one knows we were at the house." Quist smiled apologetically. "I'm afraid we have to leave *this* crime scene too, right now."

"Are you joking?" she snapped. "No, you both need to give statements and…"

"Inspector…" Quist gently gripped her shoulders. "You know now that I was speaking the truth about the supernatural and you witnessed this lethal monstrosity. Believe me when I tell you the people who created it are performing another sacrifice ritual tonight. The police follow set procedures and they won't be able to prevent the murder in time. Watson and I will track down these occultists and stop them, but we can't do that if we're making statements."

"But I can't allow you to go." Katie laughed. "How the hell am I supposed to explain what just happened and where you are?"

"Don't mention the body glowing as it died," said Watson, helpfully. "Or miniature tornadoes springing up."

"Tell the truth, up to a point." Quist heard the approaching sirens and spoke hurriedly as he turned. "You met us on the bridge and Sawtelle arrived. For some unknown reason, the doctor attacked your Constable and then chased the three of us. We were separated during our escape, Sawtelle was hit by a car whilst attempting to kill you and you don't know where Watson and I are." He pulled the teenager through the park gate. "I'm sure you'll do fine."

"No, wait. You can't just…" Katie grimaced as they vanished into the mist. "Damn it!"

Flashes of bright blue illuminated the billowing fog, the disco display heralding the arrival of the police. Two squad cars raced up Lendal Road, the rear car parking sideways to block the street as Angie Gibson and three uniformed officers jumped out of the first vehicle.

"Jesus, Ma'am," gasped the Sergeant, running over. "Are you okay?"

"I'm good," said Katie, gesturing to Sawtelle's corpse. "I can't say the same for *him*."

"What the hell happened here?" Angie peered with wide eyes at the smashed body in the gutter. "My God, is that the doctor we spoke to at the museum?"

"It is, or rather what's left of him. I have no idea why, but he tried to kill me just now. If he hadn't been hit by a car, I think he'd have succeeded." Katie handed her the bagged amulet. "He has that Badda symbol on his wrist and he was wearing this."

"Just like the one we found on King." Angie held it up, peering closely. "Another of those occult trinkets, and King's wrist design too? I don't understand, Ma'am. What's going on here?"

"I wish I knew," muttered Katie, glancing irately at the foggy parkland where Quist had vanished.

* * * *

Quist raced across the Memorial Gardens lawn.

"I'd better ring Lestrade," he said, dryly. "Those background checks on Sawtelle will be a waste of time. I think it's safe to say he's no longer a suspect."

Watson ran through the mist beside him, but came to an abrupt halt by the riverside gateway. Squinting in the darkness, he pointed shakily to the two corpses lying beside the fence. Tendrils of steam rose from the open stomach of the closest.

"Bloody hell, Guv…" he croaked. "Those are the guys we passed a few minutes ago. They're *dead* and just look at the state of them. Oh, my God, did Rakkat do that?"

"Without a doubt." Quist shook his head bitterly. "Come on. We can't do anything about this and the police will discover them soon enough. They're back there right now and we need to keep moving."

Leaving the gardens, the pair hurried along Wellington Row, the foggy waterside route they'd taken earlier, to return to Lendal Bridge.

"We were supposed to meet Mel here, but that thing turned up instead," said Watson, climbing the stone steps. "What do you think, Guv?"

"Rakkat claimed someone sent him to kill us." Quist fumed angrily. "I think we now know who that *someone* was."

"You mean Mel and Tamzin?"

"No, I mean the York Male Voice Choir." The detective glanced dubiously at him. "Of *course* I mean Melissa and Tamzin."

"I can't believe this." Watson grinned uneasily. "Sweet little things like that can't be involved with murder and the dark arts." He frowned as his boss reached the bridge pavement and turned left. "Er, isn't your car the other way? We left it in the Esplanade car park."

Quist saw the ambulance and police car where Gary Mitchell had been attacked, and crossed the road with his assistant to pass by on the opposite side.

"The girls have an apartment on Stonegate," he said, quietly. "It's virtually impossible to park in that area and it isn't far on foot. Walk slowly and natural so as not to draw attention."

"So that drooling bastard was their elemental entity," whispered Watson, glancing warily at the squad car. "I don't mind telling you, I was absolutely crapping myself, Guv."

"That's my big, brave boy." The detective gave a wry smile to relieve the tension. "Joking aside, such reactions are unavoidable. Apart from the pocket of icy cold that always surrounds them, elementals radiate a supernatural aura that humans find terrifying."

"I felt it as soon as it turned up. Those glowing green eyes really freaked me out."

"I don't doubt it. Fortunately, Rakkat has gone."

"Yeah, for *now*," snapped Watson. "But they can obviously

call it up with their magic shit and stick it in *any* dead body." He peered over his shoulder into the drifting mist. "Have you also thought there might be more than *one*? Charlotte's Dad saw Rakkat dragging a body out of that van, but he said the driver had glowing eyes."

"No, I'm fairly sure these adepts are only using Rakkat. Elementals are powerful and efficient killers, but they aren't renowned for their driving skills and knowledge of the Highway Code."

Watson shook his head. "But the glowing eyes…"

"By his own admission, Tarot was inebriated that evening and the long-haired person he noticed in the driving seat will have been wearing spectacles with the ambient light reflecting upon them. Long hair and spectacles." Quist turned to the teenager. "Now who do we know fitting that description?"

* * * *

Chapter 27

The fog was growing worse. Quist and Watson strode through the thickening haze along Stonegate, the old shop windows glowing with yellowish light on either side of the narrow street. The detective smiled grimly, remembering how the Via Praetoria Roman road lay intact beneath these cobblestones and the Prefect Aquila himself would have once walked this very same route.

"We only have Mel's mobile number," pointed out Watson. "How are we going to find her?"

Quist gestured to a window where sweets were arranged on porcelain plates. "Elementary detection." He headed for the door between this and the neighbouring shop. "Blake mentioned she'd rented rooms above a Stonegate chocolate shop and this is the only one."

The youth peered at the delicious window display as his boss pressed the intercom buzzer. Despite his unease, he licked his lips.

"Hello?" answered the speaker.

Recognising Tamzin's voice, Quist deepened his tone. "North Yorkshire Police. I'm here to speak with Doctor Blake."

"Sure," said the girl. The buzz told him the entrance had been unlocked. "Come on up."

Climbing the stairs, the pair knocked on the apartment, both smiling to see Tamzin's astounded expression as the door opened.

"Ooh, your hair's down," said Watson. "With your specs, it suits you long like that. I guess you only wear it up for work?"

"What the…" Melissa appeared behind her. "Mister Quist?"

"Indeed." The detective walked in, looking around the lounge. "You both seem shocked to see us, but I can understand why."

"More surprise than shock." The doctor gestured for them to sit on the couch. "Tamz said it was the police."

"Yes." Quist settled himself beside Watson and stroked the

208

damp leather. He sniffed his fingers, picking up the scents of blood and bleach. "If I'd said it was us, you may not have allowed us in."

Melissa sat next to Tamzin on the opposite couch and looked puzzled. "Why on earth would you think that?"

"We were supposed to be meeting you," said Watson, glaring. "But someone else turned up. Cheers for that, luv."

"*Something* turned up," corrected Quist.

"I went to the bridge, but you must have left," said Melissa. "I was late, but I…"

"No," broke in Quist. "I don't think there's any further need for pretence. We were met by Sawtelle, or at any rate, the elemental Rakkat that was using his corpse. He attempted to kill us."

The two women glanced at one another, both wondering how Rakkat could have failed. Melissa's phone rang and, glancing at the caller's identity, she grimaced and declined to answer.

"I hope you don't mind?" Quist held up a cigarette and lit it. "Whoever sacrificed those four girls had nocturnal access to the altar in the exhibition. They also appropriated the Moon Crown along with possession amulets. I originally suspected Sawtelle, especially after you insisted upon pointing a finger at him. His death tends to rule him out and the list of suspects we're left with is rather short."

"Are you serious?" Tamzin shook her head. "Why do you think *we* would want to harm you?"

"We were searching for the temples and I presume you viewed us as a threat to your project. It transpires I was correct about the location of *one* of those temples; as you evidently know, it lies beneath the museum. I deduce the Sussamma Ritual there was successful and you located the lost temple where Aquila is entombed. The month is March, this is the final night of the full moon and, if you possess the Oushane Blade, I presume you intend to use it in the Oushane Sacrament rite this evening."

"This is ridiculous," laughed Melissa.

"Wait a moment…" Watson frowned. "Two of them, Guv? Didn't you say there should be three?"

"We'll make a detective of you yet," said Quist. "For it to succeed, the Sussamma Ritual requires three adepts. A third person is involved in this and it isn't Edwin Sawtelle. Presumably it's whoever callously murdered Miles Roundhay, the person you immediately contacted after I told you we were heading to Wetherby."

"I see." Melissa smiled tightly. Her phone rang again and she switched it off irately. "This explains why I always feel sexually excited when you're around. I assume you're an adept yourself and it's some sort of love enchantment?"

"I'm no occultist," said the detective. "But I am somewhat knowledgeable in that particular field."

"As for love enchantments…" added Watson. "You're definitely *barking* up the wrong tree there, sweetheart."

"You implicated Sawtelle and his *imaginary* friends," said Quist. "You told us of his non-existent interest in the dark arts, but it's obvious now that he had nothing to do with this. If we suspected him and his fictional associates, we wouldn't be looking at you and Miss Rogers here. Miss Rogers, with her long hair and large spectacles, who was seen by Kyle Tarot driving the van near Rowntree Park."

"Not looking at us?" Tamzin laughed tartly. "Oh, I don't know. Your assistant was looking at us quite a bit."

"I liked you." Watson gave a sarcastic smile. "But I've kind of gone off you now. I've had girls send me shitty texts, but none have ever sent me anything like Rakkat."

"You amaze me," snapped Melissa. "Why the hell are you concerning yourself with this? I know it isn't some case you're working on as a private detective, so *why?*"

"Innocent people are dying." Quist shrugged. "Think of us as concerned citizens."

"Well, it's a fascinating story," said the doctor. "But here's a more plausible one that will make more sense to the police. If Edwin tried to harm you, he's obviously had some sort of breakdown. Any other explanation and you'd be considered insane."

"The problem is…" Quist drew on his cigarette. "I arranged for Inspector Bradstreet to be with us on Lendal Bridge. I wanted her to hear what you had to tell us. Rakkat attacked her too and she recognised the creature as the man she'd had in custody."

"She felt that weird cold," added Watson. "She saw the eyes change colour when it died."

"You *destroyed* Rakkat?" stammered Tamzin. "The Priestess will be furious about…"

"That's enough," said the doctor. "Don't say anything."

"I'll tell you what I've deduced," said Quist. "You two and a third adept intend to sacrifice someone with the Oushane Blade, the third adept being the *Priestess* you just mentioned. Drawing your own blood during the Oushane Sacrament would bestow eternal life, but at a terrible price; you'd no longer be human, but shapeshifting wolf creatures. The rite I'm speaking of will need to take place this evening, the third night of the March full moon."

"Incredible." Melissa swallowed dryly. "Black magic, eternal life and werewolves? This is the twenty-first century."

"Indeed," agreed Quist. "Unfortunately, if you're a competent practitioner, the dark arts work just the same now as they did in the time of Aquila. The problem is, I don't know about the woman in charge, but I sense you two would be incapable of managing the supernatural transition. You'd be out of control and far too dangerous as shapeshifters. I can't allow it to happen."

Melissa's eyes blazed. "You've no idea *what* I'm capable of. And what the fuck makes you think *I'm* not the one in charge of this?"

"Angry retorts like that." The detective smiled thinly. "Whoever the main adept is, I'm sure she'll be more professional."

"Yeah," said Watson. "The fact that you called her *the*

211

Priestess is a bit of a giveaway too."

Quist nodded. "As I said, the Oushane Sacrament has to be performed tonight, or you'll need to wait an entire year. A human sacrifice is needed, but it occurs to me, that if Watson and I are here, it won't be possible. Not with us shadowing you."

"You're very righteous, aren't you?" The doctor shook her head, seething. "I suppose that's to be commended in this day and age, but let me tell you what *I've* deduced. It sounds like these occultists have completed their objective and are tying up loose ends. From what you say, they must have viewed *you* as two of these."

"Along with the guy you shot in Wetherby," said Watson.

"How many more loose ends do you think there might be? This psychic Kyle Tarot and his daughter, for example. I saw her with you at the museum yesterday."

Quist stiffened and glanced at his assistant.

"She looked like a nice kid," continued Melissa. "Now if Tarot saw things in the park that night, such as a girl with long blonde hair and spectacles, he probably described her to his daughter. What do you suppose these occultists might be doing about that? If they're as calculating and dedicated as you imagine – shooting people and sacrificing women – I'd say Rakkat will have been sent to deal with the problem."

"The last time we saw your pal, he wasn't looking too good," said Watson. "He looked like something from the bottom of a butcher's dustbin."

"There are plenty of host bodies," said Melissa.

"Possibly so," agreed Quist. "But since Rakkat vacated Sawtelle, I doubt you've had the chance to find another."

"And with a child's life at stake, *I* doubt you'll gamble." The doctor smiled. "Okay, no more pretence. We had three hosts ready and the possession rite is short and simple. Mister Tarot and his daughter are about to meet Rakkat, but of course, you could always sit here and take the risk that I'm lying. I'll put the kettle on if you like?"

"You win, Doctor Blake." Quist jumped up angrily. "Don't worry, we'll see ourselves out."

Tamzin watched as Watson slammed the door behind them. "Rakkat failed us," she gasped. "Shit, this is all getting really…"

"Shut up. Everything's fine." Melissa checked her watch. "It's only seven-fifteen and there's plenty of time. We have the final possession amulet and it seems we *do* need our reserve host after all."

"Ryan Farmer? He lives above a shop down the street. I've been supplying him with heroin, as the Priestess ordered, and I can get him here within minutes for more."

"Do it now. Invite him." The doctor lit a cigarette, waiting impatiently as Tamzin phoned. "Tell him to use the rear stairs."

"He's coming." Finishing the call, she shook her head. "This is really scary, Mel. We're cutting out the Priestess and now we have those two breathing down our necks. They might have suspected us before, but now they *know*."

"But they *don't* know we've yet to obtain the knife and they *don't* know where Aquila is buried." Melissa sucked angrily on the cigarette. "I've no idea why they've involved themselves in this, but Quist appears to be a man of principle and luckily he fell for our bluff. That buys us time and we should get two birds with one stone, as it were. *Four* birds, to be exact."

"I'm sorry?"

"Those two definitely have to go, but we also need to be rid of this Kyle Tarot. He saw you dumping the final sacrifice and he could identify you. If the Oushane Sacrament should fail, we can't have anyone knowing what we've done. We've no idea where Tarot is and we don't have the time to find his address…"

"Exactly. With the Priestess out of the picture, we don't have the resources to track him down."

"Which is why I sent Quist to warn him." Going to her bag,

Melissa took out Watson's business card with the smiley face on the reverse. "Not only did we get those two off our backs, but they'll lead Rakkat straight to the psychic. Watson was good enough to give us his card. He handled it and personalised it too, which means Rakkat can use it to home in on him *and* Tarot. I don't know what went wrong at the bridge, but Rakkat won't fail again. "She smiled grimly. "Yes, Tamz, killing people is definitely getting easier."

"I'm still scared," said Tamzin. "I can't believe we're daring to defy the Priestess and do this ourselves."

"That was her ringing just now." The doctor let out a manic laugh. "She obviously wants to know why Edwin is dead and why we used him as a host…"

"Oh my God."

"Try to stay calm, Barbie Doll." Melissa kissed her. "You say Leanne Lloyd is definitely ready for the Oushane Sacrament?"

"Like I told you, she's expecting me to take her to a party."

"Ring and tell her to be ready. We'll be picking her up for this *party* very shortly."

The downstairs door buzzer rang and Tamzin spoke briefly to Farmer on the intercom before pressing the button to admit him.

"Less than three minutes." Melissa glanced at the time. "Oh, he's eager, but I suppose addicts usually are."

Farmer rapped on the apartment door and Tamzin let him in. The skeletal man looked to be in his early twenties and wore an anorak over a grubby T shirt and jeans. His matted hair and body odour suggested he wasn't a huge fan of showering.

"Nice," he said, glancing about and trembling. "Better than that flat of mine." He peered warily at Melissa, then noticed Tamzin was busy with her phone. "Hey, who are you and who's she ringing?"

"Relax, Ryan. I'm Mel." The doctor headed to the bureau and brought out a small container. "Tamz is only phoning her friend Leanne about a party."

"You mean a party *here*? Er, okay. Tamzin says you have some new gear? Some really good gear?" Farmer scratched nervously at his head. "Listen, I'm short on cash, but tomorrow I can…"

"Don't worry." Melissa took a packet of white powder, a spoon and a hypodermic from the box. "We can work something out later. I've tried this and, believe me, you'll remember *this* gear for the rest of your life."

"Cool." He sat on the couch, his eyes moving from the syringe to Melissa's shapely legs. "Hey, I love black chicks. Maybe I could pay you some other way?"

"Maybe." Laughing, she watched the grinning junkie tug off his anorak and roll up his sleeve. "That's an… *attractive* idea."

Finishing her phone call, Tamzin smiled to see Farmer boil the doctored heroin on the spoon and fill the syringe with the lethal concoction.

"As soon as we've completed the possession rite we need to pack our passports and other stuff," murmured Melissa. "I've no doubt the Priestess will be calling here later, but she won't find us. We won't be coming back."

"That detective Bradstreet could prove dangerous," whispered Tamzin, as Farmer injected himself. "She wasn't supposed to be there with Quist and Watson. She may now accept the reality of the Badda possession rite and work out that we're involved with…"

The drug addict collapsed sideways on the couch, the syringe falling from his dead arm and clattering on the polished floor.

"We need to hurry." Melissa rushed to the bureau to take out a knife and the last of the stolen possession amulets. "Yes, according to Quist, Bradstreet recognised Rakkat when she met Sawtelle on the bridge. It might be best if she meets him again to make *sure* she recognises him."

* * * *

Watson stood on Stonegate with Quist, veils of mist drifting silently past them like processions of sulky ghosts. It was seven-fifteen and the narrow thoroughfare was busy with crowds heading to the York taverns, all clearly undeterred by the awful weather.

"Mel and Tamzin." The shocked youth scratched his head. "I honestly can't believe it. I kind of had... you know, *romantic* plans, and now we find they're behind all this..."

"Yes, your taste in women is remarkable," said Quist. "Charlotte Lewis turned out to be barely legal and those two are sociopathic killers." Using the illumination of a wine merchant's window, he took out his phone and Kyle Tarot's business card. "As to who is actually *behind all this*, I believe that dubious honour goes to our mysterious third adept, but right now we have more pressing concerns. I have to speak to Tarot."

Gulping, Watson peered apprehensively at the passing people. *These "normal" folk were enjoying a jovial night out, blissfully ignorant of demons and dark supernatural forces. But the terrifying fact was, one of them might not BE normal – any one of this lot could have an elemental inside them and might suddenly attack.*

"Do you believe that Rakkat is back?" he asked. "Have they sent him after Charlotte and her Dad, or did they lie to get rid of us?"

"We can't be certain," snapped Quist, tapping in the number. "But I've no intention of leaving it to chance and Blake and Rogers know that. They sent Rakkat to kill us because of our involvement and Charlotte's father has made himself a similar target. They believe he can identify Tamzin Rogers as the driver of that van."

Watson fell silent as the detective connected with Tarot.

"Hello there." Quist gave a thankful sigh. "It's Bernard Quist. Where are you? I see, and where exactly is that? Alright, it's very important that you stay there. Do *not* go outside. Watson and I are coming to meet you right now. No, I'll explain when we arrive."

"Sounds like he's still in one piece." The teenager followed as his boss set off south along Stonegate. "So where is he?"

"With his daughter in a restaurant," said Quist, quickening his stride over the ancient cobbles. "The Taj Mahal on Coney Street."

"Is that an Indian?"

"Is that a genuine question?" Quist's mobile rang and, seeing the name on the screen, he answered. "Hello again, Inspector. How's Constable Mitchell? On the bridge he was…"

"He's okay," said Katie, her voice tense. "Well, apart from a broken nose. The thing is, uniform searched the route we ran along from the bridge and two bodies were found in the park. Those youths we passed at the gate. That *thing* must have killed them."

"I'm sure it did," agreed Quist. "How terrible."

"I'm here at the scene and I know what you said about the ritual tonight, but these murders change everything. This has become deadly serious and you need to come in right now to make statements. We have to speak first to decide what you'll say about that Rakkat creature."

"Yes that *is* serious." Quist hurried by Coffee Yard and Ye Olde Starre Inne. "But not as serious as the situation I'm currently facing. I'm afraid the Rakkat elemental has been, for lack of a better word, *reactivated* and there's a good chance Kyle Tarot and his daughter are in grave danger."

"How do you know?" gasped Katie, anxiously. "No, don't waste time explaining. Where are they? We can protect them."

"If I'm correct, I fear police protection would lead to several dead officers." Quist sighed. "No, I'm afraid I need to deal with this myself. I'll be in touch very soon."

"Wait a minute," hissed Katie. "You can't just…"

"Bye for now, Inspector." Quist ended the call and broke into a jogging pace, his open overcoat flapping.

"I overheard most of that," said Watson, running beside him. "Our lady cop Bradders didn't sound happy. I've got to tell you, I'm not very happy *myself* about the idea of meeting Rakkat again."

217

"I fully appreciate that," said Quist. "Believe me, I wouldn't hold it against you if you were to back out of this, but I'll probably require your assistance. If not at the restaurant, then later in locating those women and their temple."

"If that thing *does* show up, can you handle it?"

"Never underestimate the element of surprise." The detective smiled thinly. "I know what Rakkat is, but he has no idea about me."

"Okay, count me in, Guv." The teenaged grinned nervously. "But if you don't mind, I'll be standing behind you if it appears. Hey, talking of temples, who do you suppose they'll use for this sacrifice thing with the wolf knife? Another sex worker?"

"I don't know." Quist headed for St. Helen's Square at the end of Stonegate. "This is all happening so fast and we don't have the luxury of being able to stop and think. It gives those women back there quite an advantage. I now regret leaving the car; this is going to take a while on foot."

"What's this?" Watson noticed him removing his wristwatch and ring. "You're thinking of changing? Er, that's a bit risky, isn't it?"

"Risky if I *don't*," said Quist, bitterly. He slipped them into a pocket. "If we *do* meet Rakkat, I'll have surprise on my side, but I very much doubt I can deal with the creature in human form."

* * * *

Chapter 28

Coney Street lies between Lendal and Spurriergate in the city centre. Narrow and cobbled, like the majority of the streets in York, this meandering thoroughfare runs parallel with the Ouse, the establishments on its western side – including the Taj Mahal – backing onto the river via a jumble of alleys and snickleways. Quist and Watson found the Indian restaurant halfway along on their right. Not quite so grand as its marble namesake in Agra, the three-storey building boasted a small rear car park, two brightly-lit front windows and a glass door set into a corniced alcove.

Shrugging off his overcoat as he entered and draping it over an arm, Quist saw the place was busy, the room filled with lively chatter, sitar music and the mouth-watering aroma of hot spices. Watson breathed a sigh of relief to see Charlotte seated with her father at one of the furthest tables by a small bar area.

"What's going on?" Kyle smiled guardedly as the two men joined them. "You were a bit weird on the phone and you sounded like…"

"You're both okay," said Watson, sitting beside Charlotte, snapping off half her poppadum and crunching it. "That's great."

"Meaning what?" The girl frowned, her Goth make-up giving her the look of a puzzled panda. "Why *wouldn't* we be okay?"

"Good question." Kyle scowled as the youth reassuringly squeezed his daughter's hand. "You said not to go outside. What was that about and what's so urgent that you had to come straight here?"

Quist looked around to check for security cameras. Two were fixed at ceiling height in the room corners, meaning he couldn't do anything *unusual* in here. "I'm sorry about this," he said. "I really wish there was an easier way to say it, but you're both in danger. Someone wishes you harm and I believe they'll be coming for you tonight."

"Who'd want to hurt *us*?" demanded Charlotte.

"You're not going to like this." Watson lowered his voice and turned to Kyle. "The people you saw dumping that body in the park *know* you saw them and they're not too happy about it. They're sending someone to stop you talking. *Permanently* stop you."

"But I'm *not* talking about it," whispered Kyle, glancing at the surrounding tables. "We've been through all that and I told you it was over. I've given up the idea of profiting from the…"

"Listen, mate, I've met the guy they're sending." Crunching the poppadum, Watson shook his head. "Not that you can really call him a *guy*. I honestly don't think he'll be too bothered about you claiming it's over."

"The guy *who* are sending?" quizzed Charlotte. "I don't understand how you know…"

The hairs on the back of Quist's neck rose as the atmosphere turned icy. Twisting, he spotted a grubby young man approaching between the diners, stick-thin with matted hair. He saw the green eyes and instantly jumped up.

"Hello there," growled the newcomer, arriving at their table and grinning. "Well, isn't this nice and cosy? I ran pretty fast to get here and it gave me an appetite." He leered at Charlotte. "Fortunately this sweet child looks delicious."

"*Fuck!*" mouthed Watson, dropping his crispy snack and looking around for the best direction to run.

Shuddering at the unnatural cold, Kyle stared at Ryan Farmer's saliva-soaked T shirt, the grisly symbol carved into his wrist, and his eyes – his gleaming green eyes. An unexpected wave of intense fear frosted his back with gooseflesh.

"What the hell?" he said. "Who *are* you?

"Well, folk used to call me Ryan, but I go by a different name now." The man turned to Quist. "I'm guessing *you* know which name? We had such a lovely time earlier tonight."

The detective nodded slightly. He saw the Badda possession amulet hanging from Rakkat's neck and he was now all too familiar with this horrific deep voice.

"Dad, his eyes…" whimpered Charlotte. Shivering in the pocket of supernatural cold, she moving closer to Kyle. "His eyes are *glowing.*"

"Ooh, do you like them, sweet child? You'll see them up close when I eat your face." Drooling through clenched teeth, Rakkat tossed Watson's business card onto the tablecloth. "My friends would like to thank you for that. It led me straight here."

"Table for one?" enquired a smiling waiter appearing by Rakkat's side. "Or will you be joining these people?"

"No." Grabbing the Indian by his collar and belt, the creature lifted him effortlessly above its head. "But you can join *those* people."

Rakkat launched the waiter across the room like a rag doll, chuckling gleefully as he crashed down in the middle of a large table surrounded by a lively birthday party. Watson froze in horror and, dragging him from his seat, Quist positioned himself between his friends and the elemental. Kicking over their chairs, Kyle and Charlotte sprang to their feet.

"Get out," shouted the detective, snatching up his assistant's business card. "Everyone get out of here *now.*"

The mass exodus of terrified diners and waiters pouring through the front door suggested he'd wasted his breath.

"You're leaving?" laughed Rakkat, gazing at Charlotte. "I don't think so. No, we're going to play." Adopting an Asian accent, he began to sing. "*On the road to Mandalay, where the flyin' fishes play…*"

Realising the elemental was blocking the exit route, Quist pushed his terrified companions past the bar to the rear of the room. "That way," he snapped. "Through there."

Watson slammed open a pair of swing doors and ran with

Kyle and Charlotte into a kitchen area of white tiles and steel appliances. Some of the waiters had already bolted out this way in fright, but two confused cooks still remained by their bubbling pans at a central work island, staring open-mouthed at the trio.

"Fire," yelled Quist, rushing in behind his assistant. "Some maniac has set the place on fire. Go out through the back door. Get out now."

Shoving the father and daughter in front, Watson followed the panicking Indians onto the car park, but Quist halted by the stoves. It was unlikely that cameras were fitted in the kitchen, but he quickly checked, then turned to the swing doors as Rakkat burst through.

"You waited for me?" snarled the elemental. "You managed to escape earlier, but I'm here for you again and you're making it so easy." It began to circle the central workstation of boiling pans. "*On the road to Mandalay, where the…*"

"The restaurant is Indian," pointed out Quist, tossing his coat onto a table and moving slowly around the island to keep Rakkat on the opposite side. "Mandalay is in Myanmar, which means your song is as inappropriate as that ludicrous Asian accent. To be truthful, I expected a timeless entity to be more knowledgeable."

"You're not frightened. Why aren't you frightened?" Raising a suspicious eyebrow, Rakkat began a different song, changing the lyrics to include more applicable words. "*I see a Badda moon rising. I see trouble on the way*. Trouble for *you*, my dead friend, and those three out there."

"I couldn't face you the last time." Quist kicked off his shoes. "I had a police witness."

"Face me?" grunted Rakkat, spilling drool. "What's that supposed to mean? Do you actually think you can stop me?"

Shrugging off his jacket, the detective dropped onto all-fours behind the island. The atmosphere was already arctic around the elemental, but the temperature fell further as Quist's expanding furry body tore apart his shirt and trousers.

"Oh, I *see*." Rakkat giggled as the black wolf rose into view on its hind legs. "I *knew* you were different. Yeah, I could feel you were my kind of guy." Springing onto the central work station, he began singing the old Duran Duran hit. "*I'm on the hunt, I'm after you. Mouth is alive with juices like wine, and I'm hungry like the wolf…*"

Snatching a pan of fat from the stove, Quist hurled the boiling contents into Rakkat's face. His sizzling features bloated into a mass of blisters, reminiscent of a scarlet soufflé rising in an oven.

"You're mine," screeched the furious creature, leaping onto the wolf. "You ruined my song and I'm going to eat your lungs."

Quist had anticipated supernatural strength, but after seeing the dead addict's frail body, he was still astonished to feel such brute force. He fended off the frenzied clawing and chomping teeth, twisting to slam the writhing Rakkat onto the sharp corner of an industrial dishwasher. The sickening internal crunch told him several ribs had just smashed.

"Ooh, that did some damage," hissed the elemental, sprawling on top of the appliance. Undaunted, it lashed out, gouging fingers deep into the wolf's furry torso. "And so did *that*."

Lupine blood spurted, turning to crimson dust as it left Quist's body. Wincing in agony, he slid Rakkat along the dishwasher until his head cleared the edge, then pushed down hard on his chin. The creature's neck broke with a loud and reassuring snap.

"This is over," panted the wolf.

He stepped back nursing his stomach wound and saw the grinning elemental was still moving. Grabbing a handy meat cleaver, he brought it down hard to slice Rakkat's head clean off.

"Correction," he muttered, as the green eyes faded and the Badda amulet fell tinkling to the floor. "*Now* it's over."

Groaning and bending double, the wolf shapeshifted back into the form of a naked man. The bite marks and minor scratches had vanished and, gingerly checking, he found the deep claw gashes on his abdomen had virtually healed. Quist grabbed the amulet and swiftly pulled on his shoes, jacket and overcoat, buttoning the latter to conceal his nakedness. He headed for the door, then thinking quickly, paused to scoop a handful of flour from an open bag and smear it over his face before leaving.

Watson stood trembling with Kyle and Charlotte in the foggy rear car park. "What in the…" The teenager grinned nervously to see his white-faced boss appear through the fire exit. "You look like a frigging ghost. Is it safe, Guv?"

Five scared-looking Indians huddled near the door, peering aghast at his bizarre features.

"What the fuck just happened?" demanded one. "Where's the lunatic who threw Ramesh across the room? We heard the banging and smashing and…"

"Fortunately you didn't enter," said Quist, his keen hearing picking up the sound of approaching sirens. "It's safe to go back inside now, but I'm afraid it's a bit of a mess."

"Are you okay?" asked Watson.

"Yes." The detective dragged him to a narrow snickleway between the buildings. "This way, you three. Come on, we definitely don't want to be here when the authorities arrive."

"Has that thing gone?" stammered Kyle, hurrying through the mist with Charlotte. "Watson's been telling us about this, but it's too insane for words. It turned freezing cold and its eyes were glowing green because…"

"One moment." Pausing in the darkness of the alleyway, Quist pulled out his phone and rang Lestrade. "This won't take long."

"What happened in there?" Charlotte noticed his naked legs beneath the long leather coat. "Where are your trousers?"

"We fought and that thing tore off my clothes." The detective turned away for privacy as Lestrade answered. "Gareth, I need you to

224

do something urgently…"

Kyle peered incredulously at Watson. "Ripped his clothes off? Is he joking?"

The teenager shrugged. "Evidently not."

Finishing the brief call, Quist continued down the foggy alley, wiping the flour from his face with an handkerchief.

"Yes, Mister Tarot," he said. "As you've pointed out, this is difficult to accept, but that creature back there was an elemental entity using a reanimated human corpse."

"It sounds batshit-crazy, but it's true," confirmed Watson. "That's the second time tonight we've met that green-eyed bastard and both times he tried to kill us."

"We know too much about the people who sent it," explained Quist. "But you were also targets. The occultists behind those recent murders are aware that you saw one of them in Rowntree Park and they believe you can identify her. They decided to get rid of you and the elemental used Watson's business card to find us." He turned to his assistant. "Rakkat was able to home in on something you'd handled. I grabbed the card to prevent the police from finding it."

"Incredible." The youth shook his head. "So *we* were the ones who led it there?"

"Yes, Rakkat used some sort of psychometry." The detective gave Kyle a derisive smile. "As a *clairvoyant*, you'll doubtless be aware of this. Psychics handle personal items and are able to locate the owner."

"Lunatics sent a monster after us?" whimpered Charlotte, glancing over her shoulder into the fog. "What if it comes back?"

"It won't," said Quist. "Before this night is over I intend to stop the people responsible." He took out the Badda amulet and held it up. "And without *this*, they can't invoke their creature."

"That's like the one Sawtelle wore." Watson nodded. "I wonder how many they have?"

The snickleway opened into another small car park by the mist-shrouded Ouse. Quist headed for the safety handrail by the water and examined the ancient medallion.

"There can't be many," he said. "These are rare amulets brought here from the British Museum." Smiling grimly, he flung it into the fog and heard it splash down in the swirling black river. "The police have two as evidence and *that* particular one certainly won't be used again. Come on. This way."

Quist led them through a further maze of snickleways before finally emerging on the busy thoroughfare of Spurriergate. Crowds of revellers strolled past, but their interest in the flashing blue lights on Coney Street, way off to the left, told him the police had arrived at the Taj Mahal.

"An elemental entity?" Kyle hugged his daughter tightly. "It said it was going to eat Charlie's face and… I'm sorry, but I just can't get my head around this."

"Listen to me." The detective turned to him. "You never visited that restaurant tonight. To protect everyone, I had to destroy the corpse used by the creature, but the police will naturally treat the dead body as a murder. You don't want to be a part of that."

"Er, no." Swallowing dryly, Kyle nodded. "Definitely not."

"Later I'll explain everything fully," said Quist. "But we don't have the time right now. You need to take a taxi home and, for the moment, forget about everything that happened."

Charlotte laughed. "Oh, yeah, forgetting about that *thing* will be easy. So what about you two? What are you going to do?"

"The people who sent the elemental are performing a sacrifice ritual tonight." Taking his watch from his coat pocket, Quist fastened it around his wrist and checked the time. "They wanted us dead because they believe we might upset their plans, and they're right. We *will* upset them. We have to go right now and hopefully deal with this. Please take care."

"Thank you for what you did," said Charlotte, cuddling her father. "Good luck."

"You'll be fine now." Watson winked reassuringly as he followed Quist. "Who knows? Maybe we'll still have that drink together."

"Yeah," drawled Kyle. "Like *maybe* when she's eighteen."

The two men headed away from the police lights towards High Ousegate.

"So it's back to the car?" The youth glanced down at his boss's bare legs. "Hey, what about your clothes, Guv?"

"Not to worry," said Quist. "I always keep spare sets of attire in the car boot for such occasions."

* * * *

The Esplanade car park lies on the river in the shadow of the Leeman Road mail depot. It was eight o'clock and the tarmac was filled with vehicles, but fortunately empty of people. Watson sat in his boss's blue Ford, gazing politely through the window as Quist awkwardly pulled on his spare clothes behind the steering wheel.

"I can't believe Mel and Tamzin sent that thing after us again," said the teenager. "They ordered it to kill Charlotte too. Talk about crazy, cold-hearted bitches."

Quist nodded. "Doctor Blake seemed deranged when we spoke to her at the apartment. She's clearly an accomplished liar and actress, but I'm surprised I didn't pick up on her mental state during our earlier conversations. I must be slipping in my old age."

"Yeah, you're over two-hundred, but you weren't slipping when you destroyed Rakkat. Top marks there, Guv." Watson's smile darkened. "But the cops will have found the host body and they'll be looking for a murderer. The restaurant staff could identify you."

"I doubt it." The detective buttoned his shirt. "Witnesses often provide abysmal descriptions, and the only thing those gentlemen will recall is that the individual who left the kitchen resembled a white-faced Pierrot clown."

"Ah, *that's* why you covered your face in flour."

"Well, naturally." Quist paused in scrambling into his jacket to give an incredulous glance. "Did you assume I'd done that as some sort of bizarre fashion statement? Give people an obvious focus during a fleeting meet – a large mole, an eye patch, or a white face – and they'll remember that whilst forgetting subtler details. No, their security recordings are my only concern, but I won't worry *too* much until I hear from Lestrade."

"You rang him. Was that about the cameras?"

"Yes, CCTV recordings used to be stored on video tape, but through our professional dealings with Gareth, I've learnt that most companies now use dedicated hard drives. Smaller concerns, however, often link their cameras directly to the business computer. I asked Gareth if he could hack into the Taj Mahal and check."

"And if recordings of us are on the restaurant computer…"

"Hopefully he can erase them." Illuminated by the vehicle courtesy light, Quist took Miles Roundhay's street map of York from the glove compartment and unfolded it across the dashboard. "Right now we have more important things to concern us."

"Mel, Tamzin, and their loony sacrifice rite."

"Exactly. By now, I'm sure the main Badda temple will have been unearthed and that's where they'll perform this ritual tonight." Quist pointed to the Reverend's pencil crosses. "All of these possible sites lay to the west of the Roman fortress. Roundhay researched this for years and one will almost certainly be the correct location."

"Or not," said Watson, unhelpfully. "So what are we supposed to do? Visit each in turn?"

"We may have to, but there could be a way to speed this up." Lighting a cigarette, the detective took out his phone and rang Lestrade. "Hello, Gareth, how did it go with the Taj Mahal? Ah, that's splendid news. I honestly can't thank you enough."

"He got into their computer?" quizzed Watson, excitedly holding up a thumb. "He wiped the video recording?"

Quist nodded. "Now I have one more task for you. I know you can access the DVLA computer and I wonder if you could find any vehicles registered to either Melissa Blake or Tamzin Rogers? Both women reside in London."

"Well," laughed Lestrade. "I'm definitely earning my no-questions-asked payments *this* week." Several seconds of silence passed, silence save for the clicking of a keyboard. "Okay, here we go. There's nothing for Tamzin Rogers, but I've found two car owners named Melissa Blake."

"Do you have the driving license photographs onscreen? I'm interested in a black girl, attractive and around thirty years of age."

"You make it sound like I'm running an escort agency. Yeah, she's right here and she owns a silver-grey Ford Mondeo. I'll text you the registration."

"Very good," said Quist. "Once again, a huge thank you for your assistance with the restaurant."

"Mel's car?" Watson waited until the detective ended the call and checked his text. "What's that all about?"

"Those women won't be travelling to and from Aquila's temple on foot," said Quist. "They need a car and, now that we know *which* car, we can watch out for it."

"Ah, right." Watson nodded. "So we call at each of the Rev's possible sites and, if we see the Mondeo parked up, we'll know we're at the right one."

"Yes, but I wonder..." Drawing thoughtfully on his cigarette and staring at the map, Quist gestured to a pencil mark on a field near Westminster Road. "Look at this. One of the Reverend's possible sites is here to the rear of St Peter's School – Wolf Hill. Remember what I said about old place names being relevant in this type of search? Mmh, perhaps there's something even *more* relevant here."

"Hey, Charlotte's Dad mentioned this school on his ghost walk," said Watson. "He came out with some shit about a ghost werewolf being seen around the place."

"Exactly." Closing his eyes, Quist massaged his large nose. "Oh, of *course*. Roundhay was clearly aware of this ghost story and, as with all legends, he factored it into his research. If Aquila was a lycanthrope and the Romans entombed him alive, then the Prefect isn't strictly *dead*. Those spectral wolf sightings could be his latent energy exuding from the tomb and manifesting upon the ether."

"Sorry for sounding thick..." Watson let out a dry laugh. "But what the hell does *that* mean?"

"It means this particular ghost story could be genuine." Quist nodded slowly. "Tarot said this ghostly wolf was only seen on the full moon and, as you know, that's when the energy would be at its strongest. Over the years, sensitive people with the right abilities have been seeing Aquila's projected *spirit form*, for lack of better words, like some faded tape recording."

"So this could be it?" Watson tapped the map. "St. Peter's School could be the place?"

Quist started the car. "There's only one way to find out."

"Yeah, and the good news is we only have two crazy girls to worry about." Grinning, Watson rubbed his hands together. "Rakkat's gone, so we know we're not going to meet anything as scary as *him*."

* * * *

Chapter 29

Like the beautiful hybrid offspring of a castle and a cathedral, the ornate frontage of St Peter's School stands on the A19 to the west of York. A splendid mass of stained glass and Gothic towers, this is the world's fourth oldest school and the campus of ancient buildings and playing fields stretches from this main thoroughfare to the banks of the Ouse. Founded in 627, the pupils here have included Guy Fawkes and John Wright, infamous conspirators in the Gunpowder Plot, and on a brighter note – literally a brighter note – John Barry, the composer of many James Bond movie soundtracks.

The freezing fog had thickened and shrouded the school grounds as Melissa and Tamzin walked quickly along a shrubbery hedge that skirted the cricket pitch. Both women wore thick parka coats and Tamzin carried a heavy canvas tool bag.

"We couldn't have wished for better weather," murmured Melissa, clicking on a torch. "No one will see our lights."

This was the doctor's second nocturnal visit to these playing fields. The first had been on Monday after completing the Sussamma Ritual. The Moon Crown had been infused with life energy, the Priestess had placed it upon her head, and it had led the way straight here like some bizarre magical satnav.

"Wolf Hill," said Melissa, excitedly approaching an overgrown mound at the end of the hedgerow. "I remember this looked like a natural land formation, but our builder friend has certainly changed that."

Jon Oldacre, the workman hired by the Priestess, had called here the previous evening with Tamzin, stealthily approaching along the suburban Westminster Road with a mechanical digger in the rear of his van. Under the cover of darkness, the crooked labourer had secured a way into the grounds by cropping the gate padlock and his vehicle tracks now surrounded the brambly knoll. Large piles of raw earth were heaped to one side where Oldacre had excavated the small hillock and exposed the entrance to the buried temple. No buildings overlooked this area and, with Mid Spring Break ensuring the school was closed for a fortnight, no one would discover the illegal work for several days. Fortunately, for the two women, British schools seem to have official holidays every five to six weeks.

Melissa's torch beam moved down an earthen slope and over the great slab of rock that had sealed this dark place of worship for the past two-thousand years. The open doorway yawned invitingly.

"Excellent," she whispered. "Yes, we knew the temple would be aligned north with the access at this southern end, just like the Moroccan site. You say you didn't go inside?"

"No." Tamzin shook her head. "The Priestess said to wait until tonight when the three of us would enter together. As soon as Oldacre moved the slab, I paid him and we left, as she ordered. He has no idea what this is and he didn't ask questions."

"Well the plan has changed," laughed the doctor, making her way down the incline. "Aquila's temple, buried since the Roman occupation – this is incredible. Miles Roundhay was a clever man. He researched this for years and came up with seven possible locations. He was aware that Wolf Hill was a likely contender, but he couldn't know for sure."

"But our ritual confirmed it and identified the doorway." Tamzin followed her, looking around fearfully. "What if the Priestess should turn up? She'll realise what we're doing and…"

"She *won't* turn up," snapped Melissa. "It's a little after eight and she's busy until ten. Now forget about her and get your mind on this. We find the knife, we perform the sacrifice ritual and we vanish."

With her torch lighting the way, the doctor moved inside the pitch-black opening and wrinkled her nose. Tamzin gagged slightly and covered her mouth. The blast of stale gas had been unspeakable as the digger rolled the stone door aside last night, but this had now dissipated, to be replaced with a more sinister stench. This makeshift tomb had remained airtight, preventing damp, and the smell was difficult to identify. It was a musty stink that, for some reason, reminded Tamzin of evil and death. Shuddering and opening her bag, she took out three electric hurricane lamps and switched them on to light the interior.

"Amazing." Melissa's eyes widened in wonder to see how much this temple resembled the museum exhibit she was so familiar with. She kissed Tamzin. "Oh, yes, Barbie Doll, this is magnificent."

The girls trembled uncontrollably, but it had little to do with the intense cold and alarming smell. Although she was an occultist, first and foremost Melissa Blake was a Doctor of Archaeology and this was literally a dream come true. The women had just entered an intact Roman temple to Badda Oushane, the first people to set foot inside for over two millennia. This was as unbelievable and astounding as Carter and Carnarvon entering the tomb of Tutankhamun, or Donald Trump entering the White House.

"A pristine Badda temple," whispered Tamzin. "This will be perfect for the Oushane Sacrament."

"Yes, as soon as we find the blade, we'll bring the junkie in," said Melissa, grinning. "It's a shame we're leaving for Morocco tonight. This is the archaeological find of the century and, in another life, we'd be on the cover of every historical journal. Still, I'd say we can look forward to something far better."

The subterranean chamber was thirty feet in length by fifteen wide, with a marble-flagged floor, eight marble columns supporting an arched brick ceiling and intricate Badda carvings and inscriptions decorating the painted walls. A fearsome wolf statue of Badda Oushane stood behind a large altar of white limestone, with upright iron incense burners and two bricked-up doorways on either side. The one to the left bore a plaster plaque with Latin writing.

"These would have been the chambers containing the temple

lamps and ritual paraphernalia," said Melissa, her breath clouding as she walked to the plaque. Taking the Moon Tiara from her parka, she placed the iron crown on her head. "But they've been sealed."

"Sealed by the Emperor Hadrian himself," whispered Tamzin, reverently. "His men were the last to touch them."

"This is it, Tamz." Melissa ran a hand over the inscription. "Aquila is entombed inside here. The crown is burning with heat."

"Yes." Tamzin translated the plaque and nodded. "It reads: *The Prefect Aquila. Imprisoned here for eternity for crimes against Rome. SPQR.*"

"Noble intentions, I'm sure," said the doctor, taking a small sledgehammer from the tool bag and passing it to Tamzin. "But I'm afraid *eternity* ends tonight."

The brickwork was unsophisticated, but it had remained intact for two-thousand years. Taking a deep breath, Tamzin hefted the tool and slammed it into the rudimentary wall several times before it finally gave way and crumbled inwards. A crude stone coffin bound by three locked iron bands lay on the tiled floor inside, with glistening Badda artefacts surrounding it in untidy piles.

"The Priestess Hanka must be walled up on the other side," gasped Tamzin. "Wow, look how this gold has just been tossed in there. Hadrian and his men didn't care about these treasures. Their superstitions led them to believe they were cursed."

"Forget the gold." Melissa coughed on the mortar dust as she hastily sifted through the relics. "The dagger isn't here. If the Romans didn't take any of this, they wouldn't have taken the Oushane Blade either. That means it could be with Hanka."

Hurrying to the opposite side chamber, Tamzin swung her hammer again, eventually smashing down the wall that sealed it.

"Nothing," spat Melissa, angrily gazing at the identical stone coffin inside. She walked back to Aquila's chamber. "It looks like all the Badda artefacts were entombed here with the Prefect. That means the blade is almost certainly inside the sarcophagus."

"But we can't *open* this thing," hissed Tamzin. "He's still alive in there and we've no idea what he'll do."

"After all this time, he'll be in a suspended state." Melissa stared warily at the stone coffin for several seconds. "No, we've come too far and we've pretty much burnt our bridges. We *have* to do this."

"I don't like it," whimpered Tamzin. "This was never part of the plan."

"I'm not exactly over the moon either." The doctor grinned uneasily and gave her a swift kiss. "Listen to me, Tamz – we open it quickly, we grab the knife and we leave."

"What about the sacrifice ritual?"

"I don't know," admitted Melissa, irately. "No, we can't perform it here. We'll have to use one of the other temples."

"But after we're gone, Aquila will be free."

"And we'll be in North Africa and it won't be our problem. Come on, let's make this fast."

Swallowing nervously, Tamzin examined the iron restraining bands around the coffin, then brought her hammer down hard on one of the antiquated locks. It snapped off easily enough and she smashed the other two, stepping back as the doctor peeled away the hinged metal.

"Okay, here we go," murmured Melissa, gesturing to the sarcophagus cover. "I'll take this side and you push at that end."

The tombstone-like lid was unbelievably heavy, but they laboured together to slowly thrust it aside. A gust of foul gas filled the chamber as it toppled and slammed to the ground upside-down. Melissa grimaced to see scratchings on the inner surface where Aquila had futilely clawed in lupine form before the air eventually expired.

"My God." Tamzin looked inside, her jaw falling. "Oh, my God!"

The women had expected to see a corpse, but not one so

perfectly preserved. Apart from the absolute stillness and absence of respiration, the large man could have been sleeping. The muscular arms and legs were naked, but polished Roman armour encased his torso and shoulders – lorica segmentata style, pieced together in broad iron strips to allow full movement. The woollen tunic beneath this had long since turned to dust, but Aquila still retained his leather military skirt and he wore a metal galea helmet with protective hinged side pieces. The face beneath the peak was unpleasant and both recognised the jutting square jaw and cruel, twisted features from the marble bust in the museum. Momentarily mesmerised by the incredible sight, Melissa was jolted into movement by the knife in its jewelled scabbard lying beside the body.

"*Yes*." Snatching it up, the doctor slipped it into her coat pocket. "Right, it's time to go."

"Ladies," purred an eloquent voice behind them. "Are you aware that you're trespassing upon school property?"

"No." Melissa saw Quist and Watson in the temple doorway. "I don't believe this."

"Yeah, we're alive," said the youth. "Tarot and his daughter are fine too, but you won't be seeing your pal Rakkat again."

"He failed *again*?" stammered Tamzin, emerging from the side chamber. "How is that possible?"

"So you found us," said Melissa, sneeringly. "Oh, well done."

"And you found your missing crown." Watson pointed to the iron band on her head. "Hey, it suits you."

"Well, Doctor Blake, it appears I was wrong." Quist strolled inside with his assistant and gestured to the dust settling upon the demolished wall. "I assumed you'd be performing the Oushane Sacrament, but it seems you've only just opened the tomb to retrieve the dagger." He looked around. "Shouldn't your Priestess be here?"

"*I'm* the Priestess now," snapped Melissa, glaring angrily. "How did you find this place?"

"A little educated guesswork." Quist shrugged. "Now where is that knife? As I told you earlier, I can't allow you to keep it. It's far too dangerous for you people to possess."

"Fuck you," hissed Melissa. "What right have you to…"

Her words ended abruptly as the temperature suddenly plummeted. The women glanced apprehensively at one another, then turned to the sarcophagus behind them, their rapid breath forming clouds. The crackling body inside the stone coffin was swiftly changing, a huge lupine muzzle protruding beneath the helmet and thick black fur covering the bulging arms. The chest armour creaked as the torso expanded, and Tamzin gasped in fear as the creature sucked in air and red eyes snapped open. She stumbled backwards with Melissa, both mesmerised by the chilling sight of Aquila slowly clambering from his prison.

"Shit," whispered Watson.

With the elemental out of the picture, he'd assumed he wouldn't meet anything else as scary as Rakkat tonight. He was wrong. He was very wrong.

The teenager let out a terrified moan as the enormous werewolf in Roman armour emerged on its hind legs from the side chamber, its eyes smouldering scarlet and the light from the hurricane lamps glistening on its helmet and bared fangs. Watson had seen Quist's dark alter ego many times and this horrific thing looked to be bigger and far more muscular.

"Well…" muttered the detective. "This isn't good, is it?"

"Aquila," said Melissa, thinking quickly and bowing. "We are here to serve you, but those men are your enemies. They should be killed before they can…"

Ignoring her, the creature twisted furiously, growling in Latin, before lashing out at one of the upright incense burners and snapping the stand in two. Frantic and disorientated, it shouted louder, spinning around and clawing at a marble column, before racing down the central aisle on all fours towards Quist and Watson.

Grabbing his assistant, the detective leapt aside as the snarling creature raced out of the temple and into the fog.

"*What the hell?*" stammered Tamzin, horrified. "What on earth was *wrong* with it?"

"Well, he *has* been locked in there for some time." Melissa smiled tightly. "My best guess is it's driven him mad."

"And you let it out," shouted Quist, angrily. "What in God's name were you thinking?"

"I mentioned earlier how righteous you are," said the doctor, panting with exhilaration. "It seems to me you have a choice. Stay here to search for the knife and perform some sort of citizen's arrest on us…" She mockingly held out her wrists for handcuffs. "Or you could follow that insane monster and hopefully find some way of preventing whatever terrible bloodshed is about to ensue. I wonder which decision you'll make?"

Hesitating, then cursing under his breath, Quist snatched Watson's arm and pulled him out of the temple in pursuit.

"You *do* surprise me," laughed Melissa, taking the jewelled dagger from her pocket. "Goodbye, Mister Quist."

"Yes, goodbye." Gazing at the Oushane Blade, Tamzin trembled with excitement. "And *hello* eternal life."

* * * *

Chapter 30

A metal five-bar gate stood at the eastern end of the suburban Westminster Road leading into the playing fields of St Peter's School. Quist had discovered Melissa Blake's Mondeo on this tree-lined residential street a short time ago and had left his own car next to it.

"Hurry." The gate clattered as Quist vaulted back over. "We need to find that creature before..."

"We're going looking for it?" yelled Watson, following him. "Did you actually *see* that fucking thing?"

"I must admit, it was quite formidable."

"You *could* say that." The teenager ran behind him to the parked vehicles. "It was bigger than you. A monster, built like a brick shithouse in armour, and yet we're going after it? *Wonderful.*"

"Don't be ridiculous," snapped Quist. "I'm sure you can imagine the carnage Aquila is capable of. You know we can't allow him to run free in the city. You also know we're probably the only people capable of stopping him."

"*We?*" Watson let out a staccato laugh. "Yeah, I'm sure I'll be a big help. I suppose I could hold your coat or something. Hey, what's wrong, Guv?"

"Remain quiet for a moment..." Listening intently, Quist strode to the rear of Melissa's car. "Yes, it's coming from here."

The youth had heard nothing, but picked up the faint sound as he reached the Mondeo – a muffled and barely audible groaning. He watched the detective fasten his fingers beneath the boot lid, grip tightly and wrench upwards with lupine strength. The catch broke and the boot gaped wide to reveal a girl lying in the foetus position, her wrists and ankles bound with nylon cable ties. She looked to be in her early twenties and turned her head to smile dreamily up at them.

"Hey, hi there, guys," murmured Leanne Lloyd. "Are we there yet? Is this the party?"

"Bloody hell," gasped Watson. "I don't believe it."

"I do," growled Quist, snapping the makeshift handcuffs and lifting her out. "Can you smell the chloroform? Blake and Rogers brought this young woman here for their disgusting sacrifice."

Watson threw open the rear door of Quist's car, allowing his boss to lay the semi-conscious girl on the back seat.

"Incredible," he muttered, leaping in. "And just when I thought I couldn't like those two any less."

Jumping behind the wheel, Quist gunned the engine and pulled away. An avenue of semi-detached houses joined Westminster Road to the main A19 route into town and he turned onto it, passing the frontage of St Peter's School and driving as fast as the freezing fog would allow.

"She's passed out," said Watson, twisting in the passenger seat to peer at Leanne and feel her clammy brow. "She's still drugged, but apart from that, she's breathing normal and looks to be okay. I wonder who she is?"

"Aaron King was a homeless drug addict," said Quist. "From his attire and scrawny appearance, so was the man they used as a host in the restaurant. I've no doubt they chose this unfortunate young lady because she has a similar background."

"Those occultist twats really turn my stomach." The youth grimaced. "By the way, did you notice there was another stone coffin in that temple?"

"Yes, presumably containing Hanka."

"Aquila's girlfriend? What if those nutters let her out too?"

Quist shook his head. "I presume they needed to open Aquila's sarcophagus to obtain the dagger, but they saw he'd been driven mad. They have no reason to free Hanka so I'm certain they won't risk it."

"Let's hope you're right." Watson gazed through the mist at the brightly-lit brasseries and pubs as the road became the street of

Bootham. "So what was Aquila speaking back there? Roman?"

"Of sorts. It was Latin. Fortunately, I speak it too."

"Well of course you do."

"Latin was taught as standard in *my* schooldays." Quist gave his assistant a wry smile. "Who knows? I may be able to chat and reason with him."

"I'll ask again; did you actually *see* that thing? Did you notice he was bigger than you?"

"Yes, so you've already mentioned."

"So how are you going to handle him? More to the point, how on earth are we supposed to *find* him? He could be anywhere."

"Very true," admitted Quist. "But Aquila was clearly confused and wildly disorientated. I would deduce he's heading for somewhere he instinctively knows – the Roman fortress."

"Er, right…" Watson frowned. "Isn't he a couple of thousand years too late?"

"He isn't aware of that." The detective scanned the pavements as he drove, hoping for a glimpse of the running wolf. "All concept of time will have been lost and Blake was probably correct in what she said. Aquila was entombed inside that sarcophagus for centuries and the ordeal has driven him temporarily insane."

"Buried alive." The youth shivered. "Shit! It almost makes you feel sorry for him."

"Don't squander your compassion." Quist smiled grimly. "Aquila was a loathsome character, killing people indiscriminately and sacrificing innocents to his dark deity. The point is, he's now surrounded by modern buildings, bright street lights and moving vehicles with headlamps, incongruous sights which will plunge his confused, unhinged mind into deeper chaos. He's currently in wolf form and basic animal instinct will take over, hopefully leading him to York Minster. That's where I'm heading."

"Eh? Why the Minster?"

"The church building was erected above the Roman basilica, the central part of their fortress. This street follows the line of the ancient Roman road that leads there and I was hoping to spot him somewhere along it."

"Well, I hope you're right about this," sighed Watson.

"Ah, wait a moment. This is ideal." Pulling over to the kerb in front of the Bootham Tavern, Quist jumped out and opened the rear door. "Whoever you are, young lady, this is where we part company."

Watson watched as the detective scooped up Leanne, carried her across the pavement and sat her inside the doorway of the lively pub.

"The place is busy," said Quist, returning and driving away. "I could hear a crowd leaving so she'll be found and taken care of. It was too dangerous to have her in the car as we search for Aquila."

"Yeah, you're right." The teenager laughed nervously. "Too dangerous for *her*, but I'm sure *I'll* be okay."

Quist braked to drive beneath the fortified archway of Bootham Bar and cruise slowly along the narrow length of High Petergate, watching for tipsy pedestrians in the mist. With people making their merry way between the various inns, someone could easily step out in front of his car.

Watson glanced nervously at the Eagle and Child as they passed. After everything that had recently happened, it seemed like an age since Monday afternoon when they'd spied upon the adulterous couple in this inn. He shook his head in amazement. *Was it really only three days ago?*

"Hello…" murmured Quist, noticing how several pavement revellers were holding up phone cameras and gazing through the fog in the direction of the Minster. "These people appear animated. Did they just witness something odd pass this way?"

"*Odd?*" echoed Watson. "You mean *odd* like a frigging werewolf?"

High Petergate ended at Minster Yard, the vast open area that surrounds the colossal cathedral. Quist turned left across the flagstones, the western face of the Gothic building looming to their right with its twin towers soaring two-hundred feet into the fog.

"Guv," croaked the youth, his spine freezing. "There he is."

The mist swirled and briefly parted to reveal the bizarre sight of a huge wolf in Roman armour and helmet bounding across the cobbles. Reaching the Minster door, Aquila rose on two legs to slam his bulk against the aged woodwork, bursting open the smaller inset wicket entrance.

"I knew it," said Quist. "Yes, he must have run straight past those people back there. We've obviously been right behind him all the way." Watching the creature vanish inside, he turned his car into Precentor's Court, a tight backstreet leading off Minster Yard. "Fortunately the building will be empty at this late hour. We have to follow him."

"I'm sure you know what you're doing," stammered Watson, his heart pounding. "So what's the plan, Guv?"

"Actually, I don't have one," admitted Quist, parking by a wall where the passage widened. "But one thing is certain, I can't do anything about Aquila in my current form." Tugging off his shoes and socks, he stuffed them into his overcoat side pockets, along with his wristwatch and ring. "Be a good chap and keep an eye out, would you?"

Like a demented tennis spectator, Watson twisted his head left and right, glancing anxiously out of the windows and checking for witnesses whilst his boss swiftly undressed. Quist began to grunt and transform, the teenager's pulse racing faster as the air inside the vehicle turned frigid and the gruesome sound of crunching bones filled the confined space. The naked detective vanished and the terrifying shape of a black wolf replaced him in the driving seat.

"Er, like I said earlier, Guv…" Watson peered at the yellow

eyes glowing in the darkness and tried clearing his arid throat. "I'll carry your coat."

Leaving the car and throwing the lengthy coat over his arm, the youth hurried back along the street with the wolf padding at his side like some gigantic pet dog. A figure materialised out of the mist, saw the creature and choked back a scream.

"Hey, mate..." stuttered the frightened man. "I don't know what that ugly fucker is, but you should definitely have it on a leash."

Baring his fangs, Quist glared up at him.

"He isn't too keen on leashes," said Watson. "Or dickheads who call him ugly."

Gulping and quickening his step, the man vanished.

Watson dashed across Minster Yard with the werewolf trotting beside him, the damp blanket of fog protecting them from other onlookers. They entered the cathedral via the broken wicket door and saw that Aquila had smashed his way through the inner glass porch.

The youth raised his eyebrows. *This Roman twat was clearly unacquainted with modern fire exits that opened outwards.*

Although he'd spent his entire life in the historic city of York, Watson had always looked upon history and churches as boring, and hadn't visited this incredible landmark since the school trips of his childhood. He'd forgotten just how truly enormous and breath-taking it actually was. The cavernous nave spread out in front of him, its ornate ceiling suspended a hundred feet above his head.

"Aquila went that way," growled Quist, pointing towards the middle of the building. "Look at the trail of glass fragments. They were trapped in his fur and fell out as he ran."

Watson followed the wolf as it bounded along the main aisle and came to a halt beneath the central Lantern Tower.

"Hey, he's gone through there." The panting youth stared uneasily at an arched doorway. "The bits of glass end here. The fact that the door's been ripped off its hinges is also a good clue."

"Yes." Quist spotted the broken woodwork lying in the north transept where it had been flung. "This is the access to the central tower staircase."

"Why the hell would he go up there?"

"Aquila is now aware that the Roman basilica has vanished. He recognises nothing and the confusion will be overwhelming. A combination of animal instinct and military training will force him to get to the highest point and survey his surroundings. This staircase is the only way up."

"So I guess he's trapped?" Watson shrugged nervously. "We could wait here for him to come back down. Or rather *you* could."

"The tower is currently closed for renovation; we saw the scaffolding earlier." The wolf deliberated. "No, he may decide to remain up there. We're fortunate that the Minster is empty, but that could easily change and we need to follow him and end this as quickly as possible." Quist clicked on the staircase lights and glanced at his assistant. "You're young and wiry, but not fit enough to run up all the steps. Leave my coat here and jump on my back."

"Are you kidding me?" Watson let out a manic giggle. "You want me to ride you like a frigging seaside donkey?"

"We don't have time to discuss this. I may need your help, so just do it."

"Okay." Laughing apprehensively, the teenager tossed down the leather overcoat, threw a leg across Quist's broad shoulders and grabbed two handfuls of the thick fur on his neck. "If you say so, but I'm jumping straight off if we meet that thing on its way down."

Watson yelped as the wolf leapt through the doorway and bolted up the stone steps, powerful muscles rippling beneath his crotch. The spiral staircase was precipitous, twisting tightly around a central stone pillar with the steps only two feet wide. The youth had noticed a warning sign at the bottom stating there were 275 of these and that the climb should never be attempted by anyone with heart problems. Screwing his eyes shut and frantically holding on, he didn't bother to count them. Watson had no medical conditions that he was aware of, but he *was* very much aware of what awaited them up here and it would *definitely* be no good for his heart.

The constant spiralling quickly disorientated the youth, but he didn't open his eyes until cold wafts of night air signalled they'd reached the top. The staircase was normally sealed by a door in the south-western corner of the tower, but like the door at the base, this too had been smashed from its framework. The fog hadn't reached these lofty heights and stars encrusted the wintry sky surrounding a yellow full moon. The panting Quist emerged from the exit and Watson slid gratefully from his back as he rose on hind legs. Shaken and dizzy, he ensured he stayed behind the wolf.

"Well…" mumbled Watson. "*That* was a ride I wouldn't recommend for a funfair."

A walkway and waist-high parapet wall bordered the square tower summit, the latter punctuated every few feet with crenulations. These stone blocks are found on castle ramparts, where archers once sheltered behind to fire arrows, but why these were required on a cathedral was anyone's guess. Probably more understandable was the wire mesh tunnel that enclosed the perimeter walk and prevented anyone from taking a swallow dive. Watson wondered why any would-be suicide would pay the entrance fee and undertake such a strenuous climb when far less arduous options, such as the river, were readily available. The dour thought was automatic and only lasted a second, before the terrifying sight of Aquila wiped everything else from his head.

"Oh, shit," he croaked, peering anxiously around Quist's furry shoulder. "What the hell am I doing up here?"

The Roman werewolf stood thirty feet away, seething angrily with its back to them. Watson had been right in his earlier assessment

– this monster *was* larger and more muscular than his boss, which didn't bode well. The moon and Minster spotlights glistened on the military helmet and segmented torso armour as the huge creature leant on the limestone parapet staring south over the city, or rather the little of the city that was visible. The fog blanket spread out around the tower, with the Minster rooftops, the taller York buildings, and various church spires rising from the frothy white sea.

The renovation project, which Watson had noticed at ground level, was very much in evidence here. A complex of scaffolding encircled the upper parts of the tower and, with tourists temporarily prohibited, the cage tunnel had been dismantled on this southern side of the walkway, allowing stonemasons and other workmen to access the scaffold platforms. Aquila stood surrounded by cement bags, stone blocks, metal poles, coils of electrical cable and safety harnesses.

"Okay, Guv," whispered the trembling youth. "Bearing in mind he's a fucking fruit loop, any bright ideas on what to do?"

Breathing heavily from the staircase run, Quist stepped forward. "Aquila," he called out, speaking fluent Latin. "Your fortress is no more, as you can doubtless see. I believe we should talk."

"Talk?" The Prefect turned to face him, his eyes gleaming scarlet and lupine muzzle opening to reveal dripping teeth. "I have no desire to talk with anyone."

"But I fear we must," persisted Quist. "You have been a prisoner for many centuries and this is no longer the world you knew. This is no longer your time. You need to understand how things have changed and how…"

"This world *will* be mine." Aquila eyed the smaller wolf curiously and noticed Watson shivering behind him. "You are clearly the same. You too are a hunter – a disciple of Badda Oushane. Join me, swear allegiance and I will allow you to serve me."

"I'm afraid that will not happen."

"I insist." Aquila chuckled insanely. "I also hunger. Join me now and we will celebrate our alliance by feasting together upon your African slave."

"This er, *slave* is under my protection." Quist shook his head, glancing around for anything he could use as a weapon. "He is definitely not on any menu."

"We shall see." Snarling furiously and flexing its bulky muscles, the ancient werewolf threw back its head and howled at the night sky.

"I can't imagine what you're saying, Guv," muttered the petrified Watson. "But I really don't think he's listening."

Quist stiffened as the mad creature rushed at him without warning. He dropped onto all-fours and, timing it right, snatched a scaffold pole, jamming one end against the wall behind them and angling it at waist height. Blinded by rage and hurtling forward, Aquila ran straight onto the metal, skewering himself below the chest armour and letting out an insane shriek. The makeshift spear tore into the wolf's abdomen and appeared through its back.

"Bloody hell, Guv..." Watson winced at the sickening squelch. "You've kebbabed the bastard."

He gasped as his boss lifted the thrashing creature on the pole and launched it over the parapet. The youth chanced a brief glance between the wall crenulations and saw that the monster had fallen onto the wooden scaffold platform six feet below. Roaring and writhing on its side, it yanked at the metal in its guts and glared up at him with blazing eyes.

"That won't harm it," snapped Quist, jumping over the wall and landing beside Aquila. He screamed as the larger werewolf clawed at him and clamped its fangs into his arm. "Watson, grab that cable and tie it to something. *Quickly.*"

The teenager spotted the electrical wire coiled by his feet and swiftly did as ordered, whimpering in terror and fastening it around a crenulation with shaking hands. He'd no idea why his boss wanted this, but the horrific sounds of fighting, snapping jaws and snarling a few feet away didn't help his dexterity.

"Secure it," yelled Quist, rolling around on the planking with the frenzied creature's mouth locked onto his arm. "Then throw it to me. Watson, do it *now*."

The coil landed on the platform beside him and he jerked the impaled metal sideways, the agony causing the Roman wolf to momentarily slacken its jaws. Wrenching his wounded arm free, Quist wrapped the end of the cable several times around its muscular neck.

"Fool," laughed Aquila, wrenching out the pole and flinging it away. "You hope to strangle me?"

"No." The smaller wolf panted in pain. "I hope to do *this*."

He kicked hard with both hind legs, propelling Aquila over the edge of the scaffolding. Screeching and futilely raking at the rushing air with its talons, the werewolf plummeted forty feet before the cable brought it to an abrupt halt and bit deep, its own falling weight decapitating the monster. The ancient head and body crumbled instantly to a stinking cloud of black dust, leaving the armour to tumble empty.

Watson peered over the wall, sweating and trembling. "Hey, Aquila," he shouted, hearing the Roman helmet clank on the Minster roof far below "Welcome to the twenty-first century."

* * * *

249

Chapter 31

The York Memorial Gardens were closed to the public, although it was unlikely that many *normal* people would want to stroll around the foggy parkland this freezing Thursday evening. Police cordon tape and uniformed officers blocked both gateways and a white forensic tent had been erected by the riverside entrance. Katie Bradstreet wore sterile overalls and squat inside the brightly-lit shelter next to the similarly attired Jay Mortimer. She watched as the elderly Pathologist examined the two corpses.

"So how powerful *was* this Doctor Sawtelle?" asked Mortimer, frowning. "He appears to have ruptured this man's trachea with a single punch and clawed open the abdomen with his bare hands."

Katie smiled uneasily. "Then I think it's safe to say *very* powerful."

Angie Gibson appeared at the tent flap. "Both sets of prints have been identified, Ma'am," said the Sergeant, holding up her phone. "Constable Planer just rang me. You're looking at Kris Paisley and Martin Reeves."

"The names are unfamiliar," admitted the Inspector. "But if we have their prints, they're obviously on our system?"

"Yes, they're small-time drug dealers and both have extensive records for theft, intimidation and violence." Angie looked confused. "I really don't understand this, Ma'am. These sort of people often wind up dead, and I could easily imagine some rival dealer killing them, but Edwin Sawtelle? A respectable doctor from the British Museum?"

"It's bizarre, I know." Katie nodded her agreement. "He was chasing me and actually paused to do this. It only took him a few seconds."

"Well, you've just mentioned drugs," said the Pathologist. "I suppose narcotics could offer a possible explanation for the man's behaviour and strength. Most illegal drugs are capable of causing bouts of delusional insanity, especially if mixed with the wrong chemicals, but certain dangerous narcotics can also deliver ferocious boosts of strength." He gestured to the torn stomach.

"You mean PCP?" asked Angie. "Angel dust?"

"That kind of thing," nodded Mortimer, turning to Katie. "Your man Sawtelle received deep lacerations and multiple fractures to his ribs and both legs. The pelvis was shattered, the spine was broken in two places, yet he still attempted to attack you from a prone position. With high levels of something like PCP in his system, this wouldn't be as impossible as it sounds. He could still have functioned for a brief period, probably without experiencing pain."

"Maybe," lied Katie, rising to her feet. *Sawtelle had something in his system alright, and it certainly wasn't drugs.* "The toxicology report will tell us, and I can't think of any other explanation."

"An upright, middle-aged academic on some crazy drug?" Angie shook her head, looking down at the two bodies. "Chasing police officers and killing people. It's a little hard to believe, isn't it?"

The Inspector didn't answer.

"Talking of crazy," she continued, "I don't know what's going on in the city tonight, Ma'am. Zoe has just been telling me we have patrol cars everywhere. You're aware of that murder in the Indian restaurant? Apparently, the victim was some junkie named Ryan Farmer and he was *decapitated* in the kitchen. The staff are claiming he threw a waiter across the room. They're saying he had superhuman strength and glowing eyes…"

"His eyes were *glowing*?" Katie shuddered at the memory of Rakkat. "Yes, I'm familiar with Farmer. He's been arrested a few times for drugs and violent behaviour…" She paused. "Glowing eyes, you say?"

"I told you it was a crazy night." Angie laughed quietly. "Zoe says someone broke into the Minster a short while ago too. Probably kids, because they've been throwing scrap metal off the roof."

"Really?" The Inspector shook herself. "Well, neither concern us, but that reminds me, I need to call Zoe myself." Leaving the shelter and pulling down the forensic hood, she took out her phone and rang Constable Planer. "Hi, there," she said. "How's Mitchell doing?"

"Don't worry, Ma'am," said Zoe. "He's okay. He sent me a selfie from the hospital. That bust nose has given him two black eyes, but I'd say it kind of improves his looks. Then again, I've always had a soft spot for racoons."

"Very good." The Inspector laughed dryly. "Listen, I know you're busy, but I need you to do a check on the traffic cameras in Wetherby."

"Is this something to do with the shooting there this afternoon? That isn't connected to our case, is it?"

"I'm not sure, but indulge me and don't mention this to Superintendent Morton if she's about. She'll want details and, right now, this is just a unconfirmed lead I'm looking into."

"No problem, Ma'am."

"I don't have a license plate, but you're looking for a black BMW saloon being driven in the town between one-thirty and two-thirty today. If any vehicles fit the description, in particular any near Sterndale Close, I want to know who they're registered to."

"It's only a small time window," said Zoe. "It shouldn't take long. Consider it done."

Katie switched off, but before she could pocket the phone, it vibrated in her hand.

"Inspector Bradstreet?" The female caller was clearly scared. "I need to speak with you. I'm not sure what to do and…"

"Okay, calm down," said Katie. "Who is this?"

"Doctor Blake. Melissa Blake. We spoke at the museum."

"Ah, yes. I thought I recognised your voice, but you sound frightened. Listen, if you need police assistance, you should…"

"No, I'm ringing *you* because Bernard Quist said you were different and he trusted you." Melissa hesitated. "I was supposed to meet Bernard earlier tonight, but my assistant Tamzin and I were attacked by Doctor Sawtelle. It was horrible. I don't know what was wrong with him, but he…"

"I'm sorry to have to inform you," broke in Katie. "I'm afraid Doctor Sawtelle is dead."

"Oh my God," gasped Melissa. "He's *dead*? Look, this is really weird and I don't know if you'll believe me when I tell you, but Edwin was working with an occult group and he…"

"I believe it." The Inspector grimaced. "Oh, yes, I most *definitely* believe it."

"They're doing something terrible tonight. Something to do with a black magic sacrifice and I have the proof."

"Okay, do you know who these people are and where this is taking place?"

"Yes, I have all the details," stammered Melissa. "But I'm terrified. This group are powerful and I don't trust anyone. I need to meet you and speak face to face. You'll have to come alone."

"Where are you?"

"I'm with Tamzin in the multi-storey car park on Tanner Row. We're parked on the ground level."

"I know it." The Inspector checked her watch; it was eight-thirty. "Right, I'll be there in five minutes. Try not to worry."

Angie appeared from the tent. "By the way, Ma'am," she said. "What with everything that's been happening, I forgot to mention it. I've now managed to speak with all the officers who arrested Aaron King for his shoplifting and other minor offences."

"Oh, right." Katie quickly peeled off the forensic suit. "You mean to see if they collected samples of his DNA?"

"Yes, and it's a little strange. It turns out five of them took mouth swabs, so King's DNA should have been in our database."

"And yet it wasn't. That's interesting." Katie frowned as she headed for her car. "I shouldn't be long. I've a feeling this will be even *more* interesting."

* * * *

Three storeys in height, the municipal car park on Tanner Row stands at the eastern end of the thoroughfare and most design aficionados have agreed, it will never win any awards for *York's Most Attractive Building*. Katie turned her Saab into the sombre entrance tunnel facing the rear of the Grand Hotel and spotted Melissa Blake waiting in front of a line of vehicles on the ground floor. Wrapped in a parka coat and leaning against her car bonnet, the anxious-looking doctor appeared to be the only person on this deserted level. The Inspector parked in a nearby bay and walked across the garage to meet her, looking around at the cheerless concrete architecture.

"Doctor Blake." She smiled reassuringly. "Are you okay?"

"Not really," said Melissa. "This is so scary, but I feel better now that you're here."

"So what's this about?" Katie buttoned up her raincoat. "You told me you had evidence on this black magic group?"

"That's right." The doctor glanced at the security cameras that covered this area and the dangling cables where she'd disabled them minutes earlier. "It's cold. Come on, we can talk in the car."

"Hello again," said Katie, nodding to the frightened Tamzin in the rear of the Mondeo. She climbed into the passenger seat beside Melissa and closed the door. "I must say, you've picked a charming place to meet. If I were worried about a coven of witches, I think I'd have opted for a lively pub with plenty of people."

"Good point," agreed Tamzin, her voice quaking slightly.

"So what do you have for me?"

"I spoke to Bernie Quist on the phone," said Melissa. "He told me how you've come to accept the supernatural as being real? You're aware that some occultists are capable of performing genuine magic?"

"I have little choice, *but* to accept it." Katie shuddered. "I saw things earlier tonight that…"

"The Rakkat entity?"

"Yes, apparently it was called Rakkat." The Inspector pulled a sour face as she repeated the abrasive name. "I take it you're familiar with that horrendous drooling *thing* from your research?"

Melissa nodded. "As a Badda historian, I know this creature was often used as a servant by the sect. So you'll believe me when I tell you the occultists who controlled the elemental are planning an important ritual tonight?"

"Quist mentioned this to me too," said Katie. "Do you know where?"

"It's very close to here. They have a temple in a building on Rougier Street."

"When you rang me, you mentioned something about a sacrifice? A human sacrifice?"

"That's right." Melissa gestured to the silent girl in the rear and smiled at the Inspector. "And now she's here."

Tamzin launched herself forward, both hands whipping around the headrest to grip Katie's short blonde hair and clench a chloroform-soaked rag over her face. Melissa shot across to grab the officer's struggling arms, using her weight to pin her down, until the fighting quickly slowed and finally ceased.

"I can't believe we're doing this." Tamzin collapsed back in her seat, panting. "It's absolute madness."

"No, it's necessary," snapped Melissa. "Thanks to those private eyes, we've lost our junkie and Bradstreet is the ideal substitute. She's seen Rakkat, she knows the Badda rituals work and, with Sawtelle gone, she'd soon work out that we were the ones behind everything."

"Who cares?" Tamzin shook her head. "We're leaving the country straight after the Sacrament, and we could get some other drug addict. Jesus, Mel, you must know that using Bradstreet for this is so wrong. We could tie her up and leave her in her car boot. No one would find her until we're gone and…"

"Barbie Doll, I completely understand." Melissa reached back and grabbed her hand, squeezing tightly. "You feel this way because she's a police officer, not some worthless nobody like Leanne Lloyd. The thing is, this has to go smoothly and it has to be fast and efficient. I agree with you, Tamz, it didn't feel so bad using expendable addicts, but we can't possibly find another junkie in time."

"I suppose not," admitted Tamzin, gulping.

"Right now we need to forget about right and wrong." The doctor smiled sweetly at the unconscious woman in the passenger seat. "We have the perfect sacrifice right here."

* * * *

Chapter 32

The fog was dense behind St Peter's School, swirling across the playing fields and around Wolf Hill where the Priestess stood on a pile of freshly excavated earth. Smiling thinly, she gazed at the open doorway of Aquila's temple. On her last visit here, guided to this spot by the energy-infused Moon Crown on Monday evening, Wolf Hill had been a nondescript grassy hummock, overgrown for centuries with thick vegetation and knotted brambles. The mound looked very different now and she scrambled down the incline to the entrance.

The Priestess peered into the icy darkness before trying Melissa's number for the tenth time. She shook her head irately as, once again, the doctor's phone went straight to voicemail.

"Hello there, this is Doctor Blake. I'm sorry I can't take you call right now, but if…"

"Not as sorry as you *will* be," muttered the woman. "What the hell is going on here?"

Edwin Sawtelle had been killed, Blake wasn't answering her phone and there had been no one at the Stonegate apartment when she called there ten minutes ago. The two women were supposed to be preparing for tonight's ritual and Blake had been ordered to remain in contact at all times, providing regular progress reports. This suspicious silence signalled they were definitely up to something and it was time to find out what.

Pocketing the mobile and clicking on her torch, the Priestess moved inside, smiling excitedly to see the Badda wall carvings and the huge statue of the Hunter God at the far end of the temple. She froze, her gleeful expression vanishing, as the beam of light travelled down from the ferocious wolf face to the demolished walls on either side of the altar.

"No," she spat, racing down the central aisle of columns. "No, I don't believe this."

The makeshift Roman tombs had been opened and, running her torch over the stone sarcophagus inside the left antechamber, she saw it was empty. The woman nodded knowingly.

This was obviously Aquila's coffin and the Oushane Blade was gone. Blake and Rogers must have been here earlier, smashed down the wall and taken it. God alone knew where the Prefect himself was. This was HER operation and those bitches had actually stolen the knife for themselves.

"I don't believe this," she repeated, trembling with rage. "I really do *not* believe this. How dare they?"

They thought she'd be tied up until ten, but after discovering that Sawtelle was dead and suspecting something was wrong, she'd left work early.

"Oh, you'll be sorry," shouted the Priestess, her voice echoing through the temple. She laughed, but there was no mirth in the harsh sound. "You will be so fucking sorry."

And to think, she'd actually considered allowing Blake and Rogers to use the dagger with her during the Sacrament ritual.

A small sledgehammer leant against a nearby column and a holdall lay open on the marble floor tiles. The canvas bag contained various tools and battery-powered hurricane lamps.

Yes, this was planned and they'd come equipped to open the sealed tomb. The two women probably wore gloves and, with nothing to implicate them, they hadn't bothered to take these items away with them.

Seething furiously and switching on two of the lamps, the Priestess quickly searched through the piles of golden artefacts beside the coffin, on the chance that the knife might still be here. She found it wasn't.

No, of course it wasn't.

She carried one of the lamps to the opposite side chamber and saw that the sarcophagus inside remained intact, three locked iron bands holding the cover stone in place. She debated for several moments, grimacing as she formulated a rather dangerous plan.

"Okay," she muttered, snatching up the hammer. "You could have been a part of this, but no, you decided to defy me. You were stupid enough to try cutting me out of my own project."

Smashing the ancient locks and twisting off the hinged metal bonds, the Priestess slammed her petite weight against the heavy stone lid and pushed hard with her shoulder. The slab moved only slightly, but enough to unseal the coffin, create a two-inch opening and release a hissing surge of fetid gas. She fell on her backside coughing, as the unholy stench gushed into the confined space, then climbed unsteadily to her feet, sweeping back her dishevelled hair and wiping her watering eyes. Thirty seconds passed, her heartbeat accelerating at the chilling sound of crackling movement within the sarcophagus.

"Shit." Ice-cold sweat drenched her back and her legs trembled. "What the hell were you thinking? This is..."

The stone cover flew off, catapulted upwards as if constructed from cardboard. The Priestess leapt back, pressing her spine against the wall as it fractured into three shards on striking the floor.

"Oh, God," she croaked.

A terrifying figure rose from the sarcophagus. Black fur covered the body and the chest rose and fell as the creature breathed air for the first time in two millennia. The she wolf stood on two legs, its gleaming red eyes staring at the petrified woman.

"My Lady Hanka," stammered the Priestess in Latin. "I am a humble..."

"I speak your tongue," snarled the wolf. "My sorcery gifts me with *all* tongues after hearing them, and I heard your pitiful whining from my prison. Now who *are* you?"

"My Lady." She bowed low, shivering uncontrollably with fear. *This was a werewolf – an actual werewolf.* "Like you, I am a follower of the great Hunter God Badda Oushane. I am your humble servant."

Her idea had been formulated in anger on the spur of the moment. This horrific thing hadn't eaten for quite some time and this could easily end very badly.

"I see." The creature ran its gaze over the woman's strange modern attire, the large muzzle curling as it bared sharp white fangs. "Where is Hadrian and my captors? Tell me, how long have I slumbered in this foul prison?"

"Hadrian is dead. Many centuries have passed since you were entombed here, my Lady." The Priestess tried clearing her bone-dry throat. "But now I have freed you and I will serve you faithfully."

"Aquila?" The monster glared at her, its crimson eyes glinting. "Where is Aquila?"

"Your High Priest has been taken by your enemies, my Lady, but I know where they are. With your permission, I will gladly reunite you with the Prefect."

Studying her for several moments and growling menacingly, the she wolf nodded, then suddenly bent double, twisting and writhing. The temperature fell, the hideous sound of lupine snarling and shrinking bones echoing through the subterranean temple, as the monster quickly shapeshifted into the lean form of a beautiful naked girl. Ink-black hair tumbled over the dusky skin of her shoulders and pert breasts as she stepped from the coffin.

"Serve me." Hanka took a deep breath of the frozen air, her fierce expression changing to a deranged smile. "You will take me to him now."

"Of course. Please, my Lady, this way…" Still shaking, the Priestess bowed again, before leading her along the central aisle. "My chariot awaits nearby. It's called a BMW."

* * * *

Chapter 33

Fog drifted down Precentor's Court where Watson sat in the passenger seat of Quist's parked car, waiting impatiently whilst his boss hurriedly dressed.

"It was terrifying up there on the tower," said the youth. "I have to say, you were brilliant, Guv. How you handled that monster was just incredible." He peered apprehensively into the mist, checking up and down the narrow street. "But I wonder if you could speed this up? One of these days someone is going to walk past when you're doing this and get the wrong idea."

Quist smiled. "Don't let it worry you."

"Parked in a dark side street with you pulling up your pants? Yeah, I mean what's there to worry about? It's only my macho reputation at stake."

"I truly wish that were our only concern." Tugging on his jacket, the detective flicked on the courtesy light and took Roundhay's York map from the glove compartment. "We couldn't prevent Blake and Rogers from obtaining the dagger, but if their ritual is to succeed, we know it has to be performed in a Badda temple."

"We also know they need a human sacrifice," pointed out Watson. "Shit, I can't believe I'm saying that in twenty-first century Yorkshire. We freed that poor girl in their car boot so, with any luck, they might call it off."

"They may," agreed Quist, opening the map. "But with so much at stake, I doubt it, and we can't take that chance. They could easily have another young woman in reserve."

"Like a substitute footballer sitting on a frigging bench?" The youth shook his head. "Well, the obvious place for this is the museum?"

"No, Blake will consider the exhibition room far too dangerous. We know the Sussamma Ritual was performed there and

261

she's fully aware of that. We also know about the main temple where the Prefect was buried, so they probably won't return there either. No, I'm convinced they'll use the other temple – the second one, that Aquila built in the Roman Colonia. Blake has no idea that we possess this map, so she'll assume they'll be safe and undisturbed there."

"So here, you mean?" Watson tapped one of Roundhay's pencil crosses. "On Rougier Street?"

"That's right." Quist started the car and pulled away, driving out of Precentor's Court and past the Minster. "I still can't recall why that particular street rings a proverbial bell with me."

"But the site is long gone. Looking at the Rev's mark, there's a building smack on top of it."

"True," agreed Quist, negotiating the city centre roads. "But the Badda temple and its latent power remain there beneath that modern construction. All they need do is consecrate a makeshift temple right above it. They needed the Sussamma Ritual and the Moon Tiara to find Aquila's tomb, but Roundhay said the woman who used to visit him for research photographed this map. That's how they know the precise locations of the other two."

"But, like you say, they *don't* know we have it." Nodding, Watson refolded the map and stuffed it away.

The detective turned onto Station Road which ran alongside the medieval York walls, and turned off this busy main route into the much narrower Rougier Street.

"The Rev told us the girl was called *Jane Smith*," said Watson. "Do you reckon it was Mel or Tamzin?"

"I don't believe it was either of them," said Quist. "Those two are based in London and I strongly suspect it was the third member of their group. This *Priestess* they spoke of is a local woman. She visited Miles Roundhay on several occasions to gather information and then returned today and shot him."

"Why local?"

"We're almost there, so I'll explain later."

"Ooh, you're mysterious." Watson grinned. "Well, not *too* mysterious. I've seen you stark naked often enough."

For a city of such architectural wonder, Rougier Street is noticeably twentieth century, with several contemporary office blocks sporting plastic and modern glass. One building halfway along stood out from the rest, mostly due to its blackened façade and the metal shutters fixed over what remained of the windows and doors. Tarpaulins covered the lower parts and tape cordons and bollards surrounded the base with road signs instructing pedestrians to use the opposite pavement.

"Ah, of course." The detective nodded. "This is Shipton's Insurance and I remember now. They had a fire in their offices about four weeks ago."

"Do we know what started it?" asked Watson.

"It was arson." Quist smiled tightly. "Very convenient for our friends, wouldn't you say?"

"You're thinking one of those nutters torched the place?"

"Oh, I'm certain of it." He turned the car into the adjoining alleyway. "Once again, the secretive third member of their circle will have been responsible – the local woman. These people certainly leave nothing to chance. This was doubtless required as a back-up should the museum temple become compromised, as is now the case. A burnt-out shell is a much better location for occult rituals than a secure office building with alarm systems."

The alley led into a rear parking area, empty save for one silver-grey vehicle with its broken boot catch secured with string.

"Ah, here we go," said the detective.

"Yeah, Mel's Mondeo." Watson laughed. "What a surprise."

Pulling up beside it, Quist jumped out and saw that a metal shutter had been prised from one of the building's rear doors.

"An insurance company, you say?" The youth smiled

nervously and stooped to follow his boss inside. "Let's hope they insured themselves for fire."

* * * *

Waves of nausea woke Katie Bradstreet from her drug-induced stupor. The Inspector sprawled on her back and, realising she was unable to move, she quickly twisted her face and threw up. The movement set her head spinning like a faulty gyroscope and bizarre shapes whirled before her eyes, blurring her vision.

"Ah, you're awake," said a voice. "That's good."

Katie coughed and spat as full consciousness returned and, with it, the memory of her abduction in the multi-storey garage.

"What's happening?" she yelled, the chloroform dizziness finally receding. She squirmed furiously. "I'm a police officer and this is completely…"

"Stop that." Melissa Blake appeared by her side, smiling down at her. The doctor wore a white ceremonial robe with the iron Moon Crown perched on her head. "You're wasting your time struggling."

Katie tested this by writhing with all her strength, but knew it was pointless. She lay on a sturdy table top, tied down tightly with a length of rope. Her raincoat was open, her shirt had been undone to expose her flesh, but her bra remained untouched. People seeing her breasts was the least of her concerns right now.

"Where am I?" she snarled.

"In a basement." Melissa wiped the vomit with an old cloth. "Beneath the Shipton's Insurance building on Rougier Street. They had a fire here, which is why it still smells a little smoky, but…"

"And you out of your mind?" hissed Katie, her eyes darting around the cellar. The place was pitch-black, but several candles lit the immediate area. "What do you think you're doing kidnapping a police officer and why am I tied to this fucking table?"

"It's no longer a table," corrected Tamzin, appearing to her

264

left. She wore a similar white robe and the candles reflected on her large spectacle lenses. "It's now an altar consecrated to Badda Oushane. Being sick on it was blasphemous, but fortunately Mel has cleaned it."

"I was right," muttered Katie. "You *are* out of your minds. You two are completely fucking crazy."

"I know how this must seem," sighed Melissa. "For our ritual to work, it needs to be performed in a Badda temple and this building was constructed on top of one. This improvised temple of ours stands right above the one below."

"Ritual?" Struggling again, Katie swivelled her head from side to side, seeing the incense burners and the small statue of the Badda wolf God. "*What* ritual?"

"The Oushane Sacrament." The doctor held up an ornate sparkling dagger. "It's exquisite, isn't it? This relic lay undisturbed for over two-thousand years. The hilt is solid gold, with rubies and emeralds, the blade is constructed from hardened wolf bone and the sacrifice will infuse the weapon with life energy."

Katie laughed harshly. "You actually intend to use that thing on me?"

"There's no other way." Melissa nodded. "Immediately afterwards, Tamz and I will draw our own blood with the knife and become Hunter Gods."

"Werewolves," whispered Tamzin, excitedly.

"Oh, my God, you *are* insane, aren't you?" Katie laughed again. "You're talking about murdering a police officer."

"Sacrifice, not murder," said Tamzin. "I'm so sorry, but we've come way too far to stop now. This *has* to be done, but we don't take any pleasure from it."

"Really?" Katie glanced at Melissa's crazed smile and wasn't so sure. "You both need to listen to me. Murder a police officer and they *will* find you. Wherever you go and whatever you do, you'll never be safe again. Believe me, you'll be spending the rest of your life in a prison cell."

"The Sacrament will grant us incredible power," said the doctor, smiling. "I really don't think the idea of police arrests will worry us too much. Besides, we're leaving the country straight after the ritual. A short while ago I booked tickets from Leeds to connect with a Moroccan flight where we..."

"You won't be going anywhere," said Quist. "This lunacy is over."

"*What*?" Melissa's mouth fell open to see the detective walking into the cellar with Watson. "Stay back," she snarled, holding the dagger to Katie's throat. "How the hell could you possibly know we'd be here?"

"Another lucky guess like the last time," said Watson. "Oh, and Miles Roundhay's map with this place marked on it."

Katie had wondered how sharp a knife blade made from bone would be. From the feel of it on her skin, the answer was *scalpel sharp*. "Doctor Blake," she croaked. "You don't want to do this."

"No." The doctor let out a mad laugh. "*You* don't want me to do this."

"Think about it." Quist moved closer. "You can see this is finished and threatening a police officer is achieving nothing."

"I told you..." Melissa's hand twitched and a blood droplet trickled down Katie's neck. "Stay back."

"And *I* told you it's over." Quist gestured angrily to the shaky dagger. "Much as it infuriates me, I'm prepared to make you an offer. Put that down and I'll allow you both to leave here without it. You have my word, you'll be free to go, but if you harm that woman in any way, I promise you, it will be the last thing you ever do."

Staring at Watson, Tamzin stepped back, gasping in fear.

The youth couldn't understand why he frightened her so much, but then realised she was gazing past him at something behind.

He quickly turned, his eyes widening to see a beautiful naked girl striding barefoot into the cellar. Exotic-looking, with coffee-brown skin and lengthy raven hair, she appeared to be late-twenties and didn't seem overly pleased.

"Er, hello, luv." He eyed her taut curves. "Are you sure you have the right address? The pole dancing club is further along the street."

"Where is Aquila?" With hands on hips, the young woman angrily thrust out her breasts. "I want the Prefect... *now*."

"Oh, my God," moaned Tamzin. She'd somehow known who this was the moment she saw her. "How is this possible?"

"Aquila?" repeated Melissa, shaking her head in amazement. "Surely you can't be... Are you Hanka?"

Watson froze. "You're telling me this porn star was in the other stone coffin?"

"Yes, it's Hanka," confirmed Quist, walking to her. He briefly pondered how she was able to speak English, but this was a Badda High Priestess and he knew it had to be some inherent paranormal power. "I realise this must be confusing and difficult for you to understand, but..."

Snatching the detective, Hanka effortlessly launched him across the basement into the blackness. Quist grunted as his flailing body slammed hard into a wall.

"Are my commands not understood?" The naked woman stretched herself, the candlelight playing on her dusky skin. "I *said* I want the Prefect. She told me he was here and one of you will bring him to me."

"Er, yeah," muttered Watson, moving back. "There's a bit of a problem there."

"Who told you this?" asked Melissa, nervously stepping away from the altar. "We freed him, but we're not sure where he..."

"You will be silent." Hanka approached Tamzin, who stood

closer, rooted to the spot. "Where is he?" Smiling sweetly, she reached out to lovingly stroke the girl's blonde hair. "Answer me."

"I don't know," she stuttered. "But if you…"

Seizing Tamzin's head, Hanka screwed it completely around. The sharp crack of her snapping spine echoed through the cellar.

"No, no, no," screamed Melissa, losing control and racing forward with the dagger. "Barbie Doll…"

"Foolish child." Slapping the knife away, Hanka grabbed the doctor's throat in one hand, twisted roughly and wrenched out her windpipe. "You dare to attack *me*?"

Watson moaned, realising there weren't many people left to question. Petrified, he peered into the darkness, his darting eyes searching for his boss. *He knew exactly where Aquila was and he doubted this supernatural tart would be too overjoyed with the answer.*

"So foolish." Hanka chuckled as Melissa clutched futilely at her gushing throat and crumpled to the floor. She gazed at the terrified Inspector tied to the table, before turning to the teenager. "Barbie Doll?" She smiled evilly. "What is a Barbie…"

Quist flew out of the darkness, slamming his body into the woman and propelling them both across the cellar floor.

"Help Bradstreet," he shouted, pressing Hanka to the concrete and fending off her frantic clawing. "Cut her lose now."

"Yeah, yeah, right," spluttered Watson. Glancing at the dead Melissa, he snatched up the jewelled dagger and sliced Katie's bindings. "Are you okay, luv?"

"What the hell is happening?" The Inspector rolled off the table, hit the ground and sprang to her feet. "Who *is* that?"

"The last person we wanted to see," whimpered the youth. "It's Aquila's girlfriend."

Quist struggled with the frenzied, hissing woman, landing several hard blows and rolling across the floor with her to the cellar doorway.

"You are powerful for a human," snarled Hanka, leaping on top and returning his punches with lightning speed. She smiled gleefully to feel his jaw break. "Almost as strong as I, but you are not powerful enough."

Her shoulders expanded, her back arching as bones crackled and thick fur covered her skin. Quist gasped in pain as Hanka's grip tightened and sharp talons dug into his body. A lupine muzzle extended before his face and, in place of a young woman, an enormous red-eyed she wolf now sat astride his sprawling body, salivating and growling.

"Oh my God." Katie watched it lick its lips. "What in the name of God…"

"Guv…" yelled Watson. Feeling the Oushane Blade still clutched in his trembling hand and thinking fast, he threw the dagger towards Quist. "Here, grab this."

The knife skittered across the concrete and came to rest close by the wrestling pair. Pinned beneath the drooling monster and holding the snapping jaws from his throat, Quist groped blindly until he located and grabbed the weapon. He thrust upwards hard, the dagger sank deep into Hanka's muscular torso, and a deafening screech filled the cellar. The scarlet eyes blazed as the wolf grasped at the knife hilt, writhing and kicking. Quist shoved the creature off him and, pushing himself away, he watched as it shrieked again and unexpectedly vanished in an explosion of black dust.

"It's *gone…*" Katie gazed at the swirling cloud with her mouth hanging slackly open in shock. "It just disappeared."

Panting heavily and nodding, Quist climbed unsteadily to his feet and brushed the wolf dust from his coat. He ran a hand over his fractured jaw, but the bone had already knitted together.

"What the…" Watson shook uncontrollably, the supernatural scream still ringing in his ears. "Guv, what just happened?"

"I don't know," said Quist, straightening his clothes. "Well, I don't know for *certain*, but Hanka once used that dagger to gain immortality. If the knife is used a second time, it would seem the Oushane wolf energy is released and the body reverts to its normal state. In *her* case, a two-thousand year old woman."

"How did she get out of her coffin?" demanded Watson, as Quist joined them by the altar table. "How could she have found this place?"

"Never mind how it got here," shouted Katie, her heart pounding. "What the fuck *was* that thing?"

"Remember how you met an elemental earlier?" The youth grinned nervously. "Well, congratulations. You just met a werewolf."

"Are you serious?"

"You saw it," said Quist.

"Yeah." Watson glanced at her exposed bra. "You might have a copper's conservative attitude, luv, but you just watched someone change into a character from *Little Red Riding Hood*."

Fumbling with the buttons to fasten her blouse, Katie leant on the table, taking deep breaths to slow her heart rate. Her horrified gaze moved from the dagger in the pile of supernatural dust to the two corpses on the cellar floor.

"Look at the state of them," muttered Watson, cringing. "To think, I was actually going to ask Mel out."

"Before you discovered she was a sociopathic killer," said Quist. "If *that* didn't lead you to reconsider, I presume this will?"

"You're able to make jokes?" The trembling Inspector shook her head. "Listen, I honestly don't know how to thank you both. If you hadn't appeared when you did, I'd be dead. Either killed by these lunatics, or by that werewolf when it turned up…" She paused. "I honestly can't believe I just said that word."

"The main thing is you're alright." Quist gripped her quaking shoulders. "Did they harm you?"

"Never mind me." Katie looked him up and down, jerking open his overcoat to check for wounds. "You're lucky to be alive too. You were actually fighting with that monster. Thank God it didn't bite you. Is it like in the movies where a werewolf bite will turn you into…"

"Who knows?" lied Quist. "Fortunately I'm unhurt."

Taking out her phone with a shaky hand, the Inspector found several missed calls, all from her station. She grimaced to see two were from her favourite Superintendent.

"I'd rather you didn't ring your people," said Quist.

"I've no intention of ringing *anyone*." She laughed manically and left it switched off. "Not until I know what to say and..."

"Hey…" Watson gestured to the wolf dust by the cellar door. "Where is it?"

"He just explained," said Katie. "Insane as it sounds, when he stabbed her, she crumbled to…"

"Not the frigging lady werewolf." The baffled teenager peered at Quist. "I mean where's the knife?"

* * * *

Chapter 34

The King's Arms was originally called the Ouse Bridge Inn, but this was changed back in the seventies to commemorate Richard the Third, the much maligned monarch whom the people of York have always affectionately embraced. To be fair, they could name this ancient hostelry *anything*, but due to its quayside location beside the notoriously unpredictable river, it will forever be known as "the pub that floods".

Swollen from the winter rains, the Ouse flowed swiftly past the old building, the light from the tavern windows reflecting brightly on the damp cobblestones outside. The pub was busy, but despite the cosy warmth, Katie huddled in her raincoat with the collar turned up. She sat with Quist and Watson in a secluded corner behind the bar area, trembling as she drank a large whisky.

"So what happened to the dagger?" asked Watson.

"The answer to that is fairly obvious," said Quist. "Someone took it whilst we were occupied."

"But who?"

"Yes, that's the pertinent question, isn't it?" He gave the Inspector's shaky hand a comforting squeeze and sipped at his own whisky. "I'm pleased to say you're looking much better, young lady. Your complexion is less... *white*. How do you feel now?"

"How do I feel?" Katie let out a staccato laugh and lowered her voice. "I feel like I've been tied to a fucking witchcraft altar." She gulped the scotch. "They were actually going to kill me. One or two people have waved knives at me over the years, and a nutter once fired a gun, but I still can't believe those lunatics intended to murder a police officer in cold blood."

Watson held up his pint of lager. "*I* can't believe you wanted to call for a drink instead of ringing your station."

"It gives me time to get my head straight." Katie checked her watch – it was a little after nine-thirty. "I need to work out how I'm going to explain all this. The station keeps ringing, but what the hell do I say? That woman was an *actual* fucking werewolf and I watched her crumble to dust. I can't possibly mention *anything* supernatural."

"Clearly," agreed Quist, tinkling his signet ring against his glass. "I'd adhere to the truth for the most part. Blake and Rogers were evidently unhinged and part of some modern Badda sect. Through their museum work, they must have become obsessed with the cult's magical rituals and they believed those rites would genuinely work. For inexplicable reasons, they chose to kidnap *you* for some bizarre sacrifice, but the chloroform they used prevented you from seeing who rescued you."

"The last bit sounds good to me, Guv." Watson nodded nervously and lifted his lager in a toast. "If your cop pals knew we were in that cellar, we'd be held for two murders. *Three*, if you count the two-thousand year old pile of dust."

"Don't worry." The Inspector smiled tightly and gulped again at her whisky. "I've no idea who killed Blake and Rogers and cut me free."

"You now have a reason to investigate the museum," pointed out Quist. "During your abduction you overheard Blake mention how she'd sacrificed four women in the exhibition room. Your forensic people will find the blood traces I told you about."

"Yes," agreed Katie. "Now you come to mention it, I *do* recall Blake saying that." She paused, staring at them both. "This is all so crazy. Black magic rituals in museums, werewolves and elementals? My entire life has been changed by the insane things I've seen today, but you two don't appear fazed."

"Oh, it still affects me," admitted Watson. "Especially when it's happening. Believe me, luv, you never really get used to this supernatural shit, but it kind of gets easier afterwards."

"There are things you aren't aware of," said Quist. "Shortly after we spoke on the phone tonight, Blake and Rogers sent Rakkat for Kyle Tarot and his daughter. The elemental attempted to kill them in an Indian restaurant on..."

"I heard something about this," broke in Katie. "I didn't know Tarot was in the restaurant. Are you telling me *you* were there too? A man was killed, a junkie named Ryan Farmer."

"They used him as a host for Rakkat," said Quist. "Yes, from his appearance, I deduced he was another heroin addict like Aaron King. I managed to get the better of the creature and I destroyed the host body. Just like Sawtelle on the bridge, this young man was already dead when he arrived, but it would be impossible to explain that to your people. That's why the police can never know we were there."

"I heard you decapitated him," whispered Katie, glancing around. "The staff talked about him having superhuman strength and glowing eyes. It sounds like it was definitely that Rakkat thing, so how on earth did you manage to stop it?"

"It wasn't easy." Quist shrugged. "I got lucky."

"Really?" The Inspector frowned. "You'd better hope that luck extends to them not having security cameras."

Watson glanced at his boss. *Fortunately, his friend Gazza wiped the evidence before the cops had a chance to check it.*

"And then there was the Wetherby murder," said Katie. "The police found Miles Roundhay's body, but I can't mention anything about you being at the house when he died. The thing is, if you left any forensic evidence there..."

"I can assure you we didn't," said Quist. "In any case, as soon as your people find that blood in the exhibit and you arrest the occultist who murdered Roundhay, it won't matter."

"You mean the person who took the ceremonial dagger just now?" The Inspector nodded slowly. "Someone was obviously watching from the cellar doorway and sneaked in to snatch it at the right moment."

"Yes." Quist sipped his beer. "I read up on the Sussamma Ritual and *three* adepts are required for it to succeed. Melissa Blake, Tamzin Rogers and this *other* member of their group. Earlier tonight we visited the temple where Aquila was buried and the stone coffin containing Hanka's body was still sealed. This third adept called there after us, freed the creature and brought it to the Shipton's Insurance building."

"Hanka was a real-life *werewolf?*" hissed Katie. "Yes, I saw it, but I still can't believe it. You say Aquila was the same, but you managed to destroy him in the Minster?"

"It was terrifying." Watson grinned nervously at the memory. "The Guv sorted him out with a scaffold pole and he's another pile of dust like the girlfriend. Don't worry – that scary bastard is deader than VHS video tape."

Katie shook her head slowly. "I saw Hanka change into a wolf with my own eyes, just like I saw that weird stuff when Rakkat died. I watched her turn to dust, but you must know how difficult this is for me to get my head around? You're saying this occultist released Hanka and took her there to kill Blake and Rogers?"

"Yes, and us too," said Quist. "We survived, but luckily for this person, the ensuing chaos enabled them to slip in unseen and steal the dagger. I'm quite certain this is someone local. A female adept from a northern occult group."

"You were talking about this earlier," said Watson. "What makes you think that?"

"There have always been rumours of a group operating in the Pickering area," said Quist. "Inspector, I know you're aware of the ritualistic murder last year when a man was murdered on the moors."

She nodded. "So?"

"Blake referred to their third member as *the Priestess* and I believe she runs the Pickering coven."

"Again, *why*?" quizzed Watson.

"The dead man on the moors was a drug dealer."

"Eh?" The teenager looked puzzled. "That's your answer?"

"Bear with me." Quist smiled grimly. "Someone local burnt down the Shipton's building, which allowed the occultists to use the cellar there tonight. This local woman was familiar with Wetherby and the historian Miles Roundhay; he explained how a girl visited him several times to talk about the Badda cult and he gave her the temple locations. I believe that same person, driving the black BMW I told you about, killed him today before he could speak to us."

"One of my officers is working on identifying the vehicle," said Katie.

"Good. I believe this woman planned the whole thing. She had Blake and Rogers bring the Badda exhibition here from London on the correct date in March. Their superior Edwin Sawtelle accompanied them, but he had nothing to do with the…"

"If you say so," broke in the Inspector. "But who *is* this mystery woman? This ringleader?"

"I know *what* she is, but I still don't have a name." Quist took a deep breath. "As I said, the man killed near Pickering was a heroin dealer. The unfortunates chosen for the sacrifices, and the host bodies for Rakkat, were all a certain type too – sex workers and drug addicts, and every one had criminal records for solicitation, petty theft and other offences. They were chosen through some warped sense of justice, and those criminal records also enabled her to ensure the sacrifice victims had the correct date of birth. The Priestess has full access to the York police database."

Watson let out a low whistle. "Bloody hell," he muttered.

"But how can that be?" demanded Katie. "That would have to mean…" Her phone vibrated and, checking the caller identity, she hesitated for a moment before answering. "Hello there, Zoe. Yes, I know. I've been out of touch, but my mobile has been acting up. Yes,

I can imagine what Superintendent Morton has to say, but I'm fine."
She listened for a while, her eyes widening. "Okay, thank you for that.
Yes, leave it with me and I'll see you soon."

"Well?" asked Quist.

"That was my detective Constable," said Katie, quietly. "I
asked her to check the Wetherby traffic cameras for the car you
mentioned. The only black BMW in the time frame you gave me was
on Linton Road at…"

"That'll be the one," said Watson. "Roundhay's house is on
Sterndale Close off Linton Road."

"The camera recorded the license plate," murmured Katie. "I
know who was driving it." She closed her eyes. "Jesus, I really don't
believe this."

"I'm afraid you must," said Quist. "I think it's safe to say our
Priestess now has a name."

* * * *

Chapter 35

The detached house stood isolated by the edge of woodland on the northern outskirts of Pickering. It was close to ten-thirty as Katie left her car on the gravel driveway and gazed at the black BMW saloon parked by the front door. Shaking her head and feeling sick with disgust, she marched up the path and rang the bell. The woman who answered caught her breath, shock clouding her face.

"Hello, Angie," said Katie. "Zoe was concerned about you. Apparently, you left the Memorial Gardens crime scene straight after me and no one has seen you since. Your phone is dead too." Pushing past into the hallway, she noticed a small suitcase standing by the entrance. "Oh, are you going somewhere?"

Angie didn't answer and closed the door behind her superior. She wore a raincoat, and instead of tying back her long hair in a bun, as she always did when working, the red locks were down over her shoulders.

"I don't understand, Ma'am," she said. "How did you find this place?"

The Inspector walked through into a lengthy lounge. The room was filled with expensive trappings and a huge fireplace of Yorkshire stone housed a gas appliance where artificial logs blazed.

"Nice house," she said, coldly. "I knew you were renting a flat in York while you were working on my team. I was also aware of your place in Northallerton, but I didn't know about *this* house. Probably because it belongs to a woman named Susan Phillips."

"That's right," confirmed the Sergeant, following her in.

"You can thank Bernard Quist for this," said Katie. "If you recall, he's the private investigator you met outside the museum. A friend of his is a wizard with computers; far better than anyone *we* employ. Don't ask me how he managed it, but a short while ago he looked into your bank accounts. This house may be in the name of

Phillips, but *you* paid for it with money from an offshore..."

"Why the hell would he hack into my private..."

"Oh, come on, Angie," barked the Inspector. "Why do you think? I know everything and this is finished. *You're* finished."

"Susan Phillips?" Sighing, the Sergeant massaged her brow for a moment. "Yes, I have a birth certificate, passport and, as you obviously know, offshore accounts in that name too." She reached into her raincoat pocket. "I also have *this*."

Katie stared in disbelief at the Glock automatic. The pistol was fitted with a silencer and it was pointing at her midriff. "You have to be joking?" she said.

"Does it look like a joke?" Angie let out a rasping laugh. "I honestly didn't want this."

"Neither did I," said Katie, eyeing the gun. "I had Zoe check the Wetherby traffic cameras and your car left the area after that murder today. For God's sake, Angie, you're a police officer..."

"*Was* a police officer. What I've done is far more final than any resignation letter and, I'm sure you'll agree, eternal life has the edge on a police pension. You'd have worked it all out soon enough, but by then I was hoping to be out of the country."

"So you're some kind of witch," snapped Katie.

"I run an occult group, but this quest for the Badda knife was a solo project. I've spent over two years researching the Badda sect and planning this venture."

"With Blake and Rogers?"

"Hah, they were a big mistake." Angie shook her head angrily. "I needed certain ritualistic items from the British Museum and I went there to work out some way of obtaining them, either by bribery or sex with the right curators. I was prepared for it to take a while, but I had an unbelievable stroke of luck. Incredibly, Blake and Rogers were occultists too, part of a London group, and I convinced them to help. I'd no idea how unhinged Blake was until I began working with her, but we had the Badda temple brought to York at the correct time and then..."

"And then you began your murder spree," growled Katie. "You're fucking unbelievable. A murderer *and* a brilliant actor. Pretending to be shocked at the crime scenes when you were the one responsible."

"I'm not proud of it," sighed Angie. "Human life energy was needed for those rites to work, but I always made sure I chose junkies and whores for the..."

"Oh, well that's okay."

"It *wasn't* okay, but it *was* necessary. This project was supposed to run like clockwork, but Blake and Rogers decided to screw me over at the last minute. They were the ones who sent Rakkat after you, and then after the psychic and his kid. Do you seriously think *I'd* have chosen *you* for the sacrifice tonight? That was all down to those stupid bitches."

"So you got rid of them and took the dagger." Katie gazed at her. "Do you really intend to stab someone and then cut yourself to live forever as... as a *werewolf?*"

"Of course, but the time has to be right for the Oushane Sacrament and it's now passed. Thanks to Blake, I have to wait a whole year before I can perform the rite, but it will be worth it. *You* must believe this is real. I take it you saw Rakkat and I know you saw Hanka in her wolf form because I drove her to that cellar."

"It took a while." The Inspector nodded. "But yes, I now believe in the supernatural and this... *magic* you practise."

"I've been studying ritual magic since I was a teenager. It brings knowledge and power, but it also brings plenty of cash." The Sergeant gestured around the room. "Enough cash to leave all this and my old life behind. Speaking of which, I have a plane to catch. I need you to take out your handcuffs and lock yourself to that radiator."

"Be serious, Angie." Katie glanced at the pipework behind

her. "You know I won't do that."

"The alternative isn't good." Licking her dry lips, the Sergeant held the gun higher. "I really don't want to hurt you, so just do as I ask and you'll never see me again."

"I believe we've heard enough," announced a voice.

"What the fuck…" Angie twisted, pointing the Glock at the two men standing in the passage doorway. "How did you…"

"I picked the lock on the rear door," said Quist. "Watson and I entered through your kitchen a few minutes ago."

"I wasn't stupid enough to come alone," said Katie.

Angie moved back against the stone fireplace, quickly shifting her gun left and right between her Inspector and the newcomers. Quist took two steps into the lounge, leaving his frightened assistant in the doorway.

"As I told you…" Quist glanced at Katie. "The Priestess *had* to be one of your officers. Sergeant Gibson obtained the information she needed from the arrest records on your database – sex workers, all with the correct birthday, and drug addicts to use as hosts for her elemental. She also deleted Aaron King's DNA on there so you couldn't find him until his *work* was completed and she was ready to have him confess. She even found a local builder in your records who didn't mind performing illegal excavation work, with police cautions to prove it…"

"You need to keep back," hissed Angie, aiming the pistol.

Maintaining a wide berth, Quist moved slowly around the lounge to stand beside Katie. "She transferred to your CID team," he continued, "She needed to be on the scene in York and privy to the details of your investigation, to monitor everything and ensure any mistakes by her people were covered up. Sergeant Aslam being injured at just the right time can't have been luck. She obviously arranged his vehicle accident."

"*What?*" Katie stared at her for any sign of denial. "Jesus!"

"You're the Priestess of a Pickering group." Quist smiled grimly at Angie. "Last year a man named Bradley Curtis was murdered on the moors near here and the police found evidence of an occult ritual at the crime scene. I presume you were responsible? You were performing some dark ceremony for personal gain? Curtis was a drug dealer. As with this recent project, you viewed your sacrifice victim as superfluous to society."

Angie nodded slightly, her pistol trembling.

"Using that same deranged logic, Miles Roundhay was innocent though, wasn't he? Blake told you we were on our way to interview him and you got there in time to prevent him speaking. Looking at the silencer on your Glock, that will almost certainly be the weapon you used. You were also the one who set fire to the insurance offices above…"

"Yeah, great deductions, but I don't have time for any more." Angie turned angrily to Watson in the doorway. "I want everyone together. You there, get over here beside these two."

"Stay where you are," instructed Quist. "Listen to me, Sergeant Gibson, I'm sure you don't want to murder anyone else, so why not just go and…"

"*Go*?" echoed Katie. "She's going nowhere."

"My dear lady, we have a loaded pistol pointed at us. No one will be hurt if you simply allow her to…"

"I can't do that." The Inspector inched forward. "Give the gun to me and we can…"

Angie's shaky trigger finger tightened and Quist leapt in front of Katie as the silencer coughed.

"*Now*," he shouted.

The bullet slammed into his chest and everything turned black. Fortunately, this wasn't the ebony wings of death, but Watson hitting the doorway light switches as arranged. Wincing at the white-hot metal and yanking the Inspector to the carpet, Quist shielded her again as the blind Sergeant fired wildly. Enhanced lupine vision was ideal at such times, and Quist watched Angie rush through the darkness into the hall, waiting for her to leave before jumping up. His assistant heard the front door slam and clicked the lights back on.

"*Bloody hell,*" gasped Watson, appearing timidly from the corridor. "Your idea worked, Guv."

Nodding, Quist helped Katie to her feet. After listening from the kitchen passage and realising the Priestess was armed, his priority had been to separate her from Watson and the Inspector. These two were now safe, but he had to capture this woman and retrieve the Oushane Blade.

"She shot you," stammered Katie, gaping ashen-faced at her protector. "I'm so sorry, but I can't believe you jumped in front of..."

"No, I'm fine," lied Quist. He felt the bullet drop inside his shirt, forced out by the rapidly healing flesh.

"You *can't* be." Assuming shock had numbed the wound, she jerked open his overcoat to check. "How bad is it?"

Quist heard Angie's BMW start up. "Believe me, I'm *fine.*" He pulled together the leather lapels, concealing the shirt hole. "I'm glad to say she missed, but we don't have much time. I need to stop her."

"*We'll* stop her," corrected Katie, following as he headed for the hall. "I'm coming with you."

"No, look after Watson." Quist pointed to his assistant. "He's hurt."

The teenager's bewilderment at this turned to understanding. *Whatever his boss was intending to do, it probably involved a supernatural fur coat and he didn't want police witnesses.*

"Aargh, no." Groaning and overacting, Watson gripped his midriff and collapsed to the carpet. "Oh, someone help me."

"You were hit?" The Inspector rushed to his side and turned to see Quist leaving. "For God's sake be careful out there. Remember, she has a…"

"Gun?" He grinned at her and ran out. "Yes, I noticed."

The detective halted on the driveway and spotted the rear lights of Angie's car blazing red through the trees to his left. She was heading north along the narrow country lane, but from his journey here following the Inspector, he knew this route curled around the woodland and he'd hopefully meet up with her if he cut through. He glanced back at the house, darted into the foliage for cover and shrugged off his coat and jacket. Kicking off his shoes, Quist dropped into a squat and swiftly shapeshifted, his transforming furry body bursting from his shirt and trousers.

The giant wolf raced through the damp forest undergrowth on all-fours, its amber eyes glowing as it dodged between beech trees and white limestone outcrops. It bounded across a stream, sending a drinking fox yelping away and nearby badgers scurrying down their burrows in panic. The dark woodland was dense, but began to thin out as the panting creature arrived at the lane where approaching headlights illuminated the tarmac ahead. Timing it perfectly, Quist sprang onto a mossy boulder and launched himself into the air, landing on the moving BMW as Angie drove past.

The Sergeant swerved at the sound of something heavy crunching down on her roof. "What the hell?" she yelled, looking up to see talons appear through the head upholstery.

Unbelievably, something huge was riding on top of her car and whatever this thing was, it was holding on with *claws*. Accelerating and pulling out her gun, she fired upwards five times, then gasped in horror as the metal was torn apart to reveal a lupine muzzle and gleaming yellow eyes peering down at her.

"A *werewolf?*" Dropping the pistol and swerving again, Angie stabbed at it with the Oushane dagger. "You're a werewolf? Who the fuck *are* you? Have you used this knife?"

"No, I'm old school." The night air rushed through Quist's fur as he grabbed the blade, wrenching it from the terrified woman's grasp. "This is all down to the more traditional method."

Some sixth sense told Quist to look up. Glancing ahead and spotting the approaching hairpin bend, the wolf cringed. It leapt from the speeding car, leaving Angie to plough through warning chevrons, tear through a wooden fence and plummet over a limestone ravine. Landing in the undergrowth, Quist heard her shrill scream, followed by an enormous splash, as the BMW plunged into the icy river twenty feet below.

* * * *

Katie and Watson sat at the table in Angie's lounge, the Inspector examining her Sergeant's fake passport, bank statements and other paperwork. She jumped up as Quist returned.

"So where's Gibson?" she snapped. "Don't tell me she managed to get away?"

"No," sighed Quist. "She didn't escape."

"So where is…" Katie stared at his legs beneath the long overcoat. "Er, are you naked under that?"

"It isn't the first time he's heard *that* today," mumbled Watson. "It's best not to ask."

"My clothing was drenched," explained Quist. "Your Sergeant crashed her car into the river a half mile from here."

"Bloody hell," stammered Watson. "So where is she?"

"I'm sorry, but I'm afraid she's dead." Quist shook his head. "I swam down and extracted her from the wreckage, but my attempts to revive her were too late."

"Good God!" whispered Katie. "I really don't believe this. Well, there's *some* good news. Watson thought he'd been shot, but it turns out he must have imagined it."

"That's good to hear." Quist took the dagger from his pocket. "I also managed to find *this* in the submerged car."

"The magical knife," said Katie.

"Yes, the Oushane Blade." Holding it up, he nodded slowly. "The dangerous relic that caused all this madness."

"You got it back. Brilliant." Watson walked over to take a closer look. "But what are you going to do with it, Guv?"

Quist approached the fireplace, examining the dagger for a few moments, before stabbing it hard into the stonework. The house lights flickered as the bone blade shattered and a violet glow shimmered briefly around the hilt.

"The power has been released," he said quietly, tossing the gold into the gas flames to melt. "No one else will ever use it and I'm pleased to say this is finally over."

* * * *

Chapter 36

The dismal fog had dispersed over the weekend leaving York bright and breezy this Monday morning. The temperature was still the sort of thing associated with polar bears and British summer holidays, but sunlight streamed through the windows of the first-floor detective agency on Baker Avenue.

"This is the problem, isn't it?" sighed Watson. "We go through all that scary supernatural stuff – solving occult murders and saving York from Roman monsters – and then we're straight back to *this* shit. Dealing with adultery, divorces, and people who want legal papers serving." Sorting through files on the office desk, he held one up and shook his head. "This guy believes his wife has trained their Labrador to follow him when he sneaks off to see his girlfriend. He wants us to investigate the dog and see if he's right."

Looking up from the computer on the opposite side of the desk, Quist sat back in his swivel chair. "A reasonable point," he murmured. "Yes, periods of tedium interspersed with bouts of excitement and fear. I suppose I should consider how such things affect the mental wellbeing of my employees."

"What, *all* your employees?"

"Don't be facetious." Quist lit a cigarette. "You do realise that, if ever you felt it necessary, I'd arrange counselling and…"

"I'm kidding, Guv," grinned Watson. "A night out in the Duck and Diogenes with a few pints of lager and a rock band is the only therapy *I've* ever needed."

"Yes, you're a rather unique and resilient individual, aren't you?" The detective blew smoke and cleared his throat. "Um, speaking of nights out, did I mention that I've arranged to take Inspector Bradstreet for dinner?"

"Really?" The teenager smirked. "I hope you're not going to call her that in bed."

"It's dinner," sighed Quist.

"Yeah, right. Taking advantage of the wolf attraction thing, eh? Isn't that like slipping a dodgy drug in her drink?"

"Let's not go there." The detective shot him a disdainful look. "She now knows about everything that happened over the last few days…"

"Apart from the bits where you turned into a furry monster?"

"I prudently neglected to mention *that*, but she accepts the supernatural as genuine and wishes to chat about…"

A knock sounded on the door and Watson jumped up to answer it. "Ooh, hello…" he laughed. "This might be Bradders right now. Maybe she can't wait and she's eagerly panting for a bit of lupine lust and… Oh, hello there."

Charlotte Lewis threw her arms around the youth. Dressed in jet-black Goth attire, she kissed his cheek and left a dark lipstick smudge, much to the displeasure of her father who stood fuming behind her.

"Hi," she said "We've been hearing all kinds of stuff on the local news about weird murders and something about a black mass in a cellar?"

"Er, yeah." Watson nodded, unsure of how much to tell them. "The cops haven't released any details yet."

"I'm guessing you know a lot more than you're saying?" Charlotte smiled knowingly. "But the main thing *we* need to know is… well, is this witchcraft business finished?"

"You'd better speak to the boss." Watson led the pair through the reception area. "We spent most of the weekend answering police questions and making statements." He grinned at Kyle. "*You're* in the clear, by the way. Bradstreet has plenty to deal with and she's lost all interest in you lying to her."

"Ah, good morning," said Quist, standing as they entered the office. "I overheard your question and yes, I can assure you this unpleasantness is most definitely over. There's no further danger from elemental entities or anything else."

"I still can't believe that elemental thing we saw," said Kyle, uneasily. "The more I think about that weird guy in the restaurant, the more I can convince myself that his eyes *weren't* glowing with green light."

"What about the waiter he threw across the room?" asked Charlotte.

"Quite." The detective drew on his cigarette. "You have to admit, that's rather more difficult to explain away with rationality. As I often tell people, you should never dismiss the supernatural."

"I got us involved with my stupidity," said Kyle. "It's good to hear it's finished, but we still have no idea what was going on."

"I believe we can rectify that," said Quist. "You can't repeat any of this, but it's time you knew the full story."

Another knock sounded and Watson vanished into the reception. He returned with an elderly bald man in a smart business suit.

"Hello again," said Charlotte. She noticed Quist's quizzical expression and explained. "We passed this guy at the bottom of the stairs. He was waiting in the lobby down there."

"Er, yes. Good morning." Checking his watch, the old man peered at the group and took an envelope from his jacket. "Which one of you gentlemen is Bernard Quist?"

"At your service." Killing his cigarette in the ashtray, the detective shook his hand. "And *you* would be…"

"Julian Cringe of Wittering and Cringe Solicitors."

Watson raised his eyebrows. *Why did so many solicitors have strange Dickensian-style names? It was obviously traditional.*

"Then this is for you." Cringe handed over the envelope. "I'd be the first to admit how bizarre this is, Mister Quist, but we've been looking after this in our office safe for over six months. The lady paid us to hold onto it and instructed me to deliver it here to you in person at this exact time. That was the reason for my brief wait downstairs."

"I see," murmured Quist, raising an eyebrow as he tore it open. "You're right, that *is* rather bizarre."

"My instructions are then to leave." Cringe nodded politely and headed for the door. "So, much as I'm curious to know the contents, I must bid you all good day."

The solicitor left and Quist read the handwritten sheet inside.

"So what is it, Guv?" asked Watson.

"Amazing," said the detective, finding another sealed letter inside. "*Absolutely* amazing. It says Charlotte will be in the office and asks if I'd be good enough to give this to her."

"You're kidding me?" Watson laughed. "How could anyone possibly know she was going to be here six months in advance of…"

"It's from your deceased Aunt." Quist smiled at Kyle. "Vera Lewis."

"What?" The man's mouth fell open. "*What?*"

"Vera says you'd both be calling here right now and that your daughter should read this." He passed the letter to the black-garbed girl. "Although it borders upon stage magic, I believe this is a creditable demonstration of her genuine psychic power."

"Yeah?" Watson shook his head. "Either that, or Vera was the world's best guesser."

Trembling, Charlotte tore open the envelope with shaky hands and began to read aloud. "Hello Charlie my love. First of all, let me tell you that your Mum is fine, and one day, far from now, you'll be together again, as I told you. You *did* see her spirit that night in your bedroom and she loves you and your Dad so much. She says she knows how much you both miss her, but you need to live your lives to the full and your Mum wants you to know…" Charlotte sobbed. "No, this is too much. I can't say this…"

"Understandable," murmured Quist. "This is clearly a very

intimate message for you both."

Kyle looked over the girl's shoulder, openly weeping as he read the words of love with her. He pointed to the final paragraph.

"What's this?" he croaked. "Tell your Dad to check the box in the loft. The one where he cut his hand when he piled the Christmas decorations on it two months ago…" He glanced at Quist. "I know the box she means, but how could Vera know I cut my…"

"Shares?" read Charlotte. "She says grandad gave all his Corotan company shares to Mum before he passed away and she stored them in there. The portfolio with all the legal paperwork is in the bottom under the old photo albums."

"I remember something about a shares portfolio?" said Kyle. "But I haven't thought about it for years."

"Vera says they're now worth an absolute fortune." His daughter laughed and wept at the same time, Goth make-up staining her cheeks. "She says we're rich. She knows you didn't like her, but she doesn't hold that against you. Give the daft bugger a hug, she says, and tell him he doesn't need to con people for cash anymore."

"Well, as I said…" Quist glanced at his dumbfounded assistant. "You should never dismiss the supernatural."

Charlotte burst into tears and her father wrapped her in his arms, sobbing and smothering her head in kisses. The detective walked quietly to the door and gestured for Watson to follow him into the outer reception area.

"Let's give them a little privacy," said Quist, leaning against the wall and lighting another cigarette. "Doubtless this will be difficult for them to process."

"Yeah, I'll say." Watson jumped up to sit on the reception desk, shaking his head. "Well, *that* was frigging weird."

"Vera Lewis," said Quist. "What a remarkable lady."

"I have to ask, Guv…" The youth shot him a confused look. "Instead of sending us this letter now, why didn't she send one to Kyle last week? She could have told him not to drop himself in the shit by lying to the cops."

"Mmh." The detective drew on the cigarette and nodded slowly. "A valid question, my young friend."

"Better still, why didn't she send *us* a letter last week too, with the identity of the killers and the bent cop?"

"I honestly don't know," admitted Quist, smiling. "But, as Mister Tarot is so fond of saying, where the supernatural is concerned, sometimes it's best not to question too much. Sometimes it's best just to accept."

The End

Cat Flap (1)

The Music of Sound (2)

Judgment Clay (3)

   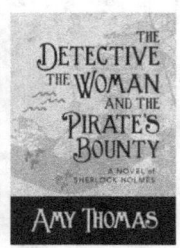

Also from MX Publishing

The Sherlock Holmes and Enoch Hale Series

The Amateur Executioner
The Poisoned Penman
The Egyptian Curse

"The Amateur Executioner: Enoch Hale Meets Sherlock Holmes," the first collaboration between Dan Andriacco and Kieran McMullen, concerns the possibility of a Fenian attack in London. Hale, a native Bostonian, is a reporter for London's Central News Syndicate - where, in 1920, Horace Harker is still a familiar figure, though far from revered. "The Amateur Executioner" takes us into an ambiguous and murky world where right and wrong aren't always distinguishable. I look forward to reading more about Enoch Hale."
Sherlock Holmes Society of London

Also from MX Publishing

"Phil Growick's, 'The Secret Journal of Dr. Watson', is an adventure which takes place in the latter part of Holmes and Watson's lives. They are entrusted by HM Government (although not officially) and the King no less to undertake a rescue mission to save the Romanovs, Russia's Royal family from a grisly end at the hand of the Bolsheviks. There is a wealth of detail in the story but not so much as would detract us from the enjoyment of the story. Espionage, counter-espionage, the ace of spies himself, double-agents, double-crossers...all these flit across the pages in a realistic and exciting way. All the characters are extremely well-drawn and Mr. Growick, most importantly, does not falter with a very good ear for Holmesian dialogue indeed. Highly recommended. A five-star effort."
The Baker Street Society

www.ingramcontent.com/pod-product-compliance
Lightning Source LLC
Chambersburg PA
CBHW070833250626
47159CB00003B/766